Ann Taylor was born in London during the war. Brought up by her father and various relatives, she was the first from her humble family to go to grammar school which she had to leave at sixteen to earn her keep.

Marrying at nineteen, Ann was in her late twenties before she had two sons. She was promptly abandoned by her husband, who she eventually divorced. At thirty-two she retrained as a teacher and went on to senior positions in both state and private schools, writing and making pottery in what spare time she could find. Now remarried, Ann lives in rural Somerset surrounded by various cats and dogs. As well as having had magazine articles published and collaborating on a 'how to' textbook with her husband, Ann has also part-owned an art gallery and continues her ceramics, as well as supporting various local activities.

Nothing Ventured is Ann's first novel.

nothing ventured

Ann Taylor

PIATKUS

Copyright © 2001 by Ann Taylor

First published in Great Britain in 2001 by
Judy Piatkus (Publishers) Ltd of
5 Windmill Street, London W1T 2JA
email: info@piatkus.co.uk

The moral right of the author has been asserted

A catalogue record for this book is available from the British Library

ISBN 0 7499 3274 0

Typeset by Palimpsest Book Production Limited,
Polmont, Stirlingshire

Printed and bound in Great Britain by
Mackays of Chatham Ltd,
Chatham, Kent

author's note

Nothing Ventured is the story of Christina Swanson: Chrissie to her friends; or Tina, Kit or Chris depending on who you talk to and when.

You might know the village of Wooburn Green, just off the A40 in Buckinghamshire. You might even have lived in a house like Chrissie's. All breeze block and gleaming, white wood to cover up the ugliness. A 'bijou residence', as described in the estate-agent jargon of the mid-sixties, it could have been anywhere in England.

It's no wonder Chrissie escapes to become Tina, frequenter of the Watford Town Hall on a Saturday night and other less salubrious venues she'd rather forget. But Kit won't allow herself to forget. And then there's Chris . . . But I won't spoil my story for you.

Christina Swanson in all her incarnations is fictitious. Of course she is. But you've met women just like her. Women who survive, whatever life throws at them. With a little help from their friends.

Let me tell you about her.

Chrissie

one

If I screw up my eyes tightly and concentrate I can still just about picture Chrissie as she was then, back in the late 1960s.

Once a lonely, timid little girl, Chrissie is now a lonely, timid twenty-five-year-old wife and mother. Correction. Not entirely alone. There's always Angel. Always Angel, inside her head.

Unlike the imaginary friends many of us invent in childhood, Angel has shown remarkable staying power, not to say bloody-mindedness. As Chrissie grew up, Angel did not pack her bags and slip away, quietly and discreetly, without a backward glance, confident that her job was done. This guardian Angel stuck around, refusing to be dismissed as superfluous to requirements. Just as well that she did, because Chrissie needs all the help she can get right now.

Dawdling over the washing up in her plastic apron and Happy Shopper rubber gloves, she gazes vacantly at the nearly new terrace of white-boarded, not-quite-identical doll's houses across the road.

Number thirty, on the end, stands out like a sore thumb. All imitation Tyrolean shutters, leaded lights and spectacularly ugly garden gnomes, it is the last word in suburban vulgarity and the only house in the row to boast its own built-on, perspex-roofed garage. 'Suppose a garage in a shared block isn't good enough for Fat Pat and Henpecked Henry,' (Hen, for short) rumble the neighbours, and they suppose right.

As Angel correctly guesses, right now Hen is supposed to be mowing the postage stamp of mossy grass masquerading as a front lawn, like most other Sunday-afternoon husbands in The Close. Like Scotch Andrew at number twenty-eight, for instance. But for once in his life, Hen has decided on a small rebellion and is giving his brand new, 1967 Ford Popular an unnecessary wash and brush-up instead.

The 'fastjet' attachment on the hose (special offer at Halfords) is really a deadly ray gun and Hen is liquidating Fat Pat, who, completely oblivious of her plight, is sprawled on her World of Leather sofa hogging the television and a packet of chocolate digestives. She would happily stare at the test card in order to keep Hen from his precious Surrey versus Middlesex (not that she needs an *excuse*, for heaven's sake), but Fat Pat has decided to watch Anna (Deborah Kerr) Shall-we-dance, dance, dancing with the King of Siam (Yul Brynner) – for the third time to Hen's certain knowledge – so he can just forget about the stupid cricket.

He blasts at a speck of bird lime sullying the Popular's shining bonnet. Take that earthling! And that and that!

Scotch Andrew pauses in his mowing and steps across the invisible line which separates his patch of grass from next door. With his close-cropped, bullet-shaped ginger head and bowling, determined gait he is Caledonian belligerence on legs.

Hello, says Angel. *Here comes trouble. In thee blue cawnah, I give you Scrappin' Scotch Andrew, and in thee red cawnah, your own, your very own, 'Enpecked ... 'Enery!* Chrissie giggles and leans forward with interest.

Fat Pat, in a caffeine-and-cake-induced fit of confidentiality, has dripped details of her latest crazed 'home improvement' plan via the bush telegraph of the coffee-morning circuit, and Andrew's snapping Scotch terrier of a wife, Moira, has only just got wind of it. At least, that's Angel's theory. Andrew has been despatched to Have It Out With Hen Once And For All, she reckons.

4

The gnomes don't know it yet, but they are to pack their fishing rods, wheelbarrows and sticks with red-and-white-spotted-handkerchief bundles tied on the end, and depart The Close for ever, bound for the salt mines of Stevenage New Town. On arrival, Pat's sister – a mere council-house tenant and therefore a deprived, second-class citizen, in Pat's eyes – will display them proudly, grateful for something to raise the tone and set her apart from her neighbours, most of whom, she assures Pat, have got no bleeding idea and are as common as muck, to boot.

Can't wait to hear what Scotch Andrew says about the concrete pond, breathes Angel. *That and the teensy concrete footbridge for the concrete hedgehogs and concrete bunny rabbits to hop over.*

Ray gun in hand, for a wild moment Hen contemplates eliminating Scotch Andrew along with the bird lime and Pat. It would be most convenient all round, considering he too is under orders from his wife to 'speak to' his neighbour on quite a different matter, the matter of Andrew's son, Alistair.

'If you don't do something, that guitar-playing, pasty-faced delinquent will drive me into an early grave,' Pat had moaned.

I wish, thought Hen, but said gently, 'Don't want to cause an upset, dear,' partly because he didn't fancy taking on Scotch Andrew but mainly because he took a perverse pleasure in winding Pat up. It didn't take much. An overly apologetic remark or a mild rolling of Hen's eyes was usually enough to set her off on a tirade that left her red-faced and gasping like a fish out of water. Hen never interrupts Fat Pat in full flow, but just thinks his private thoughts and sits it out. It is oddly satisfying.

'Typical! You're such a spineless wonder, Hen. Sometimes I wonder why I married you at all.' (So do I dear, so do I.) 'I knew it was a mistake buying a semi.' (End-of-terrace, dear.) 'These walls are like cardboard. Should've

5

gone for the Belvedere, the detached three-bedroom with choice of fireplace. But oh dear me no, the Derwent's good enough for us, you said.' (No, the bank said, actually, on my wages.)

'I wouldn't care, but he can't even play a proper tune. Just this dreadful, twanging, shrieking outpouring – it never stops.' (Rather like the sound of your voice, dear.) 'He's as pale as a ghost, and looks like death with all those spots round his mouth – hardly ever ventures out of that God-forsaken bedroom of his, that's why' (or could it be anything to do with the dubious substances he sniffs up his beak-like hooter?) 'and on the rare occasions he does emerge he walks around in a daze, blinking at the light like a coalminer fresh up from the pit and looking at us like we're creatures from another planet.' (We are from another planet, as far as he's concerned.)

'Oh well,' says Hen mildly, 'practice makes perfect, so Moira's always saying. She's convinced their boy'll make it one day and keep her and Scotch Andrew in clover in their old age.'

'In her dreams. You just speak to him at the first opportunity, and that's my last word on the subject.'

'Yes, dear.'

They were not to know that ten years on the wraith-like Alistair would become famous (or, in his case, infamous) as the lead singer and guitarist in the group, MacAli, and in another quarter-century number twenty-eight The Close would be bought by the National Trust as the early home of Sir Alistair MacFee – a place of pilgrimage for MacAli's countless, still-screaming fans, even though they were by then all in their late fifties.

Technically, of course, young Alistair was born in the front room of his maternal grandmother's grim, terraced, two-up-two-down in Dundee, but the place was demolished to make way for the new ring road long before MacAli's meteoric rise to fame. The National Trust will make do with number twenty-eight, which is, after all, close enough to the A40, not to mention Heathrow Airport, to ensure a steady flow of MacAli worshippers for a good few years, surely.

But what's this, viewers? Can the big fight really be off? The contestants haven't even touched gloves and . . . It's. All. Over. Yes, their heads are swivelling in unison as Trish, a model of deep sayuth womanhood (her parents are *American*, you know) sashays down the concrete front path of number twenty-nine, all bouncing breasts and flying blonde corkscrew curls.

'Don't get many of them to the pound,' murmurs Hen appreciatively and Scotch Andrew grunts agreement, tempered with relief.

Like Hen, he is grateful to Trish for providing a diversion, deep in his tartan heart. Being born ginger was unfortunate, but being born in Glasgow (dear old Glasgow town) was a tragedy for Andrew, who seems predestined to live his life wearing a metaphorical kilt knocking seven metaphorical bells out of his wife every Saturday night after a metaphorical skinful.

In reality he is a peaceable man, but is constrained to live up to the image decreed by the world in general and by his wife in particular, though she draws the line at Saturday night knockings-about. Scotch Andrew sighs and secretly yearns for old age. Perhaps then he can safely turn into Harry Lauder. It will be such a relief.

Back at number twenty-seven, Chrissie's husband, Dennis, has seeped into the kitchen like so much smoke. The smoke becomes a small, black storm cloud of aggression, which hovers just above Chrissie's unsuspecting head.

'How much longer?' he spits, caterpillar eyebrows bristling dangerously. 'You're supposed to be coming to bed while Janine's out of the way at thingummy's birthday party.'

Lucky Janine, says Angel. Unlucky Chrissie. She doesn't

like sex very much. Not Dennis's idea of sex, anyway. But she smiles apologetically. 'Won't be long, love.'

'See that you're not,' he commands. *Yes sir, no sir, three bags full, SAH!* says Angel, and Chrissie smiles her secret smile. Angel really is incorrigible, sometimes.

Standing directly behind her, Dennis's hands slide under the bib of plastic to grasp Chrissie's breasts. He frowns, kneading and weighing them dispassionately, like a conscientious shopper trying to decide which melon to buy, while gazing absently out of the window.

At the sight of Trish, chatting amiably with Hen and Scotch Andrew, he consigns his wife's breasts to the reject bin with such disdainful haste that Angel gives thanks for Chrissie's Trueform circle-stitched 36B, without which they might have rolled straight into the watery grave of the washing-up water.

'Just look at that slag! No bra. Nipples standing out like chapel hat pegs. And by God, if that skirt were an inch shorter you could see its knickers!'

Angel would be surprised if Trish is wearing any. Knickers are conspicuous by their absence on Trish's Whirlybird clothes line, according to Fat Pat's best friend and fellow witch, Skinny Liz, at number thirty-one. There's never so much as a cross-your-heart bra, either, though the number and variety of lacy little suspender belts and baby-doll nighties would make a tart blush – pardon my French. That Woman, the gruesome twosome are wont to pronounce in capital letters, is obviously a Stranger to Cotton and Polyester Mix. According to them, Trish is also a Stranger to Proper Tea (as opposed to teabags), Ajax ('You've only got to look at the state of her bath') and Pledge ('She wouldn't know a duster if you gave her one gift-wrapped').

Chrissie grins to herself. They are wrong about the Pledge. Trish regularly sprays the air with the stuff so that husband Nick thinks she's been furiously polishing the furniture all day. It's more fun that way, according to Trish, and she should know. She has a bloody sight more fun in her life than Chrissie does, that's for sure. Lucky old Trish. She's got everything – a beautiful son, no money worries and, above all, a devoted and loving husband.

Don't let's forget the loving husband, Nick, sneers Angel. *So unlike our own dear Dennis, isn't he? Fancy him do you? Well dream on, Chrissie, you've no chance.*

Like a pan of milk that Chrissie has taken her eyes off for a microsecond, Dennis is beginning to boil over. It doesn't take much. 'Her sort thoroughly lower the tone,' he rants, bubbling himself up into a froth that an espresso machine would envy. 'Parading up and down like a second-rate tart, flaunting herself! Don't know why she bothers. No one's impressed.'

Wisely, Chrissie remains silent, but Angel has plenty to say for herself, as usual. *Oh yeah? You're getting a good eyeful, along with the sudden army of lawn-mowing, hedge-clipping, car-washing husbands the other side of the window. Performing a public service, is Trish, especially if she diverts Dennis's attention away from Chrissie for five wonderful minutes.*

'What are you grinning at?'

'Nothing,' says Chrissie, her smile vanishing at the whip-lash of his tongue.

The caterpillars arch ecstatically as Dennis seizes on an opportunity for a bit of withering sarcasm (speciality of the house). 'Oh, we're smiling at nothing now, are we? I worry about your mental state sometimes, Chrissie, I really do. You're always laughing at nothing, muttering to yourself under your breath.' He speaks slowly and deliberately, as if addressing a slightly backward child, shaking his head from side to side. 'Well?' He folds his arms and regards Chrissie gravely.

Tell him to get stuffed, advises Angel, but Chrissie hangs her head, like a naughty schoolgirl caught smoking behind

9

the bike sheds. 'It's, it's just Trish. She's such a breath of fresh air. It makes me smile just to look at her, that's all.'

'She makes you smile,' repeats Dennis slowly, incredulously. 'What's amusing about that slag?'

Without waiting for a reply (he knows Chrissie's replies are never worth listening to) he stalks from the room.

That was a close call, kid, says Angel. *Now with any luck he'll bury himself behind the Sunday papers and sulk. Might even go right off the idea of getting you between the sheets. Hallelujah.* He's not so bad, protests Chrissie guiltily. *He's not so good either. Face it.* Chrissie snaps on the transistor radio to drown Angel out; she can get a bit above herself at times. But Mick Jagger bawling his inability to get any satisfaction is the last thing she needs, so she switches him off in mid-wail. No offence, Mick.

Outside, Fat Pat appears at her front door wearing a deeply offensive marquee of a dress in the sort of jungly print that looks as if someone has been sick down it. She grunts something unintelligible at Hen, who stiffens like a pointer at the sound of the master's voice. His beaming, Trish-induced smile vanishes as, without a word, he dutifully plods towards his wife. Flabby arms folded like a Sumo wrestler, tiny pig's trotters planted a foot apart (she hasn't been able to get her ankles together since she was thirteen), Pat says not a word, silently supervising the Ceremony of the Removal of the Wellies, a high priestess at the gates of her Cyril Lord shag-carpeted temple.

She gives Trish a triumphant glance as she closes the front door, for Trish is a threat to Decent Women, who must be Ever Vigilant against Her Sort. Confusingly, as well as being a Stranger to many of the things that Fat Pat holds dear, Trish is also No Stranger to a number of others. Peroxide, for example ('You've only got to look at those roots'), fast food ('That poor child of hers *lives* on takeaways') and of course Husband Rustling ('She was all over my Hen at the last party, all over him'), to name but three.

Chrissie smiles. If they but knew it, Trish has eyes only for her Nick, and he for her. They are the perfect couple. *Apparently*, says Angel drily, but Chrissie ignores her. She's only jealous.

Her lord and master will be home soon, so Chrissie drags on the plastic apron and scrapes potatoes and washes lettuce, lah-lahing along with the Kinks on the transistor. They have been lazing on a sunny afternoon, just like her and Trish, while their respective children, Janine and Ian, wallowed in the inflatable plastic paddling pool from Green Shield stamps, naked and water-shiny as baby seals. She glances at her reflection anxiously in the mirror. Uh oh. Nose is a shining beacon from so much sun. Dennis is bound to notice. *Who gives a shit?* shrugs Angel. Dennis, that's who.

All in a good cause, argues Angel, persistent as ever. *The kids had a marvellous time, so what the hell?* Yes, but you know Dennis . . . *Don't I just. You'll just have to get in first with some bit of nonsense to make him laugh, put him in a good mood from the off. You're a clever girl. Think about it.*

And so she does. She is a trier, Chrissie, I'll give her that. But I sometimes wonder about the clever part, because on this summer evening she is, as ever, completely wasting her time.

It's easy for me to talk, of course, but she should have given up the unequal struggle the minute she heard the front door crash back against the wall, announcing the arrival home of her nearest but, let's face it, not very dearest. Instead of trying to jolly Dennis out of one of his typically foul moods, she should have shut her trap before he shut it for her, as he was so fond of telling her. Her well-meaning chatter only fuelled the smouldering bonfire of his anger, I can see that now.

I screw up my eyes and concentrate on Chrissie. I screw

up my eyes to keep the tears from running down my silly, middle-aged cheeks.

Dennis pokes at his mandarin segments and evaporated milk looking as if he has discovered some alien, faintly repulsive life-form lurking in the Libby's.

'What's this muck? Suppose it's too much trouble to make a proper dessert. Easier to open a couple of tins. Don't suppose you had time to cook your husband a decent meal after lazing around in the garden all day with that slag from next door.' He pushes his plate to one side in disgust.

Wrong again, sighs Angel. Fancy telling him you've actually been enjoying yourself in the garden with Trish and the kids. That will never do.

But Chrissie paints an apologetic smile on her face. 'Sorry Den, er, Dennis, I mean.' He hates being called Den; thinks it sounds working-class, which he is. Thinks Dennis (he's taken to spelling it D-E-N-Y-S by the way) sounds somehow more impressive, which it doesn't. 'Let me get you something else instead,' she says.

'Such as? Tinned pears with tinned custard? Don't bother.' He stalks across the room, the very furniture seeming to cringe against the magnolia emulsion, and snaps on the television with such force that the Doulton figurine (a wedding present. Ha!) on top of it has to hold on to her hat as she struggles to keep her footing.

'Coffee then?' says Chrissie hopefully, and Dennis grunts. *We'll assume that's a yes then shall we?* says Angel, and Chrissie trails miserably into the kitchen to put the kettle on.

It isn't fair, Angel, and your comments didn't help, I have to say.

As ever, she had sat listening patiently, trying to ignore Angel's frequent interruptions, while Den let off steam. First he treated her to a blow-by-blow account of his ongoing battle of wits with the Area Manager. (*In the*

12

blue cawnah . . .) Stifling her yawns, she had oohed and ahed in all the right places, knowing in advance that Den (*bobbing and feinting in the red cawnah*) would emerge victorious. He always did. (*Is there no end to this boy's talent?*)

Moving rapidly on, he had ranted about the uselessness of the new typist ('. . . all Cathy McGowan fringe and sooty eyeliner that make her eyes look like piss holes in the snow'), the infamies of British Rail ('. . . this is not what I pay my season ticket for') and the nerve of some upstart know-nothing who had wilfully parked in *his* spot in the station car park ('. . . felt like slashing his bloody tyres; that'd teach him').

Yet when she tried to tell him about *her* day, tried to cheer him up, he just flattened her with a few well-chosen words. *What's new?* said Angel.

Dennis accepts his cup of coffee without a word, his eyes glued to the television. 'Janine's in bed, is she?'

No, sneers Angel. *She's been abducted by little green men, what do you think*. 'Yes,' says Chrissie.

'Hardly get to see my own daughter, these days. I'll look in on her in a minute. Give her a goodnight kiss from Daddy.'

Only Chrissie's coffee cup rattling slightly in its saucer (Dennis will not allow mugs) betrays a twinge of unease. 'Don't wake her up, will you Den?'

Please let her be asleep, says Angel. *Safe*. Safe from what? *Just safe, OK?*

two

Chrissie decides to do without her new Coty Frosted Sugarplum and remain bare-lipped. It's all the go, as Florrie (Dennis's mother, God help her) would say, and in any case she can't keep her lipstick hand steady, or any other part of her body for that matter, with Dennis storming around the bedroom whipping himself into one of his rages.

Her mouth is dry and her heart is pounding. *You'll have a bloody heart attack one of these days*, murmurs Angel. *That or a nervous breakdown. Or both. No wonder Dennis worries about your 'mental state'; him and me both. What would he do if you suddenly clutched at your chest and staggered around like Jimmy Cagney, finally crashing to the shag-pile, eyes bulging, mouth frothing? Tell you to get up and stop overacting, I expect.*

The wire hangers complain among themselves as Dennis raids the MFI wardrobe for what he calls a 'decent' shirt. *As opposed to an 'indecent' one?* queries Angel, *i.e. one with sexily cutout breasts, perhaps, or an off-the-shoulder collar? Right, come out with your double-cuffed sleeves high, you pervert, we know you're in there.*

Caterpillars bristling, Dennis grabs a mild-mannered, blue-and-white-striped Rael Brook Toplin (the shirt you don't iron) that never harmed a soul in its entire life and doesn't see why it should be picked on like this. 'This is the only one I could find, the *only* one, mark you, that isn't full of creases.' *Let's hear it for Rael Brook*, says Angel. 'It

14

simply isn't good enough, Chrissie. And why on earth did you agree to go to this God-awful party anyway?'

'Bit awkward to refuse, really. Living next door, we can't say we're already going out somewhere else – not that we ever do go out.' *Ouch*, says Angel, as the caterpillars twitch ominously. 'Not that I *mind* not going out very much, but—'

'Oh dry up, Chrissie! Surely you explained we've been lumbered with my parents for the weekend?'

'Well, yes, but you know Trish. "Stan and Florrie can come too," she said. "They'll enjoy a good old knees up."'

'Oh my God, it's not going to be one of *those* dos, is it – all brown ale and Mother showing her knickers at the drop of a SingalongaMax record?'

Angel wants to know whether Dennis has broken the habit of a lifetime and made a little joke. *Do we laugh? Or are we liable to get turned to stone with a look if we do?*

Chrissie isn't taking any chances, so she smiles politely and makes for the door. 'I'll wait for you downstairs with your mum and dad.'

Pausing on the staircase, she watches Dennis's parents lumbering around the room, locked in an impromptu waltz – a pair of dancing bears. Stan's eyes are closed as he softly serenades Florrie with 'The Anniversary Waltz' and suddenly Chrissie feels an intruder. She clears her throat delicately and they spring apart, like clandestine lovers caught in some guilty embrace.

'Just getting a bit of practice in,' says Florrie shyly. 'Ages since we've been to a party, isn't it Dad?'

'You can say that again, love. Still, haven't lost the touch, have I, eh?' Stan gives her a squeeze, and she blushes like a young girl.

'Gerroff. You'll muck up me hair. Had it done special. And what about me new frock, Chrissie? Not too young for me, is it? Not a bit on the short side?'

Florrie is resplendent in blue crimplene spattered with a riot of unlikely looking flowers in every colour of the rainbow and her usual iron-grey candyfloss perm has been tortured into a rigid beehive of a French pleat by a permanently gum-chewing, sixteen-year-old apprentice called Shireen from Hair Magic of Neasden. Shireen has only mastered one hairdo, so Florrie has been churned off the assembly line looking like an elderly Dusty Springfield. Well, why should Shireen put herself out for Wednesday-half-price-special pensioners?

Chrissie grins. 'You look terrific, doesn't she Dad?'

'Oh aye. Could almost fancy her meself.'

Dennis has slithered downstairs in silence. 'Suppose we'd better put in an appearance. Mustn't keep the lovely Trish waiting.' He studies his parents appraisingly, a general inspecting his troops. Angel wants to know if he expects them to salute and click their heels together. *All present and correct – SAH!*

'Mother, that frock's too short for a woman your age, and do you have to wear those awful old shoes, Father?'

'But these are me dancing boots. Light as a feather in these, ain't I, Florrie?'

'Just like a bleeding fairy elephant.'

The troops smile winningly, old hands at dealing with Dennis's ilk. Let's face it, they've had years of experience, poor sods, having had Dennis for breakfast, dinner and tea (sorry, breakfast, lunch and dinner, as he would have it) for aeons and survived to tell the tale. Stan and Florrie are the ultimate double act, their non-stop banter honed and polished over nearly forty years as if in old-time music hall. Except it is no act.

They are still in love with each other. It is obvious. Nothing can shake a partnership that has survived economic depression, World War Two, and that great natural disaster, Dennis's maternal grandmother, Lil (predictably known as Diamond Lil because of her penchant for diamanté) who moved in with them as soon as she was widowed in 1946.

'Went all through the Blitz, he did, my Bert, then 'ad to go and get knocked down by a number seventy-three in Pentonville Road, though what he was doing down King's Cross of a Tuesday afternoon I dunno. Passed away still clutching a buncha daffs he musta bought for me.'

The flowers were actually 'for some tart he'd picked up with (at his age!)' according to Florrie's Auntie Glad, though thankfully Diamond Lil was never to find out. She was discovered dead in bed one Sunday morning in 1959, with a smile on her face. 'No wonder, the amount of gin she put away last night,' murmured Stan. He hugged Florrie, whispering, 'Alone at last, eh? And about bleedin' time, too.'

Having just about scraped through Dennis's inspection, the troops muster next door, to be greeted by an already tipsy Trish, stunning in a white crochet confection which leaves little to the imagination. Tantalising glimpses of golden flesh bloom through lacy, lazy daisies and the handkerchief-pointed hem reveals an expanse of suntanned leg that reaches 'right up to her bum', as Stan would say.

'Amazing what you can do with Ian's christening shawl and a handful of diaper pins.' She gives Chrissie a broad, blue wink and hoists up the front of her creation like Les Dawson doing his Widow Twankey routine. 'It's sheer willpower that's stopping my tits popping out. Remind me to keep breathing out, or it'll really hit the fan.'

'Strewth,' murmurs Stan approvingly, 'you'll catch your death in that, me duck.'

'And you'll catch a clip round the ear'ole. Don't start, Stanley, for Gawd's sake.' Florrie means business when she calls him Stanley.

Most of the men are in the kitchen 'warming up', and, scenting booze, Stan lumbers off, rubbing his stubby paws together like Yogi Bear anticipating a picnic out of sight of the park ranger.

'Keep him off the shorts, Den, you know what he is. Only needs a sniff of a barmaid's apron and he'll be dancing on the bleeding tables.'

With a small shudder of distaste Dennis follows his father, while the two women trail after Trish like maids of honour attending the bride, as she sways into a sitting room throbbing to Jimmy Ruffin demanding to know what becomes of the broken-hearted.

In the one corner not occupied by furniture pushed up against the walls to make room for the (hoped-for) abandoned dancing to come, a MacFee tartan taffeta-clad Moira has herded a captive audience of three. She is yip-yipping at Janice (deceptively mousy-looking infant teacher and amateur dressmaker, married to 'My Ron', lives at number four, caravan parked on front garden – horrors!) and Sylv'n'Trace (some say they're, you know, more than just women friends – nudge, nudge – but we're broad-minded in The Close and what consenting adults do behind closed doors is their own business, know what I mean?) *Very* enlightened for those pre-PC days.

The three women wag their tails obligingly, 'You don't say'-ing and 'Is that a fact'-ing at regular intervals, while eyeing each other's clothes speculatively. ('That blue floral came straight out of the John England Spring/Summer Catalogue – seven and six a week for the rest of your life – and I reckon Sylv's knocked that up herself. I'd recognise that material from Brooker's sale anywhere. Must show her how to put a decent zip in.')

Fat Pat and Skinny Liz, a female version of the Little and Large comedy team without the jokes, stand by the window criticising the furnishings ('Trust her to have wood block flooring; thermoplastic tiles won't do for our Trish. More money than sense.') and casing the joint for dust, cobwebs and other signs of Trish-like slobbiness ('. . . stranger to the

18

simple feather duster and that upholstery could do with a vacuum').

Hen, Scotch Andrew and My Ron look depressed and wish they had the nerve to make a break for it to the kitchen with the other husbands ('I'll try sliding across the parquet on my belly but for God's sake keep me covered you two. Could be instant death if Pat spots me.'), but they perk up at the sight of Trish.

'That's a nice frock she's nearly got on.'

'Phwoar – wouldn't kick *that* out of bed.'

'That Nick's a lucky bastard. All that and stinking rich parents-in-law into the bargain. Yanks apparently.'

The women's reactions are rather different:

'What *is* she wearing? Can't resist making an exhibition of herself, can she?'

'Natural blonde, my arse!'

'It's her husband I feel sorry for.'

Determined to be the Life and Soul of the Party, Trish shoos reluctant men out of the kitchen and turns up the volume on the Dansette record player. If conversation becomes impossible, she reasons, perhaps they will start dancing. 'Not Dancing at a Party' is considered a crime of the utmost seriousness, second only to hanging out your washing in the front garden or lighting bonfires on Sundays, and persistent offenders are discussed and dissected enthusiastically over cups of coffee at the Monday morning post-mortems that religiously follow these occasions.

The Swinging Blue Jeans exhort everyone to do the Hippy Hippy Shake Shake and so does Trish, while clutching the front of her christening shawl for dear life.

Chrissie eyes the dining table pushed up against the wall where sausages on sticks, French bread, crisps, pâté and cheese straws jockey for the limelight. ('Try me, I'm begging for it. Ignore her – she was only a Special Party Offer from Tescos, whereas I came from Harrods Food Hall, no less.' 'That's as maybe, but it's only half eight so you'll just have to hang on for at least an hour and try not to wilt, *per-lease*, especially you Mixed Salads.')

'Not exactly inspiring, is it?' drawls Dennis, materialising at her shoulder like the demon king at a pantomime. ('The nerve, after we've made such an effort! Well really!') 'All shop-bought stuff, I notice. Trish was obviously far too busy tarting herself up to bother making an effort with the food. Lazy cow.'

Sounds like a pretty fair trade, if you ask me, murmurs Angel. *Look at Hen, Scotch Andrew and the rest. They'd let Pat and Moira off kitchen fatigues like a shot (as if they had any say in the matter!) if they thought there was the remotest chance they could end up looking like Trish.*

'I certainly wouldn't allow *you* to parade in public looking like that, Chrissie. Won't tolerate other men ogling *my* wife.'

Fat chance, snorts Angel. *Thank you Dennis, and good-night.*

Predictably, the guests fall upon the food on the stroke of nine thirty, sitting or standing about trying unsuccessfully to juggle drinks, handbags, cigarettes and insubstantial paper plates which make a career out of buckling alarmingly at any attempt to spear a sliver of ham or a slice of cucumber.

Even more predictably, the lights are dimmed at exactly eleven, and Little Eva's 'The Locomotion' is replaced by Andy Williams. 'Can't take my eyes offa yew,' croons Scotch Andrew into Moira's black beehive, while watching Trish's crocheted handkerchief points creeping steadily bumwards under My Ron's stealthy fingers. Ron's wife Janice is not amused and is wearing her Joyce Grenfell expression ('Don't do that, Ronnie . . .') *Tears before bedtime*, observes Angel. *Mark my words*.

Dennis shifts his weight from one foot to the other, a step or two behind the beat of the music, as he is propelled unwillingly around the parquet. His eyes gaze glassily over the improbably red head of his partner (no stranger to henna), who has twined stick-like arms that even Skinny Liz would die for round his neck and is hanging on drunkenly, like a drowning woman clinging to a raft, more from necessity than ardour.

He meets Chrissie's eyes as she sits by the open patio door, ever the wallflower, and smiles smugly. At least *his* wife knows how to behave in public, thanks to his years of training. She was fifteen when they met and Dennis was her first and only boyfriend. An indifferent scholar, he burned with resentment when Chrissie won a university place, her head stuffed with dreams of eventually becoming a lawyer, or some such nonsense.

But he put paid to all that by getting her pregnant and bullying her into marriage, for in the early sixties there could be no other outcome for 'good' girls.

Dennis congratulates himself on his cleverness. Chrissie might be a bit of a bore at times, but he doesn't regret making an honest woman of her, as he likes to put it. (Well, he would, wouldn't he?) Always room for a bit of extramural activity if things get dull. (He's a lad, that Dennis Charleton!) He shrugs. She would never have made the grade anyway, and was far better off as a wife and mother being kept firmly in her place. What more could any woman want, for heaven's sake?

Emboldened by several pints of Watney's finest and satisfied that Fat Pat appears preoccupied snuffling through the party leftovers, Hen slinks towards Chrissie like a trusting collie who's momentarily slipped his lead.

'Come on, Chrissie, this is supposed to be the swinging sixties. Let's groove.' (Yes, I know, but people like Hen really did talk like that in those days.) Pawing at Chrissie's arm, he pushes his perspiring face into hers, his doggy brown eyes pleading. 'Haven't had a look in with you all night. Where have you been hiding?'

At the table, Fat Pat stiffens, scenting trouble.

But Chrissie, that paragon of wifely virtue, (*Dennis would be proud of you*, sneers Angel.) disengages herself with the skill born of practice. 'I'd love to a bit later, but I must just pop next door to check up on Jan, my little girl.' *Before Dennis does*, adds Angel mysteriously.

Hen collapses into Chrissie's vacated chair, eyelids drooping, and Fat Pat sighs contentedly having unearthed a last sliver of quiche that had been kidding itself it was safely hidden under an abandoned lettuce leaf and a couple of wizened cucumber slices.

Slipping through the open patio door, Chrissie sidesteps Skinny Liz who is dutifully vomiting into a flower bed, glad to be rid of all that forbidden buffet food. Chrissie hitches up her skirts and hops over the fence into her own back garden, grateful that her small daughter has provided an excuse to avoid being clamped, cheek to sweaty cheek, in Hen's arms. *Or anyone else's for that matter*, murmurs Angel. Well, it'll only lead to Trouble. *By God, Dennis has trained you well*. Absolutely right, Angel. Ten out of ten.

Pink thumb in rosebud mouth, Janine sleeps clutching her indispensable bedtime companion, Teddy Ed, now rather balding and battered through an excess of loving. The little girl has cast off her Mickey Mouse pyjamas, which lie neatly folded over the back of a chair. Chrissie frowns. It is rather a hot night, but ... *But would a four-year-old take the trouble to fold her pyjamas carefully like that?* says Angel. *What do you think, Ed?* But Ed's shoe-button eyes give nothing away, as usual, so he's no help.

Outside a pale ghost of a moon rides above the trees, and the sickly-sweet perfume of night-scented stock hangs in the still summer air. Safe in the knowledge that Skinny Liz, duty done, has vanished, Chrissie sinks down on to a wooden garden bench and closes her eyes. The last thing she wants to do is rejoin the party, and who can blame her?

Unobserved, Nick rocks back and forth on his son's garden swing and watches her silhouetted against the light from the windows. He has been sitting there for some time observing the various comings and goings with mild interest, a bottle of Scotch at his elbow.

There is no sound except for a faint creaking from the garden swing and distant strains of Bobbie Gentry never falling in love again. Chrissie peers into the gloom apprehensively.

'OK, it's a fair cop. I'll come quietly.' Arms raised, Nick ambles across the dandelion-splattered grass (Strangers to lawnmowers, that pair.) and sits beside her. 'Guess I've been in hiding long enough.'

'Aren't you supposed to be in there playing mine host?'

'Nah, Trish is the hostess with the mostest, to coin a phrase, so who needs me? She won't even have noticed I've gone missing. Nor will anyone else, for that matter.' Nick tosses his cigarette end into the air, and they silently watch it describe a glowing arc in the darkness.

Sensing the bitterness in Nick's voice (and let's face it, she is an expert after a few years of living with Dennis, if you can call it living), Chrissie racks her brains for something vaguely comforting to say.

'I'm sure Trish has got tracker dogs combing the countryside and police frogmen dragging the canal even as we speak.'

Nick cups his hands around his mouth. 'OK baby face – throw out your gun and come out with your hands high,' he whispers hoarsely. 'We know you're in there. We got the place surrounded.' They giggle together like children and Nick waves the bottle vaguely in her direction. 'Drink, madam? Managed to sneak a drop out with me – all part of the escape committee's plan. They think of everything. Passport, false identification papers, suit made out of old army blankets, you name it.' Chrissie shakes her head.

'Well, come on,' he continues, apropos of nothing, 'how

23

did you manage to get out under the wire? What's your excuse for leaving the happy throng?'

'Excuse? Why, the best one in the world. I'm being the perfect wife and mother, ensuring the safekeeping of my only child, of course.'

'Oh yeah?' He takes another swig from the bottle and wipes his mouth with the back of his hand. 'Pull the other one, Chrissie. You just wanted to get away from the all-seeing gaze of your devoted husband for five minutes. Be honest.

'I've seen him watching you like a bloody hawk, just waiting for you to put a toe out of line. Not that you ever do, of course – but he watches and waits just the same, hoping you'll turn out to be less than perfect after all, hoping he'll detect some tiny flaw that'll make him feel superior.' She catches the white gleam of a disembodied grin, and a sour breath of whisky. 'Only the infuriating thing about it, the thing that really gets him climbing the walls, is that you are, by your own admission, the perfect little wife and mother. Why the hell do you do it, Chrissie? What makes you tick? Tell me, I want to know.'

Silence. It's not like that, she wants to protest. You don't understand. But she is struck dumb. *Nick's right, that's why*, sneers Angel. *He's absolutely spot on, only you don't want to admit it. Don't want to admit your marriage is, shall we say, less than perfect.*

With the immense concentration of a drunken man, Nick laboriously lights another cigarette, his face haggard in the brief flicker of flame.

'Sorry, Chrissie. Sorry, sorry. That was completely out of order. Just ignore me, I'm a bit pissed. Mind you, you were wasting your time checking on Janine; Dennis was with her . . . ooh, ten minutes ago.'

The hairs on the back of Chrissie's neck stand to attention. 'I was sitting right by the patio door and I didn't see him slip out.'

Nick shrugs. 'That's because he didn't. Must've gone out the front way. Shook me for a minute when I saw a shadow on Janine's curtains. Thought you were being burgled or something. Then I realised it was Dennis.' He leans towards her and puts an arm across her shoulders. 'What's the big deal, anyway?'

'I didn't see him go,' she repeats forlornly. *No, you wouldn't have done*, whispers Angel. *Not if he snuck out the front door. That way you wouldn't know he'd been out, supposedly to check on Jan.* What do you mean, supposedly? *Come on Chrissie, get real. What do you want, a signed confession in triplicate, catch him in the act? What?*

To Nick's bewildered alarm, Chrissie looks near to tears. What did I say? He pats her shoulder ineffectually. 'What's the big deal?' he repeats.

Go on, says Angel desperately. *Tell him. Tell somebody, for Christ's sake.* 'Who'd believe me?' wails Chrissie, aloud. *Nick would, I bet*, says Angel, but isn't given the chance to find out whether she's right because Chrissie jumps up and, without another word, heads back to the party. Nick watches her go, wide-eyed, then shrugs and takes another swig at the whisky bottle.

In Trish's living room, a few entwined couples are mindlessly shuffling to the Moody Blues singing 'Nights in White Satin', half-dead competitors in some lunatic marathon dancing contest. Dodging between them like a rogue pinball, Chrissie homes in on the kitchen and shakily pours herself a drink from just about the only bottle with anything left in it (Janice's home-made sloe gin which has been studiously ignored since it is well known that her brew tastes like paint stripper without the pleasant afterglow). She gulps down a couple of glasses in quick succession and leans wearily against the sink.

Nick must be mistaken, must be, the state he was in. *How we delude ourselves*, sighs Angel. He just thought he'd seen Dennis. Chrissie giggles to herself. The amount of whisky he'd put away she's surprised he didn't see little green men with lavatory brushes sticking out of the tops of their heads.

Why, only yesterday Trish had confided that his drinking was becoming a problem and for once in her life she wasn't kidding. ('. . . me and Nick used to have a wild sex life, but just lately, even that's gone for a loop. My Nick just don't wanna know n'more. Dunno whether he wants to jump me but can't get it up because of the old demon drink, or whether he deliberately gets smashed to avoid my insatiable demands. Or maybe getting really, really rat-arsed is the only way he can bear me near him.')

The marriage is obviously going through what Chrissie's mother would call a 'bad patch'. *You'd know, of course*, slurs Angel (sounding slightly the worse for drink, to Chrissie's faint surprise); *your marriage is a bad patch the size of Greater London*. Oh shut up. What do you know? Pathetic, though, for Nick to use alcohol as a prop. She frowns and, unaware of the irony, pours herself another drink.

Dennis is framed in the kitchen door, with Stan and Florrie looking anxiously over his shoulder, and Chrissie freezes like a rabbit caught in headlamps. 'You've had quite enough already,' snaps Dennis, dramatically snatching the glass from her fingers and tipping the contents into the sink. 'Time we were going. Come along Mother, Father.'

OK, it's a fair cop. You got me bang to rights, giggles Angel, as Dennis frogmarches Chrissie towards the front door. Dusty Springfield coiffure askew, Florrie drags a reluctant Stan in their wake. ('I was just beginning to enjoy meself.' 'Never mind about that, Stanley. Time we was in bed.' 'Ooh, promises.')

Back inside number twenty-seven, Stan and Florrie hurry upstairs to bed. ('Come on Stanley. Bed. Our Den's got a gob on 'im like a smacked arse and if him and Chrissie

26

are going to have words we don't wanna get caught in the crossfire, do we?')

Flopping into an armchair, Chrissie closes her eyes, a puppy waiting to be scolded for peeing on the carpet. She doesn't have to wait long.

'I think you owe me some kind of explanation.'

'Sorry, Den – I had a bit too much to drink, that's all.'

'That's most certainly not all, and you know it. I am referring of course to your little tête-à-tête in the garden with Nick,' sneers Dennis. 'How long has this been going on?' *You wish*, murmurs Angel.

'How long has what been going on?'

Face suffused with colour, he takes a couple of steps towards Chrissie and she draws back instinctively. Dennis feels powerful, omnipotent. Curled inside his Marks & Spencer underpants his penis begins to stir, for bullying Chrissie is his fail-safe path to sexual arousal, always has been.

'Your . . . your *affair*. I saw you Chrissie. I saw you laughing and joking with him. It was painfully obvious . . .'

Here we go, says Angel wearily. *Foreplay, Dennis Charleton-style. Just take a long, hard look at your dearly beloved, ranting on and on, getting himself in the mood. How much longer are you going sit there listening to this bollocks? Ask him, for Christ's sake. Just ask him and get it over with.*

'Why didn't you stop me going out to check on Jan if you'd just done it yourself?' *Good girl*, says Angel. *Go for it*.

'What?' Dennis stares at her, his mouth wetly agape, little flecks of spittle at the corners.

'You *did* go in to Jan, didn't you?'

'No, I don't think I . . . Look, what's got into you?' Angel has, obviously.

'Only Nick saw you, through the curtains.'

'Oh well, if *Nick* saw me, it must be right, of course.'

27

Dennis passes a hand over his face and sits down abruptly. *You've got him on the run*, says Angel incredulously. *You've got him on the bloody run. Hang in there, kid.*

'You *did* look in on Janine then?'

'All right, yes – yes I did. What's wrong with that, for Christ's sake?'

'And you took her pyjamas off and folded them on the chair by the bed?'

'No . . . yes . . . look, what the hell are you driving at? Jan was fast asleep. Her pyjamas were on the floor in a crumpled heap – too hot, I suppose. Can't think why you insisted on putting them on her in the first place on a night like this. So naturally I picked them up and folded them over the back of the chair.' Naturally.

Except that Dennis is of course the last man on earth who would dream of performing the smallest household chore when there's a woman, any woman, around to do it for him. Why have a dog and bark yourself is his motto.

'Made a rod for me own back, there,' Florrie had confided, long ago. 'Well, I'd more or less given up hope of ever 'avin' any kids, so when I fell for Den when I was pushing forty, my Stan was like a dog with two tails. At first, anyway.

'Den's bin waited on hand, foot an' elbow since he was a kid, and all down to me. D'you know, Chrissie, like a silly cow I used to lay out a fresh shirt for 'im every day of his life. Hot meal on the table the minute he come home. Even cleaned his bloody shoes for him, if you ever. Stan used to go mad. Jealous, see. "You don't do that for me," he'd shout. "You spoil that boy rotten. You'll regret it, you will," an' I do, Chrissie, believe me I do. He's never lifted a finger to help around the house, not since the day he was born; reckons it's women's work. Stan was right. Thanks to his stupid mother pandering to him all these years, the lazy sod wouldn't even stir his stumps to go and fetch a bucket of water if his arse was on fire, and that's a fact.'

But to Angel's astonishment, Chrissie believes him. Wants to believe him. Has to believe him. To disbelieve would lead to the unthinkable. Ignoring Angel's protestations, she smiles her relief. 'Of course. Think I'll go to bed then. I'm exhausted.'

Angel is speechless and so, for a change, is Dennis, who watches her climb the stairs with his mouth open.

He feels puzzled and cheated, like a child whose own mother's just told him that not only is there no Father Christmas, but the Tooth Fairy is wobbling on her perch too. The erection that started so promisingly has faded and it's all *her* fault.

Chrissie *usually* gazes at him dopily, her huge grey eyes brimming with tears when she's upset him which, let's face it, she seems to manage to do just by breathing lately. *Usually* she is as eager for forgiveness as a naughty puppy dog who knows from the master's tone that it must have done something wrong but can't quite remember what it was. *Usually* . . .

He scowls. What's got into the stupid bitch? (Angel, that's what. Dennis doesn't know it, of course, but Angel is growing stronger.) He pours himself a drink and considers the case for the prosecution. Chrissie made a complete fool of herself by drinking too much at the party, spent time alone with bloody Nick then had the nerve to question him about an innocent trip to check on his little girl. Question him! Then she strolls upstairs to bed without so much as a by your leave. Who the hell does she think she is? He'll have her on her bloody knees for this. She'll find out who's boss once and for all.

Dennis drains his glass and, having studiously worked himself up into a mood of righteous indignation, takes the stairs two at a time, eager as a young lover, eager to reinforce his complete domination over his property.

She will be tucked nervously between the sheets no doubt, pretending to be asleep, but he will enter her without preamble and thrust towards his climax, as ever. And she will be grateful – grateful that he still wants her, that her body gives him pleasure.

What could more could a woman want? What more did any woman have the right to expect?

three

Monday morning and the kitchen at number twenty-nine still looks even more of a wreck than usual in the aftermath of Saturday night's party. Chrissie picks her way carefully through cardboard boxes full of empties, heaps of dirty washing and Trish's two cats, Librium and Valium ('We couldn't choose between them, they were so adorable, so we took both') who are staring each other out (looking less than adorable) in a confrontation reminiscent of *High Noon*.

Tails swishing in unison, they are psyching themselves up for a brief bit of fisticuffs over who gets the lonely slice of quiche between them on the thermoplastic tiled floor. ('OK, punk, make your move.' 'Look, Lib, Val-baby, be reasonable. Can't we just talk this thing over like civilised pussycats?')

Trish digs out the kettle from underneath a pile of flattened Tesco carrier bags that might come in handy for something one day, and hastily washes a couple of coffee mugs. 'No cookies today, hon, but masses of party leftovers. For Chrissake help me shift some of these sausage rolls or we'll be eating them 'til doomsday.'

Having cleared a chair of its usual litter of magazines, out-of-date newspapers and ancient circulars, Chrissie sits at the kitchen table nursing her smiley-face mug of Maxwell House (none of your supermarket own brand for Trish) and gazes at her hostess with something approaching awe.

Even at ten in the morning, she is a living, breathing advertisement for Charles of the Ritz. ('Must take her a couple of hours to plaster all that muck on each day,' according to Fat Pat, whose moon face has to make do with 'good, honest soap and water and a dab of Velouty Powder Creme if it's lucky. Mind you, I have a perfect complexion already so don't need to resort to artifice.')

Skin glowing with health and Sunbronze all-in-one make-up, Trish turns her back on the wreckage and settles across the table from Chrissie to enjoy their Monday morning post-mortem of the party while their respective children, Jan and Ian, are safely at playgroup mucking about with plasticine, poster paints and cardboard toilet roll tubes.

'. . . And of course Nick ended up smashed, as usual, but this time I was just as bad. We got through one helluva lot of booze. Cost plenny. And I'm gonna need a skip to get rid of all these bottles or the garbage men'll go ape-shit. You know how bolshie those guys can be. "Hai'm afraid that constitutes a large load, missus, and as such is outside our jurisprudence. More than my job's worth, missus, 'onest." Union rules and all that crap. Guess I'll just bat my baby blues, give 'em a quick flash and slip the boss man a coupla quid. "Ho, I couldn't possibly, missus . . . Ho very well then, if you insist." ' Trish snorts explosively and takes a swig of her coffee, leaving a thick coating of Desert Fire lipstick on the rim of the mug. 'Still, it was worth it. Old Stan certainly had a wild time.'

'Oh yes. Wild,' says Chrissie. And Angel reckons that's because Dennis's attempts to 'keep Stan off the shorts' as Florrie had decreed, had ended in complete failure. Chrissie smiles apologetically. As we know, she's had plenty of practice and if anyone should have a degree in apologetic smiling, Chrissie should. 'I hope Stan didn't upset Fat Pat.'

'Did she *look* upset?'

Chrissie shakes her head, grinning at the memory of

Stan whirling Pat around the parquet. Like so many obese women, Fat Pat is surprisingly light on her little trotters, and Stan set her spinning like a shiny, Bri-nylon whipping top until the overblown roses on her party frock became a pink blur and he and Pat ended in a crumpled, giggling heap on the floor. ('What do you mean, "take more water with it", Stanley? I hope you're not implying I'm squiffy.')

'No. I reckon Pat had a wild time too, though she'd never admit it in a million years. But Stan paid the price.'

Trish leans forward on her elbows. 'Tell me more. Florrie get to him, did she?'

'And the rest. No, it was Dennis.'

'Might have guessed. C'mon, give.'

And so, with frequent interruptions from both Trish and Angel, she does just that.

She describes Dennis's foul morning-after-the-night-before mood (*what's new?*) and the icy disdain with which he treated them through breakfast (*typical!*) sparing no detail, glad to get it off her chest. (*Better out than in, as Florrie would say.*)

Florrie's face had crumpled like a deflated balloon when her ever-loving son suggested the eleven five Marylebone train home. Her and Stan had been looking forward to roast beef and two veg ('Don't often run to a joint on our pensions.') followed by Florrie's speciality – a golden-crusted apple tart that would have done credit to the front cover of *Good Housekeeping* magazine.

Chrissie's suggestion that they catch the half past three had been brushed scornfully aside by Dennis (*surprise, surprise*), who had invented some ridiculous tale about his boss, Bill (*Mr Harris to you, Charleton!*) and his wife, June, calling in for lunchtime drinks.

Angel had been almost beside herself. *Do me a favour! Old Harris can't stand bloody Dennis and I must say he shows excellent taste. To use one of Florrie's mixed metaphors, the old boy wouldn't cross the road to piss on Dennis if he was on fire, in fact, so I can't see him and the lovely June driving all the way down here from Woking for a couple of glasses of warm sherry and a handful of Bombay Mix. Besides, Stan and Florrie'll believe the bastard and feel about as welcome as a pork chop in a synagogue. Stan'll hit the roof.*

As ever, Angel had been absolutely right.

'Don't tell me,' Stan had roared, 'let me guess. Don't want yer working-class old mum and dad coming eyeball to eyeball with yer precious boss, do yer? Frightened we might show you up? Shitting yerself in case we eff an' blind all over the shop, scratch our arses and drink out of our saucers? That's about the size of it, innit, eh?'

'Now Stanley—'

'Now Stanley be buggered! Snobbish little git! To think we scrimped an' scraped to give him a decent education, and now he just don't wanna know us—'

'Oh, here we go. Any minute now we'll hear the old sob story about how my devoted mother worked her fingers to the bone doing a cleaning job just to pay for my school uniform.'

Chrissie had feared for a moment (*Hoped, you mean*) that Stan would 'land one on him' as he had so often threatened, 'big as you are.' *If only.*

But Florrie had saved the day, what was left of it, politely asking Chrissie to telephone for a taxi, there and then, which of course shamed Dennis into offering to drive them to the station. (*Big of him!*)

'Big of you,' said Stan, unknowingly echoing Angel. 'It's a wonder you don't expect us to bloody walk it, or run in front of the car wavin' bleedin' palm leaves.'

Standing on the pavement outside number twenty-seven Chrissie had waved and waved until the car turned out of the close. 'They looked so miserable, Trish, looking out of the rear window, like baby calves being transported to market. Resigned, sort of.'

She sighs and selects a stale sausage roll, one that hasn't been fought over by Lib and Val, with luck, while Trish shakes her head sympathetically, blonde corkscrews bobbing. 'Jeez, some marriage you got. Dunno how you stand it.' She shrugs. 'Me and Nick, we have our moments, but compared to you guys we're Mr and Mrs Perfect, I guess.'

Oh yeah? That's not how I heard it, honey-chile, whispers Angel slyly, which is enough to seize Chrissie with a sudden, irrational and destructive desire to hurt, to wipe the slightly superior smile off Trish's carefully made-up face.

'That's a joke, coming from you. Things aren't exactly all moonlight and roses in your neck of the woods at the moment, by the sound of it.'

Trish's smile falters for a brief moment. 'Meaning?'

'Meaning Dennis and I couldn't help hearing you and Nick having a mother and father of a row last night. Well, these walls are so thin that you can hear every sound under normal conditions, so when you two started screaming at each other we naturally—'

'You naturally forced yourselves to listen. Take it down to be used in evidence, did you? Jeez, Chrissie, all couples have words from time to time.'

'Yes, we heard every one of them.'

'Congratulations. Give the lady a gold clock. What's with you, Chrissie? What do you want, a framed apology?'

Trish nibbles at a Desert Fire-enamelled talon and Angel is impressed. *You've really upset her now. Biting her nails is against Trish's religion. You'd better leave it there, I reckon.* Chrissie has the grace to blush.

'Oh, I might as well level with you,' sighs Trish. 'Fact is, I've . . . we've been fighting for weeks, no months, and I just don't know what to do about it.' With shaking hands, she lights a cigarette and sucks in greedily. 'Not exactly flavour of the month with Nick, as you know. Tried everything short of shaving my head and painting a dahlia on my fanny to grab his attention, but lately, well, we just don't seem to be able to communicate somehow – inside or outside the sheets.'

'You were communicating last night.' Chrissie attempts a smile. (*Why don't you just shut up?* And why don't you just keep out of it, Angel?)

'You can say that again. D'you know, it was almost a relief to have a knockdown, drag-out fight – better than all those strained conversations and ominous silences.'

And we know all about those, don't we, Chrissie?

'Mind you,' continues Trish, with a bitter little laugh, 'I thought it would clear the air, whatever that means. Imagined the big reconciliation scene. You know the sort of thing – the hidden orchestra plays something with a lot of wailing strings and Nick and I run towards each other in slow motion, through a sun-filled meadow strewn with wild flowers. Only my graceful run doesn't end in a passionate embrace, it ends with me falling flat on my face in the cowshit and Nick rushing straight past me into the faceless arms of The Other Woman.'

'You don't really think there *is* another woman, do you? Nick doesn't look the type.' (*Whaddya expect, a large sign on his T-shirt that says, 'Fancy a shag' or what?* Oh shut up, Angel.)

'Who knows? You know men – got to get laid somehow, somewhere. Can't do without it, poor bastards. Well, he sure ain't getting any at home so it stands to reason . . .' Trish's voice trails off miserably.

Chrissie reaches for her hand and squeezes comfortingly. 'Have you tried talking about it calmly and quietly?' (*What, like you and Dennis do, you mean?*)

'Yeah, I've done calm and quiet. But it got heavy. I've just got to face it – he must be playing away, is all.'

She stands up and begins noisily washing their coffee

cups, tears beginning to send twin streams of royal blue mascara wriggling down her cheeks, while Chrissie sits in an embarrassed silence. *Well say something, for Christ's sake*, says Angel. *Trish needs you.*

'Not necessarily,' mumbles Chrissie at last. 'Perhaps he just isn't that keen on sex. Some aren't.' (*Hark at the voice of experience.*)

'Bull*shit*! Not my Nick! I should know. Was a time when he couldn't get enough of it – enough of me.' She dries her hands briskly and mops at her eyes ineffectually with the corner of her 'Making Bacon' tea towel, which features a less than tasteful motif of pigs bonking. 'I've tried every trick in the book, but it's no go. I've even suggested a goddamn marriage guidance counsellor, if you please – how desperate can you get – but Nick wouldn't have it. Told me no bloody do-gooder was going to get her rocks off asking questions about *his* sex life. Course, I had to open my big mouth and say that if anyone could get a kick out of our sex life I wish they'd tell me how they did it, because I'm damned if I know.

'The joke is, Nick told me to get stuffed – which is hilarious when you think about it. It's the very thing I absolutely can't manage, however hard I might knock myself out trying. Why do you think I trick myself out like a high-class hooker? All the local broads think it's because I'm after their property. Well, they should be so lucky. The only man I'm after getting inside my pants is my own. But nothing works any more, despite taking the advice of the women's magazines when they tell us we've got to make an effort to look nice for our Masters or we're in Big Trouble. "Dear Worried Blue-Eyes of Basingstoke, I'm sorry your husband beats up on you but you've only yourself to blame since you must have committed the cardinal crime of Letting Yourself Go . . ." You know the sort of thing.'

Oh yes, says Angel. *We know the sort of thing, all right.*

*

37

It should have been obvious even to Chrissie (a naive soul, in those days) that Trish and Nick's marriage was well and truly down the tubes. Though I suppose my mother, that undisputed queen of the cliché, would say I'm just Being Wise After the Event or speaking with Benefit of Hindsight.

Whatever, when Trish comes pounding on her door a week after the party, Chrissie has to cope with the twin shocks of seeing Trish completely devoid of make-up (*Bloody hell, she must be in a bad way*, comments Angel.) and of hearing her spill out her story about Nick leaving her that very morning carrying only a modest suitcase and his Arsenal Football club memorabilia. ('Thought more of Arsenal than he did of me.') *Probably thought more of Wycombe Wanderers than he did of you, kid, let's face it*, says Angel unkindly.

That evening, Dennis arrives home in an unusually good mood (*What's got into him? Come up on the pools, or something? Not that he'd tell you if he had.*) so, over dinner, Chrissie blurts out Trish's news without waiting for him to tell her about his day first. This is an unprecedented and daring move and Dennis's caterpillars lower menacingly. However, by the time she has breathlessly finished the tale, he is smiling condescendingly.

'Well, it's no surprise to me.' *Natch*, says Angel. *Nothing ever is.* 'I've seen it coming for months. (*And aren't you just cock-a-hoop to have been proved right? As usual.*) What does surprise me is that the marriage lasted as long as it did.'

'I know they had the odd difference of opinion, but—'

'Difference of opinion?' He treats Chrissie to one of his witheringly scornful looks, another speciality *de la maison*. 'They were like cat and dog. No wonder he walked out on her. Bully for him. No *real* man would put up with that bitch for five minutes, flaunting herself, throwing herself at everything in sight. Nick was a laughing stock. God, she was begging for it, the painted tart.'

'Yes, but—'

'But what? There can be no buts. Subject closed.' (*Whatever you say, oh master. God, you're a wimp, Chrissie. Don't bother to spring to Trish's defence, will you? She's only supposed to be your friend, after all.*) Abruptly Dennis moves towards her, fondling her rump proprietorially. 'Thank God my wife's not like her. No one can say a word against my little Chrissie.'

Hands grasping her buttocks, he pulls Chrissie towards him, crudely pressing her against his body so that she can feel his hardness. 'Come on,' he commands huskily, 'Janine's fast asleep by now so we'll have an early night for once.'

Chrissie nods obediently. 'You go on then, while I just tidy away the dinner things. Be up in a minute.'

'Don't be long.'

Upstairs, Dennis removes his Cecil Gee single-breasted with side vents and hangs it up carefully in the wardrobe. The rest of his clothes are of course left on the floor for Chrissie to pick up and launder (why have a dog, etc.). He doesn't bother to wash – it's only Chrissie, for God's sake – and tugs on a pair of crumpled British Home Stores paisley pyjamas (stripes are so working class).

Relaxing on the bed, Dennis links his hands under his head and smiles into space. It's been a marvellous day for a change. His promotion's gone through at last and old Bill Harris (*Mr* Harris to you, Charleton) has grudgingly hinted at greater things to come if Dennis plays his cards right.

He closes his eyes contentedly. Only a matter of a few weeks before he gets his company car, bigger and better than the reps' cars, in keeping with his new status. No more grinding backwards and forwards on the train with the peasants every day because you could never get into the company car park, either. Oh certainly not. He would have a reserved place in the car park and a key to the executive loo.

What's more, he won't have to butter up the fat cow in charge of the typing pool any more to get his letters typed; he will have a secretary of his very own – well, shared with two others, for the time being. Ginger hair with moustache to match. And freckles. No oil painting, certainly, and a bit of a big mouth. But he'll soon put her in her place, and if she doesn't play ball he'll get rid of her and take on some little dolly fresh from secretarial college that he can train up. Preferably a blonde, with big tits, good legs and sod her shorthand and typing speeds.

Life is sweet.

With the right kind of grooming Chrissie will make the perfect Young Executive's wife: discreet, supportive and attractive without being obvious, unlike that tart next door. Dennis crosses his ankles comfortably and smiles even more broadly. So the man-eater's without a man, eh? It's quite a laugh when you come to think about it. Well, it is when Dennis comes to think about it; nothing amuses him more than other people's misfortunes. She's just some slut and deserves her comeuppance, of course. Her type's all right for a quick poke if you felt like chancing your arm, but as a wife and mother? No way. Nick's well rid of her.

'Course, Nick'll be out on his ear as far as work's concerned. He'd never have got that jammy little number if Trish's father hadn't invented a post for him in his company's London office. Do him good to have to stand on his own feet, like the rest of us. Could be the making of him.

Dennis glances at the bedside clock and the smile fades. What the hell is Chrissie playing at? Why doesn't she hurry up and come to bed, as she's been told?

As if reading his thoughts, Chrissie ascends the stairs reluctantly and begins to undress, aware of Dennis's eyes watching her hungrily. *Well go on then*, says Angel. *Not going to just let him slag Trish off and get away with it, surely. Not even you would be that feeble. Or would you?*

Slipping on her cotton nightgown, she sits on the side of the bed and meets his eyes. 'I – I do think you're being a bit hard on Trish,' she says in a small voice.

'Hard on her? Hard on a bitch like that, who drives her husband away by putting herself about with other men?'

'Well, we don't actually *know* why Nick walked out. It's their business. We're only guessing, really.'

'My dear girl, I've seen enough little tarts like her to be able to make a pretty intelligent guess. It's as plain as the nose on your face. Besides,' he smirks, playing his ace card, 'I'm a man and I know from first-hand experience the sort of tricks she gets up to.'

'What do you mean, "first-hand experience"?'

'Well for a start she was all over me that night at their party. Practically shoving those great udders of hers in my face and suggesting – well, I wouldn't like to tell you exactly what your *best friend* was suggesting.' *Oh go on*, says Angel sarcastically. *Force yourself.*

'She'd just had a bit too much to drink, that's all,' murmurs Chrissie.

'Oh, charming! Meaning she must have been pissed to make a pass at *me*, is that it?'

'No, no of course not Den, er, Dennis, but it could explain why—'

'Balls. She's just a tramp. I saw through her the day they moved in here. You're so pathetically weak and naive, Chrissie. Never want to see any wrong in anyone. But you might as well face it, the woman's just not worth the time of day. She's certainly not a suitable friend for any wife of mine. I don't want you to have anything further to do with her. Cut her out of your life once and for all.' *And that's an order*, says Angel grimly.

Discussion over. He pats the bed in what he imagines is

41

an inviting manner. 'Come on, bed. Don't forget I've got an early start tomorrow.'

He smiles in anticipation. Yes, the promotion's going to mean more business travel, as befits his new exalted rank, a real broadening of his horizons. Dennis gives a sigh of satisfaction at the prospect and mechanically turns to face his wife. All's right with the world.

four

Trish stands at the kitchen window, a faint frown appearing between her perfectly plucked brows as she watches Chrissie, basket in hand, stumping down her straight-as-a-die concrete front path. Obviously off to Burlington Arcade, which is Trish's sarcastic name for the dismal little parade of shops that straggle along one side of what was once the triangular village green. Sadly every last protesting blade of grass has been smothered in tarmac to provide what the parish council calls 'much-needed provision for car parking'.

The war memorial still stands proudly in the middle of the triangle, watching the traffic come and go and wondering what the world is coming to. It looks sniffily towards the Bull Inn (Beer Garden. No Coach parties.), which dominates the shop side of what is still optimistically known as The Green, and curls its lip.

Dwarfed next to the Bull is Chiltern MiniMart, and they don't come much mini-er with their half-dozen tins of everything, the odd greying cauliflower and stained cardboard baskets containing one or two squashed tomatoes, and next door is a dusty-looking chemist's shop which is always packed with wailing toddlers grabbing at the plastic carousels of ancient pink hairnets, tailcombs and hairpins while young mums and rheumy-eyed old ladies wait patiently for their prescriptions.

Curl up and Dye, ladies' hairdressers (half-price for OAPs Wednesdays only), has managed to elbow its way in on the Bull's south flank when no one was looking. The windows are all peach flounces, cans of hairspray and dead bluebottles, and it stands out as the only shop that's seen a lick of paint in ten years or more. Vivid flamingo-pink gloss screams at the peach flounces but Marlene the Mouth, owner and chief stylist (*only* stylist, actually) doesn't give a stuff. 'I don't care what the Council says, I think it brightens the place up and I'm certainly not changing me curtains to match the paintwork, neither. What do they think I am, made of money?'

A sub (very sub indeed) post office is next in line, its window crammed with curling birthday cards depicting loveable kittens and cross-eyed Alsatians and postcards advertising second-hand three-piece suites, and, to complete this retail paradise, there is an old-fashioned iron-monger's which still smells satisfyingly of paraffin and candles and has the dubious honour of being the oldest shop in the row, having been there since time immemorial – well, since the twenties, anyway.

Chrissie usually pops next door to see if Trish wants anything at the shops – save her a journey – but today is different. Chrissie is different. Trish doesn't get it. She was so sweet and understanding when told about Nick's departure, but ever since – four whole days now – she has been cutting Trish dead.

A fat teardrop wobbles an uneven path down Trish's cheek. She feels alone and unloved, deserted by the best friend she ever had. Thought she had. Her mouth tightens bitterly. Odds on Fat Pat and the rest have got to her already. News travels faster than the speed of light in The Close and they'd all be pawing over her problems like old crones picking over second-hand clothes at a jumble sale, if she knew them. She'd be discussed, dissected and dusted over countless cups of instant coffee and home-made carrot cake around Fat Pat's G-Plan, glass-topped coffee table, sure as God made little apples. She could just hear them:

'Well, she had it coming . . . Such a nice man. Can't imagine how he put up with her as long as this . . . Wealthy in-laws, of course. Knew which side his bread was buttered . . . It's poor little Ian I feel sorry for, with *that* for a mother. I certainly won't be wasting my sympathy on that slag, oh dear me no.'

Trish manages a grim smile. As a newly Deserted Wife she represents even more of a threat to their net-curtained status quo now, of course. Everyone *knows* that any lone woman, especially one who looks like her, is automatically Desperate For It and that Any Man Will Do. No Man Is Safe, in fact.

Savagely, she rips off a piece of kitchen tissue and blows her nose. Well, she isn't giving up that easily. The neighbours can go take a running jump, but she isn't going to lose both a husband *and* her only friend in the same week.

Positioning herself at the window where she can watch for Chrissie's return, Trish begins to tackle her mountain of ironing with unusual vigour. The contents of her yellow plastic laundry basket are aghast, since most of them haven't seen an iron in ages, but the socks, tea towels, vests and pants are positively smug. (We're all right, Jack. She never bothers to iron *us*. You must have heard her: 'The day you catch me ironing *socks*, for Chrissake, you can send for the guys in the white coats.') Nick's things get thrown on the floor in disgust (phew, that was close) but everything else gets ironed half to death until, glancing towards the window, Trish spies Chrissie plodding up the path next door.

As she fumbles for her key, she is waylaid by Trish. 'A word, please.'

Uh oh, says Angel. 'Oh, er, yes . . . just let me take the shopping indoors—'

'No, now!' Trish steers Chrissie into her house. 'It'll only take a minute.'

45

'That's what the dentist always says.' Awkward laugh. 'Sounds as though you're about to complain about something. Have we been playing records too loudly, or are you getting up a petition to stop the Jamiesons' dog crapping on your front garden?'

'Dogshit's the least of my problems.' Trish leans against the front door, cutting off any possible means of escape. 'Come and sit down a minute. I've got to talk to you.'

'Well, I'm a bit pushed at the moment, and—'

'Please, Chrissie.'

For God's sake, says Angel. *You're being a cow.*

'Oh all right, Trish. But I can't stop for long.'

They sit facing each other, silent as strangers in a doctor's waiting room. Then Chrissie begins to burble on self-consciously about trivialities, her usual device for taking the steam out of potentially awkward situations (she never learns!) while Trish watches her without interrupting at first, figuring she'll run out of words eventually.

But Trish can never be patient for long. 'Please,' she says, holding up her hand like a policeman on point duty, and Chrissie's mouth closes like a trap.

'Why the big freeze, Chrissie? Afraid to touch pitch in case it rubs off on you, or what? For Christ's sake talk to me. I need you! I need all the help I can get.' She bursts into tears and Chrissie caves in at once.

'Oh Trish, I know it must sound silly, but . . . but I was just so angry. I know you don't mean anything. It's . . . it's Nick you want. (*Don't we all?* says Angel.) You just like to flirt around for the fun of it, but . . .'

'But what?' Trish is mystified.

'Well, why pick on Den? If you felt like propositioning someone, why my husband? I always had the feeling you didn't even like him very much.'

'I always had the feeling *you* didn't like him very much either (*Got it in one*, says Angel), so what's with the Frankie and Johnnie routine? Besides, he's the last man on earth I'd

46

– how did you quaintly put it? – *proposition*. He should be so lucky! It's the other way round, pal, I kid you not. He's always hanging round me with his goddam tongue hanging out.' She breaks off at the hurt expression on Chrissie's face. Me and my big mouth. Good old Trish does it again. Give her a big hand, folks.

'You mean *he's* supposed to have made a pass at *you*? And not for the first time? You expect me to believe that?'

Trish forces her lips into an artificially bright smile. 'Well, it has been known. We all have our moments. Mind you, it didn't amount to a row of beans. He said a few things at my party. Just the booze talking, I guess.'

'And the other times? Surely it wasn't booze the other times?'

'You know what men are.' Trish shrugs elaborately. 'They're all the same – like to admire the goodies from afar, but terrified to touch. Why, if I'd given your Den any encouragement, he'd have run a mile, take my word for it.'

'Well, it's not like Den to—'

'He's a man, isn't he? The grass is always greener, and all that. Your Den's no different from all the rest. Does their little egos good to have a flirt and no harm done. Besides, he'd hardly pick his next door neighbour if he *really* fancied chasing ass, now would he? Men never foul their own nests, they're too cute for that. No, if he meant business he'd find himself some little doll in the back of beyond and start having to go off to mysterious conferences and meetings in the evenings, all of a sudden.'

She breathes a secret sigh of relief as Chrissie's face begins to thaw slightly. 'I suppose you're right.'

''Course I am.' Trish puts an arm across Chrissie's shoulders and smiles into her face. 'Friends again?'

'Friends.' *Well, try to sound a bit convincing about it.* Oh shut up, Angel.

*

It has been a swine of a day. The washing machine repair man has failed to appear as promised ('Can't say whether it'll be a.m. or p.m., but I'll definitely be there, come hell or high water.') and Chrissie has waited in all day for nothing. Driving, grey rain has kept a fretful Jan from playing outside ('But I could wrap up in my mac and wellies, Mummy.') and Chrissie is exhausted from trying to keep her entertained all day. ('Don't *want* to give my dollies a tea party, Mummy. Want to go *out*! I hate you. I want my daddy!')

And your daddy wants you, sweetheart, whispers Angel, *which is why your mummy always makes sure you are in bed and asleep before he gets home*. Shut up, Angel. For God's sake don't start all that again.

Chrissie dries the dishes in a silence, wondering whether perhaps Dennis has bitten off more than he can chew with this promotion of his. He's been worse than ever lately, if that can be imagined, arriving home late most nights and shutting himself away at weekends in order to work. She and Jan get snapped at if they so much as breathe near him, these days. Angel wants to know what's new about that and anyway why complain? *At least it keeps him out of your way for a bit longer*, she argues. *Besides, look at what happened last night when you tried to tell him you were worried he might be overdoing things, putting in so many hours at work.*

'Old Harris hasn't promoted me for nothing, Chrissie,' he had shouted. 'Now he wants his pound of flesh. You and Jan are the first to benefit from my new salary, not that I *see* much of my little girl these days (*And that can't be bad*, says Angel.), so don't you dare whine when I have to work for it. I'd have thought even *you* would know that no one gets an extra five hundred a year and still expects to clock off on the stroke of five each day.'

'Yes I know, but you were out all hours on Wednesday night and—'

'I wish you'd *listen* for once. I *told* you there was an important meeting on Wednesday, with drinks afterwards.'

Oh yeah, sneered Angel. *Mysterious conferences and meetings in the evenings is it? You know what Trish thinks about that.* Sod Trish. What does she know? *Quite a lot, actually. She's no fool, unlike you.*

'But you didn't get in until after twelve . . .'

'Don't imagine for a minute I'm accounting to *you* for every waking moment, but if you must know we went back to Bill's place for coffee. Satisfied? Expect me to get your signed permission, do you? Well think again. What am I supposed to do, turn down my boss because it might upset the little woman? A right nellie I'd have looked. No bloody woman tells *me* what to do, Chrissie, as you know only too well!'

Predictably, Dennis had worked himself up into a fine rage, slamming out of the house and returning long after Chrissie had gone to bed. He had awoken her at one in the morning to forgive her in his own inimitable way.

Now here he is, all set to go off to their Dublin office for a whole week and Angel is cock-a-hoop. *Be great to get rid of him for a few days, why not admit it. He's been even more of a pain in the arse than usual, you know he has, so why should you give a toss?*

Dennis calls imperiously from their bedroom. 'Chrissie! Did you remember to get my grey suit from the cleaners?'

'Yes.'

'And where's my grey striped shirt?'

'I don't know. In with the stuff waiting to be ironed, I think.'

There is a moment's silence, then: 'Just get up here. Now.'

She climbs the stairs wearily to face Dennis, who stands in the bedroom doorway with a face like a smacked arse, as his mother would have put it, fists clenched at his sides and caterpillars looking as if they mean business. 'This just isn't good enough, Chrissie. You know perfectly well I intend taking that shirt with me tomorrow.'

'OK, I'll iron it tonight.'

Chrissie should have left it there, of course, if she knew what was good for her, but, prompted by Angel, she has to add, 'Though why you're making such a big deal about that particular one beats me – you've got loads of other shirts.'

'That's hardly the point. You could at least have got my things ready for the trip. As it is I'm expected to do my own packing and everything.' *You poor sod*, says Angel. Dennis gives a short, barking laugh of exasperation. 'I don't know, I work myself into the ground for you and Jan, keep you in the absolute lap of luxury, wanting for nothing, and you can't even be bothered to do the bloody ironing or anything else, by the look of things.'

Chrissie's heart begins to pound as Dennis gets into his hateful stride. *Here we go*, sighs Angel. *Stand by for blast-off.*

Lip curling in disdain, he looks around the room disparagingly. 'Just look at this place. I sometimes wonder what you *do* all day. You've got lazy, Chrissie – fat and lazy. Have you looked at yourself lately? Have you?' He grips her shoulders and spins her round to face the cheval mirror. 'You've been letting yourself go.'

Dennis is beginning to enjoy himself. He stares at her reflection, looking her up and down insultingly, an unpleasant smile on his face. 'What a pathetic mess. Well, you'd better do something with yourself in time for the annual dinner next month or there'll be trouble. Don't want you showing me up like you did last year. Proudly telling all and sundry you'd made that dress yourself. They must have thought I couldn't afford to buy you one.'

'I thought I looked OK,' whimpers Chrissie, 'and actually, Den, we were a bit short of cash at the time, if you remember, and—'

The stinging blow across her face catches Chrissie completely off guard, and she falls on to the bed, tears of shock and pain springing to her eyes. Even Angel is stunned into silence.

'You don't learn, do you? Always trying to make me feel inadequate. Always niggling on about how hard up we are. Well those days are over and I can do without you constantly trying to undermine me. Get your hair done, buy yourself a new dress, for God's sake – I can afford it.' He turns to leave. 'Oh and don't forget,' he commands almost casually over his shoulder, 'I want that shirt ironed and packed *now*.'

five

'Is that you, Chrissie?' Florrie's voice on the telephone sounds weak and tremulous. She could be ringing from the moon rather than Neasden.

'Whatever's the matter, Mum? You sound awful.'

'What am I going to do? It's Stan – he's had a heart attack. All of a sudden it happened, no warning except for a bit of indigestion. We was on our way to my sister's, on the tube, when he come over all sweatin' and grey-lookin'. I got him off the train at the next stop and made him lay down on one of them seats—' She breaks off, weeping noisily into the phone, while Chrissie waits in an agony of suspense, not daring to think . . . well, just not daring to think.

Like erratic bursts of machine-gun fire, Florrie blurts out the whole story. She had bullied and badgered the normally indifferent station staff to help ('They were wonderful, especially the kiosk man – I take back everything I've ever said about blacks.'), and an ambulance had arrived surprisingly quickly. ('I take my hat off to the NHS. They know how to pull out all the stops in an emergency.') Stan had been whisked away to a nearby large London teaching hospital, where he now rested, still grey, but thankfully still alive, in the intensive care unit.

'I had to phone to tell Den. Where *is* Den? Put him on, will you? He must be told straight away.'

'He's away on a business trip, but don't worry, we'll get hold of him. In the meantime I'm coming straight over to get you. Now come on Florrie – no arguments. You can't stay there, all alone, worrying and wondering and driving yourself frantic. You've just said Stan isn't up to visitors and has got to have absolute quiet, no excitement for a few days—'

'Stopped getting any excitement from me years ago, poor sod.'

– 'so there's nothing you can do moping about at home. Just sling a few things into a bag and sit tight until I pick you up in Den's car. He didn't think it was worth taking it across to Ireland so he's hiring one over there.'

But Den doesn't like you driving his precious company car, says Angel slyly. And of course you'll never cope with London traffic, according to him. Tough tittie, this is an emergency.

'Should be with you in, what, three-quarters of an hour or so, and don't you start worrying if I'm held up. There's major roadworks on the A40 by the Polish War Memorial.' (*Don't we just know it. Den's been moaning about it for weeks.*)

Amazed at her own efficiency (*See, you can do it when you have to. You're not the useless lump Dennis seems to think you are.*), Chrissie settles Janine in the car and drives the twenty or so miles to Neasden.

As the car pulls up at the kerb Florrie appears on the doorstep, small and suddenly vulnerable in one of her home-made, brightly flowered dresses ('Didn't take me five minutes to run it up on me Singer.'), a blue knitted cardigan about her shoulders. She carries a battered tartan holdall in one hand and a bulging string shopping bag in the other. The net curtain twitches in the window next door, and old Mother Hopkirk, Florrie's neighbour and sometime combatant of twenty years, waves her a solemn farewell. ('Don't forget, Florrie . . . anything I can do, anything. You've got me number.')

She is unnaturally quiet and withdrawn during the drive

back, in spite of Chrissie's brave attempts at conversation and Janine's childish chatter, but relaxes a little by the time they pull into The Close.

'I brought you a couple of new colouring books I've been saving, my little love,' she smiles at Janine. 'There's some sausages and bacon, oh and a bit of cheese.' Florrie delves into the string bag, triumphantly extracting lumpy paper packages, like a magician producing rabbits from a top hat. 'No point in leaving stuff to go off while I'm away. Oh, and I had some cold lamb left; Stan loves a bit of cold lamb and pickle—' She breaks off, her hand rising involuntarily to her mouth. 'Silly cow. Stan's not here, is he? Didn't think.'

Janine settles at the dining table with her colouring books ('Thanks, Nan. This one's got Yogi Bear and Boo-Boo; I love them.') and Chrissie makes a cup of tea, that panacea for all ills.

Gradually, like the old trooper she is, Florrie manages to take control of herself. 'I s'pose Den must be told.' Her eyes meet Chrissie's for a brief moment, then slide away furtively. 'Just in case,' she adds, a slight break in her voice.

'Oh, er, yes, of course.' Chrissie had almost forgotten about Dennis. *You and me both, kid*, says Angel. She crosses the room to his desk, an oversized, brass-handled mahogany affair bought on the strength of his promotion as a mark of his new status, and begins rummaging through the drawers.

'Should be a piece of the firm's headed notepaper somewhere. It'll have the phone number of their Dublin office on it . . . Ah, here it is. I'll phone straight away.'

'Harding Drew.' The voice is cool, impersonal, with the slightest trace of brogue.

'Oh, er, I'd like to speak to Dennis Charleton please.'

'Trying to connect you.'

She turns to smile encouragingly at Florrie, who perches on the edge of her chair looking anxious.

'We don't appear to have a Mr Charleton listed, I'm afraid.' The voice pauses politely, awaiting further instructions.

'No, no, he's from the London sales office. Just visiting. I don't quite know who he's with at the moment.'

'I'll try Mr Docherty, the sales director.'

Rolling her eyes at Florrie, she mouths, 'They're just trying to find him.'

'I'm sorry, caller.' The voice is polite as ever, but now with an indefinable edge of coolness. 'Mr Docherty has no knowledge of a visit by a Mr Charleton at this time.'

The Dublin operator hangs up and Chrissie's patient smile fades, her mouth falling open in dismay. She stares at the telephone receiver uncomprehendingly then turns to Florrie. 'He's not *at* the Dublin office.'

Sensing something is wrong, Janine looks up from her colouring, rosebud mouth ajar, and stares at her mother.

'Well, ring his hotel then, and leave a message, or ain't he even told you where he's staying?' *Fat chance*, snorts Angel. Chrissie shakes her head dumbly, and Florrie tut-tuts at her son's typical lack of consideration. 'He don't change a scrap; never thinks of anyone but number one. Well, you'll just have to ring the London office. *They'll* know where he is.' Even if you don't, she wants to add.

But Florrie is wrong.

Dennis's (shared) secretary is enjoying a gossip over an illegal (outside statutory break time) cup of Co-op 99 tea and fruit cake. It is the office junior's birthday and any excuse will do. Besides, she is celebrating a whole week of not having to put up with 'that git Charleton, with his everlasting "*when* you're ready, dear" and "don't let *me* interrupt your private conversation on company time, *please*".'

She is caught slightly offguard by Chrissie's phone call, and before she realises she is talking to none other than that git Charleton's wife, she has spilled the beans about his week's leave on a family holiday in the West Country. ('Christ, I reckon my face was as red as my hair when I realised it was her. I could've *died*. Should've recognised the voice from when I met her at last year's annual dinner. Such a nice little thing too, though completely dominated by that wanker of a husband of hers, poor cow. What the bloody hell is he up to, that's what I'd like to know.')

It's what Chrissie would like to know, too, not to mention Florrie – although she can certainly hazard a guess.

'Bleeding men, they're all the same. Lying, cheating bastards the lot of 'em. To think that my own son . . . my own boy . . . What's his bleeding game? Off with some tart, I s'pose. Wish I could get my hands on him, that's all. I'd knock his bleeding teeth down his throat, big as he is. There, there, my duck, that's it, you have a good cry, get it outa yer system. They're none of 'em worth it, not one of 'em.'

'Oh Florrie, I feel such a bloody fool, apart from anything else.' *That's because you are one*, hisses Angel. No comfort there then.

Florrie is a tower of strength over the next couple of days. ('Take more than 'im to get *me* down, the little shit. Wish I'd drowned 'im at birth.' *Don't we all*, says Angel.) The house is cleaner than it's been in weeks (oh all right, months then) as Florrie whirls about taking out her aggression in an orgy of hoovering, polishing and scrubbing so that Chrissie almost forgets that she is supposed to be playing the role of comforter to Florrie and not the other way about. According to Angel, getting herself worked up about Dennis's 'family holiday' has given Florrie something to take her mind off Stan, and Chrissie couldn't agree more.

As if to compensate for her son's behaviour, Florrie treats her daughter-in-law with tender consideration and kindness, like a mother whose child is convalescing after a bout of illness. In the evenings, after tucking Janine safely in bed, she sits stolidly at her knitting, wishing Trish were around to help out a bit. Bit of a tough nut, that girl, bit flash, but a good sort all the same. Sod's law that she's dumped little Ian on her ex for a few days so that she can have a bit of a holiday by the sea with a friend. Florrie sniffs disapprovingly. One of her blokes, no doubt. She's a bit of a goer, by the look of her.

With the acquired wisdom and sensitivity found only in the elderly, Florrie knows exactly when to allow Chrissie to take her back home to Neasden. The girl's bewildered apathy has given way to anger, an anger of which Florrie thoroughly approves. Now I can leave her to get on with it and get back to my Stan, where I belong. I just hope to Christ she gives Den a right earful when he eventually decides to come home. ''Bout time you stood up to the little shit,' she tells Chrissie. *Absolutely*, says Angel.

Alone with Jan – and Angel, of course – Chrissie begins to take stock. After the initial shock, she felt crushed and humiliated. How those people at his office must be laughing at her.

Fancy his own wife not knowing he'd gone on holiday, she could imagine them saying. Crafty sod. Well, good luck to him if he can get away with it. I mean, have you seen his wife? They would bray with laughter. Oh yes, he brought her to the annual dinner last year. Insignificant little thing. Totally out of place. Could be quite attractive, I suppose, if she made a bit more of an effort, but really – a typical hausfrau my dear, and dull as ditchwater. Hardly Mr Charleton's type, if you ask me. No wonder he's found himself a bit on the side.

Surely he couldn't be with another woman, not Den. He's almost puritanical about that sort of thing. *Almost?* says Angel. *That's a laugh. He's only got to see someone dancing cheek-to-cheek with someone else's wife at a party and it's light-the-blue-touchpaper time. 'What do you mean, no harm in a little flirtation at a party, Chrissie,'* he says. 'That sort of thing is absolutely disgusting, and that's that. It just leads to trouble.' But his bloody rules don't apply to himself, of course. Hypocritical little shit.

You can't really think it's some woman, Angel. Not Dennis. He's never so much as looked sideways at anyone since I've known him, you must admit. Perhaps he's in some kind of trouble, pressure of work or something, and had to get away on his own. He could have been meaning to ring but had a nervous breakdown, anything. He might have lost his memory, had an accident . . .

Yeah, says Angel scornfully, *or a UFO might have landed and spirited him away. Or perhaps there's been an earthquake or freak tidal wave and we just haven't heard about it yet. Or perhaps you're just kidding yourself.*

How dare he put you through this? What have you done to deserve it? Haven't you always pandered to his every whim, agreed with his every opinion? Haven't you always made a complete doormat of yourself, in fact?

Chrissie clenches her fists. She's bent over backwards to please him (not to mention forwards, sideways and upside-down to satisfy him sexually, as Angel is quick to remind her) but it still hasn't been enough for him. Well stuff him. (*Atta girl!*) There's nothing more to do but sit it out until Friday and see what happens when – if – he deigns to return from his non-existent business trip.

I'm sure you can just picture the blissful reunion that Friday evening. Dennis stands in the hallway feeling distinctly put out. Chrissie should be greeting him ecstatically, an enthusiastic puppy dog pleased that her master has returned. She should be dancing attendance on him, the evening paper clamped between her jaws, her tail wagging.

'It's me,' he calls unnecessarily, 'I'm back.'

Chrissie does not reply but stands at the cooker, languidly stirring the contents of her orange Le Creuset saucepan (part of a set; another wedding present).

Beginning to feel slightly nervous (and who can blame him, knowing what we know), he peers round the kitchen door at Chrissie's rigid back and is momentarily lost for words.

But not for long. Stupid bitch must be sulking about something or other. A fine homecoming. She'll just have to be brought to heel, and quickly. True to form, Dennis leaps into the attack, striding into the sitting room, throwing his suitcase down on to the long-suffering sofa and himself into his usual armchair.

'Oh welcome back, darling,' he cries sarcastically. 'How did the trip go? You must be exhausted. Let me pour you a drink while you tell me all about it. I don't know, you spend all week working your balls off and for what? Your darling wife doesn't exactly give you a rapturous reception.'

Chrissie appears in the doorway. 'Is that what you expected then, a rapturous reception?'

Loosening his tie, Dennis pauses and looks at her. She looks different somehow. There is an odd expression in her eyes and Dennis feels uneasy. She should be practically in tears by now, dashing about waiting on him and getting him the pre-dinner drink he had fallen into the habit of demanding on his return from the office. (Well, that's what thrusting, up-and-coming young executives *do*, according to Dennis.)

Something is wrong, very wrong.

'Well, I certainly expected you to at least enquire what sort of week I've had, what the hotel was like, and so on.' Giving her a reproving, schoolmasterly little smile, he adds, 'Not to mention asking what little presents I've brought back for you and Jan.'

To his complete bafflement, Chrissie does not smile apologetically, but folds her arms and regards him blankly. She decides to let Angel loose on him: 'OK. I give in. What sort of week have you had, what was the hotel like, and what have you bought me? A stick of Dublin rock, or

Spanish rock, or Italian rock, perhaps? I must say you don't look very suntanned. Spend the whole time in bed, did you?'

'What the hell are you droning on about?'

'I phoned the office. Did you enjoy your holiday with the family? Where did we go? Anywhere nice? You really must let me see the photographs sometime, so that I can see whether we had a lovely time or not.'

He opens and closes his mouth like a fish out of water. Then, attempting a rally, 'How dare you phone the office? How dare you check up on me?'

'Quite easily, and I had a bloody good reason for checking up on you too, as it's turned out.' Crossing the room, she stares into his astonished face, as if seeing him for the first time. 'Your father had a heart attack while you were away God knows where. Good enough reason for you?' She smiles coldly. 'I know World War Three hasn't been declared, nor have the Russians exploded a nuclear device over Southern England, but your father's illness did seem a pretty good reason for disturbing the great man, at the time. And in response to the question, which fails to spring to your lips – because of your extreme grief, no doubt – yes, your father *is* out of danger. He's being sent home today, as a matter of fact. With plenty of bed rest he should be fine.'

Fantastic, cheers Angel. *I'm proud of you, kid. Let's hear the bastard wriggle out of this one!*

Bracing herself, Chrissie awaits the venomous counter-blast, but to her complete confusion Dennis crumples before her eyes, melting like candlewax. His head slumps forward on to his hands and he weeps, shoulders heaving.

Fuelled by Angel's venom, Chrissie has spent a week schooling her reactions to meet any of his anticipated ploys, but this leaves her open-mouthed in astonishment. She feels like a would be hero who, with a great whoop of victory, has just gone over the top into no-man's land only to find the enemy has packed up and gone home. She has never seen him so utterly defeated.

Oh, give the man a bloody Oscar, sneers Angel. *Don't fall for it, for Christ's sake*. But Chrissie is touched, rather than repulsed, by the sight of him. He's only human, after all. *Wanna bet?* says Angel, fighting to the last.

He looks up at her, his face wet with tears, and dumbly holds out his hand. Like a sleepwalker, Chrissie moves towards him and is lost. I can't ignore the appeal in his eyes, Angel. In the name of humanity, I just can't.

They talk into the early hours that night, or rather Dennis talks, slowly and painfully at first, but gathering momentum until all the pent-up grievances, all the secret dissatisfactions of their life together, come spilling out in a half-whispered torrent. There has to be more; life owed him something . . . something . . . who could say what?

'No, no, it's not your fault, but nor is it mine. No, no, it isn't anything you've done or haven't done. No, of course I haven't been with another woman; how could you even think such a thing? God, I wish the problem were that basic. No, I don't know what the problem is. It's as nebulous as mist and I wish to God I could grasp it and shake it until it comes right. I just had to get away, get away, get away and think and try to make the mist into a tangible thing. Forgive me, Chrissie. Help me, Chrissie. I need you.'

Finally persuaded to go to bed, he clings to Chrissie and eventually sleeps close in her arms, like a child comforted by his mother's presence.

Oh Chrissie, what a fool you were.

She stares into the darkness, thoughts whirling in her head like moths around a flame until, disengaging her arms from underneath the dead weight of Dennis's shoulders, she wriggles carefully under the covers and sleeps.

six

It is two months since Nick left, and the kitchen at number twenty-nine looks like the 'after' picture on a television Flash advert, the green and white gingham curtains still reeling with the shock of their first wash and iron since being hung three years ago. Trish, immaculate as ever, bustles about in a frilly apron looking like Mrs Perfect Suburban Wifey in the Persil ads.

Except of course that she isn't a wife any more, Stepford or otherwise – or won't be once her decree absolute comes through.

Librium and Valium sit facing each other on the draining board like inscrutable bookends, taking bets on how long it will take for Trish to shoo them off on to the floor. ('Things have certainly changed around here since Nick split, don't you think, Lib?' 'Oh indubitably, my dear chap, and I wish I could say it's been a change for the better. She never drops anything interesting on the floor these days, or if she does it's whipped up and thrown into the bin before you can move a paw. Makes you sick.')

'Hey, off there, you guys. Don't you know it's unhygienic to sit on the draining board?' ('See what I mean?') Val stretches langorously, taking his time, then slithers on to the floor, but Lib the old campaigner, victor of many a nocturnal spitting, snarling catfight, will lose face if he gives in that easily, so decides on a wash – always a good ploy when a cat wants to have a think about what to do next.

Trish swipes him off in mid-lick and hands Chrissie her

62

usual smiley mug of coffee. 'Won't fret if I get on while we chat, will you, hon?' she says briskly, peeping into the oven and closing the door again with a self-satisfied little nod. 'Only Paul – he's the gorgeous hunk I told you about – six-two, divorced, own business – Paul's coming to lunch, then taking me and Ian to Windsor Safari Park for the afternoon. There's masses still to do and just look at me, I'm a mess.'

She looks perfect, of course, from the tip of her newly brunette Clairol Colourwashed head to the black patent brilliance of her Dolcis stilettos.

'What do you think of the hair? Paul prefers women to be their natural colour.'

That's a laugh, says Angel. *I thought her natural colour's supposed to be more Dead Mouse than Glowing Chestnut, but still . . .*

'Paul prefers,' mimics Chrissie. 'Or Jamie prefers, or – who was the love of your life last week? Duncan, was it? They've been beating such a path to your front door since Nick left, I lose track.' *Miaow*, says Angel spitefully. *That'll get her going.*

But Trish only laughs in her easy, all-American way. 'I guess Fat Pat's got to you, hon. She must have dishpan hands the amount of time she spends at her kitchen sink watching what she calls the "goings-on" over here. The FBI'd be real proud to have her on the team.'

Yeah, we know, says Angel. 'That's three men I've seen trotting up her front path this week,' Pat had snorted. 'Don't know why she doesn't just put a red light over the front door, and have done with it. Disgusting!'

'Still,' continues Trish, pulling up a stool and sitting alongside Chrissie, 'keeps Pat off the streets, I guess. And I do make them stand in line, y'know; one at a time and all that. Fair's fair. Anyway, you got a problem with that, hon?'

Jes' plain ole jealousy, I gay-us, says Angel, in what she

63

fondly imagines to be a southern drawl. *Cain't bear to see folk having a good time on accounta she's having such a . . . such a . . .*

Chrissie weeps silently into her coffee and Trish is contrite.

'Sorry, hon,' she says gently. 'I guess I've been so wrapped up in myself lately I haven't been giving you much of my time. Come on, tell your Auntie Trish all.'

Chrissie looks down at her hands. 'I had thought,' she begins shakily, 'I had thought things were going to get better between me and Dennis, but somehow—'

'Somehow they're just as bloody as they ever were,' finishes Trish softly. *Bloodier*, says Angel.

Trish puts an arm round her friend's shoulders and smiles in what she hopes is an encouraging manner. 'Come on, give.' The smile becomes slightly strained as she adds lightly, 'Our Dennis is being even more of an asshole than usual, I guess. Am I right or am I right?'

'You could say that . . . ever since that . . . that lost weekend.'

'Oh yeah, the lost *week*, to be precise; the one where he went away to ponder on the Meaning of Life and all that bull.'

'Please, Trish. You're not making it any easier.'

'Sorry, sorry, forget I spoke.'

'Well, we talked it inside out and upside-down, as you know, and I said we must just forget the whole thing. Dennis was really pleased—'

'I bet he was. Sorry, carry on.'

'And we agreed we'd both make much more of an effort. Things were fine for a while, but now . . . well, whatever I do it's never enough. He's at me all the time.'

Trish raises her eyebrows. 'So what's new?'

'Just this.' Chrissie rolls up her sleeve and shows the bruises that bloom like obscene purple flowers on the pale skin. She unbuttons her blouse with clumsy fingers and Trish gasps at the marks Dennis has made to vent his rage.

'He knocked me down and then kicked me,' says Chrissie woodenly. She glances at Trish apologetically. 'Mind you, I suppose I asked for it, in a way. I should have just shut up, kept out of trouble, but I would keep on after he warned me.' *OK, blame me*, says Angel dully. *It was me that egged you on. Mea culpa.*

'After he *warned* you?' Trish is incredulous. 'Don't you even *think* like that. Don't blame yourself. Whatever you said he doesn't have the right to beat the crap out of you every time you open your mouth. Jesus, I knew the guy's weird, but—'

'But he doesn't mean it, Trish. He's always beside himself with guilt afterwards; keeps on saying how sorry he is over and over again, and how he can't think what's got into him. I'd have to be some kind of monster not to forgive him, he gets himself so upset and confused. It's just that I don't know how much more of it I can take.'

Until he kills you, says Angel flatly. *Until he gives you such a good kicking that you just don't get up again.*

Trish is on her feet. She takes a few paces and leans against the doorframe, hugging herself, shoulders hunched, as if seized by a sudden chill. 'And I suppose this touching little scene always ends up in the sack, does it?'

Chrissie doesn't reply; she doesn't have to.

'I get the picture. So he's got to slap you around before he can get it up, huh? I know the type, believe me.'

'Oh no, no Trish, it's not like that. You don't understand.'

'I'd say I understand better than you think.' Trish points her finger accusingly, looking like something off an 'Uncle Sam Needs You' poster. 'And what do *you* get out of it? Go on, look me in the face and tell me you get a bang out of it. Cross your heart and tell me your idea of erotic foreplay is a quick cuff about the head and body, or for a real turn-on a good kicking.' She looks at Chrissie with compassion in her eyes. 'You hate it, don't you?'

Chrissie shudders, her face white and vacant, the eyes lustreless, like twin grey pebbles. 'It makes me feel like, like an animal being used. Used and abused, like a beast of burden.'

Which is what you are, says Angel bitterly. *He's made you one.*

'Well, what are you going to do about it? Leave him, I hope.'

'I can't,' wails Chrissie hopelessly. 'He needs me. Besides, how could I survive? Where would I go? How could I support myself and Jan – don't forget Jan.'

'How could you support yourself?' echoes Trish. 'Jeez, he's done some number on you, hasn't he? He's chipped away at your self-confidence over the years until he's convinced you you can't cope without him. You can knock spots off that mother when it comes to brainpower and he knows it. That's probably half the trouble; he's jealous of you.

'You abandoned a prospective career before it had a chance to take off because he got you pregnant – his secret weapon for putting you down. (*Takes two*, says Angel philosophically. *And you were stupid and naive enough to let it happen.*) 'You could pick up the threads again, I know you could. You're a bright lady, and don't you let anybody tell you otherwise. I'll help, you know that. Anything. I'll drive you someplace, get you set up someplace safe.' *Someplace safe*, echoes Angel longingly.

'But I couldn't—'

'You *could*! For Christ's sake, make a break now before it's too late. He needs you all right, needs you as a sexual punchbag, is all. What *you* need is the important thing – what you and Jan need.'

At the sound of Jan's name Chrissie looks up, like an animal scenting danger, and Trish is quick to capitalise on that look. 'Oh no, I haven't forgotten about Jan,' she continues shrewdly. 'What the hell kind of effect is this having on her? She may only be a kid but she's not deaf, dumb and blind. And she's not stupid, either. What a wonderful example you must be. Do you want her to grow up believing sex and violence go naturally together, like love and marriage are supposed to?'

'Please, Trish, don't—'

But Trish can't stop the words pouring out of her mouth. 'What happens when beating up on you loses its charm,' she whispers, relentless as fate. 'What if he decides to turn on Jan. What then? We already know the only way he can get his rocks off is to slap a woman around a little. For him, sex is always better that way. But what if he decides he wants to taste younger meat? What then, Chrissie, what then?'

As Chrissie looks up, Trish recoils at her expression. The skin on her face seems stretched more tightly across her cheekbones and her eyes are bright with dread at some half-imagined nightmare. Angel takes over. 'That would be the end,' she hisses sibilantly. 'I'd kill him. If he doesn't manage to kill me first, that is.'

Trish shivers. She will never forget those words.

seven

our-year-old Ian is bouncing on Trish's bed, trying to rouse her, without a great deal of success.

'It was good at the zoo, Mummy. I liked the lions best. Can we go again today and can Daddy come with us this time? Can we, Mummy, please?'

Trish groans and burrows underneath the bedclothes. She hadn't enjoyed the zoo at all. Within minutes of their arrival it had started to rain, reducing the earthen walkways to a pinkish mud into which Trish's stilettos sank at every step. 'Pretty stupid wearing those shoes. They're quite unsuitable,' Paul had commented mildly, and to his astonishment, instead of coming back with one of her usual, jokey throwaway lines, Trish had launched into the attack.

'I'm a pretty stupid person, didn't you know? Get things wrong all the time, me. Look at that so-called lunch I fixed. Goddamn disaster area.'

'Oh, it wasn't that bad.' Paul slid his arm round her waist and slyly squeezed a breast. 'And anyway, who cares? With you there are compensations.'

Trish shrugged him off irritably. 'Oh sure. That's all I'm good for, yeah? Only any use in the sack, ask anyone.'

'Well, I have to admit it wasn't your culinary skills or shining intellect that attracted me in the first place.'

'Go take a running jump, asshole.'

All of which just about set the tone for what was left of the afternoon.

68

To his credit, Paul did not simply walk away, leaving Trish and Ian to slither through the mud by themselves, though God and Trish knew no one could blame him had he done just that. Instead he went through the motions, albeit with the martyred air of a man who is only there under sufferance, furtively glancing at his watch from time to time and wondering how soon he could decently suggest leaving.

Tucked up in bed, Trish sighs. Blown that one, I guess. Exit Paul, stage left. How was the poor sap to know she was too worried about Chrissie to keep up her usual sparkling line in repartee?

She peeps out at Ian from under the covers. 'Mommy doesn't feel like the zoo again just yet, honey. Maybe another day.'

'When, Mummy, when? And can Daddy come? And Mummy, why doesn't Daddy sleep in your big bed any more?'

Big, artificial Colgate smile from Trish. 'Well, it's like this sweetstuff, as you know your daddy doesn't live here any more.'

The little boy regards Trish solemnly. 'I *know*, Mummy,' he says condescendingly, with the calm acceptance of the very young. 'But why? Doesn't he love us any more?'

Trish's eyes mist with tears. 'Well, he loves you, sweets, but he's kinda gone off your mom.'

'Poor Mummy. I won't go off you. Not ever ever.'

'You will one day. Everyone does, in the end.' Trish grabs her son and holds him close, his hair tickling her nose. 'Can't say I blame 'em really,' she adds thoughtfully. 'Let's snuggle down and have one more little sleep, shall we?' She consults the Donald Duck alarm clock. 'Jeez, it's only six o'clock.'

'Oh all right then,' he answers reluctantly, 'just one more little sleep.' So she curls her arm lazily round him while he burrows and snuffles into her body like a small animal. 'I like it here, Mummy, and you're all warm, like the sun.'

'Thank you, hon.'

In the distance, far away, a bell is chiming.

'Mummy, Mummy, wake up Mummy – there's someone at the door.'

Trish opens her eyes blearily. At this time, and on a Saturday morning? Maybe if she ignores it they'll give up and go away.

'Mumm-ee – get up, get up. Someone's come to see us. It might be Daddy.'

Yeah, and the Pope's a Protestant. But, sighing, she sits up, eyes casting around unenthusiastically for her dressing gown.

Ian is hopping up and down impatiently. 'Come *on*. There's someone—'

'Someone at the door. Yes, I know. Jeez, you don't quit easy, do you, Ian Nicholson? You're gonna make a fantastic double-glazing salesman one day.'

Dennis stands shivering on the doorstep looking like death, and Trish's blood turns to ice. Something's happened. Something bad.

Without taking her eyes off Dennis, like an animal trainer who never turns his back on the big cats, Trish tells Ian to go and watch TV in the bedroom. '*Loony Tunes* is just starting,' she adds persuasively. 'And I'll fetch you some Coco Pops.'

Satisfied that Ian is out of earshot she snaps, 'What the hell do you want?'

'Trish, you've got to help me. Can I come in?' Dennis's voice is a thin whine, and Trish is filled with a disgust she can almost smell.

She hesitates for a moment, then opens the door wide, wrapping her dressing gown more tightly around her body. Dennis stumbles past her into the sitting room and collapses into a chair.

'Well?' She stands over him, arms folded.

'It's Chrissie,' he gasps, 'she's left me. My Chrissie and my little girl. I got up this morning and she and Jan had just . . . just gone. They didn't even take so much as a suitcase with them. Just the clothes they stood up in.'

'Are you sure?'

'Of course I'm bloody sure.' Dennis bridles, his voice growing stronger. 'Come and search the place if you like.'

'No thanks.' Trish shivers, in spite of herself, and shakes her head slowly in disbelief. 'But she wouldn't just take off. Not without a word to me. I just know she wouldn't.'

'Why should she tell you, of all people? It's *my* wife we're talking about. Oh God, what am I going to do?' He makes an ineffectual attempt to snatch at Trish's hand and she takes an involuntary step backwards. 'Please, Trish, you've got to help me find her.'

'Now why would I do that? Beats me why she didn't leave you long ago. If she really *has*, that is.'

'Wha-what do you mean? What has Chrissie been telling you? And what do you mean, "if she really has"? What do you think I've done, hacked the pair of them to death and buried them under the floorboards?'

He stands up, fists clenched, his face suddenly suffused with colour. He takes a step towards her and she is rooted to the spot. 'Well,' he shouts, 'what has that bitch been telling you?'

Trish's scalp prickles and, for the first time in her life, she is mortally afraid. Her instinct is to get the hell out of it, but somehow she manages to stand her ground. She examines her fingernails carefully, trying to keep her hands from shaking.

'Oh she didn't tell me much really, just that you've found ridicule and humiliation aren't enough any more. Now you've discovered that slapping her around is much more of a turn-on. Go a bit too far, did you?' She gives a tight little smile, feeling her courage returning.

'Of course, it wasn't exactly news to me. I found out just what a sicko you were during your – what did Chrissie call it? Your lost weekend. Just practising on me, were you? Well it didn't do a thing for me and evidently it didn't do much for Chrissie either.' She shakes her head mockingly. 'You've been reading all the wrong sex books, Dennis. Don't have much luck with women, do you?'

'You bitch! It's all your fault, putting ideas into her head. You poisoned her mind against me. You've told her about *us*, you slag.'

'I've what? Poisoned her mind? You made a pretty fist of that all by yourself . . . *lover*. And as for telling her about "us", as you so romantically put it, do you really think I'd want her to know I'd sunk so low as to have a "lost weekend" with what she laughingly calls her husband? I'm hardly gonna brag about it.' Trish's eyes suddenly fill with tears. 'God knows what made me do it.'

'You fancied me,' smirks Dennis confidently. 'Don't try to deny it. You'd been flinging yourself at me for ages. You were a pushover, just as I knew you would be.'

'Yes I was; I was vulnerable and frustrated in those few days after Nick left. I needed to feel desirable.' Her lip curls in distaste. 'Unfortunately, you started sniffing around just at the wrong moment.'

'The right moment you mean.' He tries to touch her, but she reels away, grasping at the back of a chair, as if to keep her balance. 'You didn't put up much of a struggle,' he sneers. 'You were begging for it.'

Dennis's eyes are sparkling with malice and Trish struggles to regain control. 'Yeah, that's me. A pushover. But what does that make you? Wasn't much of a challenge, was I? Couldn't have done the old ego much good really. I don't suppose it was as much fun as having to beat a woman into submission. Still,' she continues airily, 'you served your purpose, I'll give you that. You were there when needed. Dial-a-Dick. All you did was satisfy an itch,

72

is all. Thanks a bunch. You can get lost now, Dennis. I've no further use for you.'

To her surprise and relief Dennis turns, without a word, and leaves, crashing the front door behind him.

She stands gazing blindly out of the window for a long time, idly registering the slanting streaks of rain beginning to fall on the windowpane.

'I'm sorry Chrissie,' she says aloud. 'Please God, let you be safe.'

She pours herself a much-needed drink and takes it up to the bedroom, where Ian still sits calmly watching television.

Her mind is racing. Would Chrissie really go without even a goodbye? Without even leaving her a scribbled note? When did she leave? In the middle of the night, with a young child, wearing just the clothes they stood up in? Oh come *on*. And on foot? Just how far could a woman and a four-year-old child get on foot, for Chrissake? I just don't believe it.

Trish sips at her drink. She closes her eyes and sees Chrissie unbuttoning her blouse, sees the bruises, the marks on Chrissie's neck and breast. Her voice rings in Trish's ears: '. . . if he doesn't manage to kill me first, that is.'

With trembling hands, Trish carefully sets down her glass on the bedside table. She picks up the telephone and dials.

'Which service do you require?'

'Police,' she says tersely.

Tina

eight

Brian's mother is ensconced in front of the brand new nineteen-inch Ferguson telly from Rumbelow's that's going to take Brian the rest of his life to pay for.

'Begrudge yer mother a few quid a week for 'er only bit of pleasure left in life, I s'pose?' she had bawled, in front of that supercilious blonde manageress and a dozen gawping potential customers. 'Tight little git; after all the sacrifices I've made for you, an' all.' She has a way with words, Doris Bullock; no getting away from it.

Embarrassed into submission, as ever, Brian had signed on the dotted line and bundled his triumphantly grinning mother out into the street before the ink on the hire purchase agreement had dried.

But right now Mother is tucked safely out of harm's way in what she insists on calling 'the lounge', because nothing short of World War Three will make Doris Bullock miss *Stars of the Seventies*, a 'showcase for Britain's up and coming young talent', as celebrity host and failed comedienne, Cheeky Cherry Wanstrow, likes to put it. Brian knows nothing will shift his mother now. Anyway, peeping through the half-open door, he can spy her stumpy, support-stockinged legs comfortably propped up on the Rexine patchwork pouffe. This can only mean she has settled into her Plumb's loose-covered armchair and is already halfway down the obligatory box of Black Magic he buys her each Saturday to make sure she won't make her usual scene about him going out for the evening. Not that it ever works, reflects Brian gloomily. Dunno why I bother.

Satisfied that the coast is clear, he tiptoes stealthily along the passage and quietly eases open the door to her bedroom, which he has just finished doing up in high camp Barbara Cartland style – as prescribed by Doris. The fuchsia satin eiderdown screams at the raspberry pink velvet curtains, and Brian worries vaguely once again that grappling with all that overblown cabbage-rose wallpaper (shades of pink, of course) for days on end has either irreversibly damaged his eyesight or given him a bad dose of greenfly infestation.

Being stealthy is difficult when you're a clumsy fifteen stone, wearing the clod-hopping platform boots that are de rigueur in 1977 and are not nicknamed 'Brian the Bull' because of your alleged sexual prowess. Of course, his mother is on to him at once. Nothing wrong with *her* hearing, especially since she acquired that expensive state-of-the-art hearing aid (the NHS is not good enough for Doris) which Brian swears must be linked to compli-cated bugging devices throughout the whole flat, if not the whole of southern England.

'Whatchoo snoopin' around in my room for, Brian?' she shrills, blindly groping for a strawberry creme (that boy oughter know by now she can only manage soft centres, what with her false plate, the selfish little sod) with-out taking her eyes off the telly. On screen, twelve-stone Deirdre from Bromsgrove is valiantly trying to remember her mum's invaluable advice ('An' don't forget to *smile* at the camera, Deirdre love. You got a *lovely* smile.') while hoofing her way through 'I Got Rhythm', which she hasn't, and never will have, despite a diploma from the Lou and Edie Wade Academy for Ballet and Tap and weekly lessons since she was six.

'You'll be admirin' yerself in my wardrobe mirror again, I s'pose,' sneers Doris. 'Fancy yerself, do yer? Watford's answer to Beau bleedin' Brummel, you are, just like yer father.'

'Just like yer father,' echoes Doris's budgie, Joey-Boy, chortling jubilantly.

And just as Brian's father had, before walking out on Doris and his young son more than twenty years ago, Brian briefly fantasises – not for the first time – about smothering his mother with one of the overstuffed velveteen scatter cushions that litter the tiny flat. He is convinced they are breeding. Trouble is, knowing her she would continue to answer her own questions, even then. 'Whatchoo tryin' ter do with that cushion, boy?' he can imagine her asking, as her face takes on an interesting blue tinge and her watery grey eyes start to bulge, 'Tryin' ter suffocate me I s'pose.' Got it in one, Mother dear, thinks Brian, clenching his huge fists, but he manages to reply cheerfully, 'Gotta make sure I look good in me new suit, Mum; I owe it to me public.'

'Ooh, getchoo. Fancy yer chances, do yer? Just like that Bill Bullock, and we all know how he turned out, don't we?'

'Know how he turned out,' trills Joey-Boy, sensing a fight building up and crapping into his water bowl with excitement.

Yes, thinks Brian wistfully, we all know how he turned out: alive and well and living in sin in Greenford with some blonde tart twenty-five years younger than him, as his mother is so fond of telling him.

Talk about rubbing it in. Wish I had me father's legendary pulling power. Here I am, thirty-four and still a virgin, living with me mum in the same bloody council flat I was born in. It's all her fault. Even if I got lucky and clicked with someone, there's no chance of bringing it back here for a bit of the other. Not with *her* breathing down me neck, there isn't.

'. . . living in sin in Greenford with some blonde tart twenty years younger than him,' Doris is concluding. 'Well, you comin' in 'ere to let me 'ave a look atcha in this famous new suit you spent a fortune on down Man at C 'n' A's, or what?'

Teetering on his grey platform boots with elasticated side gussets, Brian twirls awkwardly on the sculptured shag pile while his mother manages to tear herself away from *Stars of the Seventies* for the few seconds it takes for her to give him her carefully considered opinion of his general appearance.

'What do you bleedin' look like? You look like a fat poof,' is her verdict. Which is unkind to say the least, knowing Brian's secret worries about his own sexuality – worries which have been carefully fed and nurtured by his mother since he was in short pants. Let's face it, Doris Bullock is, and always has been, a deeply unpleasant woman.

'Fat poof, fat poof,' cackles Joey-Boy, scattering feathers and birdshit all over yesterday's *Daily Mirror* spread thoughtfully on the floor beneath his cage.

'An' whatchoo wanna pick maroon for?' shrieks Doris. 'If you think it makes you look thinner you was robbed, boy. And them trousers! You look like a bleedin' chipolata burstin' out of its skin. And as for that pink shirt . . . well, words fail me.' Which makes a pleasant change, you have to admit. Even Joey-Boy is momentarily nonplussed.

Brian's face suffuses with a colour which clashes horribly with his outfit. 'It's not maroon. It's called aubergine,' he says through clenched teeth, 'and it's all the go.' Stooping slightly to peer into the concave, wrought-iron framed mirror over the fireplace that makes him look as if he's got mumps, he straightens the fashionably wide kipper tie and pats his burgeoning *Viva Zapata* moustache lovingly. Hmm . . . the 'tache is looking more like Peter Wyngarde's on *Department S* every day, he thinks smugly, giving his man-in-the-moon reflection a self-satisfied little smirk.

Uncannily, considering she is apparently now glued to

Barry, a sales rep from Ipswich, who is revving up to give a mauve ruffle-shirted and matching cumberbund impersonation of Englebert Humperdinck singing. 'Please Release Me', Brian's mother catches the gesture. Eyes in her arse, that one.

'And whatchoo think you look like with that bumfluff all over yer top lip? Call that a moustache? Looks more like sunnink hairy's crawled outa yer nose an' died.'

'Bumfluff, bumfluff,' sneers Joey-Boy, entering into the spirit of things by pecking viciously at the slice of dried cuttlefish wedged in the bars of his cage.

'I'm still growing it,' says Brian defensively, shuffling backwards towards the door. 'Anyway, I haven't got time to chew the fat, Mum. I'm meeting the girlfriend at half-past and—'

'Oooh . . . *girlfriend*. And when am I gonna meet this . . . girlfriend?' She pauses insultingly before spitting out the final 'girlfriend', as if to imply there is no such person, and of course there isn't. Right on cue, the studio audience on telly shrieks with derisive laughter as Barry from Ipswich admits that, well, *akcherly* he isn't *akcherly* a sales rep. Not yet, anyway. *Akcherly* he spends his days stuffing bags of giblets up chickens' arses for a living if Cheeky Cherry must know, but only until something more befitting his qualifications (Grade 3 CSEs in English, Geography and Art) turns up. Cherry forces one of her 'trademark' gap-toothed, cheeky grins and is tempted to frogmarch Barry off set there and then. Bastard's getting more laughs than she is, at this rate, and that will never do, not if she's pinning all her hopes on a new series of *Stars of the Seventies* in next autumn's schedules. She needs this desperately if she is to keep their kid at private school and her husband Ronnie, a former Man U footballer, in Scotch.

'Me an' Tina aren't going steady or anything,' says Brian nonchalantly, when the audience's laughter and Joey-Boy's sycophantic cackling has subsided, picking a name out of the air. Which is a bit of a coincidence really, since Brian is actually destined to meet someone called Tina this very night; only he doesn't know it, of course. 'She should be so lucky,' he continues blithely, warming to his theme. 'We're just what you might call ships that pass in the night.' Pleased with the phrase, he repeats it: 'Yeah, that's all me an' Tina are – ships that pass in the night. She'll do 'til I meet my ideal woman – a deaf an' dumb nymphomaniac who lives over a pub.'

Even as Doris and Joey-Boy are snorting with laughter at the very thought of Brian turning into a womanising bastard (you guessed it – just like his father), it finally dawns on Doris that she will just have to change tack if she hopes to stop Brian going out.

In a last-ditch stand, she turns to face him, her tone suddenly wheedling. 'Do you 'ave to go out tonight, boy? There's a good film on the telly later on an' I get lonely 'ere all on me own.' She smiles ingratiatingly, exposing a mouthful of unnaturally white, chocolate-smeared false teeth and a quarter-inch of bright pink artificial gum. 'Or if you don't fancy the telly we could play cards – 'ave a bit of a laugh.' Giving him a gruesome wink, like some worn-out old Portsmouth tart promising young sailors that don't know any better a good time, she adds temptingly, 'I got a few bottles of Guinness in the sideboard. Whatcha say, eh?'

'Whatcha say?' wheedles Joey-Boy, putting his head on one side coquettishly.

Not surprisingly, Brian has no trouble resisting such an irresistible offer. He's heard it all before anyway; like every single Saturday night of his life for as far back as he can remember.

'It's my one night out all week, Mum,' he says firmly. 'Besides, I told you already, I've made me arrangements now. Mustn't let Tina down; she's probably legging it down the town centre, panting for me, even as we speak.'

Doris's smile sinks without trace. Scowling, she turns her back, hunching her shoulders and pulling a face as Brian forces himself to plant what passes for a brief kiss on the top of her permed-to-death head. As ever, he can't help noticing how thin her hair is becoming, her pink scalp gleaming through the frizz; as ever he silently prays to God it's not hereditary. His mother is for ever reminding him that he has certainly not inherited Bill Bullock's 'mane of beautiful, black wavy hair', having decided that the odd compliment tossed in the general direction of her absent husband is perfectly justifiable provided it is used in the good cause of discomfiting her son. Knowing my luck, thinks Brian gloomily, I'll be bald before I'm forty; I've obviously inherited her rotten genes rather than me dad's. Be all I need, going bald. Unconsciously, he pats his Kevin Keegan Afro, as if seeking reassurance.

'An' what ever possessed you to have that bloody perm?' says Doris, uncannily going straight for the jugular, as usual. 'Makes you look more of a poof than ever, if you want my opinion. *Real* men don't have perms.'

With difficulty, Brian fights an impulse to peel off one of her American Tan support stockings and throttle her with it, like that bloke in *The Boston Strangler*. He shrugs his shoulders. She would probably trill, 'Whatchoo fink you're doin' with that stocking, Brian? Tryin' ter choke me, I s'pose? After all I done for you, an' all.'

'Don't wait up, Mum,' he says airily, taking another step backwards towards the front door and freedom. 'And don't put that chain on the door like you did last Saturday night or I won't be able to get in with my key.' As you know full well, you old cow, he wants to add, but doesn't.

'I can't go to sleep until I know you're in safe, Brian,' whines his mother. 'And I don't like sitting 'ere on me own without the chain on; anything could happen.'

Joey-Boy sits dejectedly on his perch, sensing all the excitement is over. 'Anything could happen,' he says sadly.

I wish, thinks Brian. Maybe masked gunmen will burst through the door and spirit her away into white slavery the minute my back's turned; maybe she'll be overcome with fumes from that bloody paraffin heater she insists on using because she's too tight to switch the electric fire on. Maybe I'll come back and find her and sodding Joey-Boy at the bottom of their respective cages with their toes turned up, to squawk no more. Bliss.

'Don't make it too late, eh?' pleads Doris pathetically, 'I need me rest, at my age.'

She turns back to the telly as Cheeky Cherry is attempting to humiliate five-feet-four budding comedian Tony Marello from Plaistow and failing miserably. Cherry has the uncomfortable and accurate feeling she is being upstaged (she is) and doesn't like it one bit.

'I'd give you a big kiss, Tony, but I haven't got a box for you to stand on,' she giggles, flashing her famous grin at the audience. 'That's all right, darlin',' replies Tony, quick as a flash, who has heard all the 'short' jokes ever invented, 'I could always dig a hole for you to stand in. It'd be even deeper than the one you're diggin' for yourself and I could always fill it in and bury you for good while I'm about it.'

Delighted squeals from the studio audience and complete indifference from Joey-Boy, who is fluffing up his neck feathers and closing his chalky eyelids for a quick kip.

Brian mumbles something non-committal and makes a bolt for it while the going's good. What a bloody life, eh? It'd better be worth it, that's all.

He brightens slightly once his mother, Joey-Boy and number eleven Garbutt Street are safely behind him. Free at last. Maybe *this* Saturday night is going to be different.

Fat chance. Sitting at the newly refurbished Hawaiian Bar, all rickety bamboo stools, rattan screens and parched-looking rubber plants, Brian decides that, after all, this

Saturday night is turning out to be as pointless as all the others. Why the hell does he bother?

Big Beryl the Barmaid is wondering the same thing. She's worked this dive for years, and has seen it through its various incarnations as the Tudor Bar (now *that* was *classy*), Mexican Pete's (bloody great straw hats and itchy striped ponchos) and the Hasta la Vista, which was a bit of a mouthful but the red satin Spanish frock she was obliged to wear took ten years off her, or so the punters were always saying. Not that Beryl takes much notice. Say anything when pissed, they do, especially if they think they might get a free drink, or better still a free bonk, out of it. As if.

But this bloody *Hawaiian* theme is something else. At forty-two, Big Beryl feels a complete prat shivering in her red boob tube (she'd refused point blank to be seen dead in the bra made of two imitation coconut shells), plastic-grass skirt (which scratches her blotchy legs something rotten) and paper-flower lei, or whatever it's called, hanging round her neck. Beryl's only been wearing this stupid gear for a couple of weeks and she's heard enough jokes of the 'how about a quick lei' variety (from her more intellectual customers, admittedly, who are mercifully few and far between) to last her a lifetime.

She's seriously thinking of jacking it in and going for a job at the Feathers over Croxley Green way. They're always short-staffed on account of their lousy pay, according to Polish Anton, cellarman at the Feathers – and he should know – but they do get a much better class of customer.

Polish Anton has been trying unsuccessfully to get inside Beryl's knockers (he means knickers, but knockers would do just as well, come to think of it) since 'time immoral' as he would put it, in his fractured English, and reckons the landlord would welcome Beryl, with open legs (he means arms), what with her being such a consuming professor (he means consummate professional, but is too proud to

85

settle for a humdrum phrase like 'good at her job' since he determined to speak English like what he imagines to be a native.)

Ruminatively buffing a glass with a tea towel that is begging for a nice soak in Domestos, Beryl glances across at Brian, who is gazing into the mirror behind the row of optics, miles away. Now there's one poor sod who *could* do with a 'lei', thinks Brenda, whichever way you want to bloody spell it. Here every week, he is, regular as clockwork, and never gets so much as a sniff of the action.

Brian takes a long, cool pull on his umpteenth pint of bitter and lights a cigarillo just like the ones Clint Eastwood smoked in *The Good, the Bad and the Ugly*, taking care not to set light to his budding moustache. That would never do.

Well, he sighs to himself, I'm certainly not going to pull if I carry on sitting here, like a lemon, specially now bloody Jimbo's turned up. I'd better get in quick, before he does. He reckons he's bloody shit-hot with the women.

Swivelling around on his stool, which creaks alarmingly under his massive haunches, Brian leans back against the bar to study the talent once more.

Speculatively, his eyes flicker over tonight's crop of unaccompanied women, judging and weighing each one as carefully as a prospective bidder at an auction, before passing on, expressionless, to the next. I wouldn't care, thinks Big Beryl sadly, but the poor sod's kidding himself he's in with a chance. Wasting his time. Completely wasting his time.

'I could give *that* one,' says Brian, digging Jimbo in the ribs. He jerks his head in the direction of a table tucked away in the corner. 'Her with the blonde hair and the tits.'

Tina. Only Brian doesn't know that yet.

'Clocked it on the dance floor earlier, shaking its stuff. Bet it goes like a rattler.' Brian smiles slyly. 'Surprised you didn't spot it from the off, Jimbo. Don't tell me you're slipping?' He can't resist trying to wind Jimbo up; Jimbo, who reckons he's such a fucking stud and is always telling Brian how he's had more women than Brian's had hot dinners.

But Jim's response is disappointing. 'Do me a favour, Bri,' he says, with a world-weary smile. 'Slipping? Me?' He snorts with laughter and pats Brian patronisingly on his dandruff-speckled aubergine shoulder. 'You don't know the half of it, old son. And if you did, you wouldn't *blaahdy* believe it, I kid you not.'

Slipping? Him? His only slip had been marrying young. What a disaster. After all his experience, an' all.

He'd lost his virginity at thirteen to Sheila McCarthy from 5C on a school trip to the Isle of Wight and had never looked back. Jimbo had been scared shitless but good old Sheila, fifteen-year-old veteran of many a skirmish behind bike sheds and bushes in parks and recreation grounds the length and breadth of Rickmansworth, had showed him the ropes good and proper.

Actually, his deflowering at Sheila's practised hands had been a hole-in-the-corner affair – if you can dignify it by calling it an affair, that is. Over in seconds, it had happened under the pier in broad daylight, with two of Sheila's giggling friends looking on and little Reggie Moffatt waiting in line. But in Jimbo's mind his Big Moment had been softened and sentimentalised over the years until pasty-faced, unlovely Sheila, in her tatty Aertex knickers and grubby Berlei 32B lightly-padded Teenbra, was transformed into the beautiful but reluctant virgin, with Jim cast as the all-conquering, irresistibly handsome, randy man-boy.

Jim smiles reminiscently. Good old Sheila. She had certainly started something. No woman was safe after that. By the age of eighteen he was cock-of-the-walk, Jack-the-lad; he could have taken his pick of all those little tarts at the Mother's Pride factory where he worked then – or so he likes to think – but, no . . . He has to go and meet *blahdy* Maureen at Dave Cope's twenty-first down the Co-op Hall, doesn't he?

Maureen was different from the rest. Jim recognised that from the off. Refined, she was, with long silky hair in one of those velvet Alice-band things and shiny, slightly protuberant, blue-grey eyes. 'Thyroid case, if you ask me,' Jim's mum had pronounced authoritatively. She was a doctors' receptionist, and knew everything there was to know about all things medical.

Maureen had been to Rickmansworth Grammar, worked in an estate agent's office and spoke really posh. Jim was deeply impressed.

The Carnaby Street pot-smoking culture of the sixties had completely passed Jimbo by (well, he was only a boy then). So by the time Jim was nineteen, his idea of giving a girl a blinding time was to meet her down the Cricketers, ply her with Dunhills (nothing but the best when *he* was on the pull) and pour as many Babychams (known as 'leg-openers' in Jimbo's parlance) down her throat as humanly possible, until she was in no state to resist when he took her outside for a grope among the empty beer crates out back.

While even he could see that this routine was a tad unsophisticated for the likes of Maureen, he was completely thrown when she flatly turned down his carefully thought-out offer of a Saturday night down Watford Palais, which was considered the epitome of class venues in his circles.

Jimbo shakes his head at the memory. Why didn't he listen to Dave, who had tried it on with Maureen himself and told Jim what a prick-teasing little cow she was? Could have saved himself a lot of grief. But, no, intrigued by the challenge, he'd persisted until eventually Maureen graciously agreed to allow him to take her to the local Berni for a prawn cocktail and steak dinner, followed by the inevitable Black Forest gateau and cheeseboard selection. 'Christ, Jimbo,' Dave had whistled incredulously, 'you must be keen, pushing the boat out like that. Costs an arm 'n' a leg, that place.' And he had patted Jim's shoulder and given a leery wink. 'You can't miss, mate.'

But if Jimbo thought that such largesse was going to buy him the right to lay so much as a finger on one of Maureen's silken, Pretty-Polly-nyloned knees, he was sadly mistaken. Maureen was apparently 'saving herself for marriage', a quaint notion that Jim thought had gone out with the invention of the rubber johnnie. Not that he would ever demean himself by wearing one of those *blaahdy* things, as he was always telling Brian; not since his old dad had told him that wearing a condom was like doing it wearing a wellington boot full of water on your dick. And anyway, 'They're all on the *blaahdy* Pill now, Bri; or if they're not, that's their *blaahdy* problem.'

You might have thought Jim would simply have dropped the saintly Maureen like a hot brick, but, with that mixture of bull-headedness and injured pride peculiar to young men like him, not to mention sheer, crawling-up-the-walls frustration, he persisted. He was determined to have her on her back if it was the last thing he did.

But Maureen didn't give an inch, and would tug primly at her skirt, or playfully slap the hand that crept under her pristine angora sweater, until she drove Jim completely crazy. Crazy enough to propose marriage, one drunken New Year's Eve when she had *nearly*, very nearly succumbed, temporarily weakened in her resolve to stay 'pure' on account of the four (no more, in case she threw up) cherry brandies Jim had managed to force down her.

'Oh Jimbo, *darling*,' she had squealed excitedly, determining there and then that she would drag Jimbo down Bravington's the minute they opened on Saturday because she had seen the *perfect* engagement ring in the window – a sapphire (to match her eyes, if you ever! Always did kid herself, that Maureen.) surrounded by tiny diamonds. Actually they were spinels, not diamonds, but Maureen wasn't to find that out until ten years later, when she tried to sell it to a high-class jeweller in Catford. Delicately moving Jim's hand from her left breast she gazed into his eyes. 'I can't wait to be *Mrs* Maureen Hunter,' she said ominously.

And she didn't wait; not for long, anyway. Before you could say 'Do you take this woman', the arrangements had been taken out of Jim's hands entirely. Not that they were ever in his hands in the first place, of course, for Maureen's mother, a formidable matron and treasurer of the local WI (mainly on the strength of her husband being a deputy bank manager), threw herself into organising her only daughter's wedding with a military precision that made Field Marshal Montgomery look like an amateur. 'Marvellous woman, marvellous,' Maureen's dad was wont to intone, deadpan. 'Pity she was too young to serve during the Hitler War. That spot of bother would have been all over by 'forty-two if my Mavis had had anything to do with it.'

Jim didn't stand a chance.

They were married the following spring in St Lawrence's, Rickmansworth, with Maureen floating down the aisle in a blur of white tulle, courtesy of Pronuptia of Watford, four assorted bridesmaids in apricot taffeta and Maureen's mum (flowered two-piece from Evans' Outsizes which gave her all the allure of an overstuffed mattress) bawling her eyes out in the front pew. Though what *she* had to cry about Jim couldn't imagine. *He* was the one who would have been *blaahdy* crying if he'd known what marriage to Maureen was going to turn out like.

After the ham-salad sit-down reception for eighty at the Co-op Hall, after a pissed Dave Cope had fallen over while delivering the best man's speech, and long, long after Jimbo's dad had had his face slapped by the chief bridesmaid when he deliberately grabbed her tits instead of her waist during the conga ('Like father like son, eh, Jim boy?'), the newlyweds managed to tear themselves away to their not-so-secret honeymoon destination.

The Balmoral Hotel, Bournemouth, turned out to be a large redbrick boarding house 'Guest House, per-lease' with delusions of grandeur, a crazy-paved front garden (to provide the 'ample car parking' described in the brochure), H & C in every bedroom, fitted carpets throughout and a landlady ('proprietor, if you don't mind') with an expression that could've curdled milk at fifty paces.

Jim scowls into his beer. What a *blaahdy* fiasco *that* had been. He'd had more fun with Sheila McCarthy under that rainswept pier all those years ago. At least Sheila had been enthusiastic, which was more than you could say for his darling bride, who just lay there, practically *yawning*, for Christ's sake, while he did the business.

'Is that it, then?' she said brightly, when he eventually rolled off her. Then she trotted off, cool as a cucumber, to the cubby-hole of a bathroom across the threadbare landing, presumably to hose off all trace of his body fluids from her milky skin. From there, it's been downhill ever since, thinks Jimbo grimly.

Taking a mouthful of beer, he brightens slightly. Still, could be worse, I s'pose. Long as I box clever, long as I keep the pennies coming in so *she* can have a new telly, new washing machine or whatever takes her fancy every coupla years, she don't mind turning a blind 'un to what I get up to on me nights out. Crafty cow. She knows which side her bread's buttered. Got it made, she has. Money-grabbing bitch, like all *blaahdy* women. They just use men, so what's wrong with returning the favour? All they're good for. She's got me by the financial short 'n' curlies, all right, what with the two kids and a *blaahdy* great mortgage round me neck 'til I'm old and toothless, so, stuff it, I'm gonna get as much fun out of life as I *blaahdy* can. It's only fair.

Many men would envy him, Jim rationalises. Dave Cope, for a start, who'd only gone an' got one of their own bridesmaids (Maureen's stuck-up best friend from grammar school, Carole Hinkley) up the duff on his and Maureen's wedding day. At least Dave *thinks* it was him ('Too pissed to remember much, Jim, to tell the truth.') and ended up *marrying* the slag. 'Course, Carole keeps poor ole Dave on such a tight rein he's not allowed to fart without her say-so, let alone so much as look sideways at anyone else. He's been a shadow of his former self since marrying her, and that's a fact.

Jim grins broadly, showing the gold tooth he's had done to replace one that was knocked out in a punch-up outside the Cricketers years back. Then there's me, as much spare tottie as I can handle and no questions asked, plus a nice, cosy wifey at home tucked up on her Times Furnishing three-piece suite doin' her *blaahdy* knitting, for Christ's sake, for when I get desperate. And I mean *really* desperate.

Shouldn't knock it really. Slipping? Him?

Jimbo grins patronisingly at ox-like Brian and wipes his too full, too red lips with the back of his hand. 'Hardly slipping, Bri old son. In fact I'd say I'm just about reaching my peak. And as for old what's-her-face over there – Tina, or whatever her name is – well, as a matter of fact it's been had already.'

He reaches for their empty glasses and raises his eyebrows. 'Another of the same?'

Without waiting for a reply he clicks his fingers at Big Beryl, who completely ignores him. Who does that Jimbo think he is, clicking his fingers like fucking castanets? He forgets this ain't the Hasta la Vista no more.

'Two more in here, please dear,' says Jim wearily. '*When* you can spare the time.' So Big Beryl sulkily obliges. It's what she's being paid for after all, though not for much longer – God, Polish Anton and the landlord of the Feathers willing.

Brian, meanwhile, is staring at Tina, almost drooling down his British Home Stores eighty per cent, polyester tie. 'Tina, you said?' He tries to keep the excitement out of his voice, because if that bastard Jimbo thinks Brian might be the slightest bit interested he'll be in there like a ferret down a rabbit hole. Bastard.

Tina, eh? Now that really is some coincidence, because it's the very name he invented to make his mother think he really had got a girlfriend at last (not that Doris believed it, for a minute). It must be fate, thinks Brian reverently. Must be meant, somehow.

'Well,' he says, ever so casually, 'What was, er, Tina like, then? Any good?'

'Not bad, not bad at all. Wouldn't kick it out, as the saying goes.'

Gotta make Jimbo think I don't wanna know, thinks Brian feverishly. He is beginning to break into a light sweat. 'You wanna get in there then,' he drawls nonchalantly, glancing at his watch. 'It's only half ten. Play your cards right and you could have it tucked up by closing time, knowing you.'

But Jim shakes his head regretfully. 'As I say, it's been had. You know me, Bri – love 'em and leave 'em that's my motto. Besides, I like a bit of a challenge, me, and the slag was begging for it from the off. Too easy by half. Only put it to her in the *blaahdy* car park, would you believe.' (Brian doesn't.) 'Dead obliging, it was. Quick knee trembler across the bonnet of someone's motor, pat on the arse and it went home happy.'

A pack of lies, of course, for Jim never admits defeat. For him there can only be conquest. Should some slag have the bad taste to turn him down he brags that he has had her anyway. Serves her right.

'Bastard,' breathes Brian sycophantically. He pats at his Afro, straightens his tie unnecessarily and jerks his head in Tina's direction. 'P'raps I'll give it a tug then,' he says, keeping his voice dead casual. 'Nothing else I fancy, after all, an' it's getting a bit late.'

'Don't think you're quite in her league, old son,' sniggers Jimbo. 'She prefers the more experienced man. Unlike yourself, from what I've heard.' And Brian's cheeks burn with anger and embarrassment. Come the revolution, he determines, Jimbo is going to be the third for the chop – after Doris and Joey-Boy, of course.

Jimbo throws the remains of his pint down his throat and pats Brian's arm, eyes fastening hungrily on a likely prospect with a bird's nest of pink hair and matching mini that's tottering out of the Ladies having just thrown up after one too many port and lemons.

'Well, can't hang about wasting good pulling time, Bri,' says Jimbo. Not that he's had much joy so far. Talk about *blaahdy* Grab-a-Granny night! 'I fancy a piece of that, over there. Might catch you later. Be lucky. Ciao.' For Jim is the sort (as if you hadn't guessed) who thinks routinely adding expressions like 'be lucky' and 'ciao' to his goodbyes make him sound sophisticated, whereas everybody thinks it makes him sound like a right prat.

Which he is.

Brian scowls into his beer. Arrogant sod. Probably a *lying* arrogant sod. Nobody gets that lucky that often. Stands to reason.

He looks wistfully across at Tina, chatting animatedly to a pallid redhead who is practically a permanent fixture here: Jean someone, he seems to recall. Jimbo reckons he's had her an' all, the liar. Mind you, that Tina's asking for it in that gear, or so he hopes.

Ah well, nothing ventured and all that. Might be worth a go. Bollocks to what Jimbo thinks. Brian empties his glass decisively and, lurching to his feet, picks his way unsteadily across the violently patterned carpet designed to camouflage traces of beer, vomit and blood that have been spilled on it in its time.

'Evening ladies. How about letting me buy you another drink?' Brian gives a surprised little start, as if recognising the redhead for the first time. Smooth, or what? 'Why, if it isn't the lovely Jean. Beautiful as ever, I see. And who's your friend?' Eat your heart out, Jimbo.

Brian concentrates on bending down without falling over or splitting his aubergine trousers and drapes an arm across Tina's shoulders. 'What you drinking, darlin'?' he says, breathing beer and cigarillo fumes into her face.

'Piss off Brian,' says Jean flatly.

For a frozen moment, Brian imagines he is about to disgrace himself and burst into tears; can't even offer a woman a friendly drink now, without getting a load of verbal for his pains. Please God don't let Jimbo see. Not Jimbo. He couldn't bear that.

Without a word, he stumbles back across what feels like miles of carpet towards Big Beryl, who has been watching Brian's every move since earwigging on his conversation with Jimbo. She could have told Brian he wouldn't get much change out of that Jean, and so could Jimbo. Only he didn't. Sadistic bastard.

'Never mind love,' she says tenderly, pouring him another pint without being asked. ''Ave this one on me. They're not worth it; not one of 'em.'

Which only makes Brian feel worse, somehow.

nine

'Poor bloke,' says Tina, as Brian lurches away. 'He looks near to tears.' *And you'd know*, says Angel. *You're an expert on tears, after all.*

Tina's lips curve in a ghastly orange smile: Revlon's Desert Fire, same as Trish always used to wear. Don't miss a trick, do you Angel?

That particular lipstick shade had been discontinued long ago, but Tina – or Chrissie, as she was known back then – had got lucky (*for a change*, commented Angel drily, at the time) and, on her way to the hairdresser's, had found a dusty little pharmacy in Garston that had half a dozen tubes of the stuff in its 'end of line' dump bin, jockeying for position with redundant packs of Rich Cinnamon hair colourant, bottles of nail varnish (Desert Fire again. Joy!), and pots of sparkly mauve eyeshadow that promised to make the wearer look as if she'd just done ten rounds with Muhammad Ali. Or Tina's ex-husband, Dennis, perhaps.

Tina ignored the eyeshadow but bought all six lipsticks and a couple of bottles of the matching nail varnish, to the delight of the proprietor, who had only managed to get shot of three packets of hairpins and a gift pack of Old Spice left over from last Christmas all day so far.

Humming to drown out Angel's protests, Tina had set off for Rachel's Hair Fashions (appointments not strictly necessary), just past the scruffy industrial estate and next door to the Taste-E-Bite Sandwich Bar, which was also owned by enterprising Rachel. ('Well, way I see it, all these punters coming in for a quick comb-out, shampoo 'n' set or whaddever in their dinner hour are gonna miss their works canteen grub, ain't they? Obvious, innit?')

Rachel had just gone off home with one of her migraines, as it happened (she was prepared to go blind rather than admit she needed glasses) and Tina's request for a Sunkissed Blonde dye job had thrown young Debbie (only six months out of college and temporarily in charge) into a right tizzy. But luckily, old Mrs Morrison, who had apparently trained with Mr Teazy-Weazy no less – round about the turn of the century as far as Debbie was concerned – just happened to be in having what she called her pepper and salt (heavy on the salt) roots touched up. ('Look as if I've got a one-inch side parting at the moment, Debs.') Mrs Morrison had kindly hung about muttering instructions to Debbie out of the corner of her mouth when she didn't know what to do next. 'I'da taken over altogether if it wasn't for me rash,' Mrs Morrison was to tell her husband later. 'Amazing how it all comes back to you when you bin well trained.' Even though it *was* yonks ago, thinks Mr Morrison, and you only stuck the job for a couple of months before falling for our Kevin. But he keeps tactfully schtum.

Debbie breathed a sigh of relief as Tina paid up like a lamb, apparently not noticing the peroxide burn behind her left ear.

Jean coughs politely. 'Hello,' she grins, peering into Tina's face. 'Is anybody home? Are you receiving me?'

'Sorry. I was away with the fairies, for a minute there.' *What's new?* sneers Angel. 'What were you saying, Jean?'

'Only that you don't wanna waste your time feeling sorry for that Brian the Bull. He's probably married – most of them are – and anyway, he's a right pain in the arse. Has to be, if he's one of dear Jimbo's sidekicks.'

Oh dear me, yes, murmurs Angel. *Don't let's forget about Jimbo.* As if I could, thinks Tina, blushing to the roots of her Sunkissed Blonde hair.

Jean pauses to paw through the contents of a suede tote bag that could have comfortably accommodated (and has, in its time) a takeaway Chinese dinner for two and a couple of lagers to follow, eventually pulling out a battered packet of Embassy and a box of matches that had been trying to hide in a split in the lining.

'Ciggy? No? Very wise. 'Bout time I gave these the boot.' Jean lights up and inhales gratefully. 'Bloody Brian's been been eyeing you up for ages with his tongue hanging out like a randy labrador. Practically frothing at the mouth, he was. No doubt Jimbo's been whetting his appetite with the trailer so he thought he'd try his luck with the big picture.'

'But it's not as if . . . I mean, he didn't . . .'

'Didn't get his end away,' finishes Jean flatly. She shakes her head gently, treating Tina to one of her speciality-of-the-house, world-weary smiles. '*I* know that and *you* know that, but it won't stop the lovely Jimbo making out he did.'

She takes a thoughtful sip at her gin and tonic. 'Thank Christ I saw the evil bastard follow you outside that night. Left poor old Keith standing in the middle of the dance floor like a spare prick at a wedding when I rushed out after you. Nearly broke me neck on these sodding heels, but at least I managed to save you from a Fate Worse Than Death.'

And you've had enough of those to be going on with already, says Angel. *Accident waiting to happen, you are. Ought to think yourself lucky you've got a friend like Jean looking out for you.* Yeah, yeah. Thank you and goodnight, Angel.

'Thanks, Jean,' says Tina dutifully.

'Think nothing of it, flower. All part of the service. Mind you . . .' She pauses for a moment, blowing out a plume of smoke. 'Can I give you a bit of advice?'

She needs all the advice she can get, says Angel. 'Go

ahead,' echoes Tina coolly. 'Apparently I need all the advice I can get.'

'Well, you do let it all hang out a bit, if you get my meaning.' Jean nods her hennaed head pointedly at Tina's cleavage. 'Gives 'em the wrong idea, poor sods. They've only gotta clock the Sadler's Wells eye make-up and the tits hanging over the old balcony like bystanders at a traffic accident to assume they're in with a shout. What with that *and* the suicide blonde bit . . . well, you've gotta be up for it, haven't you?'

Tina's hand flies to her bright hair. 'Suicide blonde?'

'Yeah – the old peroxide job, with the roots in mourning,' grins Jean. 'If you must have it that 'orrible, brassy colour, let me do it for you properly. I used to be a hairdresser in another life.' Which she did, and a bloody sight better one than poor little Debbie of Rachel's Hair Fashions.

'You think I overdo it, then?' *Got it in one, kid. That's what I've been trying to tell you for ages*, sighs Angel.

'You could say that.' Jean takes a ruminative sip at her drink. 'Look, Teen, I know you want to meet some nice bloke – don't we all, one of these days – but to be honest you're attracting the wrong type done up like that.'

And if you say, 'It worked for Trish,' I'll scream, says Angel. Well, it did, thinks Tina sulkily. It did work for Trish. How else did she attract . . . *How else did she attract Nick?* sneers Angel. *Well, I think it's just sick the way you're trying to turn yourself into a carbon copy of Trish. And don't think calling yourself 'Tina' – same bloody initial as Trish, I notice – is going to get you anywhere. Where has the whole makeover got you so far? All you've succeeded in doing is nearly getting yourself raped!*

'So nearly getting myself raped was my own fault.' Tina frowns into her glass, her voice taking on a bitter note. 'Asked for it, did I? Got my comeuppance. Story of my bloody life, that is.'

She looks Jean up and down insultingly, taking in the skin-tight suede skirt and clinging satin blouse. 'Anyway, I don't see *you* exactly hiding your light under a bushel.'

Forget it kid, says Angel. *You won't wind up an old warhorse like Jean in a hurry*. And she is absolutely right, as ever.

'Depends what you want, duckie,' says Jean, shrugging amiably. 'I'm *not* looking for Mr Right – not just yet anyway. I spent too long sitting around feeling sorry for meself after my ex-old man left with that tart Elaine from number forty-seven. Oh, don't get me wrong; I wasn't exactly on the point of slashing me bleedin' wrists just because *he* walked out on me. That Elaine's welcome to him. Lazy sod.'

She takes out another cigarette and grins at Tina. 'No, what really got up my nose was that the bastard took every one of my Beatles LPs, ten quid out of my purse and cleaned out the joint bank account I was stupid enough to sign up for. Still, that's men, eh?'

Tina nods decisively, much to Angel's amusement: *Well of course you'd know, with all your experience. Ha bloody ha*.

'These days,' continues Jean, 'all I want is a good time while I've still got me own teeth. Mr Right'll turn up when he's good and ready, but in the meantime I'll settle for the Mr Wrongs of this world. In my experience – which is considerable, I'll have you know – they're a bloody sight more fun than the rest!'

'You're incorrigible,' smiles Tina. 'I suppose I *am* hoping to meet a nice man one day, if I'm honest.' She gazes round the room hopefully, and Angel wants to know what she is expecting, some Sean Connery lookalike in a three-piece suit to materialise out of the woodwork, or what. Complete with a bunch of flowers in one hand and a box of chocolates in the other.

Do us a favour, continues Angel. *You're hardly going to*

*meet the man of your dreams in a pick-up joint like this,
now are you?* That's all very well, Angel, but where else
am I likely to meet him? Not sitting at home watching TV
with Mum and Dad every night, that's for sure. *I suppose*,
says Angel grudgingly.

Funny kid, thinks Jean, gazing at Tina in fascination. I'd
love to know where she goes when she's off in one of these
little trances of hers. And the way she cocks her head like
that. Almost as though she's . . . listening. Having a private
conversation inside her head. Or something.

Though she doesn't know it, Jean has, of course, got
it in one. How could she possibly know about Angel,
after all?

Jean shrugs. Watch it, girl. Getting fanciful in your old
age. Frustrated agony aunt, or what? Rising to her feet, she
says cheerily, 'One last drink before they close the shutters
on us?' But there is no response. Tina is still gazing glassily
into space. With a tight-lipped, 'Please yourself, I'm sure,'
Jean heads for the bar. Dunno why I bother really, she
thinks. Why am I making excuses for her? Tina can be just
plain bloody rude at times, and that's all there is to it.

Whoops, says Angel. *Think you've upset our Jean. She's
gone stalking off to the bar with a right gob on.*

What do you mean, *I've* upset Jean? Takes two, Angel.
If you weren't yammering in my ear every five minutes I
might just have a chance to have a civilised conversation
with someone once in a while! There are times when I wish
you'd piss off out of my life altogether.

You don't mean that, says Angel smugly. *You love me
really. And anyway, you and I are stuck together. For better
or worse.*

'Til death do us part?

*I reckon so. I mean, look what happened when that
bloody shrink tried to split us up when you were in a bit
of a state after leaving Dennis.*

Tina gives a bitter little smile. Bit of a state, Angel? I

101

didn't know which way to turn. I'd tried everything short of leeches and blood-letting in an attempt to 'pull myself together', as my dad so sweetly put it. And my fresh-faced young GP wasn't a lot of help. Just crammed me full of tranquillisers and then wondered why I could hardly walk in a straight line, let alone function.

So in desperation you told him about me, says Angel. *Big mistake. His little beady eyes nearly popped out of his head with excitement. Made his day having something a bit different to get his teeth into. Must be a boring life, doling out antibiotics by the vanload and shoving cold, metal things up women's fannies to earn a crust.*

But he knew he couldn't handle the pair of us, grins Tina.

Right. So he hits on the brilliant idea of getting you a few sessions with his mate, Felix, your friendly, neighbourhood shrink. All bumfluff beard and Jesus sandals. God, what a pantomime that was.

Yeah, with me as Cinderella, you as both Ugly Sisters rolled into one and Felix as Fairy Godmother. He reckoned he was going to sort me out with one wave of his magic wand. Correction. Several waves. Wouldn't do to 'cure' me too quickly. He needed the money, judging by the state of what he laughingly called his 'consulting room'.

But even he couldn't see me off, says Angel smugly. *Because you didn't really want me to go, when it came to the crunch. Admit it.*

Tina frowns, examining her Desert Fire fingernails. OK, OK, so I wanted you to stay. At the time. God knows why. There. Satisfied?

So at your fifth session you claimed I'd simply sunk without trace and thank-you-very-much-Felix-it's-been-nice-knowing-you. Then you pissed off and decided to reinvent yourself as Tina – God help you – and start over.

That's about the size of it, breathes Tina. Besides, Felix was beginning to get into territory I didn't particularly want raked up, thanks very much. It was doing me no good at all. Still, no harm done. Felix earned himself a few bob and was able to claim a victory for himself. Probably did his career a bit of good, if nothing else.

And Tina will never know how right she was. For Felix was to publish his first paper at the tender age of twenty-seven on the strength of Tina's 'case'. His reputation made, the young man ditched his bumfluff, Jesus sandals and social-worker girlfriend as fast as a rat shoots up a drainpipe. In exchange he eventually bagged himself a pinstriped suit, a state-of-the-art consulting room in West One and a well-heeled society wife.

Hello, says Angel suddenly. *They're turning the lights down. Chucking-out time.*

Sixty-year-old Mabel Hutchings, who is the very latest in a long line of cloakroom attendants (the pay's lousy and the hours unsocial) although she prefers to think of herself as a hatcheck 'girl' like in the films, imagines for a split second that she is suddenly going blind. As realisation dawns that the dim lighting is only in aid of the Last Waltz – still the traditional finale in dance halls all over the country, even then – Mabel surreptitiously pulls a quarter-bottle of Johnnie Walker from under the counter and takes a hefty swig. Gave her a nasty turn, that did.

Come on, says Angel. *Time we were off. You know what Jean always says.* Yeah, yeah, Angel, I certainly do know what Jean always says; just gimme a break, willya? *Christ, you're even talking like Trish now.* Oh shut up.

According to Jean (and she should know), the heavy mob of Married Men always arrive in force and legless the moment the pubs shut. Faster than it takes to down a final half-pint they survey the field with expert but drunken eyes and take their pick for the Last Waltz, their only dance of the evening. That way they hope to end up 'seeing someone home', which in Married-Man-Speak means finding themselves a quick lay to round

103

off the evening, like taking a sleeping tablet to ensure a restful night.

Right on cue, and with devastating irony, the band strikes up with 'Who's Taking You Home Tonight'. Jean approaches dragging a gingery man with a slight stoop and long arms who looks like an amiable orang-utan in a Prince-of-Wales-check suit. She rolls her eyes in mock despair. 'Keith's twisted my arm,' she mouths, the drinks forgotten. 'Wait for me by the cloakroom as usual.'

The bar empties as if by magic, but before Tina can make a run for it, a man looms in her path, blocking her only means of escape. 'Dance?' mumbles Brian, having sobered up slightly after the couple of black coffees he managed to squeeze out of good old Big Beryl. Hoping that by some act of God or poor lighting Tina won't recognise him from earlier, Brian glances furtively at his watch. He mustn't be too late or his mum will humiliate him by putting the chain on the bloody door, forcing him to ring the bell to his own home, for God's sake. At *his* age.

Grateful for Jean's tutelage, Tina at once assumes that Brian is indeed a Married Man: one of the enemy. Ironic, eh? 'And another thing,' Jean had told her. 'You can always spot an MM at fifty paces because he's forever looking at his bloody watch. Dead giveaway, that is. Frightened the old woman'll be waiting for him behind the door with a chainsaw if he's in late, I s'pose.'

Thanks, but no thanks, says Angel firmly.

'Sorry.' Tina sidles past him. 'I'm just off home. With a friend.' *Who?* says Angel. *Not that six-foot-four former army boxing champion and judo black belt who eats glass as a pastime and can turn very ugly if people take liberties with his woman? Not him, surely?* The very same, grins Tina to herself.

What's funny? thinks Brian, spotting the grin (I told you, he's sobered up a bit, thanks to Big Beryl). But Brian wishes he'd stayed drunk. That way he wouldn't feel so badly about watching some woman legging it to the sanctuary of the bloody Ladies' Cloakroom rather than risk a single dance with him.

Jean eventually arrives and announces that the orangutan is giving her a lift home. ('Thinks he's on a promise, poor sod.')

'You don't mind, do you, Teen?'

'No, I don't mind.' *Liar*, says Angel. *Now you'll have to walk across the car park all on your little lonesome; and look out for the bogey man.* Piss off, Angel.

ten

Reg Swanson lays down his imitation mother-of-pearl-handled fish knife and fork (his wife, Joyce, always did have impeccable taste, if she says it herself) and sighs contentedly.

'Nice bit of skate, that, Mother,' he says, and takes out his Old Holborn tin and packet of Rizlas to roll himself one of those spindly cigarettes where the paper bursts briefly into flame when the tobacco isn't looking.

Reg can actually afford to buy ready-mades these days, but they don't taste the same, somehow. Besides, he's smoked roll-ups ever since he was ten, when he was caught by his dad having an illegal puff in the outside privy – a symphony of corrugated iron and bluebottles – at fourteen Corporation Street, Leeds, and old habits die hard.

Reg smiles contentedly. Life is sweet. Ever since his accident at Wade's Paper Mills more than ten years ago, him and Joyce have been laughing all the way to the bank. Or in Joyce's case, all the way to the town centre to indulge herself in those little refinements (like the fish knives and forks in their satin-lined box, for instance) that mark out the newly arrived middle class. ('Well, we're not working class no more, Reg. Not now you stopped being a factory worker, even though you *were* a shop steward and not just one of the *hoi polloi*.')

And Reg hadn't been a shop steward nigh on twenty years for nothing, either; he knew his rights. 'I'd still have a thumb on me left hand if that guillotine'd had a proper guard, according to sub-section 6b, paragraph 9(vi) of the Health and Safety Manual, and you know it,' Reg had shouted, looking and sounding a dead ringer for Peter Sellers as Fred Kite in *I'm All Right Jack*.

He had banged his good fist on Charlie Wade Junior's brand new Executive Office Interiors desk, the splendid old mahogany-with-brass-handles job that had been in the family for four generations having been consigned to the tip the moment old Mr Wade's funeral was over. He'd fallen off his twig while bonking the daylights out of his 'seckertary' one wet Tuesday lunchtime, and what a way to go at seventy-one!

Young Charlie (or Right Charlie, as he was derisively known among the 'lads' at the mill, most of whom were approaching retirement age and were about to be made redundant, did they but know it) had caved in at once, offering Reg a generous pension with matching compensation settlement. 'One look at the whites of me eyes and he was a goner,' Reg had told Joyce, jubilantly. 'Spineless little shit. Old Charlie Senior would never have stood for it, God rest him.'

His smile fades as he eyes his only daughter disapprovingly across the hand-embroidered tablecloth that Joyce insists upon nowadays. Since becoming middle class she doesn't believe in eating off Formica like in the bad old days. Nothing like a nice cloth for a bit of class. That and the Midwinter tea service for when they've got visitors and a growing collection of Royal Doulton figurines that look a picture on Joyce's new G-Plan teak display unit with concealed 'rose glow' lighting that makes the china crinoline ladies look as if they're about to have a collective seizure. ('And I wouldn't rule *that* out once Joyce gets her mini-vac out; nearly had me over, last time she decided to have a bit of a spring clean. All thumbs, her.') Which is more than they can say for Reg, you have to admit.

'I s'pose you'll be off gallivanting again tonight?' says Reg ominously, and Joyce groans inwardly. Here we go.

Tina smiles sweetly. 'Got it in one, Father.' And don't you say a word, Angel. I'm not letting Dad tell me when I can go out and when I can't, at my age.

Ooh, you little rebel, you. And there was me forgetting you're thirty-five, not fifteen. Another fun-filled evening with Jean on the cards, is it? Why do you bother?

And Tina is lost for an answer. Deep down, she loathes those smoky pubs, clubs and dance halls, each with its stench of stale beer, sleazy decor and pissed clientele, mainly men 'out for one thing' as Joyce would say, and does say, frequently. But the last thing Tina intends to do is admit it to herself, let alone to Angel, although she is wasting her time there, since of course Angel is unique in being privy to Tina's every thought.

What else is there, Angel, wails Tina inwardly. What else? You tell me. But Angel is silent, for once.

Joyce bustles about loading dirty plates and the obligatory bottles of Heinz Tomato and Daddy's sauce Reg can't do without ('They're so *common*, Reg.') on to her chrome hostess trolley, courtesy of Green Shield stamps. (She's getting a Brevit sandwich toaster next, page seventy-one of the catalogue. Her and Reg aren't actually too keen on toasted sandwiches but it'll look a treat on the marble Formica work surface next to the new 'Tricity 77' cooker with eye-level grill, and you never knew when a visitor might fancy a toastie.)

'Now don't start, Reg,' she says gently. 'Let her enjoy herself while she can.'

Which is all Reg needs to get started, good and proper.

'Enjoy herself! She's out every other night of the week enjoying her bloody self.' *(Oh sure,* says Angel sarcastically. *Having the time of her life, she is.)* 'Done up to the nines like some Cork Street tart, and with morals to match if I'm any judge. She'll end up dead in a ditch, the way

108

she's going on. Be reading about her in the *News of the World* next.'

And so on.

Joyce, of course, sides with her only daughter, and before the crinoline ladies can say 'pass the cucumber sandwiches' (they're *very* genteel, being Royal Doulton) Reg is in full flood.

Joyce hates it when Reg gets himself all worked up. Mainly because he starts effing and blinding and dropping his 'haitches' (as she insists on pronouncing them). Makes him sound dead working class. Common, even. Almost imperceptibly, Joyce's size four Bri-nylon blue-flowered slipperettes from Marks & Spencer begin shuffling towards the kitchen as if they've got a mind of their own.

Once again (*As if we haven't heard it all before*, says Angel. *Ad bleeding nauseam.*) Reg tells Tina that he and Joyce can't carry her for bloody ever. What's more it's about time she faced up to her responsibilites. Like looking after her daughter, Janine, for a start. And she needn't think he begrudges the boarding-school fees, either. He can afford that, thanks to the compensation money. But, for Christ's sake, how much longer does Tina intend to 'leave the poor little mare to rot with a buncha strangers in that bloody Colditz of a place? Girls only, an' all; it ain't 'ealthy. An' that bleedin' 'eadmistress! Alastair Sim in drag, or what?'

He's got a point there, says Angel, unable as ever to resist chipping in. *Though personally I rather took to the discreet little ginger moustache and the Harris tweed suit. But she'll turn the kid into a dyke, mark my words.* Oh shut up Angel. It's a bloody good school, and you know it.

Sure, sure. Excellent academic record. But its main attraction is that it's at a nice, safe distance from her loving father, Dennis bloody Charleton, says Angel slyly. Quite. *With the added advantage that you don't have to see too much of the kid either.*

109

And what exactly is that supposed to mean, Angel? *Come off it. This is me you're talking to. Janine's growing into a dead ringer for her old man as she gets older and you can hardly bear to look at her. Be honest.* That's absolute total bollocks, Angel. *Oh yeah?* Yeah. *So the main reason for picking that school was just to keep her out of Dennis's way, right?* Right. *If you say so.* I do say so.

'. . . I know you think you're doing what's best for Janine,' Reg is saying, 'though if you want my opinion you bin a bit paranoid about Charleton all along.' He shakes his head in disbelief. 'I mean, I know he gave you a bit of a rough time—'

'*Bit* of a rough time?' says Tina incredulously. 'You've got a bloody short memory, Dad. Have you forgotten how Jan and I had to keep moving from one bloody awful bedsit to another, trying to get away from him?'

'That's exactly my point,' says Reg, tapping his temple with a nicotined forefinger. 'You wasn't thinkin' straight at the start. I mean, all that bollocks about 'im takin' what you called "an unhealthy interest" in the kid! Nuffin' was ever proved.' *Only because you wouldn't have Jan questioned about it*, says Angel hotly. Too bloody right, Angel. I just dropped a few hints in the right ears.

Reg puffs ruminatively on his roll-up. 'Unless o'course you was jus' fightin' dirty to make sure you got custody,' he adds.

'Oh, bloody charming!' shouts Tina. 'All down to my fevered imagination, was it? Christ, you're beginning to sound just like bloody Dennis! He tried playing the old my-wife's-an-unfit-mother-on-account-of-she's-doolally card, as you well know. And if that wasn't "fighting dirty" I don't know what was. OK, I was pretty low at the time, to say the least, but round the twist? Never.' *Just a bit frayed round the edges.* Oh shut up, Angel.

Tina lights a cigarette, her hands trembling. 'Whatever, it didn't bloody work. *I* got custody and *I* decided to put

110

as much distance between Jan and . . . and him, as humanly possible. I couldn't risk the thought of him hanging around, waiting for Jan after school maybe. Or hovering in the background somewhere. Watching her.'

'Now yer do sound fuckin' paranoid,' snorts Reg. 'Charleton *is* the kid's father, like it or not. Only natural 'e wanted to keep in touch.'

Nothing natural about the way Dennis wanted to keep in touch, growls Angel. And Tina shakes her head wearily.

'He *could* have kept in touch, Dad. Under supervision. As specified by the court. Only he isn't interested in supervised visits. That much is very obvious. He wants Jan to himself or not at all. Have you *ever* known Dennis go screaming up the M1 to an open day at the school? Has he *ever* phoned to suggest taking the kid to Alton Towers, with Mummy in tow, of course? He's sent her one bloody birthday card in all this time. And *that* was only so that he could include a poisonous three-page letter slagging me off. Telling "his side of the story" as he put it! That went *straight* in the bin, as you know.'

Reg looks sulky. 'Yeah, yeah, I know all that, but . . .'

'But nothing. He doesn't want to know unless he can be all cosied up with Jan on her own. And that'll be over my dead body.' Tina stubs out her newly lit cigarette savagely. 'Anyway,' she adds, 'you and Mum won't have to carry me for much longer, as you charmingly put it. Dennis hasn't been anywhere near Jan for years now, so I'm planning to settle the pair of us in a little flat when I've got enough for the deposit—'

'What, on your money? Working as a glorified clerk in some tinpot solicitor's office? Waste of a good brain, that job. Waste of the education me and your mother slaved to give you.'

'At least she's working, Reg,' says Joyce gently. 'Credit where credit's due. At least she's trying. And she's still got a bit tucked away from the sale of twenty-seven The Close, don't forget.' *Ah yes*, breathes Angel. *The marital love nest, no less.*

And Reg has to admit to himself that Joyce has got a point there. Though he is too proud to say so out loud. Trying to look nonchalant, he picks up the *Radio Times* for a quick shufti at what's on telly tonight, a sure sign he's running out of steam. 'Well,' he says sulkily, determined to have the last word, 'I wouldn't care, but I've *offered* to help her out enough times, Joyce, and she's too bloody stiff-necked to take it.'

'Right chip off the old block then, ain't she?' says Joyce, unwittingly denying Reg his last word and lapsing into broadest cockney in her relief. Crisis over, thank Gawd. She winks at Tina. 'Come on, darlin'. Me an' yer dad *are* on your side, y'know. Though you'd never fink so sometimes, wiv 'im. Come 'n' give us 'and with the washin' up 'fore you go off out, eh? There's a love.'

Tina spots Jean immediately. Let's face it, she'd have to be blind to miss her in that emerald-green lurex number that wouldn't be out of place kicking its legs up in the chorus line on *Sunday Night at the London Palladium*. Jean calls it her Durex frock, reflects Tina, grinning; guaranteed to stop anything in its tracks at fifty paces. *And she is not wrong*, says Angel, *judging by the way Keith the Orang is sticking to her like shit to a blanket.*

Tina winces. Angel can be so vulgar, at times. *God, you sound more like your mother every day. You've got Joyce's 'snob' gene, all right. You wanna watch it; can be fatal if it's allowed to get out of hand.*

Tina has to laugh. Oh piss off, Angel.

Well, why don't you?

What?

Why don't you just quietly piss off. Jean hasn't even noticed you come in. She's too busy swatting Keith the Orang off the goods on display, and, boy, is she displaying

*'em. You could slide off home and read an improving book,
count your money, do your toenails – anything except stick
around here.*

But Jean is on her feet, enthusiastically waving Tina
over like a demented semaphore man who's momentarily
mislaid his flags. *Sod it.*

Looking less than enchanted to see her, Keith at least has
the grace to offer Tina a drink, and as he lopes towards
the bar, *(I swear his knuckles are brushing the ground.)*
Tina suggests she might make herself scarce, don't want
to play the gooseberry and all that, but Jean won't have
it. *Sod it again.*

'Don't be a prat,' says Jean firmly. 'It's *our* night. He's
the odd one out, not you. Nice enough bloke, but that's as
far as it goes, even though he *is* kidding himself that on the
strength of a couple of G and T's he's on a promise. Now,
schtum – he'll be back any minute.'

Keith glowers at Tina over the rim of his glass, willing
her to get lost, take a hike, get the hell outa here – anything,
(he is heavily into old American films – sorry, *movies*).
Eventually, he turns to Jean with a languid, 'Come on,
babe, let's wriggle with Mungo Jerry. In the summertime,
doo-dee-doodly-doo.' See what I mean?

'Will you be OK, Teen?' Jean enquires over her shoulder,
as he drags her off.

Tina nods. *Go right ahead. Feel free. She's having – as
Keith would put it – a ball, though you wouldn't know it
– the gob she's got on.*

Why the hell did I let Jean persuade me to come to this
DSS club, or whatever it's called, Angel?

*You heard her. She said the DSS stands for Divorced,
Separated and Singles. Said it's just the place for what she
calls 'people like us'.*

People like who? People whose only common denomin-
ator is a shared affliction, a shared handicap? Christ, they'll
be starting wooden leg clubs and left-handed societies next.

They already have left-handed societies, as you well know. Anyway, what else is there, as you so often moan.

And so Tina is stuck in this dump of a Spider's Web Motel (*How very appropriate.*) with its Chinese-restaurant decor, all wrought iron, burgundy flock wallpaper and dusty artificial flowers, wishing she'd taken Angel's advice and pissed off when she had the chance. *You just won't be told*, says Angel primly. *That's your trouble.*

Tina sighs. Yeah, you're right Angel (*aren't I always?*). Being tucked up in bed with a good book would be eminently preferable to sticking around here.

You can say that again. Let's face it, mucking out the kitchen or walking across hot cinders in your bare feet would be preferable to sitting here being eyed up like a bit of prime beef at a cattle show. I'm amazed some of these blokes don't go round slapping rosettes on selected rumps: red for the winner, blue for second and yellow for third.

Or, horror of horrors, no rosette at all, thinks Tina, grinning in spite of herself.

Don't smile, for Christ's sake. You'll only encourage 'em to stroll over, feel your fetlocks (or anything else that might take their fancy), run their hands over your withers and peel back your lip to check you've still got all your own teeth. Don't catch anybody's eye, whatever you do.

Dutifully, Tina does as she's told, avoiding all eye contact and watching the packed ranks of the divorced, separated and singles crocodile-rocking with Elton John at the far end of the room. There, a mobile disco unit throbs in time to stroboscopic lighting, giving the jerky impression that the dancers are indulging in synchronised epileptic fits or are experiencing some bizarre evangelical conversion en masse. *Repent, you sinners*, giggles Angel, *and you will walk again. Heal, hee-al, I say.*

Middle-aged men who should know better are torn between trying to tuck in their beer bellies and worrying whether, if they do, their aubergine flares (all the rage, as you know) might end up round their ankles. Arthritic hips are swivelling as they have never swivelled before ('He'll have us down casualty for a hip replacement first thing in the morning, mark my words.') and ladies of a certain age are wondering why on earth they let their daughters talk them into buying these bloody *crippling* platform slingbacks from Freeman, Hardy and Willis when what they could really do with is a nice, comfortable pair of Clark's gold evening sandals. They can't wait to get home and soak their feet in a bowl of warm water laced with Epsom salts, followed by a dusting of Dr Scholl's talc and maybe, as a special treat, a Carnation corn plaster or two.

But they are the generation who lived through World War Two, don't forget, so, regular little troopers that they are, they smile valiantly, trying to look as if they are enjoying themselves while struggling to remember the rudiments of sadly dated dance routines and honing rusty chat-up lines of the do-you-come-here-often, only-in-the-mating-season variety.

Perhaps it really is their idea of fun, poor sods, says Angel sadly.

Well it isn't mine, thinks Tina. I deserve something better. I've had more fun watching the umpteenth rerun of *Oklahoma!* on the telly or touching up my roots over Mum's new Avocado bathroom basin. ('Ex display suite at Wilkes, Reg. Forty per cent off and an absolute bargain in anybody's language, even yours. Besides, I'll go mad if I have to look at them bloody great cracks in our old bath for much longer. Look like a street map of Willesden, they do.' Joyce was born in Willesden, and has been trying to live it down ever since.)

Tina finally decides to leave. *At last*, sighs Angel. She stands and cranes her neck, hoping for a glimpse of Jean. Even if it means running the gauntlet of her disapproval (and Keith's relief, no doubt), she can't bring herself to just walk out without a word. *Must tell Mummy you're off*, scoffs Angel (she'd curl her lip, if she had one to curl). Well, you know how it is, Angel. Ever since the near-rape Jean worries about me. *So she should; need a bloody keeper, you do.* Thanks a bunch.

With Benefit of Hindsight, as my mother would say, (with initial capitals, of course; she was a great one for using initial capitals when she had anything important to say) I wish from the bottom of my heart that Tina had just got out while the going was good. If she had, she would never have met Terry Haines, living embodiment of 1977 cool right down to the *Saturday Night Fever* sideburns, bum-hugging flares and gleaming white, one-inch-soled platforms. 'Never Trust a Man who wears White Shoes unless he's a Dentist, and even then, Watch Him,' my mother always said (initial capitals akimbo), and she was certainly spot on in Terry's case.

If only Tina had been that bit quicker off the starting blocks, once she'd made up her mind to leave. If only she hadn't lingered on the edge of the dance floor in her Dorothy Perkins pelmet of a skirt and what Germaine Greer was twenty years later to call 'fuck-me shoes'. If only she hadn't remained so naive, despite Angel's and Jean's combined best efforts and her own pretence at world-weary cynicism, she might have seen Terry for what he was and given him the bum's rush from the word go, thereby saving herself a great deal of pain to come. If only.

But of course, intelligent as she was, Tina didn't know any better in those days – didn't want to know any better, I suppose. And anyway, what chance did she have against a pro like Terry Haines, darling of the why-can't-I-just-give-you-one-in-the-back-of-the-car-you-know-you're-gagging-for-it set?

The DJ, known not so jokingly as Gerry the Geriatric, fancies himself as a Jimmy Savile lookalike ('Hi there, guys and gals') and is sporting his usual grotesque blond wig framing a craggy, fifty-if-he's-a-day face, gold sovereign rings and panatella stuck in the corner of his mouth, Savile-style. He can't run to proper cigars even on his plasterer's wages ('Never 'ad a day outa work in me life, me; I'm a *craftsman*, see.'), not with all the maintenance and child support he has to fork out each week. ('I rue the day I clapped eyes on that Bernice, I'll tell yer. And as for them twins of 'ers, well, I'm not convinced they're mine, y'know. Never been bleedin' twins in my family, nor 'ers, for that matter. Let's just say our Bernice used to get out a lot, and leave it at that, shall we?')

Gerry has just crooned lovingly into the mike, in his cod-transatlantic accent, 'And now, for all you romantics out there – it's Stevie Wonder with (pause, drop voice sexily), 'A-signed, a-sealed, delivered (pause again, dropping voice to an even more incredibly sexy whisper) I'm a-yours-ah.'

Then he went and spoiled the tone a bit, admittedly, by demanding, (unfortunately while still on mike) where the berluddy hell that lager he'd asked for half an hour ago had got to, and what the berluddy hell did that barmaid think she was doing: brewing it herself, or what?

Ignoring Geriatric Gerry's little *faux pas*, and right on cue with Stevie's sentiments, our boy flashes his dimple-chinned, John Travolta smile and asks Tina to dance with just the right amount of fake humility in his voice to win her over.

Thought you said you were going home, snaps Angel, and, to give Tina her due, she does at least attempt the 'Sorry, but I'm just leaving to meet my friend,' routine, I'll give her that. But her heart really isn't in it, and Terry knows it. Instinctively. This little passion flower, to use his own charming vernacular, is ripe for the plucking, and even riper for the fucking. He can tell. No question.

Several drinks and a lifetime later, Tina is convinced she is in love. She hardly notices Jean bidding her a tight-lipped goodnight, having rowed with the luckless Keith. ('I can dance with who the hell I like. Just because you've been buying me G and Ts all evening you don't own me.') Let's face it, Tina would hardly have noticed if the roof had caved in and rescue teams had been called in to start digging in the rubble for survivors. She is hooked.

She had listened sympathetically while Terry, voice breaking theatrically at all the right moments (told you he was a pro), spoke hesitantly about his broken marriage. *Oh, bring out the bloody violins*, Angel had sneered, but Tina completely ignored her. When Terry got to the bit about his wife leaving him because they couldn't have children he even remembered to brush an imaginary tear from his eye. *Masterly*, says Angel. *Give that man an Oscar. Two Oscars*.

I could hardly have put it better myself, looking back; Terry's performance is indeed masterly. Which is not really surprising, with all the practice he's had.

But amazingly Tina swallows it. Every phoney word.

Terry looks at his watch. 'Ah well, I suppose I'll have to drag myself away to my lonely room.' *Stop, stop*, shrieks Angel dramatically. *You'll have me in tears in a minute; I'm filling up, here*. He squeezes Tina's hand. 'Look, I know this sounds like a line, (*No, Gerraway?* says Angel.) but you really shouldn't drive in your condition. You've had quite a bit to drink, you know. Let me take you home. (*No, no and furthermore, NO!*) You could easily pick up your car in the morning.'

'Why not?' smiles Tina. And you can keep your beak out of it, Angel. I'm sick and tired of you trying to rule me. I know what I'm doing. *Oh yeah, must be a first, then. I wouldn't trust the lovely Terry as far as I could—* Ah, shut up Angel.

Parked outside Tina's home, Terry is growing impatient. It's payback time. 'Aren't you going to invite me in for coffee?' he breathes, nibbling at her ear. 'I can't bear to let you out of my sight now that I've found you.'

Yee-uch! says Angel. *Not even you could believe* that

corny old line, surely to God. Tina hesitates, and Angel is quick to press her advantage.

Never invite strange men in, is what Jean always says. Even if you've been stupid enough to let a complete stranger drive you home you mustn't on any account let him get his foot in the door, or you're completely sunk – done up like a kipper.

Sod what Jean always says; perhaps for once I *want* to be sunk, Angel. Or at least come under heavy bombardment.

Ah, but what about your dad? says Angel slyly, and Tina bites her lip. Embarrassingly, Reg has taken to waiting up until she gets home ('I don't care how old you are. I won't rest easy 'til I know you're in safe.') and is probably right now nodding off on the uncut moquette settee with its embroidered antimacassars (more of Joyce's proud handiwork). Tina can just imagine the reception she'll get from Reg if she lets a man over Joyce's Cardinal-polished doorstep.

'I'm afraid I can't invite you in,' she says reluctantly, 'I would, only my mum and dad . . .'

Terry freezes. 'Don't tell me you're still living with Mummy and Daddy, at your age? I don't believe it.'

Uh oh, says Angel. *That's upset him. Got a gob on him like a vicar who suspects someone's just farted in church.*

'Only for the time being,' says Tina eagerly, ignoring Angel completely. 'I'm getting my own flat soon. Very soon.'

'That's not much good to us right now, is it?' Pecking her impersonally on the cheek, Terry leans across to open the car door. (*Think in his own little way he's trying to tell you to piss off,* says Angel.) 'Time I was off anyway. I'll give you a ring sometime,' he promises, switching on the ignition. 'Perhaps we could go out for a drink towards the end of next week.'

'That would be lovely,' agrees Tina enthusiastically. But

119

her words are drowned as Terry slams the door and roars off into the night.

And that's the last you'll see of him, says Angel smugly. *Thank Christ.*

eleven

Reg watches Tina speculatively over the top of his *Exchange & Mart*. He mostly buys new these days ('We can afford it now, Reg.') but, as I said earlier, old habits, and all that.

'Not going out tonight?'

'No.'

'But you haven't been out for over a week. What's up with you?'

'For God's sake, Dad, you moan when I go out and moan when I don't! Get off my back, willya.' And you can shut up, Angel, before you say anything. *What did I say, what did I do?*

Joyce gives her husband one of her 'now don't start' looks, so Reg merely growls, 'Pardon me for living, I'm sure,' and turns to the Used Car Section (Bargains Galore!) for comfort. Like a big kid with his dummy, reflects Joyce. He's such an old softie, really.

You've hurt your dad's feelings now, says Angel sternly. *No need to snap his head off.* So Tina gets up and plants a kiss on Reg's bald pate: 'Sorry, Dad. It's just that I've been feeling a bit low lately and—'

''Ere,' says Reg with his usual tact and diplomacy, 'not up the duff are yer?' Which is of course enough to send Joyce and the crinoline ladies into a state of shock and Tina rushing to her room without a word, face as long as a gasman's mac.

He promised to phone, Angel; promised. *Ah, stop whining;*

121

what did you expect? But he promised. And here it is, Friday night, and he still hasn't rung. *Why don't you just forget it; you're being pathetic.*

On cue, the telephone shrills, and when Joyce calls, 'It's for you, love,' from the hallway, Tina nearly breaks a leg scrambling down the stairs in her excitement. I knew he'd ring, Angel, I just knew it.

But it is only Jean, wanting to know whether Tina is coming down the DSS tonight or what, and Tina cannot keep the disappointment from her voice.

'Oh I get it,' says Jean. 'You've been sulking all week because Lover Boy hasn't been in touch, is that it?' (*Exactly*) 'Hanging about, jumping out of your skin every time the phone rings, playing Stevie Wonder records over and over again.' (*And especially 'Signed, Sealed, bloody Delivered',* says Angel, *not to mention 'My Cherie bloodier Amour'; makes you sick.*) 'I know, I've been there. Am I right or am I right?'

'Course she's right, says Angel. *Jean's always bloody right. You've been acting like a bitch on heat and making a complete prat of yourself. Admit it.*

So Tina does admit it, and Jean lets her have it with both barrels. 'Repeat after me: All. Men. Are. Bastards. (My mother would have been proud of her use of initial capitals.) Face Facts. Grasp the Nettle. You'll save yourself a load of grief in the end.'

But facing facts has always been a problem for Tina, as Angel is quick to remind her.

'No, he meant to ring,' she insists. (*Oh yeah, sure.*) 'Something's happened. He's ill, lost my phone number, gone away on business—'

'Or turned into a frog, or vanished in a puff of smoke, I suppose,' says Jean caustically. 'Forget it. Hair of the dog is what you need; something to take your mind off the bastard. Come down the club with me, why don't you?'

Now there's an offer you can't refuse, says Angel sarcastically.

Tina looks around with jaundiced eyes, the old feeling of déjà vu sweeping over her. *What the hell am I doing here? You tell me, dear. You tell me.*

Gerry the Geriatric is thinking the same thing.

He puffs moodily on his panatella while the DSS set 'Dance to the Music' with Sly and the Family Stone. 'Wall-to-wall crumpet, down that DSS club,' his mate Les had told him over a pint in the Bricklayers' Arms. 'Bit long in the tooth, some of it, but any port in a storm, eh Gerry? That's what I always say.' *Bit long in the tooth!* thinks Gerry gloomily. *Understatement of the berluddy century, that is. I mean, look at the state of that old boiler in the lurex jumpsuit and silver boots, for a kick-off. Looks as if she's bin embalmed – and by an undertaker's apprentice who could do with glasses, an' all. Farrah Fawcett-Majors she ain't. Ay-oop. They've stopped dancing. Better put another record on.*

'And now, for all you young chicks who can remember one of the sixties' Golden Greats, and one of my *personal* favourites, I give you . . . 'Rr-rr-runaway' with, ah Del . . . ah Shannon.'

And I wish I could berluddy rr-rrunaway, I'll tell yer for nothin', thinks Gerry.

Only feet away from where Jean and Tina are sitting, Keith sips at his vodka martini (just like James Bond, only Keith isn't fussy whether it's been shaken rather than stirred, which is just as well, knowing what the bar staff at the Spider's Web are like). His companion is a huge, beetle-browed Neanderthal who Angel reckons must have shares in Grecian 2000 judging by the unlikely (*Must be at least fifty, fifty-two*), dead black of his hair and fashionably drooping moustache.

Jesus, says Angel incredulously. *Orang-utan meets King Kong.*

123

Every few minutes, Orang and Kong roar with laughter, as if determined to show the world what a terrific time they're having. (*Who do they think they're kidding*, says Angel.) After each outburst, Keith glances hopefully at Jean, who sits demurely drinking her gin and tonic, studiously ignoring him.

But only a couple of minutes and one vodka martini later, Keith finally cracks.

'Hiya Dollface.' (*Dollface already! Where does he get his dialogue?*) 'Is this a private party or can anybody join?'

'Please yourself,' says Jean coldly, and Keith is so relieved at this fulsome invitation that he makes a complete Horlicks of the introductions. ('Jean, Stu. Stu, Jean. Er, Tina, Stu . . .')

Arse, elbow. Elbow, arse, giggles Angel.

'Hello,' Stu is saying shyly. 'Keith's told me all about you, Jean.'

'Oh?' She gives Keith a withering glance. 'Giving references now, is he?'

'I told you she was a card, didn't I Stu?' says Keith valiantly, and Stu nods his great head slowly (he does everything slowly, including thinking), regarding Jean with the open-mouthed smile of anticipation usually reserved for his favourite comedian, Benny Hill (as if you hadn't guessed).

'Oh yeah; laugh a minute, that's me,' sneers Jean, and Keith decides now would be a good moment to get the drinks in and sod Stu, who's old enough and ugly enough to look after himself, in Keith's opinion.

Ignoring Stu completely, Jean murmurs that the good news (as far as Tina is misguidedly concerned) is that the lovely Terry has just crawled in, but the bad news ('brace yourself') is that he is with Another Woman, a pale wraith of a creature – all Medusa curls, black eyeliner and purple lippie – that looks like something that should be safely tucked up in its coffin by now, preferably with a stake through its heart.

Angel is all for leaving, right away, but Jean persuades the hapless Stu, who has been sitting there catching flies and wondering what the hell is going on, to ask Tina to dance. Not that he needs much persuasion, having been 'Ob-La-Di, Ob-La-Da'-ing under his breath along with Marmalade trying to pluck up courage, in his plodding way, to approach Tina but afraid she will turn him down.

For Stu has had many rejections in his life, and is still smarting from the most recent one at the hands of Della, his fifteen-years-younger wife – soon to be ex-wife. She only went and ran off with a skinny little runt of an asthmatic window cleaner called Eric who didn't look as if he'd started shaving yet. Between puffs of his inhaler, he'd finally managed to persuade Della to run away with him to the Costa del Sol ('. . . and the climate'll do wonders for me asthma, Del . . .').

'I'll give him bleedin' Spain; I'll give him bleedin' Asthma!' was all Stu, (convinced that Asthma was somewhere near Benidorm) could think to say when he eventually found out about Della's six-month-long affair.

Clarice Harris (how unfortunate) next door, Debenhams net curtains and antennae twitching in unison, could have told Stu about the affair long before, if she'd a mind, only she didn't believe in indulging in idle gossip, as she was to explain to her friend Ivy across the road. ('Funny how that Eric gives my windows a ten-minute cat's-lick-and-a-promise, yet it takes him three-quarters of an hour to do that Della at number twenty-three – and I don't mean do her windows, neither. I wouldn't dream of saying anything normally, but her place ain't exactly Crystal Palace, is it? She's only got four windows in the front and three out back plus the French doors, just like you 'n' me.')

Understandably, with *his* recent history, Stu is delighted when Tina allows herself to be led on to the dance floor without a murmur. Jean is even more delighted, especially as the lovely Terry has noticed and is scowling like a man who's just lost a tenner and found a penny. That's put his nose out of joint, thinks Jean, sipping contentedly at her G and T.

The evening wears on, and so does the charade. By ten o'clock, Stu, not the sharpest knife in the drawer, as you know, is hopelessly confused. He really didn't expect it to be this easy, despite Keith's reassurances that most of the chicks that get down the DSS Club are gagging for it, bloody gagging for it and you'd have to be a fucking eunuch not to score. Not that Keith's had much luck, mind; he's been knocking himself out over that bloody Jean for ages and hasn't even copped a feel yet, but he omits to mention that to Stu. Wouldn't go with his image at all, that wouldn't.

Stu has no idea what a eunuch is, of course, but is slowly beginning to take to this Tina. To his surprised pleasure, she is all over him, hanging on his every word, of which there are not that many, it has to be said, Stu liking to think of himself as the strong, silent type.

But Stuart has a lot to learn, and he is unlikely to learn it at Keith's elbow.

Satisfied that Terry and Dracula's Daughter have left (probably for a long, slow screw against the wall, thinks Jean; and I'm not talking about the cocktail of the same name), the two women breathe a mutual sigh of relief and coolly announce that they are leaving. Yes, they've had a lovely evening, really lovely. Sure they must do it again, and soon. Thanks for the offer but no, they don't need a lift since they have their own transport. Bye-ee.

And the twin smiles on the faces of Keith and Stuart fade as their two safe bets clatter off with wings on their respective sets of three-inch heels.

twelve

'Tina? it's me.'

Heart lurching, she grips the telephone tightly. *Here we go*, says Angel.

'Me who?' Jean, you'd be proud of me. I'm learning, I'm definitely learning. *And about bloody time, if I may say so.*

'It's Terry.' He clears his throat apologetically. (*Nice touch.*) 'Look, let's start again. I can be round in half an hour. We'll go for a drink or something.' *You must be joking*, says Angel.

'Sorry, I'm booked. Why not ring the friend you were with last night?' *Atta girl; you tell him.*

'Don't be like that, Tina. I know this sounds corny' (*and I'm sure it will be*), 'but Sheila's a sort of friend of the family, recovering from a bereavement, as a matter of fact, and I felt duty bound—'

'You felt duty bound to help her overcome her grief. How noble. You're right, it does sound corny.'

'Tina, please . . . look, how would it be if I call for you tomorrow? Around eight?' *No bloody way*, says Angel firmly.

'It wouldn't.' Tina smacks the phone down and leans against the wall, chewing at a fingernail. Please God, let him ring back. *Don't listen to her, God*, says Angel.

But Terry does ring back. Several times over the next two days. ('He's persistent, I'll give him that,' says Reg.)

'Tina, I must see you again . . . soon. No, please don't

hang up. Just hear me out. Truth is, I didn't get in touch after that first meeting because, well, I knew instinctively that you were something special,' (*Oh, saints preserve us.*) 'and I suppose I was just frightened of getting too involved.' (*Frightened of getting too involved? Do me a favour. That old chestnut must have whiskers on it by now.*) 'Please say you'll come out with me for a meal tomorrow night.'

'OK,' says Tina, finally caving in, just as Angel feared she would. Well, he's suffered enough, Angel. *Suffered? Him? Oh, I give up, I just give up.*

'Great! I'll pick you up at half seven.'

Tina stands in the narrow hallway and hugs herself. Something special. Too involved. She must phone Jean tomorrow and tell her the good news.

Can't wait to hear Jean's reaction, says Angel drily. *Just can't wait.*

'Something special? Too involved?' mimics Jean cruelly. 'Oh, for Christ's sake grow up, Tina. That's the oldest one in the book. Fancy falling for that load of old toffee. Now I've heard everything.' *You and me both*, says Angel. Jean shakes her head despairingly. 'I dunno; I suppose he told you that the Death's Head he was with on Friday was his bloody cousin, or something?'

Funny you should say that . . .

'No, no, of course not.' (*Liar*) 'But she can't mean anything to him. If she did, why would he want to see me again?'

'The thrill of the chase, my fine, feathered friend. Specially now he imagines he's got a bit of competition in poor old Stu. He's just after another notch on the old bedpost, take it from me. And the moment he's had you on your back – or on your front for that matter – he won't want to know.

'He's the type,' continues Jean, beginning to get into her

128

stride, 'that leaves no female unturned in his life's work of feeding the precious male ego.'

Bravo! shouts Angel. *Give the lady a gold clock! Throw that woman a fish! You wanna listen to Jean, y'know. She talks a lot of sense.*

But listening to Jean is the last thing Tina wants to do. 'Just because I've met someone I really like—'

'Mr Right?' says Jean.

'Just because I've met someone and you haven't, you don't like it.' *Christ almighty! You sound like something straight out of 'In the Sixth at Mallory Towers'! Grow up, do!*

'You think I'm jealous? God give me strength. I'm only thinking of you. I don't want you to be hurt, that's all. Bloody accident waiting to happen, you are.' (*That's just what I keep telling her.*) Jean pauses awkwardly. 'Look, don't get me wrong, but I'm very fond of you – love you in a way. No, don't panic – not *that* kind of love.'

'Phew, that's a relief.' Tina giggles. 'I thought you fancied me for a minute there. Give us a kiss.'

'Cow.'

'Lezzie.'

'Oh, get stuffed, Tina.'

'I should say there's every chance of that in the very near future, Jean.' *Intend to play hard to get, huh?*

'Ah well, I tried,' sighs Jean. 'Just don't say I didn't warn you, that's all.'

Jean-Pierre's, the best and indeed only French restaurant in Watford back then, is just perfect. Even Angel has to admit it. Spotless table linen, soft lights and the subdued murmur of civilised conversation (even though only two other couples are in tonight). This is more like it, Angel. *Well, it's certainly an improvement on the bloody Spider's Web or the Hawaiian Bar, I must say. But then, being force-fed cheeseburger and all the chips you can eat down the Wimpy would be an improvement on them.*

Jean-Pierre himself greets Terry effusively, with much bowing and scraping. 'Ah, Meestair Haines – so *vair* vair good to see you again.'

'I often bring important clients here,' Terry is quick to explain, as Jean-Pierre shows them to a secluded table with a great show of barely suppressed excitement mingled with just a dash of humility in the face of such exalted visitors. (Well, the customers expect it, especially customers like Terry.)

Bit OTT, isn't he, that Jean-Pierre? says Angel bemusedly. *God knows what he'd be like if the Queen Mum came walking in one night. Have a bloody stroke, I reckon.*

Who cares, Angel? I'm just going to sit back and enjoy it.

That's what I was afraid of.

Smiling ingratiatingly, Jean-Pierre, who was plain Johnnie Willis, proud owner of the Fish Plaice, Loughton, in a previous incarnation, is wondering once again how Terry does it and wishing he had his kind of luck. The bloke's with a different woman every time he comes in.

What a bloody poser, thinks Jean-Pierre. Which is a joke, coming from him, when you consider that his only experience of 'la belle France' (as he insists on calling it) is a day trip to Boulogne with the Loughton Working Men's Club, ooh, way back. He *has* had 'French lessons' though. Courtesy of Elizabeth David's *French Provincial Cookbook* and an elderly prostitute who picked him up as a drunken eighteen-year old in the Bayswater Road one rainswept night in 1951.

Jean-Pierre waits at a respectful distance while the pair um and ah their way through the menu, then decides to move in. 'May I suggest the specialité de la maison, madame, monsieur,' he says. 'Potage aux champignons à la Jean-Pierre, followed perhaps by our chef par excellence's highly recommended daube de boeuf Créole.'

Then he wanders into the kitchen to place their orders and sneak a quick fag. 'Open another tin of that mushroom soup, willya Marge? And we got any of that beef stew left?'

Marge, who combines her duties as Jean-Pierre's wife and chef par excellence (she is a whizz with a tin opener), is a washed-out blonde who looks as if she hasn't seen the light of day for years. Which indeed she hasn't, having spent half her adult life grafting away in steamy kitchens all over Greater London and the other half frying cod fillets at the Fish Plaice before graduating to the comparative luxury of becoming chef at Jean-Pierre's.

'Right you are, Johnnie,' says Marge cheerfully. 'We got loads of mushroom.' She stirs dubiously at a pot on the gas range. 'Dunno whether I can eke out the beef stew, though. I'll bung in a tin of oxtail, eh? That should do the trick.'

'Good girl,' says Jean-Pierre approvingly. Gotta keep her sweet. She's a grafter, old Marge, you gotta hand it to her. She didn't get them swollen ankles and varicose veins sitting on her arse. Puffing on his cigarette, he runs a disloyal eye over his wife, comparing her unfavourably with the woman presently accompanying that Haines fella. 'That bloke's with a different woman every time he comes in,' he says, apropos of nothing. 'Disgusting.'

Terry pours another glass of wine. 'Everything to madame's satisfaction?'

'Couldn't be better.'

'Good.' He treats her to one of his dead sincere, straight-from-the-shoulder looks (can't keep his eyes off her, so he says. That always goes down well.) 'I've made a real mess of things so far, Tina, but I won't make the same mistake again, I promise.' *What a pro*, says Angel.

'You mean you're going to behave yourself from now on?' says Tina coyly. *Oh per-lease . . .*

'Oh I wouldn't go so far as to say that. I'm on the

slippery slope already where you're concerned.' Corny, but devastatingly effective, he's always found.

And the accident-waiting-to-happen gazes at him adoringly, drinking in every lying, cheating word like a parched and wilting flower too long starved of sustenance. Will she never learn?

Even when, at the end of the meal, Terry pats his pockets in alarm and swears he's left his wallet in another suit (*I can't believe I'm hearing this*), Tina parts with her credit card like an eager shopper at the January sales, while Jean-Pierre, standing on the sidelines, shakes his head in disbelief. He's only gone and tricked some poor cow into paying the bill *again*. What a bastard, eh?

Assuring Tina he will drive her straight home ('Can't have good old Mum and Dad worrying about you.'), Terry makes confidently for a disused factory car park he knows, scene of many a sexual triumph.

What are we doing here Angel? *Oh come on, can't you guess?*

Terry switches off the engine, douses the lights, and puts his arm round her shoulders with an ease born of long practice. 'Just wanted to say good night to you somewhere quiet,' he breathes, and moves in for the kill. 'Besides, it's time to sing for your supper,' he adds, the fact that it is Tina's money that paid for supper conveniently slipping his mind.

Tina is relieved of her knickers and bra as expertly as a poacher skins a rabbit, and Terry unzips his fly with the abstracted air of a man performing some routine chore.

With about as much passion as a driver matter-of-factly filling his old banger with two-star petrol (and *definitely* without the enthusiasm engendered by the promise of Green Shield stamps and free crystal wine glass with every five gallons), Tina is pumped full of Terry's seminal fluid.

She is a pushover, just as he knew she would be.

Well, says Angel coolly, *all that fuss over a little prick, as the old music hall joke used to go.*

But, tell me, dear heart, did the earth move for you? Did you hear heavenly music, or was it all over so quickly that the poor old celestial choristers didn't even have time to get their songsheets out?

It'll be better next time, Angel, I know it will. (*If there is a next time, which I doubt*, says Angel.) Once we get the chance to share a bed it'll be a different story, you'll see. (*Different story? Fairy story, more like. It was a bloody disaster, admit it.*) Well, that was my fault, Angel. I couldn't relax. Never made love in a car before, you see. (*Made love? Is that what you call it?*)

Feeling oddly embarrassed by her lack of underwear, (*And so you bloody well should be*, says Angel primly.) Tina gropes around for her abandoned bra and knickers while Terry lights a post-coital cigarette. (Well, doesn't everyone?)

'Never had it in a car before, have you?' says Terry, unwittingly echoing Tina's thoughts. He smirks as she shakes her head, blushingly. 'A first then,' he adds, switching on the ignition. *Made his night, that has*, sneers Angel. 'Come on, get a move on. Gotta get you home.'

The car purrs to a halt outside the house, and Terry reaches across and opens her door politely. *What a gent.* 'See you soon,' he says dismissively. 'I'll give you a ring sometime.'

Sometime never, we hope. Speak for yourself, Angel.

thirteen

Reg is trying to concentrate on the latest Love Rat revelations in the *Sunday Pictorial* but without much success, thanks to Stevie Wonder blow, blow blowing in the wind at the top of his voice on Joyce's old-fashioned walnut radiogram. (''Bout time we got a new one, Reg; I seen a lovely Sony down Curry's'.)

Over a cup of tea with Jean (not the Midwinter tea set, as Jean doesn't count as a proper visitor; she's more of a friend of the family) Tina is waxing lyrical about her planned move into her new flat. 'Should be in by Easter, Jean,' she is saying excitedly, ignoring Reg's murmured, 'Must be mad paying that price; I remember them places being built,' and Joyce's answering mantra, 'Now don't start, Reg.'

'Well, the girl's more than welcome to stay with us a bit longer, she knows that.' *That's not what he said a few weeks ago*, says Angel.

'Don't *start*, Reg,' insists Joyce. 'If you got nothing better to do than sit there moanin' you can come and give me a 'and peeling the sprouts.' They won't be eating Sunday lunch for another two hours, but Joyce believes in preparing her veggies well in advance so that they can have a really good boil-up with a pinch of bicarb to keep their colour – a virulent, unlikely yellow-green. Besides, the joint of beef is already turning to shoe leather, nestling among two pounds of King Edwards and steeped in a two-inch-deep vat of best dripping in the Tricity 77.

Stevie Wonder is just asking how many roads must a man walk down before they call him a man, so Reg decides to assert his masculine authority. 'I would help, love,' he says, 'but I got things to do in the shed.' He hasn't, of course, but sitting on the old Woolworth's deckchair that cost twelve and six in 1959 is preferable to helping Joyce in the kitchen (women's work, that). It can be quite cosy in that shed once he's got his little primus going, and he's grateful to get away from Stevie for five minutes, anyway. ('That girl must know every bloody word off by heart, the number of times she's played it.') Stevie is about to launch into 'Moving On' and Reg, *Sunday Pictorial* folded under his arm, decides to do just that.

Tina rolls her eyes at Jean. 'Phew, now you know why I can't wait to get into a place of my own! Mum and Dad have been great, but—'

'But they tend to cramp your style a bit,' says Jean flatly. 'Mind you, you've had a pretty good run for your money, if you ask me, what with your only daughter tucked up in a *boarding* school, for Christ's sake. (*Girl needs her mother*, says Angel, mimicking Reg.) If you think living with your parents is cramping your style, just you wait until you've got a fourteen-year-old pinching your tights, make-up and boyfriends, in that order.'

'You sound disapproving,' says Tina stiffly. *Oh well spotted.* 'I had my reasons for sending Janine to boarding school, which I don't intend justifying to you or anyone else.'

Don't blame you really, says Angel. *How do you begin to explain an ex-husband who tried to get you pronounced an unfit mother just so that he could get his mitts on the daughter you suspect he's been abusing since she was in nappies?*

Quite. And besides, Angel, I simply can't face opening up that can of worms all over again. Not ever.

Oh bloody hell, thinks Jean. Kid looks as if she's going

to burst into tears any minute. Me and my big mouth. She lights two cigarettes and silently passes one to Tina.

'Whatever,' says Tina eventually, 'I'm really looking forward to getting to know Janine all over again. It'll be wonderful, having a home that's all ours, after all these years.'

'Gonna be hard work, mind, running your own home, coping with a teenager – who I can't wait to meet, by the way – *and* going out to work to earn a crust. Reckon you're up to it?'

'I'll cope. And you never know, I might not be coping on my own for ever.' *Oh no*, groans Angel. *Not that old refrain; don't you ever give up?*

'Oh no,' echoes Jean. 'She's flipped.' (*You can say that again*). 'I do believe she's nest-building, and not just for her darling daughter. That glassy-eyed look says it all. The little homemaker getting everything spick and span for her faceless hero. You'll be ordering Readicut rug kits and china figurines like your mum's from *Woman's Own* next.' (Which latter remark causes deep offence to the crinoline ladies who are, of course, Royal Doulton and only available at the very best stores.)

'Bloody hell,' she continues, lighting another cigarette on the stub of the old one (she is supposed to be giving up, but this is an emergency), 'it's as bad a case of the someday-my-prince-will-come syndrome as I've ever seen! Just lie down in a darkened room for a while, keep taking the tablets, and it should pass.' *You ain't heard nothing yet*, says Angel ominously.

Instead of coming out with some smart response, Tina just sits there with a silly grin on her face, until it finally dawns on Jean that what she is actually suffering from can better be described as the my-prince-has-already-arrived syndrome. *Ah, Jean's finally caught on.*

'Oh no, I don't believe it. You *can't* have the bold Terry in mind, surely. No one could be that demented.'

Oh, she could be that demented, you better believe it, sighs Angel.

Jean looks at Tina incredulously. 'It's *his* Y-fronts whizzing round in the front-loading automatic of your mind, isn't it? *His* newspaper being fetched clamped in the jaws of Shep, the faithful family pet – or do you plan to do that for him too?'

'I really don't understand why you're so anti-Terry,' begins Tina.

'I know you don't understand, that's the trouble. You're so bloody wet behind the ears where men are concerned it's not true.' *Oh yes it is true, in her case.*

'And you're the expert, I suppose?'

'Well, I've certainly been around a bit longer than you. Not that I've made a fantastic success of my life, I'm the first to admit. But I think I've learned by my mistakes and, God knows, I've made a few in my time. I just want to spare you some of the pain of learning, that's all.'

Jean smiles fondly. 'You don't want to end up a cynical old boiler like me, I know;' (*You could do worse*, says Angel.) 'I wouldn't wish that on anybody, but . . . well, I've got this gut feeling that your Terry's an even bigger bastard than most, and—'

Tina holds up her hand. 'I'm in love with him, Jean. Go on, have a good laugh if you like, I don't care.'

'I'm certainly not laughing, flower. Crying, more like.' (*Me too*, says Angel, with feeling.) 'In love? In lust, you mean. You've been in the same room with the man three times, that's all – once when he was all over another woman, the so-called "friend of the family".' (*Dracula's daughter*. I know, Angel. Don't remind me.) 'You've had sex in his car once and you reckon you're in love. Be your age.'

But Tina will not listen, of course, so Jean stamps into the kitchen for more tea, making the Midwinter teacups rattle on Joyce's Ercol dresser and her ginger tom, Catnip, do a runner through the catflap and retire to the safety of the coalbunker in the scrubby rectangle that calls itself a back garden.

Calm down, baby, thinks Catnip (he obviously watches the same American movies as Keith), giving his paws a routine wash and brush up, just to show he's in control. Stay cool. That's one love-struck cookie in there; you gotta pitch clever with that one.

But Jean has worked that out for herself, without benefit of Catnip's advice, so she returns with fresh tea, more McVities' digestives ('You'll never eat your dinner,' trills Tina's mum.) and a different tack.

'Look Teen, I don't want to be a Jonah. Maybe this *is* the real thing, love with a capital L, straight out of *True Romances*.' (*Fat chance.*) 'I'd like to think so, for your sake. But, please, promise me you'll just slow down a bit until you've got to know Terry a bit better – if you ever have the opportunity that is. Stop viewing him through rose-tinted glasses the size of Greenwich Observatory.'

She pats Tina's hand, continuing gently, 'Men aren't like us. They don't automatically equate sex with love the way we do. One bonk and we imagine ourselves walking down the aisle complete with yards of flowing tulle, orange blossom in our hair and and the King's College choir singing "O Perfect Love". But to most men, sex is something they just need to do regularly, like cleaning their teeth and keeping their bowels open. When they feel the urge they just seek out a woman, any woman, to use as a kind of sexual calamine lotion to satisfy the itch.'

And that's some itch, in Terry's case, says Angel spitefully. *He wants to put something on that. Boiling oil, for instance.*

Tina opens her mouth to speak, but Jean is well away. 'Then they simply drop the woman like something they just scraped off their shoe, until the next time it suits them to click their fingers. Then she is supposed to roll over on her

138

back waving her legs in the air obligingly. Sorry, Teen, but I've got a nasty feeling Lover Boy is one of the predators – a user who regards every new woman as some kind of challenge which has got to be conquered, like Everest, just because it's there. To his sort, women are disposable, like Kleenex. Use once, throw away when soiled, and take a fresh one.'

She shakes her head regretfully, her face as solemn as a judge donning the black cap. 'I shall be very surprised if you see hide or hair of Sherpa Terry ever again. By now you're probably on his list of conquests, a notch on his bedpost. Carved proudly with his mountaineering pick, no doubt.'

Half expecting her to end with 'I rest my case,' Tina is about to attempt a rally when Jean delivers her knockout punch, her verbal knee to the groin. 'Has he been in touch since the Night of the Screw, by the way?'

Good question, says Angel.

Caught off-guard, Tina is momentarily stunned into silence, then she replies coolly, 'As a matter of fact he has.' (*Oh, may your tongue shrivel in your head, telling whoppers like that!*) 'So you see you were quite wrong about him; he isn't one of your predators.'

'When are you seeing him then?' counters Jean casually.

'Not for a week or so. He's away on business until the twenty-fifth, if you must know.'

'Oh yeah?'

'Yeah.'

And for your next trick I suppose you'll be walking on water, says Angel. Don't worry, I'll think of something.

Tina wipes her hands nervously on her skirt, takes a deep breath and picks up the telephone receiver. She has written down the number and rehearsed her lines as carefully as a timeshare salesman flogging dodgy villas on the Costa del whatever.

Brenda, the switchboard operator cum receptionist, doesn't seem to know who her own divisional sales manager is, but eventually, after Tina has patiently spelled out Terry's name, she cottons on and puts Tina through.

'Got a live one, here, Dawn. Only reckons Terry Haines down the print shop's the divisional sales manager, if you ever.' And Dawn laughs so much she spills her plastic beaker of tea all down the front of her new Top Shop blouse.

'Oh yeah,' says Dawn, 'and I'm Ursula-bleedin'-Andress. Let's hear old Monsterbollox talk himself outa this one – can't hear yerself speak down that print shop.'

Terry's voice sounds oddly muffled, and not a little irritated. 'Look Tina, I've told you not to ring me at work.' *Sound familiar? It's just what dear Dennis used to say, remember?* says Angel.

'Sorry, Terry, sorry – but I can hardly hear you. What's that noise in the background?' ('Wait for it,' whispers Brenda, listening in.)

'Machinery. I'm in conference with the works manager on the factory floor, not in my office,' he bawls. 'The switchboard had to page me so I hope this is important.' ('You gotta hand it to him, Dawn, he's bloody quick on his feet.') 'Now get to the point will you, I'm busy.'

Sounds like he's really, really pleased to hear from you, says Angel. *Why don't you just put the phone down right now? I can't stand the humiliation.*

'I – I just wanted to say hello,' says Tina lamely (*God, you're pathetic*), adding recklessly, 'and I wanted to ask when I'd be seeing you. It's nearly two weeks now and you haven't phoned.'

She bites her lip in dismay. Oh God, I sound awful, like a nagging wife, like a dog whining and scratching at a half-closed door. *A completely closed door, actually,* says Angel. *A locked, bolted and padlocked door that even the Sweeney's finest couldn't batter down in a hurry, in my humble opinion. As far as Terry's concerned you're history, is my guess.*

'I've been working my arse off all week. That's why I haven't called,' says Terry brusquely. 'Not that I have to explain myself to you. Might ring later;' (*if you're a very, very good little girl*) 'must go now.' Click.

Tina walks dejectedly upstairs to her room and sits on the bed. *Face it. You're just making a prat of yourself. Forget him.*

But, Angel, surely he wouldn't have been so loving and attentive just to 'get his end away', as Jean would charmingly put it? *You'd better believe it, kid.*

But surely he wouldn't have gone to the trouble of taking me out for a meal just for a quick tumble in the back of a car. *All what trouble? You were stupid enough to pick up the tab – sorry,* lend *him the money – as I recall. Paid you back yet, has he, or is the cheque in the post? I don't think so. And anyway, even if he'd taken you out for a bloody champagne supper at the Ritz with all the trimmings, it doesn't change a thing. Remember what Jean said: 'Some men'll go to any lengths to add another scalp to their collection.' She reckons he's the daddy of 'em all as far as bastards go, and she's right, you know she is, deep down.*

fourteen

One look at her daughter's face as Tina met her at the station was enough. *By God*, Angel had observed, *she looks more like her father than ever, the gob she's got on. Just look at those beetle brows, for a start. Hold on to your hat, kid. We're in for a stormy crossing.* And she was right. As usual.

Tina did go through the motions, I'll say that for her. Painting a bright smile on her face, she opened her arms in greeting, but it was obvious from the word go that there was to be no fond, *Brief Encounter*-type reunion on the station platform.

Hoping for hugs and cuddles and 'Ooh Mummy, it's so lovely to see you', were you? Well, yes, Angel. I was, actually.

Dream on, says Angel grimly. *She's her father's daughter, don't forget.*

Even the kiss Tina tried to plant on her daughter's cheek was coolly rebuffed, as she flinched insultingly away from the merest touch of her mother, and Tina's 'Did you have a good journey, Janine?' was met with a surly, 'You're late. Couldn't even be bothered to be on time to meet me. Typical.'

Which was a bit below the belt, even by Janine's standards. Desperate to get shot of what she privately referred to as Dotheboys Hall, she had jumped at the chance of catching an earlier train than planned. The girl couldn't wait to get back home. Just let her mother try getting rid of her again, that's all.

How were you supposed to know she'd catch the earlier train? Telepathy? Angel had snapped. *Tell her. Don't let her wrong-foot you the way Dennis used to do.*

But, anxious to avoid a row, (*Never did you any good with her father.*) Tina had meekly apologised to her daughter, to Angel's intense irritation.

'And it's Chaz, by the way,' the girl was saying. 'Short for "Charleton". The name you denied when you decided to call us both "Swanson" again. No one's called me Janine for ages. Not that you'd be interested. Where's the car, then?'

Christ, says Angel. *Some bloody charm school that place turned out to be. You were robbed. But don't let the little cow rattle your cage, kid.*

So Tina didn't. Swallowing hard, she said lightly, 'Chaz it is then,' and led the way to the car park. All of which just about set the scene for what was to follow.

Back at the new flat, Tina rushes eagerly from room to room, willing some of her own enthusiasm to rub off on to Chaz, who stands listlessly in the hallway wearing all-enveloping olive drab dungarees and matching expression.

The girl is clearly not impressed with the flat, ('Bit pokey, isn't it?') with her mother, ('You look like a third-rate tart in that get-up') with the world in general, for that matter. But especially, she is not impressed with Tina's decorating efforts in what is to be her bedroom.

'I suppose it'll have to do.' (*Think I'll have to have a lie-down; don't think I can take such touching enthusiasm.*) 'Be almost possible by the time I cover that awful wallpaper with posters. And as for the bedspread ... God, pink flowers, I ask you.' She rolls her eyes eloquently.

Think yourself lucky you didn't get lumbered with Winnie the Pooh or My Little Pony, girl. I had a terrible job steering your mother past those, I can tell you.

Tina's artificially bright smile falters. 'Well, yes, I suppose I did go a bit over the top on the bedspread, But it was so pretty I couldn't resist.'

She pauses, hoping to see some glimmer of warmth or interest on the girl's face. But no such luck. *Well, what did you expect, gratitude?*

'I could always swap it for the one on my bed. At least that's a plain colour.' Chaz raises her caterpillar eyebrows enquiringly. *Dennis to the life.* 'Er, pale blue,' says Tina apologetically.

'Oh terrific. Ah well, anything's better than pink flowers; the mere sight of them is enough to bring on my hay-fever.'

'Good. Fine,' says Tina between clenched teeth. 'I'll swap them over right now. How about helping me organise the living room when we've had a coffee and you've had a chance to unpack?'

'No way. I'll make the coffee though;' (*Big of you, I'm sure.*) 'tastes like crap when you make it.' *Doesn't miss a trick, does she? Why does she have to be so determinedly unpleasant all the time?* Search me, Angel. I guess she's just going through that so-called awkward teenage stage. She'll grow out of it, in time. *Huh! Well let's hope you live long enough to see it. All in the genes, if you ask me.*

The doorbell chimes the opening bars of 'Yellow Rose of Texas' (*That'll have to go, for a start*, says Angel.) and Jean stands on the threshold, dressed in a fluffy green coat and festooned with so many packages that she looks like an animated Christmas tree that's forgotten Christmas was over months ago.

'I come bearing gifts,' she puffs. 'Christ, those stairs'd murder me if I had to do it every day. Lift doesn't seem to be working.' *Does it ever?* says Angel. *That 'Out of Service' notice has been there that long it's curling up at the edges like a British Rail cheese-and-Branston sarnie.*

In no time, Jean has produced a few tempting goodies from her Argos wheelie-shopper to whet their appetites. ('Don't laugh. I nearly got one with a built-in seat and walking frame in keeping with my great age. Blue rinse and diamanté glasses, here I come.')

Also in no time, Chaz is eating out of Jean's hand. *Bloody hell! She's actually smiling. She's quite pretty underneath that olive-drab expression. How does Jean manage it?*

By doing her fairy godmother routine, waving her magic wand and producing those two Roxy Music posters for her room, for a start, thinks Tina sourly. ('Oh thanks, Jean. They're my favourite group, and Bryan Ferry's *such* a hunk.')

Ah, you're just jealous because Jean's pushed all the right buttons, so far. Too right, Angel. Too bloody right.

'Any danger of a coffee?' Jean is asking. And Chaz trots off to the kitchen without a murmur leaving Tina staring after her with her mouth open.

'Christ,' mutters Tina. 'You've made more headway with her in two minutes than I have in a lifetime.'

Jean splays her hands. 'Some of us have it, whereas others . . .' She shrugs.

'Yeah, you're absolutely right. I'm a washout as a mother. Now come on, I'm dying to see what else you've brought.'

'Hang on, hang on. At least wait 'til Mummy's Little Helper comes back with the coffee.' *Mummy's Little Helper*, echoes Angel. *Fat chance.*

For all of about fifteen minutes, everything goes like clockwork. Chaz's expression is transformed (*Christ, with one wave of her magic wand Jean's turned Miss Froggie into the beautiful princess!*) as the three of them giggle their way through Jean's collection of prezzies ('Half of 'em are only from charity shops, mind') and Tina begins to relax and enjoy herself. But it doesn't last.

All it takes is Jean's casual reference to the flat-warming

party to be held the following night for Chaz to meta-morphose into Miss Froggie before their eyes. *Uh oh*, says Angel. *Jean'd better put her wand on 'recharge'. Get the eyebrows.*

'Oh?' says Chaz. 'What flat-warming party? Nobody bothered to mention it to me.' She shoots Tina a poisonous look. (*Stand by for blast-off.*) 'Who's coming then? I suppose they'll all be boring old farts. Not a soul under thirty, I bet. Well don't expect me to be there. I shall be out!' And with a fine show of injured pride (her speciality), Chaz stamps off to her bedroom.

Tina winces as Chaz slams the door behind her. *I'm not surprised*, drawls Angel. *Hard-faced little cow. Any excuse to go into a strop, that's her.*

But Angel *would* have been surprised to see the hard-faced little cow's face crumple the moment she entered her room. She would have been even more astonished to see Chaz throw herself on her brand-new single bed and weep as though her heart is breaking.

In the sitting room, Tina groans. 'Thanks a bunch, Jean. I hadn't got round to telling Chaz about the party.'

'Don't worry. She'll get over it. And anyway, it's only to be expected from a bloody awful mother like you.'

'Bitch,' grins Tina.

'And definitely on heat at the moment, which brings me to my next point. Any nice men coming to your bash tomorrow?'

Tina looks thoughtful. 'Not really. Mum and Dad, of course. (*Daren't leave them out*, says Angel.) 'Few of my new neighbours – more to keep them happy in case the party gets noisy than anything else.' (*What do you mean, 'in case' . . .*) 'Oh, and the bloke next door: Frank Kelly.'

'Sounds like a place in Ireland – Ballykelly, Donikelly, Frankelly. What's he like?'

'Irish, as a matter of fact. Still got a bit of a brogue,

even though he came over as a child, apparently. About forty-five. Male nurse at an old people's home. He's already been in for coffee once or twice. Even offered to put up the odd shelf for me, but I'll believe that when it happens.'

'Sounds nice,' says Jean with interest, 'though you have prior claim seeing as you saw him first.'

'Oh, I don't fancy him or anything. He's just a nice, average bloke. Not my type at all.' *Nor is the lovely Terry, though I haven't noticed you letting a mere detail like that hold you back.*

'That's your trouble. You go for quite the wrong type. (*Let's hear it for Jean, folks.*) You seem to have some kind of death wish where men are concerned. (*I'll drink to that.*) And speaking of the wrong type—'

'No, I haven't heard from Terry, if that's what you were about to ask, and if you say, "I told you so" I'll come over there and strangle you with your own tights.'

'Only asking.'

As well you might, says Angel. *She still thinks she's in with a chance, would you believe; some people never learn.*

Jean stands up. 'Oh well, I'd better be off, I suppose.'

'And I'd better go and try to make peace with my darling daughter,' sighs Tina.

'I wouldn't. Leave her to stew in her own juice for a bit, is your Auntie Jean's advice. Give her time to cool off. She'd only give you a right mouthful if you went barging in, just at the moment.'

Tina nods. 'Perhaps you're right. You usually are.'

But for once, Jean is quite wrong. Chaz wouldn't have given her a right mouthful, had Tina walked in at that precise moment. Reg was correct when he said (endlessly) that 'a girl needs her mother'. And this is particularly true in Chaz's case. For despite her pretence at fourteen-going-on-twenty-five sophistication, deep down Chaz is just a lonely little girl. Rather like Tina was once, only without an Angel watching over her.

With any luck, and if Tina got her words in the right order for a change, they might even have ended up actually talking to each other. Especially about the past. But they didn't.

And so the moment passed. Sadly.

Chaz is sitting on her bed, hugging her knees. With a sigh, she gets up and retrieves a cigar box from her suitcase. Inside, wrapped in plastic, like some precious relic (which indeed it is), is an old birthday card sent from her father, long ago. The fluffy white rabbit on the front is holding up a placard that reads 'Happy Birthday Ten-Year-Old'.

It is the only communication Chaz has ever had from her father. And she only managed to get hold of that by foraging in the kitchen bin, when her mother's back was turned. What a cow, thinks Chaz, her eyes beginning to brim with tears. I wonder how many more cards and letters were kept back from me.

None, actually, but she is not to know this. Chaz cannot accept that her father has simply dropped her. What daughter could? So she dreams of a father whose many attempts to keep in touch have been cruelly squashed by her mother. Didn't she *see* her mother throw away this precious birthday card? Didn't she see it with her own eyes? How many others have gone the same way?

Tenderly, Chaz runs her fingers over the embossed words and takes out The Letter folded inside. The Letter that begins, 'My darling Jan' and ends, 'All my love, Daddy'. The Letter with no sender's address. Lovingly, she smooths out the folds and, sitting on the edge of the bed, she begins to read. Again. Even though she committed every word to memory long ago.

fifteen

Head pounding, Tina is in bed cursing the sun for shining too brightly. *Well, I told you to get curtains up in your bedroom, but no, Miss Froggie has to come first.* Ah shut up, Angel. *And anyway, the amount you drank last night I'm not surprised your head feels as if someone's trying to drill holes in it without benefit of anaesthetic. I can hardly hear myself think.*

Bundling herself in her old green towelling robe, Tina stumbles into the bathroom. A hollow-eyed stranger's white face stares at her from the mirror (one of Jean's charity shop purchases) as she clutches the towel rail like a seasick passenger on board ship (possibly the *Titanic*, the way she is feeling). *And don't you dare throw up all over Jean's new second-hand tumble-twist Oxfam rug, either.* Shut *up*, Angel. And please don't mention the words 'tumble' or 'twist', if you don't mind. Not in my delicate condition.

'Pathetic,' sneers Chaz from the doorway. *The well-known Dennis-sneer needs work, but it's coming along nicely, don't you think?*

'Leave me alone. Can't you see I'm dying?' Wincing, Tina slams the door in her daughter's face and drives the bolt home.

That's right, thinks Chaz, glaring at the closed door. Shut me out again, why don't you? What's new? You didn't want me from the moment I was born. And you don't want me now, really.

What happened? Grandpa get fed up paying the school fees? Or did he *shame* you into getting me out of the bloody place? Daddy said in his letter you only sent me there so's you could carry on putting yourself about like you always did when you were married. Have a good time without a kid cramping your style. And I believe him. Only got to look at the way you dress, for a start. Talk about mutton dressed up as lamb, as Grandma used to say. What a slag! And then you have the bloody nerve to walk out on Daddy just because he – what did he say in the letter? – just because he 'succumbed briefly to the charms of another woman.' S'pose that means he went to bed with her. Once. Don't blame him.

And just because of that, *you* have to get custody of me. It's not fair! Why couldn't I have gone to live with Daddy? *He* wouldn't have sent me away. *He* would have loved me.

On a sudden impulse Chaz thumps the bathroom door with her fist. 'I hate you!' she shrieks.

Tina raises a hand tenderly to her aching head. Now what's rattled *her* cage, Angel? *Search me*.

If they only knew.

There is a blast of 'Yellow Rose of Texas' from the doorbell and Tina and Angel groan in unison. *You really must change that. Even the theme tune from* Dukes of Hazzard *would be preferable, and that's saying something*. Yeah, yeah. Give us a chance, Angel.

Chaz is telling the anonymous caller that her mother is throwing up in the bathroom and it serves her right, the state she got into last night. 'Come in, if you want,' she adds sullenly. '*I'm* going back to bed.'

Unalloyed charm, as ever, thinks Tina. *Perhaps you should have had her 'finished' in Switzerland*. Finished off, more like.

There is a polite tap on the door. 'Are you OK? Thought I'd pop round and help tidy up after the party.'

It's bloody Frank, from next door, whispers Angel (not that Frank can hear her, of course). *What's his angle? No man offers help without an ulterior motive, according to Chairman Jean. Who needs him?*

I do, Angel. Miss Froggie'll be no help (*True; very true.*) and that living room looks as if the Mongol hordes have stopped for a quick pillage en route to scourging Europe. Some drunken bum's even left a cigarette burn on the coffee table Mum gave me (''Bout time we had a new one, Reg.'). *That drunken bum was you, actually, duckie, but we'll draw a veil over that*. Thank you so much, Angel. *My pleasure*.

'I'll be out soon,' says Tina wearily, steadying herself against the washbasin. 'Just make yourself at home.'

She splashes water over her face, gives up trying to brush her teeth because she keeps missing her mouth, and eventually makes her tottering way towards the kitchen, wincing at the sound of crockery being stacked.

Frank is washing up, immaculate in grey cords and crisp, white shirt with the sleeves rolled up. *What, no Blue Peter badge?* says Angel sarcastically. On the draining board beside him is an ever-growing mountain of sparkling plates and glasses. He turns to face her, looking as fresh and wholesome as if he's just walked off the set of a Hovis commercial, and dries his hands briskly on one of the clean tea towels he had the foresight to bring with him.

Obviously thinks of everything. Useful man to have around, murmurs Angel approvingly. *I was about to suggest you consider hiring him by the hour, but it looks as if he's giving his services free, gratis and for nothing.*

We'll see, Angel. I don't suppose I'll be getting an invoice in triplicate for services rendered, but if Jean's All-Men-Are-Bastards theory is correct, I may find that Friendly Frank, that broth of a boy from County Cork, expects payment in kind. Or something.

No, says Angel emphatically. *Not Frank*.

What? You've changed your tune, Angel. Only moments ago you were quoting the Thoughts of Chairman Jean at me. What happened to your '*No man offers help without an ulterior motive*' routine?

Dunno, replies Angel sulkily. *I've just got a gut feeling Frank's OK. What your mother would call a 'real gentleman' in fact. Besides, when did I ever steer you wrong?* Frequently, Angel, frequently.

'Ye gods,' chirps Gentleman Frank at that moment, 'you look terrible.'

'Thanks.' Tina sways on rubbery legs. 'Got a cigarette on you?'

'Don't use the things any more,' replies Frank cheerfully, (he is so bloody cheerful, damn him, thinks Tina. Of course he'll be a no-smoking convert, along with St Peter, St Patrick and the rest of the latter-day saints), 'but I'll make you a black coffee. Just what you need in your state of death.'

He propels her gently into the devastated sitting room and settles her on the sofa. Bloody hell, Angel. He's treating me like one of the inmates at his precious Rosedene Retirement Home. It's a wonder he doesn't tuck a rug round my knees. *Well, he's had plenty of practice with cantankerous geriatrics just like you, I'm sure. And anyway, don't knock it*, says Angel. *Just lie back and think of Ireland, if you'll pardon the expression.*

'I could always borrow a Zimmer frame from the nursing home for you,' Frank says with a grin, as if reading her mind. 'I'm sure any one of my little old ladies would sacrifice hers in a such an obviously good cause.'

'Sod off Frank,' says Tina wearily, closing her eyes.

Perhaps when I open them he'll have disappeared, preferably in a puff of smoke. *Come on. He's doing a terrific job and you need all the help you can get.* I know, but it's the ... the invasion of my privacy I can't take. *What's he supposed to do, leave you to die in peace? You're just pissed off he's caught you with your metaphorical knickers down, aren't you? Don't like our Frank or any other man seeing you in your ratty old dressing gown without your warpaint, isn't that it?* Oh piss off, Angel. *Would that I could, but I'm afraid we're stuck with each other.*

Frank hands her a steaming mug of coffee and she sits watching him plod patiently backwards and forwards to the kitchen, bearing tray after tray of debris. Only once does he pause, to enquire whether she wants more coffee. He is so . . . so bloody capable it makes her sick.

Bet he was in the Scouts. Probably a Queen's Scout – tying knots, lighting campfires by rubbing two cubs together and singing 'Ging-Gang-Goolie' for England, giggles Angel, making Tina's head pound more than ever.

By the time Capability Frank has finished, the living room looks almost normal, the only grim reminders of the festivities being a large red-wine stain on the carpet courtesy of Tina's dad and, of course, the cigarette burn on the coffee table.

Tina doubts even the indomitable Frank can do much about the carpet, but Angel is not convinced. *That'd be all in a day's work for him, I should think. I wouldn't put it past him to take out his trusty Swiss Army knife and knock you up a new coffee table into the bargain.*

'Thanks for tidying the place up,' says Tina grudgingly, when Frank reappears. 'You'd make someone a very good wife.' *Always has to be a bloody sting in the tail with you, doesn't there?*

'No one'd have me,' says Frank, refusing to be offended. 'How are you feeling now?'

He looks at her, his gaze direct and honest. To Tina's surprise, his brown eyes hold hers in simple trust and friendship, with no trace of the unspoken sexual agenda she is slowly learning to recognise in other men's faces.

Other men like Terry, for instance, says Angel slyly.

This Frank's different, I can feel it. He isn't like the others. He isn't one of the enemy. I could trust this man.

And for once, Tina agrees with her.

She smiles. 'I'm beginning to feel a bit better now, though I must look ninety.'

'Nonsense. You look like a child. All scrubbed and pink, like a peeled prawn on a bed of lettuce, in that green dressing gown.'

'You say the nicest things. How do you manage such fulsome compliments?'

'Years of not practising, I suppose.'

The 'Yellow Rose of Texas' door chimes blast forth (*They really, really must go*) and Frank goes to answer the door. She hears Jean's voice, already subjecting Frank to her particular brand of interrogation.

'Oh I see. You didn't stay the night then? Hmm. I believe you, thousands wouldn't. Just popped in to help clear up, eh? You *are* a one-off. All the men I know'd only pop round the morning after the night before to see if there's any booze left, or to catch mine hostess under the shower without her teeth in.'

She breezes into the living room and looks around critically. 'Well, I must say you've done a fantastic job. Marry this one at once, Teen. Grab him quick before he has a chance to escape.'

Frank laughs easily. 'Best offer I've had all week. But now I've done my good deed for the day I'd better go and get stuck into my own chores. 'Bye Tina, 'bye Jean.' He taps on Chaz's bedroom door. ''Bye sleepyface,' and he is gone.

'Well,' exclaims Jean, plopping into the nearest armchair, 'what a lovely fella. The place looks great, though I wish I could say the same for you. You look like something the cat dragged in, thought better of and spat out again.'

'Thanks. You should've seen me before Frank pumped me full of black coffee.'

'Hmm,' says Jean archly, 'very cosy. Not in love again, are we?'

'No, I told you. Nothing like that. But I think he's going to be a really good friend. Frank's . . . well . . . different from the rest, somehow.'

'You *sure* you're not in love? No, silly me. I forgot, you only ever fall for the bastards of this world. Glutton for punishment, you are. Speaking of which, guess who I saw last night when I popped into the pub to buy a bottle for your party?'

Tina's stomach does a slow loop-the-loop which has nothing to do with last night's excesses. 'No, who?' *Who schmoo*, says Angel. *You* know *who*.

'None other than Mr Wonderful himself – the bold Terry.' Jean holds up a hand, like a policeman on point duty. 'And before you ask, I told him you're doing fine – promotion at work, new flat . . . er, even a new boyfriend . . .'

Tina shakes her head reproachfully but Jean is un-repentant. 'Well, didn't want to give him the satisfaction of imagining you were pining away on his account, so I reinvented Frank as Mr Wonderful Mark Two. That made him sit up, I can tell you. Looked quite pissed off. Expect he thought you'd gone into a decline, joined the Foreign Legion or something. Conceited bastard. Thinks he's God's gift.' Jean stands up and begins to walk towards the door. 'Well, seeing as Frank's beaten me to the draw in the clearing-up-at-the-OK-Corral stakes, I'll be off . . . no, I really can't stop. I'll let myself out. 'Bye.'

Tina smiles slowly, a glorious champagne bubble of excitement growing inside. Looked pissed off, she thought. Looked. Pissed. Off.

After such a promising start to the day – at least as far

as Tina is concerned – it's downhill all the way. As the afternoon wears on, the fine spring weather deteriorates and so does Tina's earlier sunny mood.

She and Chaz bicker and snipe their way through the long afternoon like a pair of punch-drunk flyweights (*In the blue cawnah* . . . says Angel. *Just like old times, this*) until Tina finally concedes defeat and backs off to hide behind the *Sunday Express*, leaving Champion Chaz, bloody but unbowed, to make her noisy preparations for a celebratory night out at the local Odeon with enough Butterkist popcorn to fill a modest silo and two of her biggest fans (well, only fans, actually).

'So what if Jane's a punk,' the Champ is snarling, determined to cling to her title by green-painted fingernails that make her hands look positively gangrenous. 'God, you're *such* a snob! At least she doesn't look like a complete *tart*. Unlike you. And what if Rick *has* got a purple Mohican and an earring; what's wrong with that?'

What indeed, says Angel. *Let her go, for Christ's sake. Not that you've got a lot of choice, short of binding and gagging her and locking her in her room for the duration.*

Don't think I haven't seriously considered it, Angel. But you're right, and at least this way I'll get a couple of hours of peace, perfect peace.

As the front door finally crashes behind Chaz, Tina breathes a sigh of relief. *You can take your gumshield out and go for an early bath now; no need to come out fighting for a while at least.*

Thank God for that, Angel. I'm going to have that early bath and pamper myself doing all those unmentionable things women do when they're on their own. *Such as?* Such as do my nails, shave under my arms etcetera, etcetera; what did you think I meant? I'm not into self-abuse, as you know.

No, you just let others abuse you, says Angel solemnly. *Anyway, don't knock it 'til you've tried it, kid. Masturbate and be your own master, is what I say. Besides, in your fantasies you meet a much better class of person*. Oh shut up, Angel.

Tina potters about contentedly in her tatty old robe and slippers, and has just settled comfortably on the sofa with a cup of coffee, cigarette and Stevie Wonder's Sixteen Classic Love Songs (of course!) on her mother's old radiogram (yes, Joyce finally managed to persuade Reg to buy her that state-of-the-art Sony she saw down Curry's), when the 'Yellow Rose of Texas' gets going again. She answers the door with an indulgent smile on her face. *Probably Frank on some trumped-up errand*, says Angel. Only it isn't Frank.

'Are you still speaking to me?' *Oh no, it's the Boy Wonder. Slam the door, batten down the hatches, pretend you're out. Emigrate, even*.

Foolishly, Tina ignores Angel's advice. 'Hardly,' she drawls, trying to keep the excitement out of her voice, 'I'd practically forgotten you existed.' She is lying, of course, and Terry knows it. Like a shark sensing blood in the water, he moves forward, arrogantly confident.

'Aren't you going to ask me in? Please.' He flashes his John Travolta smile and Tina caves in at once. *I despair of you, I do honestly*.

'Mm. Nice flat.' He sits down on the sofa without being invited (Terry never bothers with such niceties), and produces a bottle of wine with a flourish. 'Madam's favourite, if I remember rightly.'

Excuse me while I puke, says Angel. *Cheap plonk he buys by the caseload from Victoria Wine, I expect*. (Which isn't so very far from the truth, though Angel doesn't know it, for in fact Terry has a very good scam going with an accident-prone, lorry-driving mate of his whose employer's stock seems to make a career out of falling off his vehicle and finding its way to the likes of Terry Haines. And at very reasonable prices, too.)

'You must have been pretty sure I'd see you.' *Is the Pope a Catholic?* says Angel despairingly.

'Always live in hope, Tina, "Be Prepared", that's my motto.' (*Be prepared, already! Regular little Boy Scout, isn't he? Never goes anywhere without his whistle, woggle and packet of three in the top pocket in case he gets lucky. Correction: forget the packet of three; our boy's much too selfish to bother with those, as you already know.*)

Terry pats the sofa and she obediently sits beside him, a rabbit hypnotised by a snake. And a particularly poisonous one, at that.

'Little bird tells me you've found yourself a new boy-friend,' he says casually. (*Sod Jean and her big mouth.*) He lights two cigarettes and passes one to Tina in a move straight out of some old romantic film starring Humphrey Bogart and Lauren Bacall. *If you want me, just whistle*, says Angel, quoting Lauren herself, *only in your case he doesn't even have to do that.*

'I'm jealous. I admit it,' Moving imperceptibly closer, he takes her hand. 'I don't suppose there's any chance for me now, is there?'

'I – I don't know,' she murmurs, her mouth inches from his.

'Yes you do,' he replies thickly. He kisses her and she is lost. Just like that. A pushover. Again.

To be fair, she does put up a token resistance, clutching her dressing gown round her body ineffectually, but she is no match for Terry, who, as we know, is an expert in his particular field. Removing the garment as casually as a chimp peeling a banana, and with about as much finesse, he pulls her unceremoniously to the floor and straddles her in moments.

The words he whispers while using her – you can hardly call it lovemaking, surely – shock yet excite her in their crudeness, as he explains with almost pedantic precision exactly what he will do, is doing, to her, while emphasising her utter powerlessness to have him stop.

There are women who go a bundle on this sort of thing, of course, and it may come as a surprise that Tina was one of them. But perhaps you shouldn't be surprised.

Difficult though it is to believe, despite living as an adult through most of the so-called swinging sixties and seventies, the only man Tina has known sexually before Terry is her ex-husband, Dennis: a user of women, and a violent one, at that. Little wonder, then, that she mistakes – wants to mistake – Terry's cynical seduction for what she can only dream of as 'the real thing', some half-baked notion of romantic love gleaned from women's magazines, tales of true love on the telly and, of course, the magic of Stevie Wonder's love songs.

At the mature age of thirty-five, Tina has less experience to draw upon than many an adolescent, with no conception of how it feels to be loved and cherished by a man. More than just an innocent, she is an emotional cripple.

I weep for her.

I can still see her, lying there on the floor, fondly watching Terry preparing to leave. He has finished his obligatory post-coital cigarette and is anxious for the off. No point in hanging about while there's still time for a couple of swift halves at the Royal Oak. That new barmaid with legs up to her armpits and skirt to match might be on duty; she looks as if she might be up for it, and that's a fact.

Glancing up at the clock (courtesy Joyce and her Green Shield stamps), like Cinderella sensing midnight must be approaching, Tina is shocked to realise that Chaz is due home any minute, a fact she thoughtlessly relays to Terry. Suddenly, as Angel is quick to notice, he is not in quite such a hurry to leave.

Throwing on her robe, Tina dabs at her hair and rushes about the room tidying up and straightening cushions, but at that moment, Chaz comes bursting in through the front door. ('All my friends have their own key, and I'm not ringing the bell as if I'm a bloody lodger!')

The girl stops in her tracks, looking from Terry to her mother questioningly, and Tina is embarrassed.

'This is Terry, a friend of mine. Terry, this is Chaz, my daughter.'

'Delighted to meet *you*,' says Terry, his eyes running over Chaz appraisingly, like a horse trader weighing up the blood stock. He turns to Tina, eyebrows raised. 'Didn't tell me you had such a beautiful daughter.'

'Takes after me,' says Tina lightly. *Bloody hell; you're jealous*. Nonsense!

'She certainly does. I expect she's already started breaking a few hearts.'

'Hardly,' drawls Chaz, deadpan. 'I *am* only fourteen.'

Not that a little detail like that makes her taboo as far as the likes of our Terry is concerned, says Angel.

Terry gives a low whistle. 'Really? I wouldn't have believed it. You're so . . . so mature for your age.'

Shooting him a look of the utmost disdain, Chaz turns on her heel. ''Night, Mother. If you're . . . entertaining . . . I'm off to bed.' Daddy was *so* right, she is thinking. She'd give slags a bad name, her.

Terry stares after her. 'Attractive kid.'

'Yes, I noticed you'd noticed.' *There goes that little green-eyed monster again*.

He grins unpleasantly. 'I do believe it's jealous. Jealous of its own daughter. Well, well.' *Spot on, that man*.

'No of course not,' says Tina, 'she's only a little girl, after all.'

'Not so little. She's certainly got a nice pair for her age.' (*Oh, spare us the details, per-lease.*) 'Although,' he adds, giving Tina's breasts a cursory feel, (*Just like Dennis used to do. Remember?*), 'not half as nice as yours.'

Terry looks at his watch and realises it's nearly closing

time. Shit, he'll miss the Royal Oak if he's not careful. 'Gotta go,' he says abruptly. He pats her rump like the Lone Ranger does after he's given Silver a sugar lump. 'See you soon.'

'When's soon?' she asks (*You're pathetic, do you know that?*), but he is already closing the door behind him.

'Has he gone?' Chaz opens her door and peers out cautiously. *Yes he has*, says Angel. *And bloody good riddance*.

'Yes,' sighs Tina. 'I'm afraid so.'

'God, what a creep! Mature for my age . . . breaking a few hearts . . . Jesus, talk about cornball! Don't tell me you fell for all that crap, Mother. I half expected him to tell me what a big girl I am for my age. Yee-uk! Hope you're giving *him* the Big E.' *If only*, says Angel.

'I like him,' says Tina shortly.

Chaz folds her arms and looks at her derisively. 'Christ, you really do, don't you? Well God help you, because I think he's a prize wanker.' *You and me both, kid*.

'Yes, I get the message – you don't have to draw diagrams. But I'm certainly not giving him what you picturesquely call the Big E on your say-so, and by the way, would you stop swearing please.' Summoning as much dignity as is possible when wearing nothing but a dressing gown and a warm glow, she sweeps into the kitchen to make a bedtime drink.

But Chaz follows her. 'What about Frank?'

'What *about* Frank?'

Chaz shrugs. 'I thought you were going to be seeing more of him. He's much nicer than that poser Terry – and you can't carry on seeing both of them.' *Or can you?* she thinks. *Very likely, in your case*.

'Why not? Frank's just a friend, but Terry's . . . Terry's something more.' *Yeah*, says Angel. *The sunshine of your life, if Stevie Bloody Wonder is to be believed*.

'One of your lovers?' sneers her daughter, pulling a face.

She gives a theatrical shiver. 'I don't know how you can bear him near you.'

'Yes, my *only* lover, actually. And I *can* bear him near me and intend to *continue* to bear him near me as often as possible. What the hell do you know about anything anyway? You're only a child and wouldn't understand. If you ask me, you're just jealous – jealous because some man's paying me some attention.' (Jealous? thinks Chaz. Jealous of you? Huh!) 'Well, you're just going to have to get used to the idea, because Terry's going to be around quite a lot from now on.'

'Remind me to be out when he comes, then. That should suit you nicely, shouldn't it. Having the place to yourself? Besides,' she adds nastily, 'I don't suppose you can stand the competition, at your age.'

And before Angel has a chance to reason with her, Tina draws back her arm and slaps her daughter mightily across the face.

Chaz stares at her for a moment, her eyes huge in a face suddenly quite white, except for the angry red mark made by Tina's palm, then she rushes, sobbing, to her room.

Oh God. You've really done it now. And all because of a worthless shit like Terry Haines. And you can belt up, too, Stevie. You've caused enough trouble.

sixteen

Jean sips silently at her coffee. For once in her life, she is momentarily lost for words. A novel situation, you have to admit.

Tina is back from the bathroom, having been violently sick, her colour miraculously returned. Jean has never seen her looking so alive and happy. God help her.

Poor little cow seems *pleased* about it, for heaven's sake, thinks Jean. What's more she imagines that bastard Terry is going to be over the bloody moon when he finds out she's up the duff. ('Terry's marriage only broke up because they couldn't have children.') Jean smiles grimly to herself. How we delude our-bloody-selves. Suppose she thinks it'll be doubles all round at the Royal Oak while the proud father-to-be lobs cigars in all directions, patting her fondly on the belly and saying she looks radiant. No bloody way.

Jean grinds out her cigarette end purposefully, concentrating on the task with a kind of furious intensity. 'And what does your first-born think about the prospect of a little Terry-clone, complete with two horns and a tail, in the pipeline, if you'll excuse the expression?' she says eventually. 'Delirious at the thought of hearing the patter of tiny cloven hooves, is she?'

Can't face telling Chaz, can you? says Angel, and Tina hangs her head, looking as guilty as an amateur shoplifter caught with half a dozen pairs of Marks & Spencer's knickers stuffed up her jumper.

163

'She obviously doesn't know yet,' says Jean. 'Well, she ain't gonna like it. She ain't gonna like it one little bit. You'd better tell her, and quick, if you mean to go through with it. (*And the silly cow does mean to go through with it, take it from me*, says Angel.) Chaz isn't stupid; she'll soon realise you haven't just tucked a couple of pillows down the front of your drawers as some kind of fashion statement. And what about your mum and dad? Told them?' She looks at Tina shrewdly. ''Course, there'd be no need for any of them to know anything about it if only you'd—'

'If only I'd what?' *Oh come on. Guess*, says Angel.

'Have an abortion,' says Jean shortly. 'What else?'

She lights another cigarette, her hands shaking. 'If you take my advice, flower, you'll slope off to some nice little private clinic for a couple of days and have it terminated. All over and done with in a flash these days; piece of piss.'

'No way,' says Tina firmly. And you can keep right out of it, Angel. And so they sit politely either side of Tina's 1960s beige-tiled fireplace like feuding in-laws at a shotgun wedding, lost in their own thoughts, while the hostile silence between them lengthens by the second.

Jean is remembering her own pregnancy, at fourteen years of age.

A late addition to a brood of four strapping boys (just when her mother thought it was safe to give her maternity wear and pile of matted, hand-knitted matinee jackets to the Little Sisters of Charity), Jean was, believe it or not, completely ignorant of what was once coyly referred to as 'the birds and the bees'. If it was referred to at all, of course. Which it certainly wasn't; not in her sternly Catholic family.

When her Liverpool-Irish parents finally cottoned on to the fact that their only daughter was pregnant, they were outraged ('. . . bringing shame and disgrace on a decent family') and her mother screamed that 'the randy little sod responsible would do the decent thing by her, by God he would.' But Jean, in her innocence, had only the vaguest notion of how babies were conceived (something to do with sitting on a lavatory seat after a man had used it, so her more worldly friend, Sylvie Gethin, had told her), and even less of an idea who, apart from her apparently sinning self, could possibly be responsible. Even after her father had taken his big, leather belt to her backside ('I'll beat the truth out of the little slut, so I will.'), she had maintained a mystified silence.

After all, how was she to connect those sweaty, nocturnal visits to her bed (which only started after her brothers had flown the nest) with the shameful thing growing inside her? How was she to know that the 'randy little sod' in question was her own father, a pillar of their small community in North Wales, who had been regularly abusing her since she was eleven years old and promised she would burn in all the fires of hell if she ever breathed a word of it.

Abortion was out of the question, of course, so Jean was packed off to a dismal Roman Catholic 'mother-and-baby' institution in the Midlands to await the birth.

The child was stillborn, a boy, and Jean turned her face to the wall, swearing never to put herself through such pain and misery again and crying that God had deserted her.

She never did return 'home', but stole away early one morning, long before the candlesticks for six a.m. Mass had even been ritually dusted off.

Faster than it would have taken Mother Superior to don her penguin outfit and say half a dozen Hail Marys, Jean had hitched a lift on the first lorry that would stop for her, unaware that God hadn't deserted her after all, because the lorry driver was a decent man who wasted no time getting a steaming plateful of eggs and bacon down her at the first transport caff he came across ('You look as if you could use a good feed-up, poor little cow.') before pressing on to London with his load of Fyffes' bananas and a hot dinner waiting for him with his wife and two kids in Walthamstow.

As far as Jean's parents were concerned, their errant daughter had simply vanished into thin air.

Jean lights another cigarette and smiles cynically. Didn't exactly bust a gut trying to find me, did they? No search parties; no headlines screaming, 'Bring back my child – a mother pleads'. She must have suspected *something* was going on, but did she lift a finger to help? Did she buggery. Too frightened of my old bastard of a father, I suppose. Still, he's probably popped his clogs by now. Let's hope it was a slow and painful death.

She sighs. Ah well. My tale of woe won't cut any ice with Tina. She'll just think it's sour grapes because I've never had kids of my own. But I'd be some friend if I just stood by and let her get on with it. The sooner she tells Terry, the better. Get it over with. Then when he breaks her heart, when he spells out exactly what she can do with his unborn child, maybe she'll see sense.

'OK,' says Jean at length. 'You're determined to keep this baby, right?' (*Is she ever*, says Angel.) 'I accept that. So why delay telling the proud Daddy-to-be? Unless of course you're afraid his reaction will be less than ecstatic, after all . . .' *That's about the size of it*, says Angel.

But Tina sticks out her chin defiantly. 'I'll ring him tomorrow. He'll be really excited, you'll see.'

Yes, you do that thing, girl. Then once he's given you the bum's rush we can book you into a nice, discreet clinic somewhere before it's too late. It won't come to that, Angel, I know it won't. *I wish I had your confidence, I do really*.

'One moment plee-arz. Trying to connect you.'

Brenda the switchboard operator puts her hand over the mouthpiece and turns to Dawn, who is shuffling invoices around her desk having decided at least she'd better *look*

166

as if she's working seeing as her supervisor (known as 'Two forty-watts' on account of small, high-strapped boobs that make her look as if she's got a couple of light-bulbs stuffed in her bra) is on the prowl.

'It's that woman again. Asking for Terry Haines,' hisses Brenda.

'Oh yeah,' says Dawn, without interest. 'What's he been up to now?' She squints shortsightedly at one of her Massey Ferguson invoices wondering briefly whether to file it under 'M' for Massey, or 'F' for Ferguson before relegating it to the bottom of the pile, just to be on the safe side.

'That's just what I'm about to find out. Bastard keeps telling me to get rid of her; tell her he's in conference, abroad on business (as if!), on the bloody moon – anything. But, sod it, this is the third time she's called this morning, and why should I carry on making excuses for that little shit?'

So with a quick 'Putting you through now,' Brenda settles down with a Golden Delicious (over years of professional eavesdropping she's become highly accomplished at eating silently) to listen in.

But the conversation is disappointingly brief, and by the time Terry slams down the receiver Brenda hasn't even finished her apple.

'Well?' says Dawn half-heartedly.

'Nothing much. All I can say is that the poor cow must have a face like a bulldog chewing a wasp if the only way she can get a poke out of Monsterbollox is to invite him round for a sumptuous feast at her place. I've never known him to be that picky: "Any time, any place, anywhere", like the Martini adverts, that's him, as a rule.'

Sighing, Brenda resumes her knitting (nice little pink cardi from a pattern in *Woman's Own*). 'I'm knackered, Dawn. And starving. How long 'til dinnertime?'

Tina flutters anxiously around the flat, looking at her

167

watch from time to time and giving little gasps of dismay. *Got to have everything just so for our big moment, haven't we? Dream on, Tina.*

She looks like a geriatric Cinderella waiting for her prince to show up, thinks Chaz, lolling on her outsize beanbag cushion (another of Jean's finds) in front of the telly watching MacAli (fronted by the very same Alistair MacFee of twenty-eight The Close; told you he'd be famous one day!) miming to their latest smash hit, 'I Wanna be Witchoo, Babe' on *Top of the Pops*.

Chaz glances slyly at her mother. God, all it needs is a few overweight cartoon bluebirds and cutesy butterflies flitting about helping her to lay the table, like in that scene where Cinders is getting ready to go to the ball. She's even dug out the real linen napkins! And candles, for Christ's sake!

'Who's coming round then?' she drawls. 'As if I couldn't guess. The PM, on his way back from the House, or perhaps the Pope?' She clutches her heart dramatically and rolls on to the floor. 'Or maybe – maybe it's the Second Coming.'

'Very droll,' says Tina briskly, determined not to let Chaz goad her into a row. That would spoil everything. *Why bother?* says Angel. *Things are going to be well and truly buggered when laughing boy arrives. Didn't sound exactly thrilled at the prospect of a cosy, candlelit dinner to me, when you spoke to him on the phone.* It'll be fine, Angel, you'll see.

'Well, I'm going out if that sleazebag's coming round,' says Chaz. 'Don't want to cramp Mummy's style, do we? I'm going round to Jane's, in case you're interested, which I doubt. Be back about ten. Oh, and don't worry, I'll cough or something so that you'll know I'm coming; don't want to catch Mummy *in flagrante* again, do we?'

'You really are the most selfish, evil-minded, precocious little—'

'Not half as precocious as your darling Terry would like

me to be,' snarls Chaz, and slams out. *She's got a point there*, says Angel.

And it's no good you trying to wind me up, Angel. Terry will be here any minute and I'm nervous enough, without you starting.

Half an hour later, just as Tina is beginning to feel positively sick with worry (*Is he going to show? Don't hold your breath.*), the 'Yellow Rose of Texas announces Terry's arrival. Told you it'd be all right, Angel.

'Right, where's the fire?' he says at once 'Can't stop long.' *What a charmer*, exclaims Angel. *How does he do it? More to the point, why do you take it?*

'B-but I . . . you said you'd come to dinner.' Tina waves a hand vaguely towards the kitchen. 'I've got everything ready.' *Yeah, the humble pie's doing nicely*, says Angel. *And the hemlock's just coming to the boil.*

'Look, *sweetie*, I've already told you I can't stop. Now for God's sake—'

'But Terry, I don't seem to have seen anything of you lately, what with your business trips and—' *Oh whine, whine; you sound like the runt of the litter nobody wants, left high and not particularly dry in the pet shop window.*

'Well I'm here now, so spit it out. What's so important that you have to drag me all the way over here at a moment's notice?'

So Tina spits it out. As Angel predicted (*What did I tell you?*), Terry is less than ecstatic. Quite a lot less than ecstatic.

'Oh yeah? Well why tell me? Unless you're trying to say it's mine. You having a laugh, or what? You didn't exactly play hard to get with me, so how do I know you haven't been putting it about all over the place? What about this boyfriend that slag Jean mentioned, for instance – the loveable boy next door? How do I know *he* isn't the proud daddy?'

'But, but you don't understand.' (*Don't try to justify*

169

yourself to the bastard, please.) 'I . . . we . . . it's not like that. Frank and I are just—'

'Just good friends? Oh come *on*. I know you too well. And don't think you can con *me* into stumping up with the cash so that you can get rid of it; I don't believe in abortion, anyway. Murder, that is.'

Ooh, get you and your high principles, says Angel.

He turns to leave, but Tina stands between him and the door. *Leave it, please. I can't stand to see you grovelling.*

'But Terry, I promise you, it *is* yours, and you always said you *wanted* children. I thought you'd be p-pleased.'

Terry looks her up and down coldly. 'Pleased? Why should I be pleased? Of course I want kids, but unfortunately we can't have any.'

'But we can, we are!'

'I don't mean you and me, you stupid bitch, I mean me and my wife.'

'But you said you were divorced,' she whispers. *And you believed it*, says Angel. *More fool you.*

'Yes, and I also said I was divisional sales manager rather than just factory fodder. And you took it all in – hook, line and bloody sinker.' He gives her a shove. 'Now get out of my way, before I lose my temper. I'm in a hurry. And don't ring me at work any more. You've been enough of a bloody nuisance already. And don't even think about getting in touch with my wife, either. We never met. Got it?'

He slams the door behind him, while Tina, utterly devastated, sits at the carefully laid table and weeps. *I rest my case*, says Angel sadly.

seventeen

Nearly visiting time. Tina dabs half-heartedly at her face with Max Factor Creme Puff and paints on a smiley mouth with the inevitable Desert Fire lipstick. *That's better, you look a bit less 'Phantom of the rue Morgue' now.* Thanks Angel, you're a great comfort. *Think nothing of it.* I don't.

'That's right. Bit of lippy'll do wonders.' A whippet-like trainee with the name 'Jo' on her plastic badge and an interrogative, Kalashnikov-style delivery lopes into the room bearing a vase of carnations. 'Who loves ya baby? But why carnations? Bit funeral-like, aren't they?' (*Very appropriate, if you ask me,* says Angel.) She glances at the florist's card. 'Who's Frank? Where do you want 'em? On your locker? On the windowsill? Which? OK to let your visitor in?'

Without waiting for a single answer to any of her machine-gun fire questions, (*Christ, she's exhausting. I'd rather do five rounds with Sonny Liston than five minutes with her.*) Jo dumps the flowers on the windowsill and breezes out again. Well, she's been on since two, and that Mrs Monks in room seven's been giving her the Magic Bloody Roundabout treatment all day. ('Can't get the patients, these days,' she is wont to confide to Win, the cleaning orderly.) Besides, Jo's feet are killing her and she promised herself a fag break round the back by the wheelie bins an hour ago.

Jean's head pops around the door. (*Well, who were you*

171

expecting? The grieving ex-father-to-be?) 'Hiya kid. She dumps a Tesco bag ('Bit of fruit, *She* magazine and spare knicks') on a chair and gazes round speculatively. 'Blimey, Frank's done you proud. Own TV, telephone . . . Christ, you've even got a bell for room service. Wouldn't get this five-star treatment on the old National Health.'

Tina's eyes fill with tears. (*Oh, pull yourself together!* says Angel.) 'I know. Frank's been marvellous. Not that I deserve it.' *You can say that again.*

Jean hands her a tissue. 'Here you are; have a good blow. How are you feeling, apart from the odd sunny showers and being a bit overcast in the southern regions?'

'Guilty as hell, if you must know.'

'Don't be a prat, Tina. Do you really need to be knee-deep in shitty nappies and baby puke after, what, a fourteen-year gap? And anyway, how on earth could you have supported two kids and yourself with no money coming in?' *With great difficulty, but it's no good telling her that, in her present mood.*

'Frank,' says Tina simply. 'That's how.' She plucks at the hem of her stiff white sheet, looking embarrassed. 'Frank said that if I really intended to go through with it he'd—' She breaks off to give her nose a good blow. (*Bloody hell, nearly took the top of me head off, then.*) 'Frank proposed marriage. Offered to make an honest woman of me, so to speak.'

'*Frank!*' Jean's eyes widen in surprise. 'Well, well, greater love hath no man, and all that.'

'No need to look so bloody surprised,' says Tina coldly. 'It is just conceivable that he might actually fancy me, with or without the bump.' *Ooh, that's made you sit up and take notice*, says Angel. *Can't have anyone suggesting there might just be a man born who doesn't think you're the best thing since Monroe bought her first bra.* Piss off, Angel.

Jean looks at her with amusement and something like

172

compassion in her eyes. 'I'd say it definitely is *not* conceivable that he'd fancy you, gorgeous as you are. Hadn't you realised that our Frank's gay?'

Bugger me, says Angel, taken by surprise for once, though she would never admit it.

'No. Not Frank. He doesn't act like a . . . he doesn't act gay.' (*How are gays supposed to act? All mincing walk, high-pitched voice and hand-on-hip-and-who's-pinched-me-roll-of-lino, as Ronnie Barker said on* Porridge *on the telly the other day?*) 'And why would he offer to marry me? He can't love me, or any other woman come to that.'

'What *is* love?' says Jean ruminatively. 'He's demonstrated much more than mere lust, has Frank. You ought to consider yourself honoured, flower.' She pats Tina's hand, astonished to find her eyes filled with tears. 'You wanna hang on to a man like that. But don't marry him, for God's sake – that would be a disaster for both of you. Just keep him close, like the true friend he is.'

'I shall,' murmurs Tina fervently. (*You'd better*, says Angel, sounding slightly choked.) 'I must admit he looked faintly relieved when I turned him down, though he would have made a wonderful father, particularly to Chaz.' *Unlike Terry*, says Angel. Which is enough to send Tina reaching for the Kleenex box again.

'You're not still hankering after that bastard Terry, are you?' says Jean, sharper than a bag of tacks, as ever, and Tina shakes her head miserably. *But she still wishes it could have been different, even now*, says Angel despairingly. *Regular bloody Rebecca of Sunnybrook Farm, she is.*

'I saw him the other day,' continues Jean, helping herself to a tired-looking banana from the fruit bowl.

'Down the club, large as life and twice as ugly,' Jean is saying between bites, 'chatting up some poor cow just like old times. Made my blood boil. I'd got a few G and Ts in me by then, so I bowled up to him and deliberately picked a fight, didn't I?' *Good on yer, Jean. Hope you*

173

bloody flattened him into the imitation parquet dance floor.

'Went white as the driven when I told him what you'd been going through. But here's the best bit: he had the bloody cheek to say you'd no right, no right mind you, and that it was *his* baby, the only one he'd ever managed to sire. Seemed to think he should have been consulted, for Christ's sake.' She shakes her head indignantly. 'I just don't believe that bastard.'

'Oh,' says Tina in a small voice. 'He does admit he is – would have been – the father then? Only he tried to say it could be Frank's or . . . or anyone's for that matter.' *Never mind about 'tried to say'*, insists Angel. *He did say. Loud and clear.*

''Course he admits it. He knows you were too besotted to look sideways at anyone else. He wouldn't have lifted a finger for you or the kid if you'd gone ahead and had it, but it would have given him a buzz to think he'd got a sprog tucked away somewhere. Good for the old ego, living proof that our Terry's got lead in his pencil after all.'

She pauses to toss her banana-skin deftly into the waste-paper basket in the corner of the room. (She wasn't shooter for the Holy Cross school netball team all those years ago for nothing.)

'Now, I don't know about you,' Jean continues, but I never want to hear that bastard's name again, so let's change the subject, shall we?' (*Best idea you've had all day.*) 'Good old Faithful Frank's ferrying you home on Friday, right?'

'Yes.' Tina manages a smile. 'He's cooking me a special, welcome-home lunch.'

'Good. You'd die of malnutrition if you left it to Chaz.'

'But I thought . . . Chaz said I needn't expect her to be at the flat when I came out of hospital, and . . .'

'Yeah, yeah,' says Jean. 'Chaz said a lot of things she didn't really mean. She was pissed off that you tried to keep

174

her in the dark about the, er, the termination for starters. Then when you said she'd have to stay at her nan's for a few days while you had the . . . had it done, she came out with the barmy idea that you were trying to get rid of her. Leave her round her nan's for ever.'

So with devastating logic she threatens to stay round there anyway, says Angel sarcastically. *Smart move!* Tina sighs. Exactly, Angel. God knows what goes on in that girl's head sometimes.

Jean pats Tina's hand reassuringly. 'Anyway. Panic over. Good old Frank talked her round. She's even been helping him get the flat ready for the return of the prodigal. Pound to a penny he'll have her doing hospital corners before the week's out, and rumour has it she even hoovered the sitting room yesterday. Vacuum cleaner nearly died of shock.'

'Never!'

'Cross my heart and hope to die.' Jean stands up, looking business-like. 'Now then, I'll pop in tomorrow but not Friday, obviously. See yah.'

I don't think I can stand much more of this, Angel. Frank's been fussing round me like an egg-bound Rhode Island Red all day. *Ungrateful cow.*

From her position on the sofa (with a *rug* over my knees and my feet up, Angel, for heaven's sake) she can make out the low rumble of Frank's voice and Chaz's answering laughter as they tackle the supper dishes. She pulls a face. *You're just jealous that Frank gets on with your daughter better than you do*, says Angel. Too bloody right; doesn't everybody get on with Chaz better than I do? Where have I gone wrong, Angel? How can I make things better?

Well, you could start by telling her the truth about the abortion. Face to face. She didn't believe all that garbage about a D & C ('. . . just because Nan and Granddad have swallowed it, don't kid yourself I have,' Chaz had growled). *Give her some bloody credit.*

175

She knows now, doesn't she? So what's the point? Anyway, she's made it crystal clear that she finds the very idea of her mother having sex ('At your age!') about as repellent as a case of the clap, especially with . . . with Terry ('And with that creep, of all people!'), let alone . . . let alone terminating a pregnancy. ('Abortionist!')

So Angel breaks the habit of a lifetime and shuts up. There's no talking to Tina when she's in this mood.

Having finished the washing-up, Chaz announces she is off to Jane's house, she of the newly beetroot-tinted, spiked hair and nose ring. 'We might go on to a party at Rick's, if you must know . . . Don't try and pretend you care a damn where I'm going or what time I get in, per-lease. You're only saying all this to impress Frank. Anyway, you're a fine one to talk; less than perfect role model, aren't you Mother dear?'

'She'll be all right,' says Frank mildly, as Chaz crashes out. 'She's a sensible kid.'

'Unlike her mother, you mean?'

'If you like.'

Bloody typical, thinks Tina. You can't even have a decent row with Frank.

Can't handle it, can you? murmurs Angel. *You've only ever known aggressive, confrontational bastards, after all.* Like Dennis, you mean? *Exactly. Like Dennis. Not to mention, ssh, you-know-who.*

And Angel is right. Frank can handle Tina's tantrums with one hand tied behind his back, deflecting her waspish attempts to goad him into an argument with the ease of a cow flicking bothersome flies from its rump.

Which is not surprising, considering all his years expertly nursing the elderly sick. Frank is now the epitome of patient tact and diplomacy. ('Now come on, Ethel. You'll catch your death wandering around naked as the day you were born. Let me help you get dressed again, there's a girl. That pink dress takes years off you, you know.' 'Ooh, Frank,

176

you are a one. If I were twenty years younger – oh all right, thirty then – you wouldn't be helping me get my clothes *on*, I can tell you.')

But by nine o'clock, even Frank's considerable patience is growing thin. He is exhausted, wanting nothing more than to collapse into bed. Neverthless, he insists on making Tina a milky drink and, after ensuring that she has drunk every drop and receiving her irritated assurance that she will go straight to bed, he finally leaves.

Thank God he's gone, Angel. Breathing a sigh of relief, Tina has just obediently climbed into bed, when there is a rap at the front door. (The 'Yellow Rose of Texas' has been unceremoniously ripped out in mid-chime by Chaz, who swears she found herself humming it in front of Rick last week. Embarrassing and distinctly uncool.)

Wonder who that is, Angel. *Frank's probably left his keys here, or something.*

But it is not Frank at the door.

'I had to see you,' says Terry, slurring his words slightly. 'Let me come in, Tina; just for a minute.' And Angel is shocked into silence.

'It's late,' replies Tina coldly, 'and you're drunk.' *That's it*, says Angel, recovering her composure. *Don't let him get his foot in the door, whatever you do.*

She begins to close the door, but Terry pushes forward, his eyes pleading. 'Just for a minute, please. I must talk to you, I must.'

I don't like the look of this, begins Angel, but it is an Oscar-winning performance (nothing changes) and Tina falls for it. 'Make sure it *is* only a minute then.'

Terry flashes a pale shadow of his John Travolta smile. 'You've changed your tune. Used to be all over me.' *Oh Christ*, groans Angel. *Never say die, eh?*

'Times change. People change,' says Tina woodenly. *Good girl.*

'Look, I know this sounds a bit of a cheek, but I could

do with a black coffee. (*Bit of a cheek? The bastard's got more front than Blackpool!*) I've – er – I've had a drop too much to drink ... Dutch courage ...' He hangs his head boyishly.

Muttering under her breath, Tina busies herself in the kitchen. Angel is beside herself. *He's got a bloody nerve ... turning up here ... you must be mad ...* Don't worry, Angel; one black coffee and he's out of my life for good, I promise.

Hello, says Angel. *He's even had the brass neck to switch on the bloody radiogram by the sound of it. Sodding Stevie Wonder, no less. Ready to party, is he? Surely that bastard doesn't think he can pick up where he left off? You better get your arse in there and inform him things have changed.* Too bloody right, Angel.

Terry has wasted no time making himself comfortable on the sofa. He has switched on the solitary standard lamp, and on the coffee table beside him are two large tumblers and a bottle of whisky, taken from Tina's drinks cabinet.

'Just what the bloody hell do you think you're on, Terry?' demands Tina, hands on her hips.

'Oh come on, Tina. This isn't like you.' Casually, he lights a cigarette. 'Sit down. Have a drink. We've got a lot to talk about.' He gives her a ghastly smile, patting the sofa cushion next to him.

I don't like the look of this, says Angel again. *And suddenly he doesn't sound drunk, to me*, she adds nervously.

'I don't want a bloody drink,' says Tina. 'Least of all whisky. Can't stomach the stuff, as you well know. I only keep it – only *kept* it—'

'Only kept it for me,' finishes Terry. 'How touching.' He leans to one side and fills each tumbler half full of whisky.

Suddenly Tina shivers. Terry's fixed smile is beginning to unnerve her. Thank God Chaz is out, she thinks irrelevantly. And if you say you don't like the look of

178

this once more, Angel, I'll scream. But Angel isn't saying a word.

'Just go, Terry. Please,' says Tina bravely, her voice wobbling slightly. 'We've got nothing to say to each other any more.'

With surprising speed Terry is upon her, twisting her arm behind her back and forcing her down on the sofa. Manoeuvring her into a sitting position, he seizes a glass of whisky and pushes it to her lips.

'I'd say we've got loads to say to each other. Wouldn't you? *Darlin'*. What about a toast? What'll it be, eh? How about, "To our child." The one you murdered. Come on. Drink up.'

With Terry firmly holding the back of her neck, Tina hasn't got much choice. So she takes some of the Scotch in her mouth, grimacing as it trickles down her throat. Help me, Angel, she begs silently. Please help me. But there is no response.

'Come on, Tina,' says Terry encouragingly. 'You can do better than that.' He raises the glass. 'Down the hatch.' He takes a hefty swig and wipes his mouth with the back of his hand. 'There, that's the way to do it. Now it's your turn, you murdering bitch.'

Tina clamps her lips together determinedly. But her resistance doesn't last long. Not after Terry replaces the glass carefully on the table and punches her in the mouth a few times.

'Come on, Tina,' says Terry again. 'Drink up.' And he forces the neck of the bottle through her lips, pouring until Tina splutters and gags helplessly. Inside her head, Angel begins to weep.

Help me, Angel. I'm . . . I'm drowning.

But Terry isn't going to let Tina drown. That would be too easy.

Grabbing her by the hair, he gazes into her face. Stevie Wonder is singing about a pretty little girl he adores. But

Tina is far from pretty at the moment. Not with tears and snot mingling with the blood and Scotch trickling from her mouth and down her neck.

'Christ, look at the state of it,' says Terry in disgust. 'To think I quite fancied it once. Still, one more time, eh? For old times' sake.'

He drains one of the tumblers of Scotch and pulls her to the floor. She beats her fists feebly against his chest when she realises what he is about to do. 'Terry, please. Not this,' she croaks.

'Why not? Was a time you couldn't get enough of it.' And Tina closes her eyes in despair as he straddles her.

Where are you, Angel? Don't leave me. Please. Not now.

Tina has no idea how long she's been lying here. She feels cold. Cold as death. She stares blankly at the ceiling, her face expressionless.

Terry hadn't taken long. As ever. But before rolling off her, he had coldly punched her full in the face. Maybe he'll go now, she had thought dully. Now he's got all that rage out of his system.

And she was right. Up to a point.

Terry had picked up one of the tumblers and gulped down the remains of the Scotch. Then, pausing only to aim half a dozen kicks at Tina's inert body, he had left. Not that Tina actually knew how many times he had kicked her. She had passed out after the fourth one.

Now Tina raises a fluttering hand to her face. Think he's broken my nose, Angel. Not to mention a few ribs. Come on Angel, I know you're in there. Say something, for Christ's sake.

Live to fight another day, will I? More to the point, do I deserve to? Well come on, Angel. Speak up.

She lies back wearily and closes her eyes, fresh tears squeezing between the tightly shut lids. Now even Angel has deserted her. She is completely worthless, that's why. Congratulations, kid, she can imagine Angel saying. You've scored the hat-trick – you've proved you're a waste of space as a wife, as a mother and as a human being. Now how about a lap of honour for the fans, eh?

Tina is deaf to the sound of a key turning in the front door lock. Chaz quietly lets herself in, bracing herself for a row, rehearsing her excuses for being out so late ('. . . well, we had to wait for Rick's dad to come back 'cos he'd promised to run me home, but he turned out to be a bit pissed so I had to wait ages for a taxi . . .').

All is silent apart from the click, click of Stevie Wonder's *Sixteen Classic Love Songs* revolving uselessly on the radiogram.

Typical, thinks Chaz, curling her lip. My caring mother can't even be bothered to wait up for me. So much for all that 'what time will you be home?' garbage. She doesn't give a toss *what* I do.

The door to the dimly lit sitting room stands open, and Chaz peeps in. Her horrified eyes photograph the scene for posterity. Her mother on the floor. Naked. Blink, click. The room as tidy as Frank had left it. Blink, click. No sign of a break-in. Blink, click. Two glasses and bottle of whisky. Blink, click.

With difficulty, Tina levers herself up on her elbows. 'It was Terry,' she gasps. 'He forced me.'

'Oh yeah?' snarls Chaz. 'Since when has anybody had to force *you* to open your legs? Got a bit out of hand, did it?' She wrinkles her nose in disgust. 'I can smell the booze from here. You stink of it.' She turns to go, salt tears stinging her eyes. 'I never want to clap eyes on you ever again, you . . . you old slag.'

Hopelessly, Tina turns her head away. She doesn't even see Chaz leave the flat. But Frank does.

Waking for some reason he never was able to put his finger on ('Second sight, I reckon,' Jean was to comment later), Frank had found himself unable to get back to sleep. He was just putting the kettle on for a cup of tea when he saw Chaz pass his kitchen window, on her way home. Frank had smiled indulgently. She's late, the little madam, he thought. I'd box her ears if she were mine. Still, she's home safe, that's the main thing.

Only she isn't home safe, because only minutes later, Frank hears Tina's door crash open against the party wall and Chaz comes hurtling past his window again. She is running this time. Running as if all the hounds of hell are after her.

By the time Frank throws on a dressing gown and makes it to his front door, she is long gone, the sound of her footsteps echoing down the concrete stairwell. He stands on the doorstep for a moment, his mouth open in surprise. What in the name of God . . . ?

Chaz has left her mother's front door wide open, so of course Frank decides to investigate.

Tina does not remember him carrying her to the bathroom, doesn't remember him weeping as he tenderly bathes her poor, battered face and body. He pats Tina dry as she sways, dripping and dull-eyed, on Jean's charity shop rug, and eases her into a crisp, cotton nightgown. 'Terry,' she murmurs, as Frank lays her on her bed. 'No more, Terry. Please.' Then she passes out again.

That animal could have done her serious damage, so recently after the abortion, thinks Frank. He must ring a doctor, the police. The man must be punished. He pauses, his hand on the telephone. No, perhaps not.

Can't put Tina through all that. Examinations by heavy-handed police medics. Photographs. Questions, questions, questions. Better check her over myself. He sighs and gently pulls down the top sheet.

Examining her as impersonally as a surgeon might, at last he is satisfied that no permanent physical damage appears to have been done. She will get over it. In time.

Gently covering Tina once again, he wanders into the sitting room, where he sets mechanically to work on his hands and knees, his tears mingling with blood and semen and 1001 carpet cleaner.

eighteen

'. . . And I'm sick to death of you and Frank pussy-footing round me like a pair of old maids trying to impress the only thing in trousers they've seen for twenty years,' rails Tina. 'It's been nearly three weeks now, and I'm perfectly OK. Good as new. Why don't the pair of you just piss off and leave me alone!'

'You're *looking* a lot better, I suppose,' says Jean doubtfully, 'but Frank and I—'

'Frank and I, Frank and I,' mimics Tina cruelly. 'You two planning to elope or something? You deserve each other, that's for sure – Dr Kildare and Florence bloody Nightingale.'

With great difficulty, Jean manages to bite her tongue and say nothing. Frank reckons all this snapping and snarling of hers is par for the course. 'Keep calm,' he had advised. 'Keep calm, whatever she says or does. She's just kicking out at us because we happen to be around. It's a healthy sign. Just roll with the punches and try to let her get rid of all that anger.'

So Jean has tried. How she has tried. At least Tina has been showing a bit of her old spirit for the past few days. That was something to be thankful for, she supposed. Not like just after it happened, when she would sit for hours, like a zombie straight out of some low-budget Hammer House of Horror film, moving her lips soundlessly. And listening, always listening for a response that never came.

She was trying to coax Angel back, of course. But Jean didn't know that.

Jean glances across the room at Tina, who is impatiently flicking through a magazine, ignoring her. Perhaps the time's right to ease up a little. Maybe Frank and I should gradually start to bow out. Gently get Tina used to being on her own for longer and longer periods. Got to start somewhere. We've been watching her like bloody hawks lately. Which would drive me clean round the bend, personally.

She stands up decisively and picks up her bag. 'I'll be off now, then. I'll, er, I'll pop in tomorrow afternoon. Frank's coming round this evening and—'

'Oh really,' snaps Tina, 'he's on nights this week, is he? And if you tell me once more that it's all for my own good, I'll scream. Why won't you and St Frank just give me my life back? I'm a big girl now, I promise you. Grown up at last. Isn't that what you always wanted?'

So Jean lets herself out sadly. Tina will be back to her old self before too long. Just a matter of time, according to the gospel of St Frank.

The moment Jean has gone, Tina's face assumes its now customary blank stare. She picks up the *Dalton's Weekly* hidden down the side of her armchair and flicks through the pages until she comes to the 'Short Holiday Breaks' section. 'It's such a relief to have come to a decision, Angel,' she says to the coffee table (which doesn't have a clue what she is talking about, of course; it's not the brightest of pieces of furniture). 'It's really good to have something to do, something positive to plan,' she adds conversationally.

Quickly, Tina finds the ad she is looking for, circled neatly in pencil. Here we are: 'Bluewater Guest House . . . five miles from the centre of Swanage . . . TV and H & C in all rooms.' Yeah, that'll do. She picks up the telephone and dials the number.

*

185

Tina drives slowly through Corfe, not that she's got much choice. Loads of tourists rubber-necking at the castle even in the pouring rain. Still, no hurry. Soon be over. All better. That's what Mum used to say as she kissed her grazed knees when she fell over as little child. 'Mum's special medicine'll make it all better,' she would add, popping a sweet into Tina's mouth. She giggles. I'm going to have some *very* special medicine. That's *definitely* going to make it all better, Mum.

'And you can keep your nose out of it, Angel,' she says winding her window down to speak to a mystified woman in a see-thru plastic mac with tastefully matching rainhat who's standing on a traffic island waiting to cross the road. 'Because I've definitely made up my mind.'

It is all beautifully symbolic. Swanage is an ideal choice. It was the scene of many a carefree childhood holiday. 'The Swansons are off to Swanage,' she would chant, excitedly, driving Joyce and Reg mad. Sorry, Mum. Sorry Dad, but this particular Swanson is off to Swanage for the last time. I'm going to be carefree again. If it's the last thing I do. She giggles again. Actually, it *is* the last thing I intend to do.

The cherry on the cake is that her ex-husband, the unlovely Dennis, had chosen Swanage for his various dirty weekends. Why, he had even bedded her very best friend Trish in good old Swanage-by-the-sea, so he'd told her all those years ago. Regular blow by blow account, it had been.

'Well go on, Angel,' she says, this time to a 'Keep Left' sign that had been standing by the side of the road minding its own business and had never been spoken to like that in its entire life. 'Go on, laugh. Regular blow by blow account. Get it? Very appropriate in Dennis's case.'

Trust him to pick the very town that had held so many of her happiest memories. Trust him to spoil them for her. Oh yes, Swanage is perfect, just perfect.

The doorbell at Bluewater chimes the opening bars of the

'William Tell Overture' and Tina grimaces. Christ, makes the 'Yellow Rose of Texas' sound almost acceptable. Still, who gives a shit. Certainly not Angel; she's obviously long gone, and I'll be joining her soon.

'You'll be the young lady who phoned yesterday,' smiles the landlady, a stout bottle-blonde in a floral nylon overall. (Suicide blonde, thinks Tina, grinning. Like me. Must be a lucky omen.) 'Just for the weekend, isn't it?'

'That's right. Just for the weekend.' A *dirty* weekend, she wants to add, where a very dirty deed is about to be done.

She had been saving the sleeping tablets prescribed by Dr Frank for ages, and neither he nor Jean had a clue. Dutifully pretending to take them, she would hold the capsules in her mouth and trot off to the lavatory to transfer them to the large, empty paracetamol bottle hidden at the very back of the bathroom cupboard, behind the packets of Elastoplast and dusty containers of Andrews Liver Salts, Vaseline and Vick. She had even talked them into increasing the dose, claiming the capsules weren't working.

But the real masterstroke had been stealing almost half the contents of a bottle of tablets from Jean's handbag while she was in the kitchen making tea. When she returned, Tina was still sitting where Jean had left her, gazing listlessly out of the window. She never suspected a thing.

Emptying the paracetamol bottle on to the side table in her room at Bluewater, Tina counts the tablets carefully. Terrific. More than enough to do the job. What do you think, Angel? Oh don't answer, then. Deserted the sinking, stinking ship along with all the rest, have you? Along with my only daughter, my unborn child and my erstwhile lover. Well, see if I bloody care.

Sitting on the bed, she surveys the room critically. One smudgily patterned carpet (slightly threadbare in places) that looks as though the previous guest has been sick all over it (he had, after a late night at the Lagoon nightclub on Marine Parade). One pair of shocking-pink curtains from the 1972 Grattan Catalogue Summer Sale. Calamine-lotion-coloured walls over woodchip wallpaper. One pink washbasin with badly repaired crack, vomiting for the use of (but if you can't make it in time, the carpet will do). One battered black-and-white Murphy TV that looks as if it should be in a museum. One plastic tray (amazingly not pink) containing the smallest electric kettle Tina has ever seen, a white mug with a red rose pattern and three packets of instant coffee, creamer and sugar.

'Bit of a dump really, Angel,' says Tina, addressing the TV, whose blank screen stares blandly back at her, refusing to pass comment. 'Stupid of me. Could have stayed at the Ritz or somewhere. Not as if I'll be around to pay the bill in the morning. Could have chosen somewhere really classy for my swan song.'

She begins to giggle. Swan song. Swanson's swan song in Swanage. She laughs silently, until the tears course down her cheeks. 'I really am a dead loss, Angel. Well, nearly, anyway. And so will you be, soon.'

Not if I can help it, says Angel nervously.

'Oh, you've decided to come back and help me in my hour of need, have you?' snarls Tina. 'Makes a pleasant change. Where were you when I needed you? Answer me that. Well, you're about three weeks too late if you're kidding yourself you can talk me out of it.'

And Tina snaps the television on loud to drown out Angel's protestations. She shivers, suddenly feeling cold. Cold as death.

Kit

nineteen

Emma Tilbury is on reception because Mrs Janet Discretion-is-my-middle-name Johnson, the regular receptionist, is at the dentist's. Not that Emma believes a word of it. Pound to a penny she's gone for an interview.

Still, who can blame her? What with old Iron Drawers Swanson breathing down her neck all the time Emma wonders how much longer she'll be able to stick working at Simon Chivers & Partner, Solicitors, herself.

She is just in the middle of pouring out her grievances to her friend Julia over the phone when a client walks in. Emma totally ignores him and carries on chatting (well, it *is* supposed to be her lunch hour!). Eventually, she says a grudging goodbye ('S'pose I'll *have* to go, Jules; I got some bloke waiting.') and glances up at the visitor disapprovingly.

'Appointment?' she drawls.

'Yes. Two o'clock with Mr Kit Swanson, but I'm a few minutes early.'

'Name?' says Emma, adding sternly, 'And it's *Ms* Swanson, by the way. She's very strict about that.' Man-hating old dyke, she wants to add, but doesn't.

'The name's Nicholson. Peter Nicholson,' says the bloke politely, thinking how Emma wouldn't last five minutes in his outfit and how she'd be out the door so fast she'd think her arse was on fire.

But how is he to know Simon Chivers & Partner are having to be a little less selective when recruiting junior

191

staff these days? How is he to know that the Kit Swanson he is about to meet has been responsible for the premature departure of a succession of tearful females who somehow did not measure up to her exacting standards in one way or another?

Emma Tilbury is but the latest in a long line of hopefuls who will eventually (in precisely a week, actually) slam out of Ms Swanson's office, having told the lady (as did her predecessor, give or take a few swear words) exactly where she can stick her poxy job and who does she think she is anyway, fucking Margaret Thatcher?

Unaware of the drama to come a week from now, Emma speaks briefly into an intercom on her desk and a disembodied voice barks some unintelligible instruction. 'Take a seat,' she says shortly. 'Ms Swanson'll see you in a minute.' *Todally* typical of the old cow to keep people waiting, she thinks, unaware of the irony; point of principle with *Ms* 'Iron Drawers' Swanson, that is, whatever time they turn up.

So he sits, studying the solitary print of 'When did you last see your Father' on the wall facing his chair with an absorption born of sheer boredom, while Emma furtively scans a copy of *Smash Hits* magazine which she at least has the decency to conceal in the top drawer of her desk because, fair's fair, it *has* just gone two now and she *is* supposed to be working.

After only a few minutes the intercom buzzes sharply and, with an elaborate sigh, she closes the drawer and reluctantly escorts the visitor to Kit Swanson's room. Up and down like a tart's knickers in this dump, thinks Emma disgustedly. Why I can't just point people in the right direction I can't imagine. Iron Drawers' office is only a step down the corridor, after all; hardly Hampton Court bloody maze.

Like the waiting room, Kit Swanson's office is bland in the extreme. Spartan, even.

A bookcase that looks as if it could house a family of four in some comfort dominates the room. It is stuffed to the gunwales with such an impressive array of perfect, legal-looking, leather-bound tomes, that Peter Nicholson wonders briefly whether it is really a cunningly disguised door, leading to a secret torture chamber beyond, where Simon Chivers & Partner extract fees (or teeth, if necessary) from unwilling clients.

The piles of tatty folders tied with pink string, to be found gasping like landed fish on every surface in the average solicitor's office are under lock and key ('Quite right too – we are supposed to be confidential, you know.') in a formidable, battleship-grey filing cabinet capable of withstanding fire, flood and assaults from crack teams of SAS gunmen, not to mention the occasional rampaging divorce co-respondent bent on sabotage and/or revenge.

Apart from three desperately uncomfortable-looking straight-backed chairs lined up against the wall like wallflowers at a wedding, plus a sternly practical wooden desk which is bare, except for a telephone and a plain manila folder with Peter Nicholson's name on it, there are no other furnishings in Kit Swanson's office. As *Private Eye* magazine would say, er, that's it.

The room is completely lacking those homely human touches – the family photographs on the desk, the obligatory half-dead, not-very-busy-lizzie plant, the postcards from lucky/unlucky colleagues holidaying in foreign climes/ a caravan in Bognor – that homely humans tend to introduce, bit by bit, into the workplace from the first moment they set foot on the heavy-duty contract lino tiles (or carpet tiles, if they are salaried staff).

But this office is not occupied by a homely human. This is the lair of Iron Drawers.

She stands to greet him, elegant in an understated pearl-grey suit that discreetly murmurs 'money'. ('One glance at the Harvey Nicks label should be enough, thank you.

Hardly need tickertape and a champagne reception. Too, too vulgar.')

As Kit Swanson extends her hand, their eyes meet and Peter Nicholson experiences a sudden, almost painful shock of recognition.

They shake hands formally, like the strangers they have become, her handclasp firm and dry, the hands square and freckled, as he remembers. She wears no nail varnish, no jewellery, no make-up, the Desert Fire lipstick and Max Factor Panstick having being jettisoned long ago, along with the backcombed-to-within-an-inch-of-its-life, Sunkissed Blonde dye job of yesteryear. Though, of course, Peter Nicholson is not to know this.

The sleek, prematurely silver hair is her most striking feature. ('Beautiful colour, madam,' says Marco of Marco Hairfashions, when she is expensively 'tidied-up' on the first Saturday of every month without fail. 'But perhaps a little, well, ageing. Perhaps I could interest you in a tiny colour tint? No? As madam wishes.') Expertly cut in a deceptively simple bob, the hair frames her familiar, high-cheekboned face, with its small, pointed nose that used to quiver endearingly, as Peter Nicholson recalls, in moments of high emotion. She used to remind him of a particularly cute Disney mouse.

But there is nothing mouse-like about her now, he thinks. Cat-like, yes, with those watchful grey eyes and that still, tense posture that give the unnerving impression she is about to spring on something small and furry at any minute and do it to death. If she had a tail it would be swishing ominously, he decides, with a slight shiver of apprehension.

Pull yourself together, Nicholson, he thinks. You're a big boy now. She'll thaw out when she realises who you are.

Only she doesn't.

'Well, well,' she says flatly. 'I had no idea you were Peter Nicholson.'

Liar, says Angel from inside her head.

'Why should you? I don't suppose you knew my first name was Peter. Everyone's always called me Nick.'

Of course she knew your name was Peter, says Angel. *As if she could forget.*

She sits down abruptly, so Nick follows suit. Well? Is she shocked to see me, after all these years? Pleased? Disappointed? Indifferent? The woman gives nothing away, absolutely nothing.

Hardly surprising. How could he know about the years of practice concealing her true feelings, presenting a seemingly emotionless facade to the world at large?

It's safer that way, the reinvented Kit had decided, long ago, taking a firm line with Angel – who had been getting distinctly above herself, by the way. No one can touch you if you keep them at arm's length. No one can hurt you if you don't let them in.

No, and no one can help you either, Angel had replied tetchily.

I don't need help from anyone, Angel. Least of all you. And anyway, where were you when I really did need help?

At least I stopped you from topping yourself, Angel had said resentfully. *If it weren't for me—*

If it weren't for you I'd be six feet under. So you keep reminding me. Just don't expect me to be grateful, that's all. I'm in control of my life now, Angel. You're irrelevant, like the genie in the bottle with its cork firmly in place. You're just something I've learned to live with, like a permanent, nagging headache. End of conversation.

In your dreams, sunshine, said Angel, with a glimmer of her old, feisty spirit. *You'd love to keep me firmly corked for good, I know that. You've turned into a control freak, just like your ex, the lovely Dennis. And has it made you happy? I don't think so.*

'Well,' says Nick awkwardly, breaking the oddly hostile

195

silence between them, 'looks as if you've carved out a successful career for yourself, Chrissie.'

Kit stiffens. It is twenty years since anyone called her by that name.

'Trish always said you had a good brain,' Nick is saying. 'That you were wasting your life with that scumbag Dennis . . .' His voice trails to a halt, as he becomes aware of the gaze still riveted upon him. Now there is no mistaking the hostility in her eyes. 'Anyway,' he continues, with a small, nervous laugh, 'it's nice to know I'll have friend on my side.'

'A friend? You were hardly a friend. Merely an acquaintance.'

'All right then, an acquaintance on my side,' says Nick breezily. (God, what's the matter with the woman?) 'Assuming you will agree to handle my case, of course.' He smiles, trying to lighten the almost palpable tension in the air. 'You must think we're mad, Trish and me, taking twenty years to decide to get divorced—'

'I have no opinion,' interrupts Kit coldly. 'The facts of the case are my only concern.'

Jesus, thinks Nick. The woman's bloody inhuman. You'd think she'd be slightly curious, at the very least. Trish was her best friend, for Christ's sake.

'OK,' he says, barely controlling his anger, 'Trish and I want a divorce so that she can remarry. Factual enough for you? I imagine it'll be a rubber-stamp job after all these years so perhaps you'll do the necessary, Chrissie.'

'The name's Kit Swanson. Chrissie Charleton died twenty years ago as far as I'm concerned. And quite frankly it would be unethical for me to handle your divorce in view of our previous relationship.'

Relationship? sneers Angel. *You wish. You didn't have a relationship with Nick. Wanted to though. Boo bloody hoo.*

Kit stands up and extends her hand, dismissing him along

196

with Angel. 'Perhaps you'd like to make an appointment to see our senior partner, Simon Chivers, on your way out. I'm sure he will be happy to act for you.'

So why didn't you refer Nick to Simon in the first place, I ask myself, whispers Angel. *Just had to see him again, didn't you? Couldn't resist. And don't try to tell me it was just idle curiosity.*

'Fine,' says Nick shortly. But it is not fine; not fine at all. How did timid little Chrissie metamorphose into this ball-breaker of a woman? He would love to know.

On impulse, he gives Kit the slightly mocking smile she remembers so well and, to her dismay, suggests they might meet up, for old times' sake. 'After all,' he adds winningly, 'we've got a lot of catching up to do.'

'Absolutely not,' is the icy response. (*End of conversation?* sneers Angel.) Kit sits down again and pulls a file from her desk drawer. 'Now if you'll excuse me, I am rather busy.'

Nick stands over her, an odd expression on his face. 'If you imagine I am trying to proposition you, you delude yourself. I don't know what happened to change you over the past twenty years and, frankly, I don't want to know. (*He's lying,* says Angel intuitively.) All I can say is that the new, improved *Ms* Kit Swanson isn't a patch on the Chrissie Charleton I used to know. I'll let myself out.'

And he turns on his heel leaving Kit Swanson sitting at her desk brooding on the past – a past she has tried to suppress for so many, many years.

Happy now? says Angel, and a solitary teardrop trickles down Kit's cheek and plops on to the manila folder in front of her.

Obviously not. So why not go out for a drink with the man? What could be the harm in that?

What harm, Angel? Only the harm – not to mention the pain – of opening up old wounds. It'd be like opening up a vein with a rusty razorblade and letting myself bleed to death. I couldn't bear it. And she shudders at the memory of her last night with Dennis.

Ah, sighs Angel sadly. *The night of the great escape – minus Steve McQueen to spirit you away on his trusty motorbike.*

Yes, Angel. The night he told me he'd been having an affair with . . . with Trish. The night I finally admitted to myself that as well as having to beat me to a pulp before he could—

Get it up?

Quite. Get it up, as you so crudely put it. As well as that he was beginning to . . . to want Janine – Chaz, I should say.

Beginning? says Angel. *Beginning to want Chaz? Oh come on. The signs were there long before that night, but you simply refused to see them. All those little smacks for the slightest thing, just so that he could make the kid cry and had an excuse for sitting her on his lap to 'comfort' her, kissing and stroking her all over. It was sick. And there were other clues . . .*

Tears begin to course down Kit's cheeks. Please, Angel. I really don't want to . . .

But the cork in the bottle of Kit's iron control is beginning to look distinctly wobbly, and Angel marvels at the notion that one visitor from the past, namely Nick, could be just the catalyst she needs to pop her cork altogether.

Come on, she whispers. *Let go. Let it all out. Better out than in, as your mother always says.*

Kit shakes her head in despair. What's the point in dredging it all up again, Angel? You know what happened.

Tell me again, says Angel gently. *Trust me.*

If I close my eyes, I can still picture poor little Chaz trying to come between us, that night. Still see the look on Dennis's face when he knocked her aside. I was so terrified that if I fought him off he'd . . . he'd turn on the child, so I just . . .

Just lay back and thought of England.

No, Angel. I just lay back and thought of escape. I knew I had to get away, and quickly, for both our sakes. Mine and the child's. I'd already learned from bitter experience that it was less painful in the long run if I just let him . . . let him get on with it.

Only when I was sure Dennis had fallen asleep, only then did I creep to Chaz to comfort her. We didn't dare switch on a light, for fear of waking him, so—

So you just pulled on the first clothes that came to hand and legged it, says Angel. *Just about the wisest thing you ever did in your life. Not that there have been too many of those.* Thanks a lot, Angel.

Mind you, you would probably both have died of exposure if it hadn't been for that lovely man who picked you up just as you made it to the A40. Eat your heart out, Steve McQueen; who needs you and your motorbike for the Great Escape when you can have Ron Bridges and his Unigate lorry.

Kit's face softens, bringing about a surprising transformation. Yes, let's hear it for Knight-of- the-Road, Ron. Not to mention his wife's friend, Rose McMahon.

'Well, I had to stop, didn't I,' Ron Bridges was to explain to his wife, Pam, at the time. 'Couldn't just leave them there, that time of night. Pissing down, it was, an' all. The kiddie was about our Sal's age and the pair of 'em looked scared shitless.

'Wouldn't get in the cab at first – just stood there, like a coupla drowned rats – but in the finish I got them to let me give them a lift somewhere, anywhere, for the kid's sake, if nothing else. Poor little bugger was all in, and the woman looked as if she'd just had an argument with a bloody concrete mixer.

'Shoulda taken her straight round the 'ospital, or the police, by rights, but she wouldn't 'ave it, 'case her old man found them. Terrified, she was, Pam. Wouldn't even let me take them to friends, in-laws or nothing. Said that'd be the first place her old man'd look. So I just drove, thinking what I'd like to do to the bloke if I ever got my hands on him, and that's when I had this idea.

'I suddenly thought of Rose, your mate that runs that battered wives' refuge over Slough way. It wasn't that far off my route 'ome, and I knew she'd be safe there. Rose'd know what to do.'

Thank God for Rose, breathes Angel. *Took you and Chaz in without a murmur.*

Kit allows herself a grim smile. No wonder Simon gives me our 'battered wife' cases, Angel. I met enough of them at Rose's safe house, all those years ago.

When I let Frank bully me into picking up the threads of the career in law I abandoned when I got married (*Before Dennis put the tin lid on it by getting you up the duff, you mean*, says Angel.) it was the thought of some of Rose's 'clients' that drove me on.

Grinding through university and law school, the only thing that kept me going was the thought that I could one day put something back, make a difference for some of those poor, hopeless souls who think they somehow 'asked for it' every time the old man decides there's nothing much on telly tonight so it'd be a bit of a laugh to beat up the missus.

Just like Dennis did, observes Angel. And Kit nods gravely. Indeed.

Then, to add insult to injury, (and I use the term advisedly) they get bulldozed into pitiful divorce settlements because they're too beaten down by it all to resist.

Absolutely, Angel. And if they can't stand on their own feet, then I'll do it for them. I'll hammer those men into the ground, if the women won't.

Is that all men, or just the ones that have developed a taste for using their wives as punchbags, for a pastime? asks Angel slyly.

Just the wife-batterers, of course.

I see, breathes Angel. *Even though the entire staff of Simon Chivers & Partner imagine 'Iron Drawers' is just an embittered, forty-five-year-old lesbian who's anti the entire male race as a matter of principle.*

'I don't give a toss what they think, Angel,' snaps Kit aloud, throwing a couple of files into her briefcase and preparing to leave for home. 'My work is the only important thing in my life.'

Ah well, sighs Angel. *At least you've got that. Rose would be proud of you, I must say.*

Oh, I hope so, Angel, I do hope so.

Not to mention Frank, and your parents. Your dad was like a dog with two tails the day you passed your law exams.

Yes, I know he was. God rest him.

twenty

That morning, nearly five years ago, when the results of Kit's law examinations were published, Reg Swanson had arrived at his corner Spar shop before Wilma and Dick Barraclough had had time to get the papers unbundled, let alone get much more than a sip of tea and a bite or two of their usual bacon sandwiches down their necks.

'Watchoo doin' 'ere at this time, Reg?' Wilma had demanded. 'It's still the middle of the bleedin' night to most of our customers. Or 'as your Joyce finally seen sense and chucked you aht at last?'

And she had cackled so much that she was overcome with a coughing fit and had to sit down on a slippery pile of *Good Housekeeping* magazines while Dick patted her back. 'It's no good, gel,' he had said, shaking his head. 'You'll 'ave to pack them fags in. Be the death of you, they will.' And he was absolutely right.

Twenty-five years on Wilma is to die from what the medics will call a 'smoking-related illness', but not before she outlives Dick and reaches the grand age of eighty-six. She will consider smoking forty fags a day for as many years well worth it, and besides, she is ready to go now that Dick's gone and her only daughter pissed off to live in Canada with her third husband and Wilma's grandchildren years since.

'Well,' Wilma had said, recovering, 'what can I do you for, Reg?'

Reg had looked round furtively, just to make sure none

of his neighbours were lurking behind the piles of newspapers and crates of cat food. Wouldn't do for that nosy git Jack Stubbs from next door to know what he was up to. He'd never live it down. Not that idle Jack would be up and about at this hour, but you couldn't be too careful, with him.

Reg had cleared his throat awkwardly. 'I'll, er . . . I'll 'ave a copy of *The Times*, please, Wilma.'

And Wilma had sat down again in a hurry. 'What? *The Times*? But you bin 'aving the *Mirror* weekdays an' *The News of the World* an' *People* Sundays since Adam were a lad. What's up? You gettin' ideas above yer station, Reg? Or do you want it for the Executive Appointments page? Fancy a job as boss of ICI or Ford's do yer?' Which witticisms had sent Wilma into yet another explosion of coughing loud enough to wake the entire street.

Reg had sighed. 'Very comical. I only want it to find out if my girl's passed her law exams, so just bung us a copy willya? The suspense is killing me, an' my Joyce is no better. Been up since four, she 'as. Drivin' me nuts.'

'As the patient said to the doctor when he found out he'd got a steering wheel growing out of his willie,' Dick had said, grinning his toothless grin. 'Driving me nuts. Get it?'

'Yeah, I get it,' said Reg. 'Just like I got it the other three times you told me. Right bleedin' comedian you are, Dick Barraclough. Now just give us the paper, for Christ's sake. Joyce'll think I've decided to run orf with annuver woman if I 'ang about chewin' the fat for much longer.'

'Please yerself, I'm sure,' Wilma had said stiffly, handing him the newspaper. 'An' by the way, congratulations.'

Unable to keep a straight face longer than seconds at a time, she had grinned, showing a mouthful of nicotine-stained gnashers that could have done with a good soak in Steradent. 'She's passed. Your girl's passed. We already looked.' And she gave Reg a big, bacon-flavoured kiss on the chops, just to show there was no ill-feeling and she'd only been pulling his plonker, that's all.

It had been a real red-letter day for Reg and Joyce. 'Always knew our kid had it in 'er.' Reg had said proudly, before retiring to the shed after a celebratory cooked breakfast (unheard of on any normal Friday) to read the latest *Exchange & Mart* because Joyce would get that bloody Hoover out every single morning and you couldn't hear yourself think.

Reg had put on quite a bit of weight over the past few years, and when he plumped heavily down in his usual ancient deckchair it chose that particular morning to decide it had finally had enough. The rotten canvas gave up the ghost at last, spilling Reg, *Exchange & Mart*, mug of tea and all, on to the floor.

The *Exchange & Mart* was perfectly OK, apart from a few tea stains on the 'Properties for Sale' page, which didn't really matter because Reg and Joyce had no plans to move house at their time of life. ('It might not matter to you. Bet it'd be different matter if it'd been "Used Cars".') The Leeds United mug that had contained Reg's tea had merely bounced on the floor without breaking but at the moment Reg's broad backside hit the deck he'd had a massive stroke which had pulled his face down on one side, like someone rucking up a carpet, rendering him incapable of speech.

Not that Joyce would have heard him if he had been able to shout for help, what with the Hoover and Jimmy Young ('. . . orf we jolly well go, ladies') on the transistor. But after Joyce had put the Hoover away, after she had washed up the breakfast things and put the kettle on for another cup of tea, she had glanced at her pine kitchen clock and realised that an hour had gone by already and Reg was still out in the shed.

'Silly old sod's fallen asleep, I reckon,' she had murmured to her favourite Royal Doulton crinoline lady, who didn't answer because she deplored bad language and was a bit miffed at having to slum it in the kitchen while her glue was drying following Joyce's latest bit of carelessness. 'I better go out and get 'im indoors,' said Joyce.

But by that time, it was too late.

'There 'e was, stone dead on the floor,' she had told Kit later. 'The minute the funeral's over I'm burning that fuckin' deckchair and the shed with it. And I'm not stayin' in that 'ouse a minute longer than I 'ave to. Not without my Reg. I couldn't bear it, I couldn't really.'

Over endless cups of tea in Joyce's sitting room, mother and daughter had discussed moving house, while the surviving crinoline ladies (several of their number having fallen victim to Joyce's over-enthusiasm when wielding her trusty mini-vac) tut-tutted on their shelves. ('I dread to think how we'll survive a move. I'm only here today thanks to almost an entire tube of Bostik and a matchstick holding my head on,' muttered one, while another, being slightly younger and less set in her ways, rather fancied a change of scene: 'Oh, I don't know. As long as they use a reputable removing firm and plenty of bubble wrap we should be all right; where's your spirit of adventure?')

Eventually, Joyce and Kit had decided to pool their resources and buy a tiny, run-down, end-of-terrace house in west London, only a few stops away on the tube from Simon Chivers & Partner, Solicitors, where Kit had become articled.

Joyce had been less than impressed when first she clapped eyes on the property. 'What a dump. Dunno why they bothered to board it up. Even the squatters have given it the go-by an' I don't blame 'em.' She had stood in the narrow hallway and sniffed disparagingly. 'Though by the smell of cat's pee I reckon the local moggies have been having a high old time here.' As indeed they had.

On cue, a large, ginger tom with only half his whiskers and a distinctly rakish air had chosen that moment to saunter brazenly past. ('What's this? Don't get many visitors to our exclusive club during the hours of daylight. And are you members, by the way?') He had rubbed himself against Kit's legs, arching his back in ecstasy as she automatically bent down to stroke his broad, battle-scarred head.

'But Mum,' Kit had said. 'I can see great potential in the place. Trust me.' And when she had explained her plans for the house, when Joyce saw her daughter looking excited and animated about something for the first time in years, she was completely won over.

Catching something of Kit's enthusiasm, and secretly glad of something to do, something to fill the aching void left by Reg's death, Joyce threw herself into realising Kit's plans.

The small army of workmen that invaded the place was putty in her hands. 'The daughter's a bit snotty,' one of them pronounced, 'but the old girl's a diamond; haven't had to touch my Thermos all the time I been working here. I told her the other day she oughter think about opening a caff and she just laughed and said she'd soon go broke at her prices. Won't stand no Barney Rubble, mind. Knows what she wants, that one, and makes sure she bloody gets it.'

And, months and several thousand cups of tea later, Joyce did get what she wanted, and the old-fashioned two-up, two-down had been transformed. Two separate sitting rooms had been created ('One for you and one for me, Mum.') either side of the narrow hallway, and the dismal scullery – which had looked like a stage set out of *The Prisoner of Zenda* – had been extended to provide what Joyce called her 'dream kitchen'. In theory, mother and daughter were to share the kitchen, but Joyce had made no bones about claiming it for her own right from the start.

'Well,' she had said to two of the workmen, Matthew

and Geoff (christened Mutt and Jeff by Joyce, of course), over tea and chocolate Hobnobs, 'I'm gonna be the one spendin' mosta me time chained to the kitchen sink while my gel's out at work, so you just ignore 'er. To go with the Pearl White melamine units – come up lovely with a bit of Flash when they get grubby, they will – I want Georgian Blue on the walls, right?'

'Right,' said Mutt, rolling another cigarette. 'Any chance of another cuppa, missus?'

'Only when you finished paintin' my granddaughter's new back bedroom we put over the kitchen extension an' after I bin up to give it the once-over,' said Joyce firmly. 'Should be able to knock that off by one, knowing you. I got a nice bit of apple tart to go with yer dinner, today.'

So Mutt and Jeff had simply got on with it, as per instructions.

Joyce was almost sorry to see the house finished, in the end. It had been so exciting, even though they were living in dust and grime for what seemed an age. But once comfortably settled in, once she had been made redundant from her job of building supervisor, negotiator and tea lady all rolled into one, she had taken on a new role in life.

Reg had gone – God rest him – so, just as her daughter had reinvented herself as Ms Kit Swanson, solicitor, Joyce saw herself reborn as the one destined to do the pushing.

'Well, Reg,' she would say to the pot (Royal Doulton, naturally) containing Reg's ashes, 'you've gone an' left me – not that you could 'elp it, I know that – so looking after the girl, encouraging her, is down to me now. You always said she needs a bit of a kick up the arse, at times, an' you was spot on. In a world of 'er own, 'alf the time. Miles away, she is, almost as if she's listening to her bloody voices all over again.' (Which of course, she is, though Joyce doesn't know it.) 'I bet she'd even forget to eat if I didn't put grub on the table when she comes home from work.

'Mind you, Reg, I can't talk, can I? If she walked in

and caught me having a good old chinwag with you, she'd probably have me carted away by the men in white coats.'

I don't think so, somehow, do you?

twenty-one

It is unheard of at Simon Chivers & Partner for Kit Swanson to leave the office early, but on the afternoon of Nick's visit she does just that.

Can't settle to anything, I suppose? murmurs Angel. *Not after coming eyeball to eyeball with the love of your life after all these years. Thrown you all of a heap, has it?* Oh, shut up, Angel. That's a ridiculous suggestion.

Angel, as we know, doesn't miss a trick. And nor does Emma Tilbury, who, while being too *todally* gobsmacked by Kit's sudden departure to bother to hide her Duran Duran fanzine (she finished *Smash Hits* long ago), nevertheless manages to clock the fact that Iron Drawers looks miffed, to say the least.

'Something must have upset her, to leave work early,' she will confide to a bored Jules that evening, twisting round on her bar stool and shouting to be heard over Lulu, who is giving Emma a run for her money Twist-and-Shouting on her own account as her contribution towards Sixties Night.

Jules is sick to death of hearing Emma banging on about Iron Drawers, but says nothing, stirring idly at her Tequila Sunset with the plastic swizzle stick provided because, well, she *did* pay for Jules's drink, which is going to have to last all night, the state of her finances at the moment.

'All right for some,' moans Emma. 'Goes flouncing off in the middle of the afternoon, if you don't mind, while I'm still stuck on that bloody reception desk *todally* bored out of my mind, like, *for ever*, thanks to the non-return of Janet 'Discretion' Johnson from her so-called dentist's appointment . . . I *don't* think!'

Emma was absolutely spot on, as it happens, although she is not to know Janet has been successful in her job interview. At the exact moment Kit is in mid-flounce, Janet is celebrating her success over a pot of tea for two (her married lover will be joining her any minute) and a plate of fondant fancies at the Nell Gwynne Tea Shoppe – all faded gentility and muslin curtains, and a surly, burly, mob-capped waitress who looks as if she could willingly wrestle Jackie (Mr TV) Pallo to the canvas any old day of the week, no trouble. The tea shop is tucked discreetly down a side street a hundred yards from Donaldson & Son, rival solicitors to Simon Chivers & Partner, and half empty this Friday afternoon (and indeed most afternoons), so an ideal venue as far as Janet and her lover, Alex, are concerned.

Alex will not be surprised that she has got the job, since he is the '& Son' at Donaldson's and only went through the pantomime of interviewing her for the sake of appearances, as he is technically still married to his wife of fifteen years. ('Only four weeks to go to the *decree absolute*, Janet; then, who knows?') Janet knows all right, but says nothing (as we know from Emma, Discretion is her Middle Name). She sips at her tea and reaches for another fondant fancy. No need to bother dieting for much longer, she is thinking. Not now I've as good as got him in the bag. He owes me.

Alex Donaldson had acted for Janet in her divorce, five years ago, and has been 'comforting' her ever since. ('There there, Mrs Johnson – or may I call you Janet? I know the very man to make the necessary discreet enquiries. Excellent chap. Now, you're understandably upset, so why don't we discuss the matter over a lunchtime drink? What do you say, hmm? . . . Good *girl*.) Their affair has been conducted with the utmost discretion (of course!), but

210

Janet is growing increasingly restless; five years of being 'the other woman' began to pall long ago.

Five years of hanging up the phone when Alex's wife answers it, five years of clandestine meetings and lonely Saturday nights – not to mention all those desperate Christmases and New Years spent in the bosom of her ghastly, expatriate-Cockney family in Southend – will all have to be paid for, and Janet is not the girl to be denied her pound of flesh for very much longer.

Gazing into space, a beatific smile on her Mocha Pink lipsticked mouth, Janet pictures herself sailing down the steps of Ealing Registry Office as the second Mrs Alex Donaldson, in the tasteful ivory shantung silk dress and jacket already hanging in her wardrobe, sheathed in plastic. She will wear gardenias in her hair and will emerge, triumphant, in a cloud of confetti and Ma Griffe cologne.

There will be no bridal attendants smirking in the background; they would only detract attention from The Bride. It is to be Janet's Big Moment, and Janet's alone; no satin-clad, nose-picking page boy or cute little muslinned moppet of a bridesmaid is going to steal *her* thunder.

Not like at her youngest cousin's wedding last summer, when four-year-old Darlene's antics in front of the altar (dropping the pink-to-make-the-boys-wink frilly knickers which matched her bridesmaid's dress, and showing the entire congregation her little pink bottom) had turned Janet even pinker with embarrassment. And when Uncle Ted called out, bold as brass, 'Just like her mother, little Darlene; shows anybody her knickers at the drop of a corkscrew,' Janet had wished the stone-flagged floor would open up and swallow her whole. Little Darlene, that is, not Janet, of course.

She shudders. The Southend tribe will *not* be invited, *of course*. Alex will have to meet Mum and Dad some time, she supposes, grudgingly, but it will be *after* the wedding, she will make sure of that. Her family are big on weddings

– and any other excuse for a free booze-up with, hopefully, a free punch-up to follow. If they get so much as a sniff of her impending nuptials they'll turn up mob-handed, the men in their high-days-and-holidays, off-the-peg shiny suits and the women in their crimplene dresses, white high heels and 1960s C&A bargain basement hats. Horrors! Janet wouldn't know where to put herself.

She can just imagine Uncle Ted, with a few brown ales inside him. He would wink his rheumy old eye, dig Alex in the ribs and bawl: 'Bit quick, wunnit? When's the christening then, eh? Eh?' and Auntie Glad would say, 'Ooh Ted, you are awful,' to screams of raucous laughter from the rest of the family, who would be falling about at the very thought of that snotty, tight-arsed, grammar-schoolgirl of a Janet allowing her precious self to get anything as vulgar as pregnant.

Janet frowns. Alex had better bloody marry her, and soon, after all she's been through to secure his divorce. It was thanks to her flash of genius in using Alex's 'excellent chap' of a private detective that a tidy quantity of dirt was dug up on that sainted wife of his. ('But Janet, you don't understand. Valerie will never give me a divorce; she's a Roman Catholic – lapsed, admittedly – and thinks the world of me. Besides, I simply couldn't do it to her, I just couldn't. I always considered her the perfect wife – er, before I met you, of course.')

Amazing how quickly Valerie Donaldson's religious principles went down the tubes the moment news of her own extra-marital activities reached Alex's outraged ears. He had been all injured innocence and hurt pride, which was pretty rich, you had to admit, coming from a serial philanderer like him, who, according to Cynth, the waitress at Nell Gwynne's, has had more affairs than she's had Nell Gwynne Special Double Chocolate Creme Puffs. Which speaks volumes when you consider that Cynth weighs all of fourteen stone in her stockinged feet, with a bosom that has her muslin pinny fraying at its frilly seams.

Janet does not know that Alex has been bringing what Cynth calls 'his fancy women' to Nell Gwynne's (not to mention other venues the length and breadth of the southern counties) since he was a fresh-faced newly wed, and I doubt whether she would want to know. She is not interested in Alex's past, only his present and, of course, his future. Though there have been the odd dalliances over the Earl Grey even during Janet's time, as Cynth would have borne out had Janet bothered to enquire.

Having delivered irrefutable proof of his wife's infidelity on a plate, like Salome producing the head of John the Baptist, Janet has finally driven Alex into a corner from which he sees no immediate means of escape, despite years of ducking and diving, skilfully juggling his various women like so many spinning Indian clubs. Now it looks as if one of them is about to fall to earth, giving him a nasty blow on the head on the way down.

He has given in to Janet's point-blank request for a job at Donaldson's. ('We'd better lie low for the time being, just in case Valerie has you watched . . . no I'm sure she wouldn't stoop to such a thing, either, but better safe than sorry. But, just think, we'd be able to see each other every single day perfectly legitimately in a boss/secretary relationship . . .')

Divorce stares him in the face, but remarriage to the lovely Janet? Alex thinks not. As Angel would have said, *Out of the frying pan and into the fire, or what?*

All is not entirely lost, Alex is quite sure; he will Think of Something, just as he has so many times before. Devious as ever, he appears to accept this unforeseen glitch in his romantic arrangements with a boyish shrug of his shoulders, while resolving that he must be more careful in future.

He smiles at Janet and dabs at his mouth with a paper serviette embossed with the words 'Nell Gwynne Tea

Shoppe', cake crumbs and a touch of Mocha Pink lipstick from Janet's enthusiastic greeting when he arrived. 'Must rush off, Poppet,' (he calls them all Poppet – saves a lot of embarrassment should he slip up on a name, he's found). 'I've got a client due in ten minutes; sweet little twenty-eight-year old – a Mrs Greenaway whose husband's run off with the next-door neighbour's wife. I feel so sorry for the poor little thing.' Blonde, 36C cup, at a guess, he doesn't add.

'You're *such* a softie,' smiles Janet, laying her soon-to-be-engagement-ringed hand (she hopes!) on his arm. 'Only don't you get *too* sorry for her or I shall be jealous. When *I'm* making your appointments I shall rule out anyone under thirty-five,' she adds, laughing to show that she is making a joke, for her Alex is so ingenuous he might think she means it (which she does, of course).

As Alex leaves, blowing her a kiss at the door, her smile fades. He *is* a softie, her Alex. And a bit on the weak side; no getting away from it, but she can't afford to be too choosy, not now she's pushing forty. He'll pop the question soon enough, or her name isn't Janet Patricia Johnson-soon-to-be-Donaldson.

She shivers suddenly. God, I'm only six years younger than Iron Drawers, and look how she's turned out – married to the bloody job and not a man in sight that would give her the time of day. If I don't get married soon, I'll turn out all bitter and manipulative, like her.

As if.

Kit turns her key in the front door and automatically calls out to her mother. *Honey, I'm home*, trills Angel, but Kit ignores her.

Joyce has been watching *Collector's Corner* on afternoon television, gasping with exasperation at some woman from Chesterfield who's got nothing better to do with her time than collect egg cups.

'Egg cups, I ask yer,' she has just told Reg's ashes. 'I can understand someone collecting Royal Doulton, or sunnink like that.' She nods towards the crinoline ladies, who exchange smug little smiles. '*My* collection'll be worth a fortune one o' these days, Reg. A real investment, they were.' Not that the crinoline ladies are entirely convinced. ('Oh yeah, a fortune in Bostik, maybe. I just hope she's got shares in the company; now that really would be an investment, the amount she's got through on us, over the years.')

Joyce struggles to her feet when she hears Kit's call. Her arthritis has been giving her gyp lately and she is feeling guilty at being caught out watching telly in the after*noon* something she has always hotly denied doing. ('. . . I've got far better things to do with my time than sit in front of the box all day.') Not that Kit has noticed. Girl looks quite peaky. Must be, to leave that bloody office so early.

'Cuppa, love?' she offers, but Kit shakes her head wearily and says she'd rather have a stiff drink, the day she's had. Then she disappears into her private sitting room, shutting the door behind her.

'Obviously got the right 'ump with some poor sod, Reg,' observes Joyce, and stumps out to the kitchen to make herself a cup of tea ready for the start of *Fifteen to One*. She can't stand that William G. Stewart, but watches his programme regularly, living in hope that one day there might actually be a question she can answer – ideally something on Royal Doulton or embroidery.

Kit pours herself a drink and sinks gratefully on to one of a pair of black World of Leather chesterfields. Her room is oddly sterile. No ornaments, no flowers, no family photographs gracing the mantelshelf – only a handsome black marble clock, solemnly ticking away the hours in solitary splendour. It is as bland as a Trust House Forte bedroom after the cleaning staff have sloughed away all the usual traces of humanity left by its temporary residents.

In Kit's sitting room there is none of the usual clutter indicating that a human being lives in this room; no bills shrieking 'Pay me; pay me now!' are lodged casually behind that clock, no lumpy Tesco bags containing half-finished knitting lurk behind the chesterfields, and no magazine or newspaper mars the glossy perfection of Kit's twin, glass-topped tables. The room is too perfect, too orderly.

As Angel is wont to remark disdainfully, *Cosy it ain't*.

And Angel is right. It isn't a home, merely an illusion of one; a tasteful but anonymous stage set guaranteed to give nothing away about the leading (and only) player.

Joyce's sitting room, by contrast, is a jumble of furniture she couldn't bear to part with from her old home.

In pride of place is Reg's old, well-worn armchair that, when he was alive, she was for ever trying to ditch. ('Wish you'd let me chuck the flippin' thing out, Reg. I got my eye on a nice three-piece suite in beige Dralon down Times's'.) But now that he is gone, she is glad Reg talked her out of dumping it on the nearest skip, because now the old veteran sits proudly on one side of the fireplace, drawn up close to the fire, just as Reg used to like it.

Apart from the mantelshelf, which is reserved exclusively for the Royal Doulton pot containing Reg's ashes, every available surface is cluttered with framed photographs of the family, pot plants and knickknacks collected over the years – not to mention those of Joyce's dwindling collection of crinoline ladies who managed to survive the move intact, give or take an arm or two.

It is here that Joyce has gratefully retreated after she and Kit have eaten their evening meal of liver and bacon in the kitchen.

Joyce sits in her Cintique recliner facing Reg's chair and takes up her latest embroidery project ('. . . a nice, cross-stitch runner for the sideboard, Reg'). She has switched off the telly in disgust; her usual 'soap' has been cancelled because of bloody football again, and she is buggered if

216

she's going to sit there watching it just because Reg never missed a game of footie in his life if he could help it.

'There are limits, Reg,' she says, wagging a finger at the Royal Doulton pot. 'I'm not so far gone that I think you can actually see the telly, still. You wouldn't 'ave liked it anyway. Only a bunch of bloody overpaid foreigners kicking a ball about this time; not even England.

'Anyway, Reg,' she continues, sucking on the end of a piece of embroidery silk and stabbing shortsightedly at the eye of her needle, 'I really wanted to talk to you about our kid and I can't concentrate with all that singing and carrying on. And as for all that fallin' all over each other kissin' 'n' cuddlin' when they score a goal . . . well, just ain't natural, is it Reg? Buncha nancy boys! Makes me feel sick. You wouldn't like it one little bit. Send your blood pressure *right* up it would – if you were still alive, o'course, darlin'.

'Well, anyway, as I was sayin'. I'm really worried about our kid, Reg. She's changed so much . . . well, we all change. But. She's had some hard knocks, more than most, but all that was a very long time ago . . . And that terrible business with that bloke. Terry, or whatever his name was . . . Enough to put her off men for life. Pity she can't meet some *nice* man. Pity that lovely Frank turned out to be a . . . turned out to be not that way inclined. Her boss Simon – now there *is* a smashin' fella – perfect gentleman. Thinks the world of her, but, 'course, he's married already.'

Joyce shakes her head sadly. Kit can be like a cold, hard stranger sometimes. So secretive, so unyielding, even with her *own* daughter, Chaz, as she insists on calling herself, though what's wrong with the name Janine, Joyce can't imagine.

'Even after I bust a gut talking Chaz into going back to her mother – y'know, after she tried to top herself – nuffin' changed. An' they bin at each other's throats ever since, far as I can make out. Gawd knows why. Chaz never give nuffin' away, an' that's a fact.'

But Reg is no help, of course, God love him. So Joyce shuts up about it; she's just got to a complicated bit in her embroidery and anyway, Cilla Black's on ITV soon; Reg used to love her.

In the room just across the hallway, Kit looks guiltily at her briefcase, a silent reminder that there is work still to do. Almost reluctantly she pulls out Nick's file and opens it. *Correct me if I'm wrong*, says Angel, *but I thought you weren't taking on Nick's case? What's the point of bringing the file home at all?*

And Kit drops the file back into her briefcase as if it were a red-hot coal. No point, Angel; no point at all.

She feels unaccountably edgy, even nervous, filled with a fluttery, inexplicable sense of unease. *Nick's got a lot to answer for*, begins Angel slyly, inside her head, so Kit crosses the room and snaps on the television to drown her out. Oddly enough, Angel is greatly encouraged by this; it is years since Kit has had to resort to such ploys to shut her up. Very interesting. Kit is obviously weakening.

Kit flicks through the television channels, and finally switches off in disgust. Nothing but football, repeats, football and repeats.

You're obviously in no mood for work, wheedles Angel, grateful for the silence, *so why don't you just ease up, for once? Have a nice soak in the bath; have an early night. It'll set you up a treat, as your mother would say.* And to Angel's surprise, Kit agrees to do just that. *Hmm. Things are looking up.*

Ascending the stairs to the bathroom, Kit pauses at her daughter's bedroom door.

The girl had been a difficult child, a surly teenager and had developed into an irresponsible, selfish adult. Kit sighs. But I did try, Angel. I did try so hard. *All in the genes, as I've so often said*, says Angel.

What, you mean Chaz is too like her father? *Something like that.* Oh, I don't know, Angel. She shrugs. The world is full of mothers and daughters who just don't get on. God knows why. They love each other – deep down. More out of a sense of duty than anything else. But they don't actually like each other very much. *Yeah*, says Angel, choosing to humour her for a while. *You know what they say, you can choose your friends but you can't chose your relatives.* Quite.

Sounds a terrible thing to admit, but I was almost grateful when she eventually left for university. *What do you mean, 'almost' grateful? You couldn't get her out of the door fast enough!* Now that's not fair, Angel! I just thought that a spell apart might give us both a bit of breathing space, that's all.

And of course you had to say it, didn't you? Out loud. And what did Chaz reply? Something like, 'Can't wait to pack me off to university, can you? Just like you couldn't wait to pack me off to boarding school.' God, I'd no idea how much she resented that school.

Nor did I, Angel. She shakes her head sadly. If only she'd told me. If only she'd discussed it.

Takes two, says Angel flatly. *Didn't exactly bust a gut trying to get the kid to talk about it, did you? Big Mistake. Chaz looked dead choked when she left, that day. But I don't suppose you noticed. Too busy feeling sorry for your bloody self. As ever.*

Oh piss off, Angel. It's all ancient history, anyway. And my relationship with Chaz is dead in the water. Has been for years. Too late to do anything about it now. Far too late.

Feeling like an intruder (*Which is just what you are, through your own pig-headedness*, says Angel crossly.), Kit gently pushes open the bedroom door. She has left the room just as it was (*Like some bloody shrine!*). Bottles of nail polish, jars of face cream and a porridge of odd earrings

219

and broken beads litter the white painted dressing table. A battered, threadbare Teddy Ed wearing faded dungarees still lolls on the bedspread, snuggled up to his faithful companion, Frenchie, the Poodle Nightdress Case, another of Joyce's proud creations.

Ed's lopsided button eyes regard her quizzically. Kit sits on the bed and lights a cigarette. She finds it quite painful to enter this room (*So why do you do it?*), cluttered as it is with relics of the past, in defiant contrast to her own quarters, which, as we know, are about as informal as your average boardroom. This was Chaz's private place, where she had fled to sulk (*or lick her wounds, maybe?*) after one of their screaming matches.

Kit shakes her head wearily at the memory of their fights. Chaz did make a *bit* of an effort at first, she admits to herself. Felt sneakingly sorry for me after the . . . after the suicide attempt, I suppose. *And what a pantomime* that *turned out to be*, says Angel. *Poor old Detective Frank finds the name of that God-forsaken B & B circled in Dalton's Weekly and drives through the night to save you. Only to find you tucking into the full English breakfast. You had egg on your face that morning, kid. In more ways than one!*

Yes. Thank you so much for reminding me, Angel. And if you tell me once more that it was *you* who saved my life, I'll go and slash my wrists, just to spite you.

Promises, promises.

Anyway, as I say, Chaz was all sweetness and light at first. But it didn't last long. If I expressed the slightest interest in what she was doing she accused me of poking my nose into her affairs. (*What's new? Typical teenage behaviour, if you ask me.*) If I suggested she might stay in with me, once in a while, or even bring friends round, she said my home was like a bloody mausoleum (*she's got a point there*) and slammed off out, God knows where. There was just no pleasing her.

So when she came back from university I really tried, Angel. I was ready to make a completely fresh start. You can't deny that.

Yeah, yeah, I know. But you fell at the first fence when she informed you she planned to work on that Israeli kibbutz for a year before looking for a job. What was so awful about that? Anyone'd think she'd set her heart on becoming a fan dancer at the Windmill, a madam at a Marseilles brothel, or even worse – wait for it, wait for it – an estate agent who does a bit of tax inspecting on the side!

But Kit is not amused by this feeble attempt at levity, and continues as if Angel has not spoken: What really got to me was the way she just shrugged when I said she'd be welcome here after her year in Israel. She made it perfectly clear she wouldn't be coming back. Ever.

And what did you do? Put your arms round her? Tell her you'll miss her? Tell her you love her and don't want to lose her? Oh no, not Iron Drawers. When was the last time you showed that kid – or anyone else for that matter – any loving affection? I sometimes think the only person you love is yourself, though even that's a moot point.

Kit blinks rapidly and blows her nose. She mustn't cry. She mustn't be sentimental. Forget the past. Concentrate on the present. It's the only way.

OK, let's do that thing. Let's concentrate on the present. At least Chaz has kept in touch with letters and postcards while she's been away. Odd, stilted little messages they may be, but what do you expect? And you must admit that the letters have got . . . well, a bit warmer than they used to be. That's a great leap forward, surely?

I suppose so, Angel, but I'm a bit worried about this Kris Andersen – Andy – that she keeps going on about. She can't seem to stop mentioning him in her letters. It's Andy this, and Andy that until I want to scream. 'Andy's terribly good-looking in that flaxen-haired, blue-eyed, Danish

221

way,' she said in one of her letters. 'Andy's parents live in a village just outside Copenhagen', and so on, ad nauseam. And now she plans to bring Andy to England to meet me; God knows why.

Sounds like a love job, to me, says Angel flatly. *Andy's probably going to ask for your daughter's hand in marriage, is my guess. I gather the Danes go a bundle on all that formal stuff, so you and he should get on like a house on fire.*

And anyway, you ought to be grateful to this Nordic Adonis. It's obviously his influence that's persuaded Chaz to visit at all. Think yourself lucky. At least it's a chance to see her again.

Perhaps it will be all right, Angel. Chaz has certainly never sounded so happy. But—

But you're just jealous because, yet again, someone else has won Chaz over where you failed so miserably. Why can't you just be happy for her, like any normal mother?

I am happy for her. Really I am. But I'll be a lot happier once I've had a chance to, well, look him over.

And what makes you think Chaz'll give a stuff whether you approve or not?

I'm only too well aware of that, Angel. But I just want to see them together, see if they're right for each other.

Oh, and of course you'll know instantly. You're such an expert on men, after all.

Please God let Chaz be a better chooser than I've been, that's all. Every man I've ever remotely fancied has turned out to be a bastard.

Oh, I don't know, says Angel nonchalantly. *What about Nick?*

Kit stares remotely out of the window. Yes, there's always Nick. Damn him. It's put me on edge meeting him again after all these years, that's all. I'll get over it. And before you ask, yes, I did remotely fancy him once, I admit, and no, I definitely do not want to see him again and that's flat, so just do me a favour and shut up about Nick, will you, Angel?

She stands up and walks briskly into the bathroom, turning on the bath taps in order to drown Angel out.

But Angel will not shut up. *Come off it. This is* me *you're talking to. You didn't just remotely fancy him, you found him bloody nigh irresistible.*

OK, OK. But he obviously found me totally resistible then, so he'd find me even more unappealing now. Besides, if we did meet he'd want to know the story of my life for the past twenty years and—

And you'd have to admit to some man you had no more than a nodding acquaintance with years ago that you're no longer the fresh-faced, virginal innocent of yesteryear. You're pathetic, do you know that?

twenty-two

Kit has just emerged from the bath. The phone rings.

She smiles involuntarily when she hears Simon Chivers' voice. He has that effect on everyone. Everyone except his wife, Paula, that is, who is immune to his particular brand of old-world, Wilfred Hyde-White-style charm.

'My dear Kit,' he booms, in his hail-fellow-well-met, minor-public-school voice, 'I know you'll think me a frightful old fool,' (*He must be joking; he's got a mind like razor wire*, says Angel fondly. *Just enjoys playing the archetypal absent-minded professor, like the loveable old ham he is.*) 'but I didn't get the chance for so much as a word with you at the office today. Ridiculous really. Work in adjoining rooms and hardly see each other these days, and a day without basking in the warmth of your intellect is dull indeed.'

Somebody loves you, then, says Angel drily. *Unlike everyone else at Simon Chivers & Partner.*

And Angel is right, of course. When Kit joined Simon Chivers, her largely male colleagues had been jolted out of their dusty complacency by her sheer, driving energy. They grew jealous, bickering among themselves like starlings scrapping over a dry crust when, to their surprise, Simon Chivers, that arch-sexist, who had doubted the wisdom of allowing a mere woman into his male-dominated domain, was quick to recognise Kit's abilities and shrewd enough to capitalise on them. ('I don't believe it. She's got Burrows vs Burrows. Old Simon must be losing it, to have his head turned by a nice pair of tits and good legs. That's about all the woman's got going for her, if you ask me.')

But eventually she has earned their grudging respect. While still resenting her, secretly they recognise her worth, even to the extent of quietly applauding her achievements – though not, of course, in her hearing; that would never do. ('Got to hand it to her, I suppose. She certainly gets results.')

Simon had watched Kit grow in confidence with the air of a kindly uncle watching over his protégée, which indeed she was. But now his interest in Kit is something more than just professional; he has grown fond of her, to his own slight embarrassment. He enjoys her company, as well as her intellect, and wants more of it. It is with this in mind that he is phoning Kit on this particular evening.

'Paula and I are having a bit of a do tomorrow night,' he is saying nonchalantly. 'Nothing too formal – just a few thousand close friends . . . ha, ha. Rather short notice, I'm afraid . . . one of Paula's mad impulses. Never mind, still gives you time to make yourself look beautiful, as ever. Do say you'll come.'

He pauses expectantly and is relieved when Kit agrees to be there.

'So glad, so glad', burbles Simon. 'See you tomorrow then. Around eight?'

'Do say you'll come,' mimics Paula spitefully, as Simon hangs up. 'Oh Kit, do grace our little party with your presence, oh do.'

Paula grinds out her cigarette savagely, gratified to see the smile on her husband's face disappear. 'Plenty of time to make yourself look beautiful. God help her, she'll need more than twenty-four hours to do that. It'd take a team of plastic surgeons working round the clock to make her look half presentable.'

'Why the vitriol, Paula? What is it about Kit that seems to bring out the fishwife in you? Jealousy, perhaps?'

'Jealousy? God, no. Don't kid yourself. It just makes me sick to watch you fawning over her, like a dog after a bitch on heat, and an old dog at that. She's only an employee, for Christ's sake, not a bloody partner. Though that's obviously what she's angling for.' She lights another cigarette, her hands trembling with agitation.

'You've only just put one out,' says Simon mildly, pouring their drinks.

'Oh full marks for observation. Well now I'm having another one. I can afford it, after all.' She puffs away defiantly as Simon hands her a gin and tonic. 'Bashing the Scotch a bit, aren't we?' She nods pointedly at his glass. 'You're turning into an old lush.'

Simon takes a gulp of whisky and looks at his wife with ill-concealed distaste. 'Helps to deaden the pain, my dear.' He raises his glass mockingly. 'Besides, as you yourself just said, you can afford it.'

Paula's thin-lipped mouth closes like a trap. Foiled again, thanks to bloody Simon. How is it he always manages to cut the legs from under her with a few well-chosen words just when she is spoiling for a scrap? For Paula loves a good old, knock-down, drag-out row, like the street-fighter she still is, deep down, despite the expensive education bought for her by her bookie's-runner-made-good father, Nippy Norman Parkes.

By the time Paula was in her early teens, Nippy Norman had built a sizeable business empire (a chain of betting shops, as if you hadn't guessed), not to mention an excruciatingly tasteless mock-Tudor mansion in Chigwell, to the horror of his nouveau-snob, nouveau-riche Essex-boy-and-girl neighbours, though of course the phrase hadn't been invented back then.

As a newly arrived member of the gentry, Norman swore that his little princess would grow up to be a lady if it was the last thing he did, and by God he gave it his best shot and several suitcases packed with used notes.

He enrolled Paula at one of the most exclusive girls' schools in the land (the first of many, since Paula had an alarming propensity for telling headmistresses to 'fuck off' if they looked sideways at her) in order to improve her command of English and give her some much-needed 'polish'.

Later, he even persuaded Paula to keep her mouth shut for long enough to hook a husband (the hapless Simon Chivers) who was practically an aristocrat, for Chrissake. ('Yeah, I know the family ain't got two 'alfpennies to rub together, my gel' (not helped by the gambling habits of Chivers Senior in one of Norman's shops, by the way), 'but they're in *Burke's Peerage*. That's good enough for me an' it bleedin' well oughter be good enough for you. Ungrateful little cow. And don't let me 'ear you swearing no more, my gel; dunno where you bleedin' pick it up.')

Sadly, Norman Parkes did not live to realise his ambition of making a lady of Paula. He was to die, choking on an eel bone, of all things, while seated at a marble-topped table in Manze's pie 'n' mash shop in Chapel Market, though at his ostentatious funeral the most popular theory was that Nippy Norman had sustained fatal injuries falling off his wallet.

Paula is, and always will be, what her father would call 'common as muck'. No doubt he is revolving at high speed in his expensive burial plot in Highgate Cemetery as he ponders the waste of all that lovely loot.

Sighing, Simon reaches for his *Daily Telegraph*. He is wondering what has happened to the Paula he met and married all those years ago. She was such a golden girl in her youth, one of the beautiful people, as the old song went. What was more, she was refreshingly different from all those twinsetted, horse-faced debby types Mother had tried to force on him. Indeed, the very fact that Mother thought Paula 'highly unsuitable' gave her added allure, in Simon's eyes. Inexperienced where women were concerned, Simon had been dazzled by her wit, her beauty and, he had to confess, by her money.

Now her easy wit has soured into a vinegary shrewishness, the slightly racy, exciting style of speech has become simply crude and vulgar to his ears, and the dazzling good looks have faded. The only thing that remains virtually unchanged is her money. And when all's said and done, money does serve to make one's unhappiness less unbearable.

She is a rich woman, she constantly reminds him, while he is at heart still a shiny-arsed clerk, who would still be pen-pushing in some dreary office if she hadn't taken him in hand and made something of him. Not that making something of Simon appears to have given Paula much joy.

If only he'd been able to give Paula the child she craved, things might have been different. As it was, his inability in that department had become yet another stick to beat him with. ('Call yourself a man? Well there's nothing wrong on *my* side, I can assure you; breed like rabbits, my lot.')

Which was cruel of Paula, in the circumstances, but of course Simon does not know about the abortion (and resultant sterility) forced on her by an outraged Nippy Norman when he discovered his daughter was up the duff at the tender age of fifteen following a torried romance with a nineteen-year-old gardener at her latest academy for young ladies. 'I'll give 'im "We plough the fields and bleedin' scatter",' Norman had roared. 'Well 'e needn't think 'e can scatter 'is seed in my daughter's direction and get away with it. I'll 'ave 'is bollocks for this. I'll cut 'em off with 'is own fuckin' prunin' shears . . .' Etcetera, etcetera.

Simon studies Paula covertly as she sits, bolt upright, sipping at her drink and gazing fiercely into space.

The once silky, corn-coloured hair is dyed to a hideously

228

improbable gorse yellow, heavy lines of dissatisfaction turn her thin slit of a mouth downwards at the corners, and the baby-blue eyes that once gazed up at him in lazy rapture now glitter with the hard brilliance of twin sapphires. The tiny figure, however, trim in skin-tight, shocking-pink matador pants with matching top, remains oddly youthful, thanks to years of near-fanatical dieting.

'What are you gawping at?' she demands charmlessly.

'Just thinking how slim you look in that outfit,' replies Simon truthfully. 'It's new, isn't it?'

'God, fancy you even noticing. Get the flags out.' She runs her hand along her thigh, and allows herself a smile of satisfaction. 'Your precious Kit couldn't wear something like this.' (She wouldn't be seen dead in something like that, thinks Simon.) 'She's getting an arse on her, that one – really beginning to go to seed.'

'Oh I wouldn't say that,' protests Simon mildly. 'She's still a very attractive woman. And she's not my precious Kit. She's not my anything.' Unfortunately, he wishes he had the nerve to add.

'So you say. And if she's that bloody attractive why hasn't she got a man? Striding about in those ghastly masculine suits she always wears, giving orders like some kind of . . . some kind of Nazi stormtrooper.' Paula smiles slyly into her drink. 'It's common knowledge she's a dyke; plain as the nose on your face, though of course you can't see it.'

She sits back, smirking, as Simon's mouth falls open in astonishment. There, that'll get him going. But to her fury, instead of rising to the bait, Simon begins to laugh.

'Really Paula,' he splutters, 'you do talk the most unmitigated rubbish at times. How can you make such a statement yet persist in your delusion that I lust after Kit? How could a man married to a woman with your sweet, feminine disposition possibly, er, "fancy" such an obvious – what did you call her? – such an obvious dyke?' He shakes his head disparagingly. 'Let it rest, will you, my dear? You're making yourself look ridiculous, quite ridiculous.'

As Kit arrives at the 'bit of a do', with its cast of thousands and outside caterers, Simon trots towards her, holding out his arms in welcome. 'So glad you could come, Kit dear.' He gives her a dutiful peck on the cheek and holds her at arm's length. 'You look superb, as always.' Eyes drinking in the cool elegance of Kit's Grecian-style, white silk dress, the understated make-up and simple jewellery, he ushers her into the sitting room. He glances towards his wife, comparing her unfavourably with Kit. No contest, he thinks sadly.

Paula's face is already flushed with gin and high spirits, contrasting unhappily with both the blonde floss of hair and the flame chiffon dress bought specially for the occasion.

For a woman who is for ever proclaiming her wealth from the rooftops, complete with sandwich board and loud hailer, Paula still manages to look like *Coronation Street*'s favourite barmaid, Bet Lynch, out on the spree and out of control. Money is no substitute for good taste, reflects Simon primly. You've either got it, or you haven't. And Paula hasn't.

There she stands, shrieking with shrill laughter, one bejewelled hand clutching a large gin, the other clinging to the arm of the man at her side as if afraid he might vanish if she releases her vice-like grip. He looks to be forty-ish, already inclining towards an effete plumpness and with thinning, unnaturally black hair – thanks, or perhaps no thanks, to regular applications of Grecian 2000. While apparently hanging on to Paula's every vulgar word, his slightly bulbous eyes swivel around the room like Marty Feldman's on a bad day, as if permanently weighing up alternative prospects (which of course he is).

There is a ripple of polite laughter from the small group surrounding Paula, who has obviously just reached the punchline of one of the risqué anecdotes taken from the seedy rag-bag she calls her repertoire. Simon sighs. He's heard them all before and so has everyone else. Why she doesn't just produce a tape, to be played at every party in an endless loop, he can't imagine. He glances at his watch. About an hour and several gins later, he judges expertly, Paula's stories will reach even greater heights, or depths, of vulgarity. He shudders slightly, and moves discreetly away, as far as possible from his wife's sycophantic little entourage.

Kit ambles casually among the knots of chatting guests, occasionally smiling and nodding recognition of the odd acquaintance, snippets of other people's typically shallow, 'party' conversations bouncing off her like ricocheting bullets off a Sherman tank. '. . . So I looked him straight in the eye and said . . . There was an Englishman, an Irishman and a Scotsman . . . Oh, you didn't use *that* route, surely? Absolute death, my dear . . .And the Irishman said . . . You should have turned off at Beaconsfield . . . Yes, it is rather nice, isn't it? I must give you the address of my dress-maker – wonderful little woman, and not expensive . . .' And so on.

Like Simon, Kit surreptitiously glances at her watch. *Just stick it out for an hour or so*, advises Angel, *then you can decently leave*. Roll on, thinks Kit.

Idly sipping at her drink, she wanders round the room, a temple to Paula's idea of late twentieth-century chic. *Imitation leopard-skin sofas!* cries Angel, aghast. *And lava lamps, for heaven's sake! Yuk! How does Simon stand it?* God knows, Angel. There are one or two good pieces hanging on by their ball-and-claw toenails, though. Probably relics from Simon's family home. *Obviously*, says Angel. *Paula would hardly spend good money on second- or third-hand tatty old Chippendale or Sheraton when she*

231

can buy something brand new for a fraction of the price, let's face it.

And I bet this beautiful display case of butterflies is Simon's too, thinks Kit. (Paula was always telling Simon to get rid of it, since a load of dead insects hung out to dry in a glass-fronted box isn't her idea of modern decor, but when Simon told her how much it was worth, she decided to tolerate it after all.)

'Beautiful, aren't they?' The forty-something man with the dyed black hair has managed to escape from Paula's clutches and is gazing earnestly at Kit.

'Yes,' answers Kit shortly, refusing to meet his eye. I don't like the look of him, Angel. *You wouldn't like the look of Robert Redford if you were ever lucky enough to meet him,* scoffs Angel, *though in the case of this particular bloke, you're probably right. There's something distinctly iffy about him. Don't know quite—*

'The one in the middle, slightly apart from the others, reminds me of you,' persists the man. He pauses significantly, waiting for some sort of response, some stirring of curiosity. Never fails, that approach, in his considerable experience. Kit does not display so much as a flicker of interest, but he presses on anyway.

'I've been watching you flitting from group to group,' he says, placing a hand on her arm. (*Hands OFF!* says Angel instinctively.) 'You never settle for long, just like that beautiful white butterfly. Even in death it isolates itself from the others.'

Christ, exclaims Angel. *Beautiful white butterfly, already. Anything to liven up the usual corny old chat-up lines, I suppose. Will they stop at nothing, these days?*

'Really?' says Kit coldly, removing his hand from her arm.

She glances over his shoulder as Paula teeters purposefully towards them on her stick-like legs looking like a flamingo-feathered version of Rod Hull's Emu with even

232

more attitude than usual. 'I do believe you're wanted,' says Kit, standing discreetly aside as Paula whisks him away to do the Walk of Life with Dire Straits.

The man shoots her a reproachful look over his shoulder. *I know that look*, says Angel. *Dead sincere, straight from the shoulder, and about as honest and reliable as the gaze of your average second-hand car dealer.* Kit shivers suddenly. There is something familiar about the man, Angel. Something unpleasant.

'Ah Kit,' booms Simon, 'let me get you another drink.' He follows the direction of her gaze, answering her unspoken question. 'Oh, that's Paula's latest,' he says cheerfully. 'James Something-or-other. Don't suppose he'll last, none of them do, though her taste has deteriorated over the years I must say. I suppose he's quite handsome in the rather coarse, flashy style that Paula seems to admire, but, really, he does seem utterly out of place here. Obviously an artisan in gentleman's clothing, if you'll excuse my inherent snobbery.'

Kit laughs uneasily and glances again in James's direction. She immediately wishes she hadn't, for he is staring back at her, his eyes appraising her blatantly. His pink tongue flickers momentarily over too-red, too-full lips and Kit flinches as if stung. *Yuk*, says Angel again.

Paula wriggles closer to James, wrapping her anorexic arms round his neck. 'Must you keep eyeballing that bloody woman. She's old enough to be your mother.'

'She'd have to have given birth at about ten to be my mother, dear. No, I'd put it at about nine or ten years younger than you at least.' James studies Kit's rear view appreciatively. 'About forty-five I reckon, and *blaahdy* well preserved with it. Ve-ery tasty. Nice tits, good legs and a lovely arse on it. I like a woman with a good arse; something to grab hold of.'

He notes with amusement the peevish expression on Paula's face. Just as well to keep the old girl on her toes.

Keep 'em guessing, that was the secret of his success. But don't overdo it, old son, don't *blaahdy* overdo it.

He drops the hands that encircle Paula's waist and squeezes her buttocks. Paula stiffens. 'Down boy,' she giggles. 'Not now. Not here.'

'Why not,' he whispers, 'no one'll notice in this crush. Besides,' his lips brush her neck briefly, 'you know you love it.'

Paula's cheeks flush with pleasure. 'You're such an animal. No woman is safe.'

'You're certainly not safe', he murmurs into her hair, his eyes firmly riveted on Kit's backside. Now where have I seen that arse before? Never forget a face, me.

'How about a bite to eat?' Simon takes Kit's arm and steers her towards the dining room, where the outside caterers Wendy and Sue, decked in traditional black dresses and white pinnies, are filling hungry party guests' plates from a table groaning with a selection of goodies that wouldn't be out of place on display at Harrods Food Hall – which is where most of them came from anyway. 'There you go, madam. Don't forget to leave room for dessert,' says Wendy, adding under her breath, for Sue's benefit: 'That's the third helping she's had, greedy cow. Her old man'll have to put wheels on her to get her out the door, I reckon.'

At the centre of an appreciative gaggle of gourmets, Paula is receiving their fulsome praise with an air of queenly condescension. *Shame she has to ruin the Lady Bountiful, noblesse-oblige routine by telling everyone how much everything cost*, observes Angel. *Right down to the last silver of smoked salmon and crumb of Stilton.*

James fidgets at Paula's side, out of his depth and out of his class. The braying, well-bred home counties accents on all sides are beginning to give him the right hump. Chinless wonders, he thinks scathingly. Smug, self-satisfied bastards the lot of them, especially supercilious Simon, looking down his *blaahdy* nose as if James is something that just crawled out from under a stone. Not to mention that flaming Kit woman. Where the hell have I seen her before?

Across the room, she is smiling politely while Paula's old man is obviously boring the pants off her. James grins. Bet the stupid old fart wishes he could *literally* get 'em off, randy old sod. Look at him, edging closer all the time, smiling into her eyes, casually touching her arm. He can't keep his *blaahdy* hands off her.

And she just stands there, pure as the driven. The fucking Ice Maiden. Miss *blaahdy* Touch-Me-Not.

He knows what she needs all right, and friend Simon certainly can't give it to her. Useless old bugger can't make it when it comes to the crunch; he has that on good authority from Paula. Look at the stupid bastard, knocking himself out over that *blaahdy* Kit, but wasting his time, definitely wasting his time. Can't even hang on to his own *blaahdy* property – the lovely Paula – so what chance does he have of getting anywhere with the Snow Queen?

Perhaps he ought to show the old boy how it's done; draw him a diagram or something. Be a laugh to rub his *blaahdy* nose in it, the middle-class git. Bet he could grab her right from under Simon's aristocratic nose. First his lady wife, then the lovely Kit that really would be a smack in the chops. Give Paula food for thought into the bargain.

It'd be a piece of piss. All the *blaahdy* same, women. And the toffee-nosed ones were the worst, once you got right down to it. Loved a bit of rough, they did, every one of 'em, once you managed to get through their *blaahdy* cut-glass, jolly-hockey-sticks mentality. Gave 'em a bit of excitement – just like midnight feasts back in the jolly old dorm. James smiles. He loves a bit of a challenge, always has.

He's long since tired of those common little tarts who

drop their drawers after a coupla G and Ts, though underneath her designer-label gear and expensive layers of slap, Paula has turned out to be no different. Glancing at her briefly, he notes with distaste the scrap of food lodged between her two front, lipstick-smeared teeth. Got no *blaahdy* class, the old slag. No *blaahdy* class whatsoever.

James sighs. But it's a *rich* old slag, he is thinking. Let's not forget that, old son. Can't afford to give it the *blaahdy* sailor's farewell. Not yet, anyway. Mustn't kill the goose that lays the golden eggs, when all's said and done.

Kit would be an interesting diversion though. Now she *has* got a bit of class about her. Still quite tasty, an' all. And he knows her from somewhere. Where though? It is beginning to *blaahdy* bug him something rotten.

Between bites of food (and sometimes during them), Paula is treating a captive audience of three to a blow-by-blow account of her battle with 'those Nazis at the Planning Department' who are having the temerity to jib at her latest crazed plans for 'improving' the house. Not that it needs any improvement, but Paula doesn't feel 'fulfilled' unless she has some 'project' or other on the go – usually one which involves the expenditure of vast amounts of money.

The eyes of her audience begin to glaze over as she sprays them with crumbs of flaky pastry together with precise costs right down to the last penny. James takes the opportunity to slip his lead for five minutes.

Simon looks up with a small frown of displeasure as James approaches. 'Ah James,' he says without enthusiasm, 'I believe you've met Kit already?'

'I have had that honour, yes.' He gazes sincerely into Kit's eyes.

Where have I seen this odious creature before, Angel? *Search me. Who gives a stuff anyway?* I do. I don't like mysteries.

But the ever-vigilant Paula is not going to allow James to

desert her for a minute. 'So there you are, you naughty boy. You've been neglecting poor little me.' She holds out her skinny arms invitingly. 'Come and dance with me at once,' she commands, pouting like a geriatric Shirley Temple. James tries to pretend he hasn't heard her, but Paula is an old campaigner. No one puts her off that easily.

'Please,' she wails piercingly, clawing at his arm. Heads began to turn but Paula ignores them. 'Please James, don't be mean. It's my party, cost me a fortune, and now my favourite man won't even give me a little dance in return.'

James turns to face her, shaking off her hand irritably. 'For Christ's sake,' he hisses, 'do you have to mention money every time you open your *blaahdy* mouth? And what do you mean, "in return"? I've stuck to you like shit to a blanket all evening. Isn't that enough? Am I supposed to ask your *blaahdy* permission before I even speak to anyone else, is that it, or would you prefer to put me in a *blaahdy* strait jacket and have done with it?'

Paula's smiling pout sinks without trace. A dull, angry flush spreads from neck to hairline and Kit is suddenly sorry for the little woman. She is making an utter fool of herself, Angel, but haven't we all, haven't we all? *Yeah, and no one deserves to be treated like that, not even unlovable, unloved Paula.*

James turns to Kit with an ingratiating smile. 'Care to dance?'

He must be bloody joking, says Angel.

'I think not,' replies Kit icily, and, turning to Paula and Simon, she thanks them for a delightful evening (*Liar*) and leaves.

'Ciao,' says James sarcastically. 'Be lucky.'

237

twenty-three

Simon presses his fingers to his temples. One of his migraines coming on, he is sure. Hardly surprising, considering Paula's frame of mind this morning. What *is* the matter with the little woman?

Pacing up and down like some demented creature locked for too long behind bars in a zoo, Paula is treating him to a blistering tirade that could strip paint at fifty paces. When she occasionally pauses, it is only for long enough to light yet another cigarette or gulp air and gin in equal quantities, before launching into the attack once again.

With no handy chair or whip with which to fend her off, Simon briefly considers hiding behind one of the leopard-skin sofas and playing dead. For Paula is only interested in savaging live prey. She derives no satisfaction from mauling carrion.

Better to just sit it out, thinks Simon, trying to keep calm. Mustn't get too agitated; you know what the quack said. Say nothing, that's the ticket. Usually works when she's in killer mode. She'll eventually lose interest and make one of her dramatic exits. And the sooner the better, the way I'm feeling. My head hurts, and I've got that pain in my chest again . . .

'. . . leaving everything to me, as per usual,' Paula is bawling. 'Christ, if it weren't for me behind you, I hate to think where you'd be by now . . .'

Idyllically happy, I should imagine, thinks Simon.

'. . . and have you any idea how much effort I put into

that party? How much money I poured down the throats of all those influential guzzlers?'

Ah, money . . . I wondered how long it would take for you to mention that. Again.

'. . . and you chose to give them the frozen mitt. I was so embarrassed, I can't tell you . . .'

But you will, my love, you will. God, I wish this pain would ease up.

'. . . could have died of embarrassment, *died*. But do you care? Do you give a toss how hard I work? Do you buggery! The only person you gave the time of day to was that bitch Swanson.'

Simon looks up at the mention of Kit's name, and Paula is on to it at once, a stringy ferret past its best pouncing on a defenceless mouse.

'Oh yes, that's got to you, hasn't it? That's sunk in. Everyone noticed, everyone. Making a bloody spectacle of yourself, at your age.' Paula sits down heavily and lights another cigarette.

Ah, thinks Simon. She's stopped pacing about. At last. Must be running out of steam. Steady now. She'll fire one more devastating broadside, hurl one more verbal hand grenade, and then storm out. Brace yourself, old chap. Just hang on in there, as the saying goes these days.

Paula glances across at her husband irritably. Why the hell doesn't he retaliate? He sits there, wimpishly sipping his bloody drink, totally ignoring me, the way he's always ignored me. A right wash-out he's turned out to be. I'd think more of him if he gave as good as he got, bawled back at me, smashed me in the mouth or something.

'Call yourself a man?' she sneers, scrabbling for a toe-hold in Simon's apparent wall of indifference. 'Your darling Kit's falling about laughing at you behind your back. Do you really think she'd look twice at a wet like you?

'She was pissed right off, stuck with you all evening. I could tell. Why else d'you think she left so early? Oh, that's got you interested, hasn't it? That's got you sitting up and taking notice. She was bored shitless listening to you droning on. I know, I was watching her. Couldn't take her eyes off James for a minute. She's not interested in *you*; she's after a *real* man, like the rest of us, one who can give a real woman what she wants.'

Paula leans back and puffs on her cigarette, smiling her tight little smile of triumph.

Pouring himself another drink, Simon tries to stop his hands from trembling. She's gone too far this time. He can't remain silent, he simply can't. He takes a long pull at his Scotch and sits down hurriedly, before his legs give under him. He really is feeling most peculiar.

'I was under the impression,' he says carefully, 'that you seem to think – totally without foundation of course, like all your theories – that Kit is some kind of a . . . er . . . dyke, was the rather coarse expression you used? Hardly one's definition of a "real woman", I would have thought.

'And your notion of a "real man" leaves me at somewhat of a loss, too. Where you come from, I imagine a "real man" is a tattooed Neanderthal in string vest and non-designer stubble who gets drunk as a skunk every Friday night before reeling home and beating up the, er, "old lady", is I believe the expression, in your circles.'

Old woman, thinks Paula, irrelevantly. The wife is always 'the old woman', where I come from. Granny Parkes – her Dad's mum – was the only one to be called 'the old *lady*'.

But she says nothing, stunned into silence by Simon's unexpected show of defiance. She sits, mouth agape, slowly shaking her head from side to side, reminding Simon briefly of the fairground sideshows of his youth, where punters were invited to lob tennis balls into the crimson maws of grinning, papier mâché clowns' heads.

Except Paula isn't grinning. The worm appears to have turned at last, and Paula doesn't like it. Not one little bit.

Slightly slurring his words, Simon continues. 'As for your suggestion that Kit would actually be attracted to your "real man" . . . well, the thought is laughable, quite laughable. Unlike yourself, Kit would show rather more, um . . . discernment, I would hope.

'And incidentally, my dear, while we're on the subject, I'm rather worried about the decline in your taste of late. If you must throw yourself at anything in trousers that crosses your path, at least have the courtesy to be a little more selective. It's so embarrassing when your little friends – most of whom seem to have trouble walking upright – can communicate only in grunts and appear woefully lacking in the usual social graces.'

'If you think I'm sitting here listening to this . . .' begins Paula, finding her voice at last, half rising from her seat.

'Oh I haven't finished yet,' says Simon airily. 'Have the kindness to hear me out.' And to his surprise (not to mention Paula's) she sits down again.

'Now, where was I? Oh yes. Your . . . accusation regarding Kit's supposed pursuit of your friend James would in any case appear to be completely without foundation, since it was patently obvious from last night's little exhibition that it was he who seemed quite taken with Kit, rather than the other way about. Perhaps there's hope for the fellow yet if he shows such excellent taste.'

Simon smiles at her thinly. 'Perhaps you'd better look to your laurels, my dear. You're not getting any younger, as they say, and I'm afraid your James seems to prefer women who are a *teensy* bit nearer forty than sixty. Besides,' he adds, picking up his newspaper, 'your latest, er, acquisition, hardly strikes me as the faithful type, not once he's bled you of all that money you rather vulgarly flaunt.'

'James isn't a bit interested in that bloody woman, for your information,' shrieks Paula, thoroughly rattled. 'It's me he wants, me! And not just for the sake of my money either, unlike you. I sometimes wonder why the hell you stick around at all, money or no money!'

'So do I, my dear, so do I.'

'Anyway, I've had a bellyful of this,' says Paula, snatching up her handbag (Gucci, no less). 'I'm off for lunch. With James. At the Regency. That'll cost him a packet, so don't try and tell *me* he's only after my money.'

'Have a wonderful time, dear,' replies Simon pleasantly, 'and don't forget to take your American Express, Diners card, et al. You'll no doubt be needing them.'

Only when the door slams behind Paula does Simon lay down his newspaper. His heart is pounding against his ribs. He gulps the remains of his drink and leans back against the sofa cushions, his face suddenly bathed in perspiration. Gazing at the empty glass in his hand, Simon shakes his head. Must give this stuff a rest, my lad. That and these continuous dog fights with Paula are doing you no good whatsoever. She's been quite unbearable since meeting that odious James fellow.

Meanwhile, James is lounging in his state-of-the-art, leather recliner in his upmarket flat just off Albany Street. He slips off his shoes and waggles his toes. This is the life, he thinks, sipping at his whisky. He holds it up to the light, admiring the warm, rich colour. Yes, this is definitely the life, all right, and all thanks to good old Paula. He raises his glass. 'To good old Paula, and all who sail in her.' Where would I be without her?

Still working as a glorified *blaahdy* shop assistant, no doubt. Still existing in that God-awful bedsit while his ex-wife, Maureen, and the kids lived in *blaahdy* luxury in the house. His house. *Blaahdy* palace, that place. Wall-to-wall shag pile throughout, MFI's finest fitted kitchen with eye-level grill, washable vinyl wallpaper, cocktail cabinet with concealed lighting . . . and in the master bedroom, James's pride and joy, a velvet upholstered and buttoned

242

headboard. He'd given Maureen everything, everything. And she'd copped for the *blaahdy* lot.

It would break his heart to know that the velvet headboard was the first to go after he left – ritually torched in the back garden by a jubilant Maureen. The cocktail cabinet had been next, followed by all other traces that James had ever lived there.

James sips moodily at his Scotch. Maureen's solicitor had known his *blaahdy* stuff, all right. Encouraged her to suck him dry; not that she needed any encouragement. Cow.

And all because of one tiny little slip on his part.

He'd been a *blaahdy* good husband to that woman, but she never appreciated it. Never appreciated him. No wonder he'd been forced to turn to other women for a bit of light relief (not to mention sex). Lots of women. So many that he'd practically lost count. Years it had gone on, *blaahdy* years, with that doughy Maureen none the wiser.

She'd been right pissed off when he lost his licence through drunken driving. Not that he was exactly *drunk* – more unlucky, really. He was only a couple of pints (well, all right, four then) over the odds, but was stopped by some young copper still with bumfluff on his chin who turned all *blaahdy* self-righteous when James tucked that tenner into his driving licence and let's-say-no-more-about-it-officer. Big mistake.

Maureen just had to get used to the *blaahdy* idea that she would have to be James's personal chauffeuse whenever he clicked his fingers. 'Bout time she did something to pay for her *blaahdy* keep, seeing as sex had been Out of the Question from the moment she'd got her regulation two pregnancies under her belt, so to speak.

At just after midnight that Saturday (the night of James's second Big Mistake – if you don't count marrying Maureen in the first place), he'd found himself stranded outside a gambling club in the back streets of Watford in the pissing rain, legless, potless and, of course, car-less.

Naturally he'd rung Maureen from just about the only telephone box in the entire south-east of England that hadn't been vandalised, and told her, with his legendary tact and diplomacy, to get her arse over there pronto, and don't spare the horses.

Maureen wasn't best pleased, to say the least. She had been tucked up in bed underneath her Marks & Sparks duvet, happily watching Vincent Price in some old horror movie on telly (James even gave her a colour telly in the *bedroom*, notice). But, sighing, she switched Vincent off in mid-maniacal laugh and got dressed, taking her time since it was raining stair-rods by this time and she didn't see why her devoted husband shouldn't get a good soaking in return for making her turn out on a night like this.

As Maureen was to tell her horrified mother later, 'If you've never tried getting a six foot two drunken man into a Mini when you're five four and stone cold sober, let me tell you it was no joke.' And things were to get worse. Much worse.

'Having somehow managed to get the great lump upstairs (talk about one step forward and two steps back every inch of the way), I flopped him on the Slumberland and eventually got his clothes off, with him making all manner of lewd sexual promises he had absolutely no chance of keeping, in his condition. Thank God.

'Well. I'd just got him tucked up, and was beginning to nod off, when he had the bloody cheek to start getting amorous, if you ever! So I said to him, I said, "You can take your fifteen and a half stone over your own side of the bed, thanks very much."' Maureen paused here for dramatic effect, before continuing, 'And he said, and I quote: "If that's how you feel about it I'm pissin' off home."'

Which was just about the last straw, as far as Maureen

was concerned. 'You *are* home,' she had said coldly, 'though not for very much longer.'

Unknown to her ever-loving husband, Maureen had been turning a blind eye to his sexual adventures for the entire duration of what she laughingly called their marriage. At least he left her alone, that way, and he always came home to her in the end, complete with wage packet, of course. But this time he had gone too far.

It was war.

Maureen would settle for nothing less than, as she picturesquely told her solicitor, 'the bastard's bollocks on a plate, preferably still warm'.

So James had ended up in seedy lodgings with his boot-faced landlady, Mrs *blaahdy* Interfering Briggs for ever sticking her nose into his affairs – and I use the term advisedly. But did James let that hold him back? Did he let that cramp his style? Oh no. Not him.

Christ, the tales he could tell. He smiles reminiscently. The women he's had, in and out of marriage. Love 'em and leave 'em, that had always been his motto in the old days. Still is, given half a chance, only Paula watches him like a *blaahdy* hawk all the time. Worse than being married, in a way.

Still, can't have everything, I suppose. He shrugs his shoulders philosophically. Paula's becoming a right *blaahdy* drag, be honest. But having loved her (after his fashion) he isn't prepared to leave her. Not just yet anyway.

He gazes smugly around the flat, enjoying its showy splendour. This is a far cry from Holmes Street and Mrs Doors-Locked-By-Eleven Briggs. Paula has spared no expense on the place, he has to hand it to her. Impulsively, James gets up and wanders into the bedroom. He opens the wardrobe door and feasts his eyes on the neat row of expensive suits, each one custom-made by Simon's own tailor. That had been an amusing touch; he liked that.

'Oh nice one Paula,' he had grinned, 'using your old

man's own tailor, eh. What a *blaahdy* laugh. I bet you've even had the cheek to charge them to his account.'

'Of course,' she had replied. 'I pay all the bloody bills, anyway.'

Lovingly running his hand along a sleeve, James relishes the smooth richness of the fabric. Oh no, Paula has her good points; couldn't let her off the hook just yet.

That very first day in Harrods Food Hall, where James used to work, he knew she fancied him rotten. She'd been about as subtle as a *blaahdy* charge of cavalry, and anyway, he had an instinct for these things. Known for it. Women simply couldn't leave him alone. Fact.

And his instinct had proved absolutely right. Paula was in and out the shop like a fart in a colander, on one piddling errand or another, making a complete prat of herself. ('Hello. It's your girlfriend. Again. Must be desperate to fancy you. Loaded, mind. You only gotta clock them rings on her fingers. Must be a coupla grandsworth there, easy. You wanna get in there, boy.')

So James did.

But, scenting money, he was unusually subtle about it, for a change. Instead of rushing in, bright-eyed and bushy-tailed at the chink of coin on coin, James had played Paula like a fish. He was all earnest attention one day, and polite indifference the next, until he drove her quite frantic. As James was to comment to Old Tom (who should have been pensioned off from the Food Hall years ago, in James's opinion), 'Poor cow didn't stand a chance from day one.'

Right again. Paula was captivated.

As far as she was concerned, here was a 'real' man. James was exciting, different. Not for him the ball-breaking domestic treadmill. Bollocks to routine and responsibility, that was his motto. He was footloose and fancy free, answering to no one (apart from Mrs *Blaahdy* Briggs, of course, but Paula was not to know this). Here, at last, was a man who pursued excitement and novelty with all the dedication of the true addict. Just like Paula herself, in fact. They were made for each other. Two peas in a pod.

Except that, unlike James, Paula had the money to indulge herself. James fancied a piece of it from the off – a big piece – and, so far, Paula had been generous. Extremely generous.

He frowns. Mind you, she's been getting a bit too *blaahdy* big for her boots lately. Demanding. Acting as if she owns him. No *blaahdy* woman will ever do that. Besides, he has a gut feeling that the moment Paula feels she has completely conquered him she will tire of him: an oddly masculine trait that James recognises only too well. The secret of his success lay in keeping Paula guessing, keeping her on her toes, bewildering yet delighting her with his abrupt swings of mood and behaviour. 'You can't buy me,' he would say coldly, during one of their fights. But you can carry on trying, he would think. Stupid, thick cow.

Glancing at the handsome Rolex on his wrist – Paula's latest gift – he smiles unpleasantly. She will be here soon, *blaahdy* panting to take him to lunch, grateful that he still wants her after she upset him at last night's party. He had gone through the motions of inviting her to lunch, of course, and she had coyly accepted, but they both knew who would be picking up the tab. Serves her right for embarrassing him in front of her supercilious husband and that toffee-nosed, superior bitch, Kit, or whatever she called herself.

Who the hell did she think she was, freezing him out like that. Both she and Paula deserve a *blaahdy* lesson. No woman ever got the better of him.

Wandering over to the mirror, he gazes at his reflection, turning his head to study the jawline and running a plump hand along the fleshy neck. You've still *blaahdy* got it, son.

247

Make no mistake about that. You've still got the old magic touch. They're all the same under the *blaahdy* skin. Just a matter of tactics. Horses for courses. Knowing how to handle 'em, that's the key.

Play your cards right and you can give Paula a kick up the jacksie and topple Kit from that *blaahdy* pedestal she's stuck herself on in one easy move. The notion amuses him. Kit's cool, distant manner represents an irresistible challenge to a man of his peculiarly destructive temperament, and is spiced with the tantalising knowledge that he has met her before, somewhere, sometime. And under very different circumstances from last night's party.

Thoughtfully, he lifts the telephone receiver and dials the number he has gleaned from the address book placed so obligingly on Paula's rattan telephone table by the front door of her house.

Kit slams the telephone down irritably. With luck that's the last we've heard of him.

I wouldn't place any bets on it, murmurs Angel.

But that's the fourth time he's phoned in two days. Will the man never take no for an answer?

I doubt it, says Angel shortly. *He's one of the predators: men who stalk women for sport. The greater the put-down, the greater the challenge.*

His initial attempt had been all boyish charm and where's-the-harm-in-a-friendly-drink. When that didn't work he tried (*God help us*) what Angel called the 'Some Enchanted Evening' routine – the eyes-meeting-across-a-crowded room ploy.

With a predictability that almost made Kit smile, James had then switched tactics completely and suggested maybe there was something slightly suspect about Kit's fiercely-guarded independence. Well, Paula was always banging on about the woman being a dyke, and James was just the man to show Kit the error of her ways.

As a last-ditch stand, he had resorted to his knock-'em-in-the-aisles, sure-fire recipe for success with all women, any woman. He had 'talked dirty', to use his own phrase, working on the assumption that if Kit hung up, she must surely be gay, since no woman in his considerable experience could resist him when he used this particular tactic. If Kit listened, he reasoned, she was a goner.

Kit listened politely, but she was not a goner.

Go for it, girl, urged Angel.

So, when James finally ran out of words, Kit did just that.

Clinically, she gave James the benefit of her theory – arrived at over many years of careful research, she assured him – as to exactly what made men like James tick.

Their overweening vanity persuaded them they were irresistible to women, she explained; usually the result of being an only son sadly over-indulged at the maternal knee by a mother who, herself married to an abusive husband, poured all her repressed sexuality into the child sucking at her breast. Sometimes unhealthily so. The child then grew into a man who saw his life's work as humiliating and using as many women as possible in an attempt to punish his mother.

What utter, half-baked claptrap, Angel had murmured, at this point. I know that, and you know that, Angel. But James doesn't. Anyway, don't stop me, I'm beginning to enjoy myself.

'Of course, as if the deep psychological scarring thus produced in such a man were not enough,' sighed Kit, going for the jugular, 'men of this type – your type, James – are often physiologically flawed also . . .'

'Physiologically flawed?' James had interrupted nervously, in spite of himself.

'Yes. In plain English, James – since your grasp of vocabulary is obviously limited – there is usually, and I speak from personal experience here, a direct correlation

249

between the man's drive to conquer as many women as possible and a severe inadequacy in the size of his equipment.'

Bracing herself for the final, verbal knee to the groin, Kit had grated, 'In other words, James, men like you usually behave that way because, deep down, you know that the pitiful smallness of your penis renders you incapable of satisfying a real woman, but you are doomed to be for ever banging away trying to prove yourself. I pity you, I really do. Perhaps you ought to consider taking up masturbation. It would be far more rewarding in the long run, though it would deprive womankind of a good laugh when you drop your Y-fronts.'

With that, Kit had gently replaced the receiver, leaving James trembling with anger and humiliation. Castrating bitch, he had raged, shakily pouring himself the inevitable Scotch. No *blaahdy* woman talks to me like that and gets away with it. She's going to be *blaahdy* sorry, mark my words.

Half an hour later, the telephone rings again. *Told you he'd be hard to shake off*, says Angel.

'Get lost, James,' says Kit, and hangs up.

But it rings again. 'Who's James?' says a half-familiar voice.

'Oh, a man I had the misfortune to meet recently. Who is this?'

'It's me, Nick.' He pauses, but there is no response. 'Look, I'm sorry I was abominably rude to you in your office the other day. There was really no excuse for it. Hardly the way to renew an old acquaintance . . .'

'I thought I made it quite clear—' begins Kit coldly.

'Oh, you did, crystal clear, but, well, I'm a persistent sort of bloke, I'm afraid, and—'

'And I'm afraid you're wasting your time. Now if you don't mind—'

'If I don't mind you're rather busy. Yes I know.' To Kit's amazement, Nick bursts into laughter. 'Jesus, you really have got a chip on your shoulder, haven't you? What happened to make you build a wall round yourself like this? What is it you're so desperate to bury? Tell me, Chrissie, I want to know.'

Tell me, I want to know, echoes Angel. *Remember the night of Trish's party, all those years ago . . .*

Tell me, I want to know. The phrase coughs and splutters dismally in Kit's head, a firework lying forgotten in the damp grass of her memory, barely alive, yet threatening to burst back into life in a shower of sparks.

Go on then, says Angel. *Tell him. Light the blue touch paper and retire.* But Kit is afraid. Afraid of unleashing a display of emotion that could get out of hand.

'I really don't want to discuss the past,' she says stiffly, her voice carefully controlled, even though tears are springing to her eyes.

'It might help to talk about it,' begins Nick tentatively. 'We all need someone . . .'

'Not in my case. We really have nothing to say to one another, and I am more than capable of dealing with my own problems – past, present and future – by myself. I've had years of practice, after all.'

Don't get any better at it though, do you? I'd demand my money back if I were you.

Kit replaces the receiver and sits with her head in her hands. Give it a rest, Angel. I've got to wipe out the past. Stamp on it with my heel until there are no more sparks.

The telephone shrills again, and Kit awakens with a start, mouth dry and neck aching. Must have dozed off. Always did sleep in times of strain, like an animal. She picks up the receiver warily and listens.

'Mother, it's me.'

'Chaz! Where are you?'

'I'm in Copenhagen, staying with Andy's parents for a few days. Can't stop and chat, so just listen. We're coming to England soon, on Saturday, OK? I know it's short notice, but we need to see you. Something to tell you.'

'What is it? Tell me now.'

'No time – long story. Just be patient. I'll explain on Saturday. OK? Don't know what time yet but I'll ring again.'

'Yes, yes, of course. Can't wait to see you.'

'Great, see you soon. 'Bye now.'

Kit feels ill at ease, emotionally and physically exhausted. Leaning back on the sofa cushions, she closes her eyes.

Chaz is planning to marry. It's obvious. But she's so young, so very young. *Twenty-four*, Angel's voice reminds her coldly. *Quite old enough. You were only twenty-one when you got married, though girls who got themselves up the duff, as Reg would say, didn't have much choice in those days.* Yes, Angel, and look what a mess I made of it.

I know, I know but she's much more sensible than you, always has been.

What has sense got to do with it? Women are such fools where men are concerned. Kit's mouth makes a small moue of distaste. They fall in love, or rather delude themselves that it's love, and offer themselves as hostages, sacrificial objects on the twin high altars of emotionalism and marriage.

Jean always used to say women were fools to equate sex with love, and she was right. Sex has nothing to do with love. How could it? It's greedy and violent, self-seeking and selfish, messy and filled with pain. It's everything that love is not. Love is gentle and unselfish. Love is—

How would you know? says Angel coldly. *You won't let yourself fall in love because it would mean a loss of control. And anyway, you can't face the thought of the sex bit.*

It's possible to love without sex.

In your dreams, sunshine. If you love, really love a man, you want sex too.

Then I'll do without love, Angel. The price is too high.

twenty-four

Kit wonders why she let Simon talk her into this. Glancing across the room she catches the eye of Tony the barman, who shrugs his shoulders and rolls his eyes expressively (well, he *is* half Italian on his mother's side).

Mr Chivers is almost a permanent fixture at the club, these days, but it's a free country and he's a paid-up member, so why should Tony worry? Except that he does.

Nice old boy. Perfect gent, that Mr Chivers. Unlike some of the types you get in here these days. Take the three not-so-wise monkeys at the corner table, for instance; all red braces and Filofaxes and not a 'please' or 'thank you' between them. Buncha jumped-up barrer boys is all they are. Tony's half-Italian lip curls. Place is really going downhill.

Accompanied by his two acolytes, Jason and Paul-boy, Damian, king of the barrer boys, is celebrating the safe delivery of his first-born child – well, the first he is admitting to – in the only way he knows how. ('See ya dahn the Club, lads – it'll be shampoo 'n' cigars all the way. Just to wet the baby's 'ead, like.')

Loudly, he demands yet another bottle, and Tony paints on an ingratiating smile, all gleaming white teeth, Brylcreem and Latin charm, though the closest he's ever got to Naples, the city of his mother's birth, was when he went on a package holiday to Rimini two years ago.

'Certainly, sir,' he beams. 'Coming right up, sir.' Well,

it's a living, he reflects gloomily, and I've been trying to offload that case of cheap fizz from Romania for bloody ages. These peasants'll never know the difference until their bloody teeth start going black and falling out.

Opening the bottle with a theatrical flourish, he casts an anxious sideways glance at Simon. He's really bashing the Scotch these days. Started getting a bit loud when he's in his cups, too. Still, the woman he's with looks as if she can handle herself. And the old boy an' all if it comes to the crunch.

'Come on, Kit,' Simon is saying. 'I've had a hell of a week. We both have. Deserve a little drinky-poo before . . . before going home.'

Little drinky poo? snorts Angel. *He's already had the best part of that bottle stashed in his office filing cabinet, or I'm losing my grip.*

Kit swirls the drink around in her glass thoughtfully. 'You can't put off going home for ever, Simon, and, well, this stuff isn't really helping you is it?' *Does it ever?* says Angel sagely.

'Wish I *could* put it off. Paula's always been a difficult woman, but just lately . . .'

He tosses back his drink and gestures to Tony to bring him another. *Bloody hell*, says Angel. *He's knocking them back a bit quick, isn't he?*

'It's that bloody James Hunter,' says Simon. He gives a short, mirthless snort of a laugh. 'Hunter by name and Hunter by nature. He's certainly got old Paula shot, stuffed and mounted, if you'll excuse the expression. Silly little woman. Do you know, she's spent a fortune on that bastard . . . bloody fortune. He's bleeding her white, the damned vulture . . .'

Tony sets another glass in front of Simon and he seizes on it hungrily.

'Shouldn't be doing this.' He winks at Kit roguishly. 'Doctor says I must lay off. Bloody killjoy. What does he know?' (*Probably what's best for you*, says Angel primly.) 'And before you say a word, Kit, this drink is my last. Well, almost ... Silly little woman,' he mutters again. 'Hate to see her making a fool of herself with that ... that creature.'

Gulping down his drink, he beckons Tony, who studiously ignores him, busying himself replenishing small dishes of peanuts which do not need replenishing.

'What about some service!' roars Simon, oblivious to disapproving stares from the barrer boys. 'For Christ's sake, what do you have to do to get a drink in this place, tap-dance on the bloody tables?'

So, glancing apologetically at Kit, and with an almost imperceptible shake of his Brylcreemed head, Tony obliges with yet another Scotch.

'Bleeding her white,' mumbles Simon into his glass. 'After the buy-out of her father's business she was sitting pretty. All that's gone – even her shares. Overdrawn up to the hilt, now. And bits and pieces of her good jewellery have gone missing. Thinks I don't know about it, but I keep my eyes open.' He taps the side of his nose. 'Poor old simple Simon's not as simple as she thinks.'

Gazing at Kit, his eyes are haggard. 'Been throwing her money about like a drunken sailor, Kit, and it's almost all gone. I've managed to salt a little away over the years in a separate account, but that won't last long. I can see us having to sell the house at this rate, and as for the business ...' He shrugs eloquently. 'She never stops reminding me that although she's *only* the sleeping partner, it's her money and she can do what she likes with it. I just don't know what to do any more.'

Simon covers his face with his hands and begins to sob, the sounds loud and ugly in the genteel quiet of the bar. The fashionably cropped heads of the barrer boys swivel round in unison.

What the hell are they gawping at? says Angel, so

256

Kit stares back challengingly until they drop their eyes in embarrassment. ('Fuckin' stroll on,' mutters Damian under his breath. 'Wouldn't like to get the wrong side of *that* in 'urry.')

'Come on Simon. I'd better take you home.' Her eyes meet Tony's, and he nods approvingly.

'No. Not yet. Please. I couldn't face it.' Simon's voice is almost a whisper. But he allows Kit to lead him gently outside and tuck him into her car, like an invalid. He sits staring vacantly ahead as Kit drives, occasionally casting anxious glances at her silent passenger.

He's a terrible colour, says Angel, and she is right; his skin is a ghastly grey-white, his lips tinged with blue. *And he's sweating like a pig*, she adds unnecessarily.

You can't inflict Paula on him, in this state. She'll wipe the floor with him. Take him home and pump him full of black coffee first.

Good idea, Angel. Luckily, Joyce is visiting an old friend and won't be back until late and—

I don't believe you sometimes. Don't tell me you're worried about what Mummy will think about you bringing a man home, at your age. For God's sake, this is an emergency.

Over coffee, Simon brightens slightly, apologising for being such a nuisance, for burdening Kit with his problems, for being disloyal to Paula.

'You've been so good, such a comfort. If only Paula were more like you.'

'Come on, Simon. That's the booze talking. You sound as though you're about to proposition me.'

'I could do worse.'

'Nonsense,' says Kit briskly. 'I'd drive you mad inside a week. Besides, you obviously care for Paula – despite everything – and she cares for you, I'm sure. You need each other, whereas I . . . I can manage perfectly on my own.'

'We all need someone.'

Not her. Iron Drawers doesn't need anyone but herself. God help her.

'Not me,' says Kit breezily. 'Now then, what about some more coffee?'

'In a bit, in a bit. Just sit and talk to me. It's not often I get the undivided attention of an attractive woman.'

'Fine. What would you like to talk about?'

'You, basically. Despite our . . . professional relationship, I really know so little about you.'

And you never will know, says Angel flatly. *So don't waste your breath asking.*

'I know you claim you can manage perfectly well on your own,' Simon is saying, 'and I'm sure you're right, but have you never ever considered, well, remarriage, my dear Kit?'

'Absolutely not,' says Kit firmly. *What did I tell you?*

'Now then,' she continues brightly, changing the subject (*As ever*), 'you seem to be rallying. Still look a bit chewed around the edges, but almost fit for human consumption.'

'You're not going to throw me out?'

'Well, Paula will be wondering what's happened to you.'

Glancing at his watch, Simon shakes his head. 'I doubt it. She'll be out wining and dining James at some expensive watering hole by now.'

'Tell you what, we'll compromise. You must be starving – God knows, I am – so I'll get us a quick snack and *then* I'll throw you out. How's that?'

Simon smiles gratefully. 'I'd like that. Thank you.'

The doorbell rings shrilly. Kit raises her eyebrows at Simon. 'That'll be my mother, though it's a bit early for her. She's probably forgotten her key. Again.'

But her welcoming smile fades as she realises the identity of the visitor.

'Surprise, surprise,' he says jovially. 'Aren't you going to invite me in . . . Tina?'

258

And the colour drains from Kit's face.

Confidently, James pushes her to one side and swaggers into the hallway. He smiles broadly, and Kit notices for the first time the gold tooth glinting in his mouth.

Now who do we know with a gold tooth like that? Who did we use to know?

'It's finally dawned on me where I seen you before,' says James. 'Bumping into an old mate triggered it. You must remember Terry . . .'

Who the hell is he? whispers Angel helplessly, as James, all cocky arrogance, strolls into the sitting room.

'Oh,' he sneers. '*Very* cosy. *Blaahdy* tea and sympathy is it? Consoling the cuckolded husband, eh? You don't *blaahdy* change much, do you Tina?'

Simon begins to rise from his seat, but James places a heavy hand on his shoulder and pushes him effortlessly back down again.

'Been knocking it off for long, have you, you old bugger?'

'I can assure you there's no question of Kit and me—'

'Turned you down, did she? What, our little Tina, everybody's friend? Must be getting *blaahdy* choosy in her old age, doing the old Virgin Queen routine all of a sudden. Was a time when anybody'd do. Isn't that right, Tina?'

Who the hell is he? whispers Angel again.

'I know I was only one of many,' continues James, 'but don't tell me you don't remember me. Me, of all *blaahdy* people. Now you've really gone and hurt my feelings. Thought I was a bit special. Gave you something to remember me by, didn't I? And you were more than willing in those days – *blaahdy* famous for it.'

Closing her eyes, Kit feels sick and dizzy. This isn't real. This . . . this invasion simply can't be happening. It is as if she is being raped, all over again.

Rape! explodes Angel. *It's him. Remember? The bastard who would have raped you in that bloody car park all those years ago, if it hadn't been for Jean riding to the rescue, like the Lone Ranger. James, Jim, Jimbo. Of course.*

Kit's eyes snap open and she stares at him, remembering. Dear God. A hand flutters to her throat, her eyes wide with horror.

'Jim,' she croaks. 'The car park at that awful club. You tried to—'

'Got it in one,' grins James. 'Jimbo to my friends, in those days.'

He turns to Simon. 'You wouldn't have recognised it back then,' he says conversationally. 'All blonde frizz and tits hanging out to dry. Picked it up at a dance hall. Real knocking shop of a place that was, eh Tina? Years ago it'd be now, but I never forget a face. All over me like a *blaahdy* rash it was, proper little tease. Then just when I was getting all ready to shoot my bolt it only decided it'd gone off the *blaahdy* idea. Well, I wasn't having that, what man would, so I put it to her in the car park. Loved every minute of it, she did, in spite of making out she didn't want it. Went like a *blaahdy* rattler.'

'That's not how it was,' whispers Kit. 'You know it wasn't like that.'

But James ignores her. 'Yet now it has the nerve to come on like some kinda vestal *blaahdy* virgin, looking down her nose at me like I'm a bit of dogshit she picked up on her *blaahdy* shoe.'

He takes a step towards Kit, who backs away, the look of horror still frozen on her face.

'Come on Tina,' he says softly. 'You used to be much more sociable in the old days. Famous for it, like I said. And your last little fling with poor ole Tel was the talk of the pub for *blaahdy* weeks.'

She closes her eyes again. *No, please God. Not that. Please don't let him drag all that up again*, says Angel.

But there is no stopping James now. He is really enjoying himself. Two for the price of one, or what?

Turning to Simon, still sitting white-faced on the couch, James continues, 'Only got itself up the duff by my mate, Tel. Or so it said. Though it could've been anybody's *blaahdy* kid, the way it used to put itself about. But ole Tel believed it, poor sod. Like a dog with two tails he was, for a while. Then the slag has to go an' have a *blaahdy* abortion. Murdering bitch!'

Simon's mouth is working, but no sounds come out. His grey-white pallor has returned, and beads of perspiration bathe his brow.

I don't like the look of Simon, says Angel, an edge of panic in her voice. *Pull yourself together. Fight back. You've got to do something, for his sake.*

'. . . an' even after, when Tel goes round there to try an' *blaahdy* talk to her, like,' James is saying, 'she expects him to just pick up where he left off as though nothing's *blaahdy* happened. Pissed as a fart, she is, and—'

'Right. That's enough,' says Kit sharply. 'Get out. You've said what you wanted to say. Now just go, and leave us alone.'

James glances at her contemptuously. 'Get out? Who's gonna *blaahdy* make me? This stupid old sod? I've been pissed on from a great height by wankers like him all my life. Now it's my turn to get the *blaahdy* boot in and I'm loving it, *blaahdy* loving it. Just look at him, shitting himself wondering what he might have picked up from a slag like you. Or haven't you let him *blaahdy* have any yet?'

By now, Simon is gasping, sprawled on the couch, but James shows not a trace of pity, of humanity. He moves cruelly in for the kill.

'Or couldn't you *blaahdy* get it up, is that it? Old Paula's told me what a useless bugger you are. No wonder she turned to me. I know how to keep 'em happy. Your lady wife can't get enough of it, even willing to pay for the *blaahdy* privilege, poor cow.'

With a tremendous effort, Simon raises himself on one

elbow. 'D-don't you dare speak about my wife . . .' he begins bravely.

'Oh, mai waife,' mimics James. He pushes his face into Simon's. 'Your precious *blaahdy* wife's nothing but a common slag, like all the rest, only it's a rich slag, and that's the only reason I put up with the shrivelled tits and the skin that looks like a wrinkled body stocking that needs a *blaahdy* good iron.'

'G-get out,' croaks Simon feebly.

'Don't get yer Y-fronts in a turmoil, *old boy*. I'm going anyway. You won't be *blaahdy* seeing me again. Either of you.'

He gives Kit a look of sheer malice. 'And don't kid yerself I came here to try my *blaahdy* luck with *you*. No danger. I couldn't fancy you now, not now I know where *you've* been. I just wanted to put your *blaahdy* nose out of joint, see you squirm, you castrating bitch. Being able to put friend Simon right about you at the same time was an added *blaahdy* bonus. Buy one, get one free.'

James turns to leave, but he cannot resist one more pop at Simon. 'And don't worry, I won't be sniffing round your lady wife for much longer. Getting a bit too much of a *blaahdy* effort, even on my wages; I've had more fun sandpapering me bollocks with a bit of wet 'n' dry than I have with her.'

And besides, says Angel dully, *like a hound scenting thunder in the air, he senses that the* blaahdy *money's running out*.

Simon's lips tremble slightly, parting as if about to speak, his arm lifting momentarily in a gesture of . . . anger, resignation, defeat? But James is already slamming out of the door.

Kit does not watch him go. Transfixed, she can only stare at Simon with a horrified intensity. *For Christ's sake*, screams Angel. *Don't just stand there with your mouth open. Do something. Help him. And hurry!*

Obediently, Kit moves towards him on rubbery legs that feel as if she is wading through treacle. Sitting beside him, she takes a handkerchief and gently wipes his brow. A spasm crosses his face – half smile, half grimace, his lips twitching involuntarily, his eyelids fluttering, and Kit is momentarily frozen in panic.

She feels faint and dizzy, as if about to pass out, but Angel will not let her. *Don't give in to it!* she yells. *Brandy! See if he'll take a little brandy.* Somehow, Kit manages to stand up, dimly surprised that her legs will actually support her weight, and sloshes brandy into a glass. She raises the glass to Simon's lips, but his mouth hangs slackly open, a trace of spittle at the corners.

Feverishly, Kit kisses his eyelids and chafes his hands in hers. *It's no good*, says Angel. *Ring for an ambulance; it's his only chance.* But Kit merely shakes her head in despair. With the utmost tenderness she closes Simon's mouth and wipes his face. Too late, Angel. Too late.

Angel's cries of anguish sear through Kit's head, but she is dry-eyed. Like a zombie, she sits rocking Simon in her arms, for how long we shall never know.

Suddenly Kit is dimly aware of the telephone ringing insistently at her elbow. Like a sleepwalker, she picks it up and listens.

'Mother,' shrills Chaz. 'We're here, we're in England! Andy and I got a chance of a cheap flight tonight instead of tomorrow, but don't worry about putting us up tonight. We're staying with friends who live near the airport. We'll be over in the morning. Must dash now. See you tomorrow. 'Bye.'

Kit tries to speak, but no sound emerges. Dully she replaces the receiver and at last she weeps. She weeps for the manner of Simon's death, and for the obvious happiness of her daughter, but above all she weeps for herself, her pathetic, hopeless, bitter self.

twenty-five

Once the mourners have filed solemnly into the chapel for Simon's funeral, Kit slips unobtrusively into a pew near the door, exhausted by the emotions of the past few days.

The young priest's voice drones on in a fly's buzz of sound. The pink mouth opens and shuts, meaninglessly spilling the automatic platitudes that go with the territory. 'Even in life we are in death ... beloved brother, er, Simon . . .' Etcetera.

Don't suppose the reverend gentleman even knew Simon, says Angel gloomily. *What a bloody fiasco. You'd think Paula might at least have spared him this.*

Not her, Angel. Never mind about Simon's last wishes, spelled out in black and white in his will. *Which you drew up, of course.* Kit nods. As an agnostic, the last thing he would have wanted was a pantomime like this.

But this is Paula's big moment. Her chance to play the grieving widow to the hilt in her brand new, Harvey Nicks widow's weeds. I'm surprised she didn't leave the price labels showing.

Yeah, I noticed. The full Jackie Kennedy bit, complete with all-enveloping black veil. Still, it put her off her stroke seeing you here.

Don't remind me, Angel.

Paula had descended from the big, black Bentley and stood for a moment, head bowed, presumably in silent prayer. (*Nice touch*, said Angel. *Very theatrical.*) But when

264

she saw Kit, she abandoned the act, her whole body rigid with hatred.

'How dare you come here,' she had hissed. 'How dare you show your face, you whore. James has told me all about you.'

Surely he isn't here, Angel had said incredulously. *I thought he'd crawl back under his stone now that the golden goose has got egg-bound.* And Kit had smiled sadly. No doubt decided to stick around for a little longer, Angel, under the circumstances. He'll be hoping Simon's left a few quid tucked away that he can help the grieving widow to squander.

As if reading her thoughts, Paula had stiffly explained that James had thought it inappropriate to attend the funeral. 'But he's been marvellous,' she had added, almost triumphantly, 'helping me through my grief and advising me on the disposal of Simon's property (*I bet!*). He's the only true friend I've got left. Thank God Simon was so prudent. At least I won't be left completely destitute.'

Not immediately, anyway. Not until James has sucked you completely dry.

Quite. And even in the face of death she can't stop talking about money, Angel.

Yeah. The day of her own funeral she'll probably sit bolt upright in her coffin and demand to know who's footing the bill and why the piggin' mourners haven't provided more impressive wreaths.

Simon's brother (*Didn't know he had a brother*) stands to read the lesson. But Kit isn't listening. She is completely lost in her own thoughts. She can hardly believe it is only five days since Simon died. So much has happened since that terrible night.

Long after the ambulance had been and gone, Kit had sat, wide-eyed, staring at the indentations made by the weight of Simon's body on her couch. She had answered countless questions, posed by innumerable faceless people, until finally she was alone again.

She was oblivious to Joyce's key turning in the front door; doesn't remember spilling out the whole tragic tale to her dumbfounded mother. Sitting dumbly while Joyce fussed around her, Kit had found herself quite unable to move.

Joyce had very nearly panicked. Then she remembered Reg. He would know what to do. Leaving Kit gazing into space, she tiptoed across the hall to her sitting room.

'Sorry to sit in your chair, love,' she had said, gazing earnestly at the Royal Doulton pot containing Reg's Ashes, 'but this is an emergency. I thought I betta get closer to you than ever to tell you the latest, so I 'ope you won't mind this once.' Briefly, she filled Reg in with what happened. 'And the girl's bin sittin' there like a tit in a trance ever since. I dunno what to do with 'er, I don't straight.'

But Reg was no help. At least, Joyce didn't think he was, at first. Just as she'd given him up as a bad job and heaved herself to her feet, she had knocked over the little table by the side of Reg's chair. 'Oh now look what I've bin 'n' gorn 'n' done. I'm getting bloody clumsy in me old age.' ('*Getting* clumsy,' tittered the crinoline ladies. 'She was clumsy from the day she was born, that one'.)

Joyce was particularly fond of that table even though it had always been a bit wobbly on its pins and Reg's promises to 'give it a goin' over' had never amounted to anything. So there it had sat, at Reg's elbow, handy for his baccy tin and *Exchange & Mart*, which, as we know, was essential reading as far as he was concerned.

Reg had even been settling down to read the magazine the day he died, of course, so for ever after Joyce had ensured that, side by side with his Old Holborn tin and packet of Rizlas, the latest *Exchange & Mart* always sat where it belonged, on Reg's side table. Besides, she didn't mind flicking through the 'Properties for Sale' section herself, when she had a minute. ('Nice to keep up-to-date on prices, Reg, 'specially after puttin' in so much effort with this place. They reckon this is an up 'n' comin' area round 'ere, y'know.')

Joyce had set the table lovingly to rights, and stooped to retrieve Reg's 'baccy tin and *Exchange & Mart* from where they had fallen.

And that's when it happened.

The magazine had of course been turned to the property section, and as Joyce replaced it on the table, there, staring her in the face, was an advert for a splendid farmhouse in County Cork. Which probably won't mean much to you and me, but it did to Joyce.

'You done it again, Reg, you clever old sod,' Joyce had smiled. 'County Cork is where that nice Frank come from as a boy. I'll give him a bell in double quick time. Frank'll know how to handle the girl. Always did.'

Kit smiles to herself. Dear Frank. He never let her down. Ever. *Stroke of genius on Joyce's part*, says Angel fondly, unaware of Reg's intervention, of course.

Not that Kit remembers Frank arriving. All she remembers is her mild surprise at waking up on one of the chesterfields, with the grey light of a new day dawning through her curtains and Frank snoring gently on the other couch.

Well don't just lie there, Angel had admonished. *There's loads to do. Chaz is coming home – Chaz and Andy, her Great Dane*. And Kit had stumbled to her feet and wandered into the kitchen to make coffee.

'And what do you think you're up to, madam?' Frank had enquired at the door. 'You should be in bed.'

'God, you sound just like Joyce. I'd love to go to bed, but Chaz and Andy are due and—'

'And there's heaps to do. Yes, I know. Leave it all to your trusty uncle Frank.' He had opened his arms wide and Kit had allowed herself to be held comfortingly, tears beginning to stream down her face. Frank had stroked her hair. 'You go and have a bath and make yourself look beautiful, there's a girl.'

Chaz had duly arrived, full of laughter and excitement, shyly introducing Andy to her mother, pride and love shining in her eyes.

To Chaz and Andy's identical bewilderment, Kit had thrown back her head and laughed hysterically, the unnatural hilarity quickly giving way to wrenching sobs which threatened to pull her apart. Frank had of course taken control at once. 'A brandy I think, Chaz,' he had commanded, and Chaz had rushed to do his bidding.

Eventually, Kit had calmed a little, and, kneeling at her side, Andy had taken her hand and gazed into her eyes anxiously. 'Am I so terrible? You look at me with dismay. Am I not as expected?'

'H-hardly,' Kit had stammered trying to remember how to smile. 'You see, I was expecting a man. Chaz omitted to tell me she was in love with a woman.'

Kit is suddenly aware that people have begun leaving the chapel. The funeral service is over. Waiting until everyone (*Especially bloody Paula!*) has shuffled respectfully out, Kit quietly says goodbye to Simon for the last time. Then she goes home.

Turning her key in the lock, she is surprised to hear Frank's voice call to her. 'Come and sit down, love,' he says. 'You look terrible.'

That's my Frank, says Angel, with a smile in her voice. *Always ready with the fulsome compliments.*

'Joyce has gone off sightseeing with the girls,' grins Frank. 'She was tempted to take Reg's ashes with her, apparently, but I managed to persuade her against. Be terrible if she dropped them, I told her. 'Specially south of the river. She'd never forgive herself if Reg ended up scattered all over Lambeth.'

Frank pours Kit a coffee and sits down beside her. 'Now then,' he says, sitting down beside her, 'where do we go from here? I take it you won't be going back to Simon Chivers & Partner?'

No chance, says Angel, and Kit shakes her head.

'You've no ties at all then,' says Frank gently. 'You're free as air to do whatever you want. Chaz is off to Copenhagen to work for Andy's parents in their hotel and . . .'

Kit smiles thinly. 'Poor things. They thought I'd finally flipped when I reacted to Andy the way I did.' *And that's the understatement of the bloody century,* says Angel. *You and your fertile imagination.* And yours, Angel. And yours.

'I'm not surprised,' says Frank, beginning to laugh. 'When you get hold of the wrong end of the stick, you really go for it, don't you?' She stares at him blankly. 'I mean, really my love, first you convince yourself Chaz's Big News involves yards of flowing white tulle, orange-blossom and confetti . . . and where did you get that idea from, by the way? Been reading the tea leaves, or what?'

He pauses, wiping his eyes with a handkerchief. 'Then when you finally clap eyes on gorgeous Andy you jump to the inescapable conclusion that Chaz has turned into a raving lesbian just because of years of your anti-male propaganda. You really do punish yourself, don't you? Gays are born not made, my dear, sweet, short-sighted innocent. I should know.'

'Well, how was I supposed to know that their Big News was about Chaz's job plans?' says Kit huffily. 'Why didn't she give me some warning that she was off to work in Copenhagen? And don't tell me she was worried about my reaction to her living abroad because since when has she ever considered my feelings? Besides, she's always made it crystal clear she never intended to live with me ever again.'

To Kit's annoyance, her eyes begin to fill with tears. *Oh there there*, says Angel sarcastically. *Put a bloody sock in it, do. You'll cope, as you're so proud of telling everyone.*

'Anyway,' she continues grumpily, 'I'll cope, whatever Chaz has decided to do. I wish you'd all stop treating me like a child.'

'But you *are* a child in so many ways, which is probably part and parcel of why I love you so much. You bring out my frustrated paternal instincts.'

'Oh come on, Frank. I'm forty-five years old, for heaven's sake.'

'And I'm twelve years older, and still as daft as I was as an adolescent, but you . . .' Frank shakes his head mockingly. 'Jean was right all those years ago. You're really not fit to be let out into the world, even at your age.' The smile fades suddenly. 'You need someone to look after you, you know, despite your much-vaunted independence. Perhaps now is the time to consider it.'

Oh God help us, says Angel. *Frank's not going to propose again, is he?*

'Oh come on, Frank,' says Kit wearily. 'We've been here before. We both know it couldn't possibly work. I'm just not cut out for marriage to you or anybody else.'

'I wasn't suggesting marriage to *me*, you idiot,' grins Frank. 'It's the "anybody else" I was thinking of, and not necessarily with marriage in mind.'

Kit opens her mouth to reply as the phone rings. *Saved by the bell*, says Angel drily.

'Chrissie?' says a familiar voice. 'No, please don't hang up. It's Nick.'

As if she didn't know, says Angel.

Kit's stomach does its old forgotten, treacherous forward roll, which does not, of course, escape Angel's attention. *That's a relief. You can still jump at the sound of a man's voice, then?* Yes. Don't learn, do I Angel? Frank's right. I'm simply not fit to be let loose.

'Chrissie?' he says again. 'Are you there?'

'Yes,' she whispers.

'How are you?'

'I'm fine.'

'Good.'

Nick clears his throat. 'Look, I'm off to the States in a few days' time – part business but mainly to see my son, Ian. Please say you'll see me again before I go. I promise I won't mention the past, Scout's honour.'

'No way.'

Why the hell not? demands Angel. I mustn't weaken now, Angel. You know very well that every man I've ever even mildly fancied has turned out badly for me. I'm simply a hopeless judge.

Watching her, Frank observes Kit has gone quite pale. Silently he pours her another coffee and hands it to her.

'Please don't ring me again, Nick Nicholson,' she says crisply. 'There would be no point in our meeting, no point at all. I'm getting married again very soon, as a matter of fact, and have got rather a lot to do.'

'Congratulations,' says Nick coolly, 'and good luck.'

Frank looks at her quizzically as she replaces the receiver. 'Anyone I know?'

'W-what?'

'Your husband-to-be. Who's the lucky man?'

Kit bursts into tears. 'Oh no one, of course. I just made up a phantom lover to get rid of . . . of someone. Obviously you realised that.'

'Obviously, but why? You look as if you'd like to meet this, er, Nick, again in reality, so why give him the bum's rush?'

'Just keep out of it, Frank. I knew Nick a very, very long time ago, and by a coincidence he turned up at the office recently, wanting us to act for him. That was one meeting

271

too many and I have no intention of ever, ever seeing him again. It's, it's too painful.' She slams out of the room and rushes upstairs to her bedroom. *Just like a bloody spoiled teenager*, sneers Angel.

Frank sits nursing his drink, looking thoughtful. Then he begins searching through Kit's briefcase.

Kit has just got out of the bath, preparing to go out for a few drinks with Frank, when the doorbell sounds.

'I'll get it,' calls Joyce. 'You carry on making yourself look pretty.'

Fat chance, says Angel.

There is a low murmur of conversation downstairs. Kit shrugs. Probably one of Mother's friends; either that or she's having one of her heart-to-hearts with Dad's ashes.

As she descends the stairs, Joyce emerges from the kitchen. 'There's someone to see you,' she says, looking oddly pleased with herself. 'I've given him a drink and put him in the garden as it's such a lovely evening.'

'Who is it?'

'Search me,' says Joyce unconvincingly, disappearing back into the kitchen.

Kit is mystified. She wanders out into the garden, experiencing an odd sensation of déjà vu.

The sun is setting to mark the end of a perfect day, the sky streaked with orange and gold. The perfume of night-scented stock strikes a chord in her memory, and she finds herself wandering mindlessly toward a faint creaking sound in the distance. The path leads to a small patio, placed to catch the sun and equipped with white-painted garden furniture.

A lone figure swings gently to and fro on a garden chaise, his cigarette glowing in the semi-darkness.

'I thought you'd never come,' says Nick comfortably, patting the seat at his side.

Kit sits down, dumbstruck, suddenly and ridiculously

shy in his presence. Even Angel doesn't know what to say, for a change.

'Your old friend Frank is a diamond,' he says simply.

She nods wisely. 'Obviously he set this up. It's just like him. Devious old bugger.'

Placing his arm about her shoulders, Nick smiles into her face. As if it were the most natural thing in the world, Kit leans towards him to receive his kiss. A tiny breath of laughter escapes her lips as they bump noses.

'Out of practice,' murmurs Nick, finding her mouth at last.

There were no exploding stars, no bells jangling, no swell of a hidden orchestra.

Well, what did you expect, bloody Vesuvius erupting? You've not been at the Mills & Boon novels, have you?

No and no, Angel. I'll just settle for this wonderful feeling of exhilaration and sense of deep, deep contentment, thanks very much.

'Throw down your gun and come out with your hands up,' grins Nick. 'I gotcha surrounded.'

Go on then. And Kit can hear the laughter in Angel's voice. *You always were a pushover, deep down.*

'Anything you say, officer.' Kit smiles. 'I was getting sick of being on the run anyway.'

You and me both, says Angel.

Chris

twenty-six

Chris (for Nick refused point blank to call her Kit) became Mrs Christina Nicholson on 12 February 1988. It was to have been a discreet affair: just the two of them plus Frank and of course, her mother, Joyce.

But Joyce wasn't having any. Reg's ashes got a right ear-bashing (so to speak): 'We gotta make sure the girl gets a better send off than that, ain't we, Reg? I bought a lovely new 'at 'specially – real feathers.' She had donned the hat and looked at her reflection in the mirror over the mantelshelf. 'Whadjer think? Don't make me look too much like a pearly queen, I 'ope. Anyway, as I was saying, young Mandy that comes to 'elp with a bit of 'ousework twice a week (not that I akcherly need any 'elp but she's a single mum, see, poor little mare, an' needs the money) – well, she said she could put on a lovely spread, wedding cake, the lot. Make a bit of a do of it, eh? Whadjer think, Reg?'

Reg's Ashes hadn't offered any objection, of course, so Joyce had made up her mind that a bit of a do was what Chris and Nick were going to get. Whether they liked it or not. ('Good ole Frank'll help me out, Reg. He's a smashin' fella, for a nance.')

Thanks largely to good ole Frank's machinations, Chaz had secretly flown over from Copenhagen. ('Well, Reg, fancy not even givin' her own daughter an invite! Quiet ceremony, me arse! Wants 'er bleedin' brains tested sometimes, that girl of ours.') Nick's son, Ian, and his wife Anita had made the trip from Boston.

But the real cherry on the cake was getting Jean along. She and Frank had remained in touch for many, many years, but Kit, as she was known by then, had resisted all his efforts towards a reunion. ('Absolutely not, Frank. I really don't want to rake up the past and there's an end to it.')

So Frank had patiently waited for a suitable opportunity to present itself, and the forthcoming wedding had provided a perfect one.

Jean had turned up, hennaed to death, as ever, on the arm of her second husband, who turned out to be none other than Brian the Bull. Remember him? He of the aubergine suit, platform boots and ghastly mother with live-in budgie? Not that you'd have recognised him, ten years on.

'They're not all bastards after all, Teen – er, Chris,' Jean had confided happily. 'My Bri's turned out to be a little gem, haven't you, darlin'?' And Brian had nodded bashfully. 'Year or two younger than me, but who's counting?' *I am*, Angel had giggled. *And the age gap is about eight years, actually.*

'His mum popping her clogs was the making of him, I reckon,' Jean had murmured. 'He was a different bloke after she went.'

Brian had smiled to himself. You can say that again, Jean, he thought. Mum caught pneumonia after rushing out one wintry Saturday night in her nightie looking for that bloody budgie, Joey-Boy. He had escaped through an open window (in January!) after someone forgot to close the door to his cage . . . Apparently.

After the simple ceremony, after all the celebrations were over and the last guest had quit the premises. Joyce had settled comfortably in her usual chair to tell Reg all about it.

Chris and Nick had gone off to Cookham for a few days, where Nick had a little cottage he used for weekends, and at last Joyce was alone. Apart from the Doulton-potted Reg, of course.

'She's a good girl, that Mandy. Said I'm not to lift a finger. She'll come in tomorrer and do all the clearing up. Mind you, Reg, I s'pose I could at least take the balloons 'n' stuff down. Save 'er one little job. I'll start with the ones over the mirror.'

The crinoline ladies had been distinctly uneasy as Joyce pulled out Reg's side table and placed it in front of the fire. Standing first on a small footstool, Joyce had climbed precariously on to the table and stretched to reach the balloons, whose strings were sellotaped to the back of the mirror.

It had all happened in seconds. With a slight creak of protest, the table gave way. Joyce's arthritic fingers scrabbled at the mantelshelf to save herself. But it was no good. Reg's Royal Doulton pot fell to the ground and so did Joyce, cracking her head on the cast-iron fender in the process.

Mandy had let herself in at nine the following morning with her own key. She found Joyce, dead as a doornail, still clutching a broken shard of Royal Doulton.

An ambulance was called. So was the happy couple, of course. By the time Chris and Nick arrived, Mandy, glad of something to do, had thrown herself into tidying up, keeping her last promise to Joyce.

'Least I could do,' she was to tell her mum later that day. 'Bad enough having to come back off your honeymoon to find your mum dead an' gone, without coming back to a messy place. I did Joyce's room first. Would have upset Chris even more to see that broken table and china all over the place. By the time I'd given it a good hoover round, you'd never have known there'd been a terrible accident.'

Which was how Reg's ashes came to end up in the pristine dustbag of Joyce's brand-new, never-been-used-before Electrolux. ('Well, it was a bargain, Reg, and we were well overdue for a new one.')

twenty-seven

After their truncated honeymoon, followed by Joyce's funeral, Chris and Nick were to make the London house their home. A real home, where real people lived and laughed and made love.

Happy now? Idyllically, Angel.

And they were.

Nick and Chris simply delighted in each other. That was apparent from the start. The patient tenderness of Nick's lovemaking was a revelation to a woman who had spent so many years in the emotional wilderness. Or, as Angel robustly put it, *Didn't know what you were missing, did you kid?* No, I didn't, Angel. Neither of us did. But we're going to make up for lost time. Depend on it.

And they did. Not that their relationship was just about sex. It was a true meeting of minds, a joyful blending of personalities that neither could possibly have envisaged. 'If only we had run away together twenty years ago,' they would sigh, almost in the same breath, 'we could have saved ourselves an awful lot of pain.'

Not to mention alimony, Angel had said at first, acerbic as ever. But, in time, even she softened slightly, only occasionally commenting on the pair's seeming ability to read each other's very thoughts. *Bloody hell, I'll be out of a job at this rate!*

Don't be daft, Angel. You'll always be around. Always.

Oh do leave off; I'm filling up with tears, here. You're coming over all soppily sentimental in your old age, kid.

Though I must say that this time your change of persona has been a change for the better. Am I glad to see the demise of Iron Drawers. Difficult, prickly bugger she *was.*

Yes, grinned Chris. But she was bloody good at her job. And she helped a lot of desperate women. Iron Drawers might be dead and gone, but her work's going to continue, if only on a voluntary basis. I owe her that much.

Go for it, kid, said Angel, sounding slightly choked. *And let's face it, now that you've found your own happy ending maybe a little of the new, improved you might just rub off on others less fortunate.*

Now who's coming over all soppily sentimental, Angel? *Ah, shut up.*

Nick and Chris sit side by side on the garden swing installed at the cottage in Cookham. *I know this is meant to be terribly romantic*, says Angel, *but it's bloody February and I'm freezing my whatsits off, here. Or would be, if I had any whatsits to freeze.* Shut up, Angel. Have you no sense of occasion?

'What a way to spend a fourth wedding anniversary,' grins Nick. 'Working on the cottage, for heaven's sake. My back's killing me.'

He's complaining about his back a lot, these days, says Angel anxiously. Oh, give it a rest, Angel. You can be such a doom merchant, sometimes.

'Don't know when to stop, that's your trouble,' says Chris lightly, pecking him on the cheek. 'And you certainly know how to give a girl a good time, I must say. Never mind, a nice hot soak in our brand-new bath'll iron out the kinks.'

'Is that an invitation?' laughs Nick.

'If you like.' *Oh do me a favour. The weight you've put on round the beam you'd need an Olympic-sized pool to indulge in sexual wallowings these days.* Spoil-sport.

Nick raises his glass. 'Happy anniversary, Mrs Nicholson. May there be many, many more.'

I'd drink to that, says Angel. *If I could.*

But, sadly, Chris and Nick were not to enjoy many, many more anniversaries. With the pain in his back growing rapidly worse, and after consulting countless specialists, Nick was finally told he had inoperable cancer.

They sold the London house and moved into the cottage in Cookham. There, two weeks before their fifth wedding anniversary, Nick died.

Day after day, Chris had driven herself on. Somehow. But the nights were worse. She would stare into the blackness, forcing herself to stay awake. Well, Nick might need me, Angel. *Yes, and you'll be a fat lot of use if he does. For God's sake try to rest. You're exhausted.*

But Chris didn't listen. And when Nick finally gave up the unequal struggle, still she could not sleep, even though her body craved it. Wandering from room to room, she would steadily drink herself into oblivion, despite Angel's protests.

Alcohol's not the answer. Never was. You ought to know that by now. Ah but it *is* the answer, Angel. Enough of this stuff will shut you up, for a start. Which would be bliss. Just get off my back, will you?

Late one night, exactly a week after Nick's death, Chris had sat nursing the inevitable gin and tonic, listening to the creaking conversations that all houses hold after midnight. She was dully aware of the steady tick-tick of the black marble clock, the rain lashing monotonously at the window . . . and a scratch, scratch, scratching at the kitchen door.

Filled with curiosity, Chris had opened the door and there, slumped on the doorstep, was a pathetic bundle of soaked black fur, drenched and bloody and desperately in need of sanctuary. Without a second thought she had scooped it up and placed it carefully on the draining board for a closer inspection. *Poor little sod looks more dead than alive*, Angel had said. And, as ever, Angel was right.

But Chris wasn't about to give up on the creature. After all those months of frenetic activity nursing Nick, interspersed with bouts of mind-numbing hopelessness and despair, Chris felt herself to be living in a void. She needed some aim, some goal, upon which to focus what little energy she had left. She knew at once that she would nurse this creature back to health if it was the last thing she did. And he was to be her triumph and her salvation.

Eventually he had emerged as a handsome, mature tom cat with only half his rightful allocation of bristling white whiskers. He wore his battle scars proudly and demonstrated his undying gratitude to his saviour by never leaving Chris's side if he could help it. He would follow the Boss about like a dog, sitting adoringly nearby when she settled, staring his amber stare.

I swear that moggy thinks he's a dog, Angel had remarked. And he had at once been christened Rover, a name which seemed in keeping both with his oddly canine disposition and the wandering, gypsy life he had presumably led before singling out Chris's cottage as the ideal retirement spot.

twenty-eight

Five years on, and Chris sits in her cottage garden. On the garden swing, of course, where she feels closer to Nick, somehow. She stretches and yawns in the sunshine, Rover as ever curled up contentedly by her side.

His grey-speckled muzzle twitches occasionally, as he dreams of black nights long past. Then he was young and sleek and lithe, invisible and invincible in the velvet dark. Neither mouse nor vole was safe when *he* was about, as he stalked the night searching out tiny, timid creatures that squeaked and scampered. ('Those were the days, I can tell you. Those were the days, all right. Had all my whiskers, not to mention all my teeth, back then.')

Chris reaches out a lazy hand to scratch between Rover's chewed and battered ears. He awakens briefly to push his head adoringly into the Boss's hand before dropping back into a blissful snooze.

Predator turned pussycat, thinks Chris fondly. Gets to all of us in the end, I suppose.

Oh do leave off, says Angel. *Ole rockin' chair's not gonna get you just yet, surely. Where's your get-up-and-go?*

Got up and went, sighs Chris. Got up and went long ago.

Rover stirs as the back gate clicks open, his big, square head swinging briefly towards the sound. ('Oh, it's her. The Boss doesn't look exactly ecstatic to see her either. Time to put in a few more zeds, I think.')

284

A young woman, immaculate in Donna Karan suit and toting matching luggage, picks her way along the path. She ducks her head occasionally to avoid overhanging boughs of old roses and lilac, cursing under her breath as stray tendrils threaten to catch at her perfect hairdo.

Kit, to the life, sighs Angel. Yes, and no doubt as unyielding, thinks Chris. Why do visits from Chaz make me feel so apprehensive, Angel? Even now.

You've just grown apart, I suppose, says Angel uncomfortably. *After all, you haven't exactly seen that much of Chaz over the past few years. What with her whizzing all over the world, busy with her career.*

Come on, Angel. Not like you to pussyfoot around. We haven't *grown* apart. We were never that close in the first place. Face it. I know I have.

'Good to see you,' murmurs Chaz. She gives Chris a perfunctory peck on the cheek. 'I'll just dump my things in the spare room and freshen up. Then we'll talk. I've a lot to tell you.'

'I'll make some tea,' says Chris stiffly, 'and we'll have it in the garden. Might as well enjoy the sun while it lasts.'

'Whatever you say.'

As her daughter disappears upstairs, Chris leans against the kitchen sink, gazing out of the window. Nothing's changed, Angel. The old reserve . . . it's still there. *I know. You can cut the atmosphere with a knife. Even Rover senses it. Just look at him: his tail's puffed up like a loo brush.*

'Daydreaming again, are we?' Chaz reappears and stands, gazing around the kitchen disdainfully. Looks as if she's got a nasty smell under her nose, thinks Chris. *Haven't we all? We're used to being up-wind of the pig farm down the lane. Chaz isn't.* No, it's not that, Angel. She disapproves. I can feel it.

But, as ever, Chris has got it quite wrong where her daughter is concerned.

Chaz's searchlight gaze takes in Rover's tatty basket,

the mud-caked wellingtons by the back door, a plate of half-eaten catfood and the dirty dishes stacked hopefully in the sink. Jesus, she is thinking, Mother's really letting it all hang out, these days. Thank God. And thank Nick. She's been so much more relaxed, so much more *human* because of him.

With a dancer's grace, ('Not bad for an old boy, eh?') Rover picks his way delicately through the profusion of pot plants and cuttings that clutters the windowsill and sits, bolt upright, watchful as ever, studying her with his inscrutable, owl-like gaze.

'This cottage is a mess,' remarks Chaz, grinning.

God, she even sounds like Kit, says Angel sourly, missing Chaz's grin entirely. *A place for everything and everything in its place.*

'Suits me,' says Chris defensively. ('And me,' thinks Rover, deciding on a quick wash and brush-up before dinner.) Blowed if I'm going to start making excuses for the way I live, Angel.

'And why you tuck yourself away in the wilderness is beyond me.' Chaz places a hand tentatively on Chris's arm, as if afraid she might bite. 'I do worry about you, you know.'

'No need,' says Chris shortly, and Chaz removes her hand in a hurry. Whoops, she thinks. Perhaps I spoke too soon. She can still be as prickly as a whole litter of hedgehogs when she feels like it.

There is an awkward silence, until Angel prods Chris with, *Well say something. Make a bit of an effort, for God's sake.* So Chris does.

'While I don't have to work full-time any more,' she says self-consciously, 'I do keep my hand in as legal adviser for the refuge.'

'Your battered wives,' nods Chaz encouragingly.

'Quite. And of course, there are my sessions at the Law Centre and Citizens' Advice Bureau to stop me getting bored.' She pauses. What else is there, Angel? *You tell me*, says Angel drily. *You're always banging on about what a rich and varied life you lead.*

'I've also got my books, the garden, my friends and Rover here,' says Chris, almost defiantly. 'My life isn't as busy as it was, of course, but I'm really quite content.'

'Quite content!' Chaz is appalled. 'Jesus, you sound so smug and complacent. You used to be so . . . so energetic.'

Exactly what I keep telling her, says Angel.

'Well, time to slow down a little, at my age.'

'At your age? Good grief,' wails Chaz. Daringly, she takes Chris by the shoulders and shakes her gently, much to Rover's consternation. He gives a low growl of disapproval, which Chaz ignores.

'You're fifty-five years old, for Christ's sake, not seventy-five, eighty-five.' (*You tell her, girl!*) 'You're talking as if your life is drawing to a close already. And you used to be such a fighter.'

'Not any more,' says Chris firmly. She inclines her head towards Rover, still sitting on the windowsill. 'He and I are two of a kind – and we've got the battle scars to prove it. No more fighting for either of us. All we want now is a bit of peace and quiet.' She gives the ghost of a smile. 'Unlike most males I've ever met, Rover doesn't answer back. He also gives me his unquestioning love and devotion without expecting anything in return.'

'Oh no? What about a little matter of food, shelter and undying affection? He wants it all, that one. He knows when he's on to a good thing, the old fleabag.' Rover gives her a look of the utmost disdain and begins to wash, his usual tactic when offended or embarrassed.

To Chris's puzzled surprise, Chaz begins to laugh.

What's the joke? Search me, Angel. But whatever it is, it's certainly helping to ease the atmosphere around here. *And that can't be bad.* Quite.

'Well come on then,' says Chris. 'What's funny? The suspense is killing me.' *Me too*, says Angel.

'All will be revealed over that cup of tea you promised me. Oh Mother, I can't wait to tell you my news. Though I really don't know how you're going to take it.'

And who can blame her? Until Nick came into her life, her mother's mistrust of all men – except Frank, of course – was well known. With Nick's death, maybe she had reverted to type, for all Chaz knew.

Mysteriouser and mysteriouser, says Angel, as Chris stands, open-mouthed, watching Chaz carry the tea things into the garden.

'Now then,' says Chris firmly, pouring the tea. 'For God's sake spit it out. It would be sheer sadism to make me wait a moment longer.' *And me*.

'Well, the reason I made the trip over from New York was because I wanted you to be the first to hear my news.' She pauses maddeningly, smoothing a non-existent crease in her skirt. 'Don't drop dead with shock, but, well, the fact is I'm going to be married. In Boston. In his family's home. Obviously I want you to be there.' *Obviously?* says Angel. *By God, that's gotta be a first*.

Spluttering into her teacup, Chris's face is a picture of astonishment. 'But, but you always swore you'd never marry. All men are bastards, you always used to say.'

'No, *you* always used to say.' Chaz sips her tea thoughtfully. 'And now that I'm a big girl, now that I've had a few knocks myself, at last I begin to understand why. And not before time. God, Mother, I really have had a string of desperate relationships. You can't imagine.'

Oh yes she can, says Angel. *She can well imagine. Been there, done that, bought the T-shirt. And more than once*.

Purposefully, Chaz puts down her cup and saucer. Now or never, she is thinking. Once more into the breach, and all that. She takes a plastic-wrapped package from her handbag. 'Not to mention my desperate relationship with you. You'll never know how hard I've tried to make that work, Mother.' She places the package in Chris's hands. 'Not that this exactly helped. It's been wriggling around like a maggot in a rotten apple for far too long.'

Happy Birthday ten-year-old, says Angel dully. *Complete with poison-pen letter in Dennis's own fair hand. By God, to think that the kid's been hanging on to it all this time.* B-but I thought I'd thrown that away. Buried it years ago. *Evidently you didn't bury it deep enough.*

'You believed it all, then,' says Chris flatly. 'Every rotten word.'

'I was only a kid, Mother. And it all fitted. You sending me away to that bloody awful boarding school just to get me out of the way, so my father said, the way you used to dress, the way you were with that awful bloke . . .'

'Terry.'

'Yes. Terry. From there it didn't take much of a leap of the imagination to buy my father's tale that you had been . . .'

'At it?'

'Yes. At it. From the moment you and he were married, according to his letter.'

'And you believed it,' says Chris again.

'Well, you never gave me any reason to *dis*believe it,' snaps Chaz, suddenly angry. For heaven's sake, she wants to scream, all I want is for you to take me in your arms and stroke my hair and tell me everything's going to be all right and Daddy's letter was one great, fat lie. 'Why the hell didn't you *tell* me he was violent from the start? That you were afraid of him? Why didn't you *tell* me that's why you ran away? I would have understood.'

'You never asked,' says Chris simply. Thank God, Angel. She doesn't know the full story, even now. *Well, now would be the perfect time to tell her*, says Angel wisely. *Better out than in.* As my mother used to say. Yes, I know.

Sorry, Angel. No way. How can I tell my daughter that her father was a child abuser?

'I shouldn't have *had* to ask you,' Chaz is shouting. 'Besides, after the . . . the suicide attempt I tried, I really tried. Nan and Granddad more or less told me the real reason for you leaving my father. All about his . . . his affair with another woman, and how he used to knock you about. And I had a good, long heart-to-heart with Frank. But it wasn't enough. I wanted to hear it from you. But you were so, so cold and unapproachable. There never seemed to be a right moment, so it all just . . . just sort of drifted.'

To Chris's immense surprise, Chaz her daughter, Chaz her child, great big successful about-to-be-married Chaz, begins to weep. Instinctively, Chris does what she should have done years ago. She holds her in her arms and comforts her child, rocking her just as she had done when she was a very little girl.

'I'm sorry,' murmurs Chris. 'I'm so very sorry, baby. I had no idea.' *Too wrapped up in yourself, as usual*, sniffs Angel. 'Things are going to be different from now on.' *Not until you tell her the whole story, they won't*, says Angel. *While there's this half-truth between you, you've no chance*. It'll be all right, Angel. Trust me.

Gently extricating herself from Chaz's arms, Chris says, 'I could do with a drink after all this high emotion. How about you? G and Ts all round?' And Chaz nods.

By the time Chris returns with the drinks, Chaz is gazing dreamily into the distance, a half smile on her face. *Dreaming about Mr Right*, says Angel intuitively. Obviously. Not that I thought she'd ever marry that Jonathan fellow. I didn't really like the look of him when she brought him over on her last visit. *Nor me. Don't ask me why*.

Settling herself down beside Chaz, Chris says breezily. 'Well. This is a surprise. I never thought you and Jonathan would—'

'Never thought I'd be daft enough to take the plunge and actually bind myself legally hand and foot to one of the enemy?' grins Chaz. 'And it's not Jonathan, idiot. He and I split up long ago, and I was too embarrassed to tell you yet another one had bitten the dust.' She smiles. 'This time it's different. This time *he's* different.'

'But how can you be absolutely sure he's right for you?' asks Chris nervously.

'How could you be sure Nick was right for *you*?'

And Chris looks down at her hands, almost shyly. 'I just knew, somehow. There'll be another like him.'

Chaz smiles. 'Wrong again, Mother. I've found one just like Nick. Which is hardly surprising, considering they're extremely closely related.'

But Nick's only close relation was his son, Ian, gasps Angel. And Chris's mouth drops open in astonishment. *Stop gaping like a landed fish, for God's sake*, says Angel.

'I'm going to marry Ian,' laughs Chaz. 'We met up again at your wedding, remember? Got on like a house on fire straight away and decided to stay in touch. It was largely through Ian that I landed the New York job.' She gives a modest shrug. 'After that we became even closer friends.'

'But what about Anita? His wife?' *Trust you to look for the fly in the ointment.* Some bloody fly, Angel.

'Ex-wife,' says Chaz. 'We'd already taken to meeting up for lunch now and then, when he was over from Boston on business, and after he and Anita split up . . . well, he needed his hand holding.' She laughs. 'Not that I was a lot of help – talk about the blind leading the blind. I was in the throes of breaking up with Jonathan so the pair of us used to end up crying into our beer together. I *had* decided that—'

'All men are bastards?' says Chris, smiling.

'Absolutely. Only, as I say, Ian's different.' She takes her mother's hand. 'You . . . you will come to the wedding, won't you? You and Frank? Where is he, by the way? I thought he practically lived here these days.'

'Try keeping us away,' says Chris happily. (*What will we wear?* muses Angel. *Never been mother-of-the-bride before.* Ah, shut up, Angel.) 'And Frank doesn't *practically* live here, he *does* live here. He's just gone to visit his sister in Devon for a few days. Should be back the day after tomorrow. I can't wait to tell him your news. He'll be absolutely delighted, I know.' Chris pauses. 'Please don't think I'm interfering,' she continues tentatively, 'but have you considered asking Frank to give you away at your wedding? He's as old-fashioned as they come, and I know he'd consider it a huge honour.'

And the smile on Chaz's face disappears abruptly. Whoops, she thinks. Now for the tricky bit. There may be trouble ahead, as the old song goes.

'Well, actually, much as I'd love that, I'm old-fashioned too, deep down, and really think that . . . that my father is the right person to give me away.'

'What!' says Chris. 'Do you mean to tell me that after all this . . . after all his poisonous lies you still . . .'

'He *is* my natural father,' says Chaz quietly. 'And I want him at my wedding.' She takes Chris's hand. 'I know it's a lot to ask but can't you bury the hatchet, after all these years? For me?'

But Chris's voice is like ice. 'No, I can't. I hope I never want to clap eyes on the man again. Not even for you.'

'Just like that,' says Chaz coldly.

'Just like that. And anyway, who knows where he might be living these days. Could be dead for all I know.' *You wish*, says Angel.

'Well, I was rather hoping you might try to find him for me.'

'No bloody way,' says Chris flatly. And for once Angel doesn't argue.

292

twenty-nine

Why don't you switch the television off? says Angel. *No one's watching it.* Got to do something, Angel. It's as silent as the grave in here. *Oh well, in that case I suppose the umpteenth repeat of 'Phantom of the Rue Morgue' is really quite appropriate.*

With a sigh, Chris reaches for the remote control and switches off. 'Weren't watching this, were you Chaz?'

'No, not really,' says Chaz, glancing up from the magazine on her lap. Laugh a minute, this is, she is thinking. Why do I bloody bother? Come all the way over here to tell Mother my good news and for what? She doesn't change.

Blown it again, says Angel. *Your only daughter's in your company for just a few hours and you're at each other's throats.*

What am I supposed to do about it, Angel? Give in, like always, I suppose. Well eat your heart out, because this time she's asking too much. I won't be bullied – not any more.

Her mouth sets in a stubborn line and she glances across at her daughter, who sits with an identical expression on her face.

Like looking in a bloody mirror, comments Angel.

'I can hardly keep my eyes open.' Chaz yawns and stretches elaborately. She throws the magazine down. 'Might as well turn in.'

'As you wish,' says Chris coldly. *Don't let her go to bed*

without thrashing this thing out, says Angel. *For God's sake explain to her. She might actually* understand *why you don't want to help her dig the bugger out of the woodwork all over again.*

Chris shudders. Even if I could find the strength to do it, Angel, the thought of sitting in the same room with the man is intolerable. How could I discuss our daughter? With him. How could we possibly make polite, stilted conversation while avoiding any reference to the past; avoiding that at any price?

Perhaps he's changed, says Angel hopefully. *Perhaps time has mellowed him, rounded him. Perhaps he married again, who knows? Maybe he married some strident virago who's led him a dog's life and sandpapered away those spiky edges and spiteful corners.*

Smiling maliciously at the thought, Chris closes her eyes and tries to picture him older, plumper maybe, thicker about the jowls and midriff, the hair touched with grey. To her astonishment she finds she just can't conjure up his face in her mind's eye, however hard she tries.

She can separately visualise the springy, dark hair, the sardonically raised, bushing eyebrows and the deeply clefted chin that she once found so attractive. But when she tries to fit the pieces of the jigsaw together, all that emerges is the kind of bland identikit picture seen on *Crimewatch* each month.

What, 'Have you seen this man?' says Angel. *'If you have, ring 999 at once and do not approach him'?*

Quite. Run screaming in the opposite direction, if you know what's good for you.

Honestly, Angel, I can hardly picture Dennis's face any more, and quite frankly I really don't want to. So why rake over the ashes, after all these years?

'But why rake over the ashes, after all these years?' wails Chris.

'Why not?' says Frank shortly. 'If it's what Chaz wants, why ever not? Can't you forget your own feelings, just this once, and think of her?'

No she can't. Selfish cow. Oh shut up Angel. Whose side are you on anyway? *Not yours, that's for sure. I'm with Frank, not to mention Chaz. Remember her? Your only daughter? The one who's getting married?*

'Trust you to side with Chaz against me,' mutters Chris. *Pathetic. Bloody pathetic!*

Frank shakes his head. 'Silly woman. When have I ever said or done anything that wasn't in your own best interests?' He gazes steadfastly into her eyes, strong and vital as ever, the generous mouth curved into the smile she knows so well.

Never, says Angel. *He's never let you down. Not once. Ironic isn't it? The only man – apart from Nick, of course – who's been a true, loyal friend all these years and he turns out to be gay. You don't deserve a man like Frank.*

Chris sighs. 'Why on earth do you put up with me? Why didn't you take off long ago?'

'Not me,' grins Frank. 'I thought I'd be able to escape your clutches when you married Nick, but like a fool I stuck around.' He looks at her fondly. 'Can't think why. Must be a glutton for punishment. Good thing I did, mind, the way things worked out.' *Yes,* says Angel. *Where would you have been without Frank, especially during Nick's illness?* Where indeed.

Frank puts an arm casually about her shoulders. 'Look, your only daughter's scouring Oxford Street and all points west for her trousseau, or whatever it calls itself, at this very moment, full of hope and excitement. She's getting married for the first time at the ripe old age of thirty-four and I want – we both want – the occasion to be perfect for her, don't we? Well, don't we?' He takes a deep breath. 'Chaz is going to be centre stage on her wedding day, not you. And if she wants her father to give her away then I think you ought to put your own feelings on the back boiler and help her find him. I know that's not what you want to hear, but—'

'I can't, Frank. I just can't.' *What a wimp*, says Angel disgustedly.

'Nonsense. You were terrified of him, I know. But that was thirty years ago and you're a big girl now. Face him, Chris. Lay the ghost, once and for all. I'll do everything I can to help, you know that.'

Chris blows her nose. 'I suppose you're right. As usual,' she murmurs grudgingly. 'Though where to start I can't imagine. I've no idea where he lives now, or anything. Don't want to know really.'

'Shouldn't be that difficult.' He passes Chris a battered business card. 'Remember this fellow? You used to use him occasionally back in the dark ages when you worked as Kit Swanson, ace solicitor. I met him once, years ago, when he did a little private investigation job for one of my old ladies at the nursing home. He might be able to help if he's still in business.'

Chris frowns at the card. 'Yes, we did use him. So did Donaldson and Son.' She grins suddenly. 'You're a scheming old bugger, Frank. Knew you'd be able to talk me round, didn't you?'

'Well,' says Frank modestly, 'I had great hopes.'

The insignificant little man in the shabby raincoat rolls himself a victory cigarette and takes a cautious sip of the thick brown liquid in front of him that's passing itself off as a cup of tea.

He looks around Nic's Caff disparagingly, noting the chipped Formica tables, the steaming, grease-spattered urn and the grimy fingernails of the overweight Cypriot who shuffles to and fro on flat, waiter's feet dispensing doorstep sandwiches and plates of egg and chips to the handful of punters.

Christ, nothing changes. Why do you come to this dump?

he asks himself. 'Cos it's cheap. Admit it. Never did make the big time, did you? Sleuth of the bloody century, you were going to be, and here you are, pushing sixty-five and still snooping about following middle-aged men in pinstripes sneaking off for a lunchtime lay with little tarts from the office.

Still, don't knock it son, don't knock it. It's the wages of sin that keep you in beer and tobacco. Long live sin, that's what I say. I'll drink to that. He takes an enthusiastic gulp at his tea, grimacing as it hits the back of his throat. God, you could strip paint with this stuff. It's probably been festering in that bloody urn since VE day.

Nic smacks a plate of what purports to be mixed grill in front of him, and walks away with an air of disdain. Well, he knows what goes on in the kitchen. He knows all about the cook's personal hygiene habits, or rather the lack of them. And so he should. He's married to her, after all.

Alf Robbins gazes at his gruesome plateful in disbelief. Frizzled egg, grey sausage and a rasher that defies description, jostle cheek by jowl with a congealing dollop of baked beans and a cindery object that was once a lamb chop. Mercifully, the whole dismal repast is partially hidden under a layer of chips which at least bear a passing resemblance to actual food.

Some celebration meal, thinks Alf glumly. Still, Ms Swanson – sorry, Mrs Nicholson as she is now – had been well pleased with him. Fancy her remembering him after all these years, when she was a lawyer in a smart office up west and he was Alfred X. Robbins, Private Investigator – Discreet Enquiries at a Discreet Price. The 'X' didn't actually stand for anything, but had been inserted on his business cards to lend a touch of class, or so he had imagined.

Alf had dispensed with the 'X' long ago, along with the trench coat with the collar turned up and the trilby hat. He had kidded himself they made him look like Mike Hammer on an important case, but in retrospect he admitted to himself that they had made him look like a prat.

Besides, the name of this particular little game is to be utterly insignificant, to blend into the background, to be the sort of bloke no one would look at twice. In this, at least, Alf Robbins has become singularly successful.

It has been quite tedious, tracking down Dennis Stanley Charleton, last known address twenty-seven The Close, Wooburn Green, Bucks. But Alf is a patient man, as dogged as any bloodhound once he gets his quarry's scent in his nostrils. Having tracked Dennis to ground, he has triumphantly reported his findings to Mrs Nicholson and discreetly awaited further instructions.

Old Dennis Stanley had been easier to find than he had imagined. Surprising how many people live thirty years of their lives in an area extending to as many miles in any direction. The man had changed jobs a number of times. Too many times, in Alf's opinion. Yet good old Alfred Robbins had manage to track him down. Didn't let Mrs N. think it had been too easy, though. Might try to cut down his fee. No, he'd blinded her with science, letting her think he has triumphed against outstanding odds.

The dossier Alf has built up makes interesting reading. Very interesting. The man once married to his client is obviously a complete shit and Ms Swanson/Nicholson's well rid. Wonder why she wants to get in touch with a sort like him after all these years.

None of your business, Alfie old son, he reminds himself sternly, none of your bloody business. You've done your job. Now take the money and run.

Alf munches away ruminatively. But why did a woman like her want to unearth the past? She's hardly the black-mailing type, though God knows there's enough there to make old Dennis Stanley a bit hot under the collar, in the right hands. And it would serve the bastard right.

He stops chewing and smiles slyly to himself. Not that

298

Mrs N.'s been given the chance to make use of the information, even if she wanted to. She only asked him to *find* the man. She didn't ask for the story of his life for the past thirty years. Alf had only given her the edited highlights, as it were, just sufficient to make her feel her money's been well spent. He is keeping the full story to himself for the moment. You never know – it might come in handy sometime.

Pushing his plate away, Alf mops at his mouth with a paper napkin, one of the few attempts at refinement in Nic's Caff. What the hell could a sort like Mrs Nicholson – a real lady if ever he saw one – have seen in a bloke like Dennis Stanley Charleton in the first place? Hardly her type. Bit downmarket for Ms Kit Swanson, as was.

He frowns. He had been quite hurt when she had insisted on meeting him in a pub for what he grandly called his 'progress reports'. Didn't want him soiling her precious cottage with his tatty presence, was that it? Oh he'd found out where she lives, all right. No danger. Always makes it his business to know where to get hold of the punters on their home ground, just in case they try bouncing a rubber cheque off him. Which has been known, Alf admits ruefully to himself.

Her superior manner at their little tête-à-têtes had got up his nose a bit, too. Like the Queen Mum talking down to some grubby tradesman. Still, he'd felt almost sorry for her when he finally told her he'd managed to locate her mystery man. She'd gone quite pale, close to tears, and he'd gone scuttling to the bar to get her a medicinal brandy and water. Pulled herself together, though, like a trooper, and told him to fix up a meet.

No she didn't, lying sod. Why do you have to think in outdated American slang all the time? OK, Blue-eyes, so she asked if it would be possible, as one last favour, to arrange an appointment for her with Mr Charleton in the name of Christina Swanson. Their rendezvous should of course be at a discreet distance from her cottage yet near enough to the man's home to ensure his agreement.

'Certainly ma'am,' he had smiled. One last favour, indeed. It was going to cost her, so who's worrying?

He'd been to see friend Charleton and fixed up the time and place: a pub about fifteen miles from the cottage, aptly called the Crock of Gold, which is what his services had cost Mrs Christina Nicholson.

No one could say Alf Robbins hadn't got a sense of humour.

thirty

Just concentrate on your driving, says Angel. *And stop worrying*. How can I, Angel? I'm dreading meeting Dennis again. Really dreading it.

Well, Frank did offer to come with you ... I know, I know, and I turned him down. This is one battle I've got to fight by myself. *With my help, of course*, says Angel. *Don't forget about me*. Would that I could, Angel.

'Huntersley welcomes careful drivers'. The sign looms suddenly, like a portent of doom, and Chris wishes she had Frank sitting solidly beside her in the passenger seat after all. *Pull yourself together*, says Angel. *And don't go roaring straight through the village in a cloud of dust like the Lone Ranger, never to return, however strong the temptation*.

'It's a large, thirties-type, tarted-up roadhouse,' Alf Robbins had said. 'About halfway down the main drag. Can't miss it.' And, sure enough, there it is. All fake oak beams, hanging baskets, obligatory cartwheels and imitation leaded-light windows.

She drives cautiously past, as if expecting Dennis to materialise out of thin air and force her to a halt, like the demon king in a pantomime. Turning round at the end of the High Street, she parks down a side road facing the Crock of Gold.

Well, don't want to come eyeball to eyeball with him in the car park, Angel. *No. That'd be a real anticlimax*.

Glancing at her watch, she pulls a face. Typical. Ten minutes early, the story of my life. For Chris is one of those people who are always maddeningly punctual; the kind who have to suffer the self-imposed indignity driving round the block several times in order not to be embarrassingly early for a dinner party.

She looks at her reflection in the interior mirror. Hmm, not bad. Totally white-haired, of course. Ever since the . . . ever since my mid-thirties. Still slim. Well, slim*ish*. Though not as slim as when . . . when *he* knew me.

Christ Almighty, exclaims Angel. *It's only bloody Dennis. Who gives a stuff what he thinks of you?* Who indeed, Angel.

Head down, Chris strides briskly towards the saloon bar, like a local celebrity who doesn't want to be recognised and pestered by autograph hunters. *No dark glasses?* says Angel. *Getting bloody paranoid, you are*. Oh shut up Angel. I'm just too strung up to bandy words with you at the moment.

Indeed, Chris is so strung up that she doesn't notice Frank's battered Vauxhall tucked discreetly among a handful of other vehicles at the far end of the car park.

He had arrived half an hour ago and had been halfway down his second Guinness when the man-who-just-had-to-be-Dennis turned up. Only when Dennis had installed himself comfortably at a table by the window did Frank take a seat at the far end of the bar. From there he had a perfect view of Dennis's table. Just in case things got tricky for Chris.

Frank glances at his watch as Chris pushes her way through the swing door. He smiles. Trust her. Bang on time, as ever.

The pub is fairly busy for a Thursday lunchtime. The two youngish barmaids duck and bob busily behind the bar, casting occasional irritated glances at mine host. But he continues to lean across the counter setting the world to rights with a trio of like-minded regulars who are murmuring, 'You're right there, Sam,' and 'Isn't that just

302

what I said last night?' at intervals, like film extras given only limited lines to say so as not to outshine the star.

The plump, balding man sitting by the window half rises from his seat, raising his arm authoritatively to attract attention. Chris realises, with a shock, that it is Dennis.

Christ, he hasn't changed, says Angel. *It's a wonder he doesn't click his fingers at you as though you're his bloody skivvy*. Oh no, Angel. Those days went long ago. You'd better believe it.

Chris walks slowly and deliberately towards him (*That's right. Take your time.*), as uncomfortable under his scrutiny as she was thirty years ago.

'Well,' he says, all smiles, bad breath and false bonhomie, 'long time no see, eh? I must say you're looking well.' His eyes flicker up and down her almost proprietorially. 'Kept yourself in good shape for a woman your age.' Hmm, he thinks. Done all right for herself, by the look of it. Good clothes and jewellery. Probably worth a bob or two. Better keep her sweet. For now.

'Thanks.'

He continues to gaze at her, and there is an awkward little silence.

'Er, how's Florrie?' ventures Chris at length.

'Oh, Mother's fine. As far as I know.' He scowls into his beer. 'Went to live in Aussie-land with her sister Eileen after Dad died. Not that I hear from her much. Doesn't want to know me these days. My own mother.'

And who can blame her? Pity she didn't drown him at birth, says Angel viciously.

Chris clears her throat. 'Well, aren't you going to offer me a drink?'

'Of course. How remiss of me,' says Dennis apologetically. Getting cocky in her old age, he is thinking. We'll see about that. I'll soon cut her down to size. 'Sweet sherry is it?' He gives her a cloyingly sentimental look. 'That's what you always used to drink.'

303

'Not any more. I'll have a gin and tonic please.'

Dennis nods briefly, his smile fixed into place, and lumbers towards the bar.

My God, he looks old, says Angel. *And he's only, what, fifty-six, fifty-seven?*

The mop of springy dark hair has receded almost to the point of non-existence, except for luxuriant tufts above each ear, which meet at the back of his head. The firm jawline and strong features Chris had once so admired are now lost in folds of flesh, the nose already traced with that telltale, blue-veined discolouration which hints at years of alcohol dependence.

That or heart trouble, says Angel. *With any luck he might drop dead before the wedding.* I wish. Except that, knowing him, he'd stay alive just to spite me.

Dennis places the drinks on the table and sits down opposite her. 'Well now, Chrissie. Tell me all about yourself. What have you been up to all these years?' He smiles roguishly and pats her hand with a podgy white paw.

'That would take far too long,' she says briskly, recoiling instinctively from the touch of him, 'and I can't spare the time. Besides, I didn't arrange this meeting for a cosy chat about old times.'

Her ex-husband's smile fades, and he flushes the familiar dull brick-red she remembers so well. 'Touchy and stand-offish as ever, I see. Just making polite conversation, that's all.'

'I haven't come here for polite conversation, Dennis. I've come to discuss our daughter.' *Good girl*, says Angel. *Don't give him a bloody inch.*

Dennis switches on a fond smile, as if suddenly remembering he'd had a daughter once. 'Of course,' he beams. 'And how is Janine?'

Chris blinks. *No one's called her Janine in twenty years*, says Angel.

'She's fine,' says Chris. 'Alive, well and living in the USA. She's very happy and, er, about to get married.'

'Getting married? Left it a bit late, hasn't she? I'd have thought we might have one or two grandchildren running about by now, for all I knew. Not that you ever bothered to keep in touch,' he adds sulkily. 'Never answered any of my letters.'

What did he expect? demands Angel angrily. *Cosy postcards every five minutes saying 'Wish you were here'?*

Dennis stares moodily into the distance, his daughter's wedding plans apparently forgotten already.

Here we go, groans Angel. *Pound to a penny he's going to start banging on about how there's never been anyone like you and how he wishes things could have been different*. And she is absolutely right.

Chris stares at him as he rambles on, undisguised loathing in her eyes. How could I have loved this fat, repulsive slug of a man, Angel? *More to the point, how could you have been afraid of him. He's pathetic*. Absolutely. And to think I was so worried about meeting him again.

'Can we get back to the point of this meeting,' says Chris brusquely. 'Because frankly, Dennis, you're boring me to tears.'

He clenches his fists. Cheeky cow. 'You've grown very hard, Chrissie,' he whines. 'Hard and bitter. You used to be so—'

'Weak? Feeble? Subservient? Not any more.' Avoiding his eyes, Chris takes a deep breath. 'Chaz – our daughter hasn't used the name Janine for donkey's years, by the way – Chaz had the ridiculous idea that her father might actually want to be involved in her wedding plans.'

'So that's it. By involved I take it you expect me to throw money. Well, no chance. If she wants a big flash wedding it's down to you. You look as if you can afford it.'

'No, Dennis.' Chris shakes her head pityingly. 'Actually the ridiculous idea I was talking about was Chaz's notion that you might wish to give her away at her wedding. Father of the bride, and all that.'

'I don't see what's so ridiculous about it,' snaps Dennis. 'I am her father after all. Unless of course you know something I don't know.'

I don't believe it, says Angel incredulously. *He's still trying to put the boot in, after all these years.*

'No Dennis,' says Chris icily. 'Adultery was your game, not mine, though I must say I wish to God she were *not* your daughter. I'm only here because I promised her I would try to find you, God help me.'

He lolls back in his seat, a curious little smile on his lips. 'So she wants to see her old dad again, does she, and you've helped to track me down? Why the change of heart, Chrissie? You've gone to enormous lengths all these years to keep me well away from your precious daughter – *our* precious daughter.'

'My choice, Dennis. I had custody, not you.'

He lunges forward suddenly, like a snake about to strike. From sheer habit, Chris draws back, and, in his seat at the far end of the bar, Frank tenses, ready for action.

'Yes, thanks to your lies!' shouts Dennis. 'You poisoned my own daughter's mind against me!'

'For heaven's sake keep your voice down,' says Chris coldly. 'You know as well as I do that you could have faced criminal charges of assault against Chaz if I'd chosen to pursue it, and don't you forget it. And as for poisoning her mind against you, don't worry, she has no idea why we left you in such a hurry.' She gives a mirthless little laugh. 'Oh don't imagine I kept it from her for your sake, believe me. I just didn't want Chaz to grow up knowing she'd got a child molester for a father.'

'Still playing the drama queen, I see,' sneers Dennis. 'I showed her no more than the usual fatherly love and affection, that's all, and you can't prove a bloody thing against me.' He tips the remains of his drink down his throat and gives her a nasty little smile. 'Anyway, you've got a bloody short memory, Chrissie. It was all in your mind, remember? Always was. And if you think you can just wipe out the past—'

'I don't suppose your own past bears too close an inspection, Dennis,' counters Chris hotly, unable to keep from interrupting him. And, to her surprise, Dennis shuts his mouth abruptly.

Bloody hell, says Angel. *He's gone white as a sheet.*

'If that's some kind of threat you can forget it,' he says menacingly.

Threat? What's he talking about, Angel? *God knows, and He won't split.*

Without consulting her, Dennis suddenly stands up and swaggers to the bar to replenish their drinks. Frank relaxes slightly. Panic over. For the moment.

Gripping the arms of her chair, Chris fights to regain her composure. Get me out of here, Angel. I feel sick. Why don't I just make a dash for it? Drive off in a cloud of exhaust fumes and pretend I've never been here. *Don't you dare*, says Angel. *Dennis'd love that. He'd love to feel he can still put the wind up you, even after all these years. Besides, you've come this far; now stick it out – for Chaz's sake.*

Dennis returns with their drinks and sits down heavily opposite her once again. 'What's the blushing groom-to-be like?' he asks nonchalantly. 'Or haven't you had the pleasure yet?'

He's changing the subject, says Angel. *Always used to do that when he was in a corner. You've got him on the run, kid.*

Chris smiles. 'Oh, yes, I have had the pleasure, and so have you, long ago. You remember Trish? Silly question, of course you do.'

'*That* slag! What's *she* got to do with anything? I'm

307

amazed she didn't pop off years ago. Hopefully from some sexually transmitted disease.'

'That slag, as you call her, happens to be the groom's mother, actually,' smiles Chris. 'And you will be relieved to know that she is alive and well living in the USA with her Italian-American husband.' With that, Chris sits back to watch Dennis's reaction. His face is an absolute picture, Angel. Perfect. She almost laughs out loud.

'What are you smirking at?' snaps Dennis. (*Just like old times*, giggles Angel. *Had to ask his permission to smile in the old days.*) 'Don't tell me you're pleased that Son of Slag is contemplating marrying our daughter?'

'Well, yes,' grins Chris confidently. 'He's a lovely young man. I couldn't wish for a better son-in-law.' She looks at Dennis curiously. 'Anyway, what do you mean, "contemplating" marrying Chaz? Ian's not "contemplating" anything. The wedding plans are well in hand now.'

Gotcha, thinks Dennis. Gotcha, you supercilious bitch. 'Oh dear, oh dear,' he says, and to Chris's astonishment, he begins to laugh. *What's his game?* growls Angel.

'It really is too much.' Dennis pulls out a grimy handkerchief and makes a big show of pretending to mop at his eyes. 'You obviously don't want me at our daughter's wedding, my dear Chrissie. That is all too plain. Well, your wish has been granted. I won't be there. But then neither will you.'

'What the hell are you talking about? Of course I'll be there.'

The laughter stops as abruptly as it has begun. 'No you won't. There won't be any wedding for you to attend.'

Chris stares at him in complete mystification. *Surely he doesn't imagine he can stop the wedding?* says Angel. *What possible influence can he hope to have?*

That's got her worried, thinks Dennis smugly. 'Remember the so-called business trip to Ireland, Chrissie?' he says softly.

'Of course I do. You made me look a complete idiot.'

'You *were* a complete idiot. Probably still are. Fancy you not realising that my little playmate was none other than the lovely Trish, your erstwhile best friend and confidante.'

'Yes, thank you for that Dennis,' says Chris quietly. 'You claimed you could have taken your pick of all the silly little girls at the office, but you had to choose Trish. You really enjoyed regaling me with all the lurid details, too, as I recall. Even had to spoil my memories of childhood holidays in Swanage by choosing that very spot for your tacky little affair.' Chris blows her nose. *For Christ's sake don't weaken now*, says Angel. *Don't give Dennis the satisfaction.* 'That's all water under the bridge now,' Chris goes on airily. 'Doesn't change a thing. Chaz and Ian are going to be married in a few weeks' time and there's no reason on earth why they shouldn't.'

'Oh, but there is.' Dennis smirks at her. 'Still don't get it, do you? Christ, you always were thick. Me and Trish were having an affair long before that week in Swanage. Trish couldn't keep her hands off me from the moment she and Nick moved in next door.'

Don't listen to him, commands Angel. But at the mention of Nick's name, Chris is hooked. She blanches, staring at Dennis in disbelief.

And that's wiped the smile off *her* face, thinks Dennis triumphantly.

'You were fat, pregnant and boring,' he says, moving in for the kill. 'Nick couldn't provide enough for a slag like Trish so . . .' He shrugs.

'I don't believe it. Your . . . affair with Trish didn't start until after Nick left her.'

'Don't want to believe it, you mean. That's you all over.'

He finishes his drink in one gulp, and thumps his glass down on the table. 'There can be no wedding, you thick bitch, for the simple reason that *I* am Ian's father. *I* got Trish pregnant, not that useless sod, Nick.' He smiles cruelly. 'Even you must see that it's not a very clever idea for a half-brother and sister to marry each other.'

Dumbfounded and desolate, Chris sits, her shoulders bowed. *Lying b-bastard*, whispers Angel brokenly.

Dennis stands up and gazes down at her. 'I'm off. Don't waste your breath telling me it's been a pleasure seeing me again, after all these years. The pleasure's been all mine, I assure you. If only to put the record straight.

'Now you can crawl back to our precious daughter and tell her she'd better find someone else to marry.'

thirty-one

After leaving the Crock of Gold Dennis had waited patiently in his car for Chris to emerge. Then he had simply followed her home – at a safe distance, of course. Wouldn't do for the bitch to know what he was up to.

Parking a few yards past Chris's cottage, he had made a note of the address. Never knew when it might come in handy.

Indeed, Dennis had been so preoccupied that he'd scarcely given the scruffy black Vauxhall a second glance, as it negotiated carefully round him and drove slowly on down the lane.

At the wheel of the Vauxhall, Frank had frowned. What's the bugger up to now?

Not that Dennis had a clue who Frank was, of course. He had just dismissed the Vauxhall driver as some stupid git who'd lost his way. Stood to reason. Anyone who could afford to live round here wouldn't be driving an old heap like that. Obvious to someone as sharp as Dennis. 'So sharp you'll cut yer bleedin' self one of these days,' his mother always used to say.

Very nice properties round this neck of the woods, he had thought. *Very* nice. Trust bloody Chrissie to land on her feet.

It's not fair, he had thought, driving back to his dismal lodgings in Uxbridge. Why should I have to live in squalor while she plays lady of the bloody manor in leafy Cookham? Eh? Answer me that.

But of course, no one did.

*

Lolling on his bed, Dennis is beginning to feel a little more cheerful. Especially since downing at least three tumblers of vodka from the bottle of Smirnoff's at his elbow following his meeting with his ex-wife.

At least he's managed to put *her* nose severely out of joint, Dennis is thinking. And that's just for starters. He's even been handed a heaven-sent opportunity to take a pop at that slag Trish, into the bargain. Can't be bad.

He raises his glass towards the ceiling. Thank you God. And thank you Chrissie, for being stupid enough to pay that poor man's Colombo – complete with dirty mac – to seek me out. Hope you're satisfied. I know I am.

Topping up his glass, Dennis smirks to himself. Chrissie needn't think he's going to scuttle obligingly back into the shadows after she ruined his life all those years ago. Oh dear me no. He hasn't finished with her yet. Her or her precious daughter. Needn't think she can just do another disappearing act, either. He's found out where she lives now, did she but know it.

Dennis lights a cigarette and leans back against the headboard, sipping thoughtfully.

It's all her fault his life has gone sour. Hers and that slag Trish's.

Everything in the garden was rosy once. His career had started to take off, he'd had his foot on the first rung of the property ladder, he'd had a submissive wife and a pretty little daughter. What more could any man have wanted?

Then that slag next door had to start putting ideas into Chrissie's head, ruining everything. Chrissie, the only woman he'd ever really loved (or so he has convinced himself), had done a runner, taking his daughter with her. Then she had the bloody cheek to divorce him and force the sale of his home.

And now he is reduced to this.

He glances around his seedy room, seeing as if for

the first time the stained, threadbare carpet, the cheap, ill-fitting curtains and the ghastly, ivy-patterned wallpaper. Poison bloody ivy, more like.

To think he has to live like this, while she's queening it in a des. res. that must be worth tens of thousands. No, hundreds of thousands. And what has he ever done to deserve it?

Tears of self-pity fill his eyes as he gulps down his drink, and pours himself another.

The house in Wooburn Green had sold readily enough, but by the time the mortgage vultures had been paid off and that bitch took her share, there was hardly enough to buy a rabbit hutch, let alone something suitable for a man of his standing.

Renting a luxurious flat close to his London office, he had lived well, while the money lasted, eating in the best restaurants and seeking out women who shared his particular sexual tastes. Life had been sweet.

He frowns. Then he had to meet bloody Sharon at that office do. Christmas party for the staff and their spouses – for 'partners' hadn't been invented back then. In those days a partner was someone who had a financial interest in a business. End of story.

Sharon had been all over him from the off, never mind that she was the thirty-year-old second wife of Dennis's boss. 'Well, Bill just don't satisfy me, Den,' she had confided drunkenly, as Dennis groped her enthusiastically over the photocopier in Despatch. 'Know what I mean?'

Dennis had known exactly what she meant. He was just the man to satisfy her all right. And, over the few weeks of their affair, she'd accumulated the bruises to prove it. Bruises that old Bill Harris clocked one night when she was getting undressed. He'd gone ballistic and given Sharon a few more to add to her extensive collection.

Dennis shakes his head. Bad news that was. Sharon had

tried crying 'Rape!' but couldn't make it stick. Especially when Dennis produced those six by eight glossies of the innocent rape victim posing in that bondage gear he'd bought for her, complete with rubber cut-out bra and matching crutchless knickers.

The managing director had suggested Dennis should quietly resign, but, like a fool Dennis had insisted on a handsome 'redundancy' payment in return for the negatives. Big mistake.

With a sardonic this-is-going-to-hurt-you-more-than-it's-going-to-hurt-me expression, the MD had produced a file from his desk drawer. Seemingly the company had clear evidence that Dennis had been fiddling his expenses for some time. (Well, wasn't everybody? thinks Dennis indignantly. Perk of the job that. Well-known fact.) Dennis was coldly asked whether he would prefer to be prosecuted and fired in disgrace, or simply tender his resignation and disappear on the spot.

Needless to say, Dennis had opted for the latter.

He scowls at the memory. Landed in the shit by yet another stupid bitch. The story of his life. If only he hadn't been so attractive to women. They were always throwing themselves at him, just like that slag, Trish, so many years ago. She had been the start of all his problems.

His affair with her had meant nothing, nothing at all. All men cheat on their wives, given half a chance. Well, men like Dennis do. And after Nick walked out on her Trish had been bloody gagging for it. Dennis smiles. Never one to look a gift horse in the mouth, me.

And Chrissie turning up after all these years had turned out to be a gift horse and a half, all right. Dennis pours himself another drink.

Planting that rubbish about fathering young Ian had been a master stroke. That had wiped the smile off her face, the smug, self-satisfied bitch.

Trish would deny it, of course, and Chrissie would want

to believe her. But there would always be that little worm of doubt, wriggling and niggling away.

He chuckles. Love to be a fly on the wall when dear Trish finds out. Her and her Wop husband.

Trish's second husband, Gus Pannitti, is immensely proud of his hot-blooded Italian ancestry. Indeed, he has made a career out of it, affecting the sharp-suited, blue-chinned tough-guy image popularised in films of the *Godfather* genre.

Like the screen characters, his parents, Sophia and Antonio, had hit Ellis Island as poor immigrants in the twenties and, like them, had made good in America, land of opportunity. But in a modest way, you understand. In a very modest way.

Sophia and Antonio never lost their musical Italian accents, but when Gus and his brothers and sisters – all seven of them – opened their mouths, it was pure Bronx. Not surprising, considering they were all born over Toni's Deli on the West Side. Though as a young man Gus was to embroider upon his humble beginnings, giving just enough of a hint of Family connections (with a capital F) to give him what he saw as 'an edge' in his business dealings.

And it had worked. Gus's brothers and sisters were now scattered all over the USA: in Chicago, Detroit, San Francisco – you name it. But Gus had stayed in New York, duty-bound to care for Toni's Deli and Toni himself, who had never been the same since Sophia's death bearing their final child. Giuseppe.

When his father died in the early seventies, thirty-five-year-old Gus began to carve a successful career for himself in business. No, not the food business. Gus had sliced enough salami and mixed enough tubs of Toni's Real Italian Salad Dressing to last a lifetime. Gus had gone into the used car business and had never looked back.

Over the next twenty years, Gus married (disastrously),

became a father, got divorced (inevitably) and poured all his considerably energy into building both a substantial business in the motor trade and a handsome near-mansion in the affluent suburbs of Boston.

Five years ago, Gus met and married Trish. Best goddamn thing he ever did, in his view.

As you might imagine, Gus is not a patient man under normal circumstances. But these circumstances are not normal, not normal at all.

Ever since she came off the phone, Trish has been so upset that he has been unable to get a coherent word out of her. So he simply waits, makes coffee, and does his best to comfort her, knowing that eventually her tears will turn to blistering anger and he will discover the reason for her distress. As usual, he is right.

'I just don't believe that asshole,' rails Trish. 'Coming back to haunt us after all these years with such a crock of shit. Poor Chrissie! As if she hasn't suffered enough. Wasn't it enough for him to rub her nose in our solitary dirty weekend – which, God knows, I've bitterly regretted for my entire goddamn life . . . Wasn't that enough? Not for *him* it wasn't. And now he's trying to say that my . . . my darling Ian . . . How can the guy do that stuff? And to his only daughter?'

Encircling her with his arms, Gus kisses her lightly on the mouth. 'Now, honey, why don't you just drink your coffee, have a cigarette, take a deep breath then tell me the whole bangshoot? I've gotten too old to play guessing games.'

Trish nods and, for once, does exactly as she is told.

When she finally stops talking, Gus's face is grim. 'Guy ain't got a leg to stand on. If he tries to stop the wedding, a blood test'd prove once and for all that he can't be Ian's daddy. No way. Oh, no, honey, not that *I* expect proof, believe me, but it might come to that if this guy gets nasty.'

'*Gets* nasty? He's already bad enough. I'm amazed Chrissie actually wanted to get in touch with the shit, but according to her old friend, Frank – the one who phoned to tell me all this – she did it for Chaz. Kid wants her ever-loving daddy to give her away at her wedding, like any normal daughter would.'

'Even though she knows the old man used to beat up on Chrissie?'

'Apparently, yes.' Trish takes a thoughtful sip. 'Mind you, I often used to wonder whether there was more to it than that, whether something else happened that I never did find out about. Maybe she was worried he might start beating up on the kid ...' She shrugs. 'But I guess I'll never know now. Jeez, if only Dennis Stanley Charleton had fallen off his twig long ago. Would have saved us all this ... this pain.'

'*That* could be arranged, believe me.' Gus gives a harsh little laugh. 'I got friends and family all over that'd be only too pleased to rid the world of a shitheel like him. It wouldn't even cost much, either.'

Trish glances at him, open-mouthed. There he goes, she thinks fondly. Going into his Mafiosi routine again. He's still a great big kid, her Gus. Wouldn't harm a fly in reality. Or would he?

'You *are* kidding me, Gus?'

'Sure, honey, sure,' says Gus easily, patting her arm. 'Guy like that don't deserve to walk God's earth, though. Certainly don't deserve a fine daughter like Chaz. How can he hurt his own flesh? Sure beats the hell outa me. And why does he hate you so much that he'd tell such a pack of dirty lies about you?'

Trish sighs. 'Thirty years ago I had this, this one-night stand with him, to my eternal shame. Then, not content with encouraging my very best friend in all the world to leave the shit while she was still in one piece, I called in the cops when she finally made her escape.' She shivers. 'I

317

was convinced he'd killed her. He's quite capable of . . . of that. Believe me, hon, that's more than enough for a man like Dennis Charleton to hate my guts and want to hurt me, even after all this time.'

'Ain't no one gonna get to my girl,' growls Gus.

But Trish is lost in the past, tears trickling down her face. 'I never saw Chrissie again. Never had a chance to explain, to try and put things right.'

'Never mind, hon, in just a few weeks your Chrissie will be flying across the pond for the wedding and you'll be meeting up with her again. Then you'll be able to put her right once and for all. How d'ya like them apples?'

'I'm terrified,' says Trish.

Gus smiles easily and opens his arms wide. 'Come here, dummy,' he says softly. And Trish allows herself to be enfolded, burying her head into his shoulder. Gazing into the distance, Gus's smile fades abruptly.

Trish would have been shocked to witness the expression on his face.

'Well that just about settles it,' says Frank flatly, putting down the receiver. 'I've had a long conversation with your friend Trish and she said it's an absolute pack of lies. Poor lady was distraught. She was horrified by the suggestion that Ian could be anything but Nick's son. Said it was typical of the sort of poisonous lies your charming ex-husband was capable of dreaming up. There, I've only given you the important bits, but does it make you feel any better?'

'Hugely. Sorry to ask you to do my dirty work for me,' (*Yet again*, says Angel) 'but I had to know, straight from the horse's mouth, so to speak. I was too . . . too bloody chicken to speak to Trish myself after all these years.' (*Pathetic!*) 'I just knew the bastard was lying through his teeth' (*Oh yeah. Sure you did*), 'but just wanted . . .'

'Just wanted confirmation,' concludes Frank gently.

Chris nods. 'Chaz and Ian must never know about this,' she says firmly. *Oh come on*, protests Angel.

'But here's your chance to make Chaz realise what a shit he really is,' says Frank incredulously. 'Might help her understand why you couldn't endure living with a man like that.'

Couldn't endure living with him! says Angel indignantly. *There was more to it than that, as we know.* Yes, Angel, which is exactly why I don't want the corpse of my marriage to Dennis dug up for inspection. It would mean opening up a whole can of worms I'd rather Chaz never knew about.

'Chaz must never know, Frank,' says Chris stubbornly. 'And that's my final word on the subject.'

'But what *are* you going to tell Chaz?'

'I'll think of something. Make up some reason why Dennis can't be at the wedding. Tell her I couldn't find him. Anything.'

'That's all very well,' says Frank slowly, 'but to be honest – and I'm not just being alarmist – I can't see Dennis Charleton giving up that easily.' Why else did the man follow you back to the cottage after your meeting at the Crock of Gold? he wants to add. Why else did he make a note of the address?

More to the point, thinks Frank grimly, why didn't I trail the bastard back to his home that afternoon? Why didn't I find out where he lives, instead of rushing to the cottage to comfort Chris, who he'd found breaking her heart over Dennis's revelations.

'But what can Dennis do?' says Chris. 'It's not as if I'm about to give him Chaz's address so that he can tell her his poisonous little story. What possible harm can it do to just forget he exists? I've done it before and I can do it again.' *Bravo*, says Angel.

But Frank gazes at her bleakly. 'I'm just not prepared to take the risk. I won't tolerate even the thought of him hurting you and Chaz any more. We've got to be sure of getting him completely out of your life. And for good this time.'

'You sound as if you're about to bump him off or something,' says Chris, smiling in spite of herself.

As if, says Angel. *I just can't imagine sweet, gentle Frank doing anyone a mischief. Not even Dennis.*

Alf Robbins is like a dog with two tails. He is on his way to meet another new client! And within days of being paid off by Mrs Whasserface Nicholson for services rendered.

Be able to retire soon at this rate, thinks Alf. No you can't, you soft sod. There's hardly enough in the kitty to settle your rent arrears, let alone jet off to spend your declining years in a retirement villa on the Costa Dorada with a blonde on each arm and all the Piña Coladas you can drink.

Still, at least I'll be able eat somewhere a bit upmarket from Chez Fat Cypriot for a few weeks. McDonald's, for instance. Or Burger King. That'd be really living.

The new client, a Mr Kelly, had agreed to meet at Alf's usual pub, since, like all the others, he wished to avoid home ground. They're all the same, thinks Alf wearily. Still, can't blame 'em for being a bit twitchy, I s'pose. They'd usually got themselves in a right old state by the time they resorted to Alf's services. Bloody paranoid, some of 'em.

Alf arrives at the Oaks and strolls to the bar to get himself a drink.

'Your usual, Alfie?' says Carole, the publican's wife, all jet black bouffant and blue eyeshadow. And all because some drunken customer once told her she looked like Elizabeth Taylor.

'Yes please, dear,' says Alf. 'And I'll have a packet of cheese 'n' onion and one of your panatellas to go with it.'

320

'Oooh,' squeals Carole. 'Come up on the lottery 'ave yer? 'Cos if that's the case p'raps you wouldn't mind settling your slate. Me 'n' my Barry could retire in clover on what you owe.'

'Yeah. Later, darlin', later,' says Alf airily. 'No prob.' Christ, he is thinking, me and my big mouth. Bleedin' vulture she is, that Carole. One sniff of the folding stuff an' she's on to it like a bloody ton of bricks. She's wasted here. Shoulda got a job with the bleedin' Inland Revenue.

Forcing himself not to break into a run, Alf heads for his usual corner seat next to the archway leading to the snug. Ever since an eighteen-month spell inside, as a young man (which *really* put the kibosh on his youthful ambitions to join the Met, good and proper), Alf has always believed in sitting with his back to a wall. Next to an exit, preferably. That way it's easier to make a quick getaway if things get sticky.

Not that Alf is expecting any trouble from the as-yet-unknown Mr Kelly. It's just that old habits die hard, and that particular old habit has served him well. Up to now, that is.

Alf puffs happily away on his panatella, watching the main entrance. What's it all about this time, Alfie, he wonders, smiling at his little witticism. The client had sounded really wound up about something, that was for sure. Probably suspects his wife's playing away, poor sod. Still, can't knock it. Other people's little adventures form the bedrock of Alf's business, such as it is. Long live sin, he thinks, lifting his glass.

As the man slides into the seat beside him, Alf splutters into his beer. Bloody hell. Must be losing me grip. No wonder I didn't see the feller come in. He's slipped through from the Snug. Must have been in there all along, watching me across the bar. Make a good private eye, he would. Bloody sight better than me, an' all.

'Right,' says the man, without preamble. 'I need to get

in touch with a Dennis Stanley Charleton and I believe you can tell me where he is.'

It gets better, thinks Alf. Two enquiries about the same geezer in as many weeks. I can't miss, here.

'I can certainly make enquiries for you, no probs,' smiles Alf encouragingly. 'It'll cost you, of course.'

But his new client is not smiling. 'Don't mess me about. Please. You've been in touch with Charleton very recently, for another client, so there'll be no question of any further fee. Just give me an address and I'll be off.'

Alf's smile becomes even broader. What does this bloke take him for? Some kind of mug? He shakes his head in mock bewilderment.

'I'm afraid it just doesn't work like that, squire. New client, new fee – that's my usual system. Know what I mean?'

Mr Kelly gives a weary sigh. 'And my usual system, I'm afraid, is to resort to violence when I don't get what I want immediately.' Without warning, his hand dives under the table and grips Alf's testicles, squeezing and twisting spitefully. 'Know what I mean?' he smiles.

Behind the bar, Carole's lipglossed mouth hangs open. ''Ere Bah,' she whispers theatrically. 'Don't look now, but that bloke over there's only gone an' grabbed old Alf by the balls!'

'Takes all sorts,' says Barry philosophically, busy with his crossword.

'Oh, I don't think Alf's that way inclined.'

Barry folds his newspaper carefully and lays it down on the bar. Can't get a minute's peace in this place, he thinks, what with old Carole rabbiting on. 'Joke, Carole, joke,' he says resignedly. 'P'raps Alf owes the fella money an' he's being persuaded to pay up. You know what they say, grab 'em by the balls and their hearts and minds follow.'

'But he's gone a terrible colour, Bah. Hope he ain't gonna pass out on us.'

'Not before he pays his fuckin' bill anyway,' says Barry grimly. 'Bet Alf'd soon stop pissing about if I tried that bloke's methods.'

In his corner seat, Alf has indeed stopped pissing about. 'I'm sure we can come to some arrangement, Mr, er, Mr Kelly,' he gasps.

'I knew you'd see sense.' The man relaxes his grip. 'What sort of an arrangement?'

'Well,' says Alf carefully, 'the client who got me to trace the bloke in the first place didn't want to know anything about him, not even an address. Just wanted me to arrange a meeting. Which I did.'

'And got paid for it.'

'Oh, yes, absolutely.'

'But?'

'But in the, ah . . . in the course of my investigations, I accidentally uncovered rather a lot about friend Charleton. Stuff that might be of interest. To the right person, that is.'

'Go on. I'm still listening.'

Alf pauses to mop his brow. *Bloody hell. I'm sweating like a pig, here.* 'Well, er, it seems friend Charleton's had rather a . . . rather a chequered career, to say the least. I've built up quite a tidy little dossier on him, as a matter of fact. It's in my car outside . . .'

Alf lets his words hang in the air, while his companion frowns thoughtfully.

'How much?' asks the sinister Mr Kelly.

'Well, shall we say two hundred?'

The man gives Alf a humourless smile. 'No. I think we'll say more like eighty, don't you, Mr Robbins? Expecting to get paid twice for the same piece of work is really rather greedy, and I do so *detest* greed. Fortunately for you, though, I'm feeling in a generous mood.'

Alf gulps. 'Eighty it is then. I'll just go to my car and—'

Gripping Alf's forearm, Mr Kelly shakes his head menacingly. 'Oh no, Mr Robbins. *We'll* go to your car together, and when I'm satisfied that the so-called dossier is worth having you'll get your money.'

'Anything you say.'

Jesus Christ, thinks Alf. Wouldn't like to be in friend Charleton's shoes when this bugger catches up with him, that's for sure.

And where did he learn his stuff? The bloody IRA? He's certainly got the right accent.

thirty-two

Frank wishes to God he'd never pushed Chris into meeting up with Dennis Charleton. She's been a bundle of nerves ever since, despite his attempts at reassurance.

Right now she is pacing the room like a cat on hot bricks, thanks to yet another phone call from Chaz.

'What on earth am I going to do, Frank? I keep stalling, saying I haven't had any luck finding Dennis, but I can't keep that up for ever. The wedding's only weeks off and she's getting twitchy.'

Frank gives what he hopes is an encouraging smile. 'Not half as twitchy as you're getting. For heaven's sake, Dennis has made his nasty, cruel little move and I wouldn't mind betting that's the last we'll hear from him.'

Eh? says Angel. *He's changed his tune.*

Chris stops pacing and looks at Frank curiously. 'But only a couple of days ago you were talking as if he'd go to almost diabolical lengths to ruin Chaz's future. Now here you are dismissing the whole thing as some kind of minor hiccup. What's brought this on?'

Diabolical lengths, thinks Frank. What a good idea. He shrugs, picking up today's *Daily Telegraph*. 'Oh, you know me,' he says vaguely, 'ever the optimist.'

Weird, says Angel.

Frank sits pretending to read while Chris makes her preparations to leave for one of her sessions at the Citizens' Advice Bureau.

Only after she has pecked him distractedly on the top of

the head and left the house does Frank move. Standing at the window, he watches Chris's car disappear down the lane. Then he goes upstairs and takes a brown manila folder from his bedroom chest of drawers. This'd better be good, he thinks. It's cost me eighty quid.

Making himself comfortable with a large drink and a cigarette, Frank begins to read.

Looks as if Alf Robbins has done a good job, he thinks approvingly. See what he means about Dennis's 'chequered career', too.

From the home that he had shared with Chris, long ago, Dennis had moved to an expensive flat in Connaught Street, just off Hyde Park – an area that Alf Robbins knew very well, as luck would have it. For Alf had been born in St Mary's Hospital, Paddington, and, until his brush with the law at the age of twenty-two, had lived cheek by jowl with his hugely extended family in the warren of streets to the rear of Paddington Station.

Over the years, Alf had built up and maintained a useful number of contacts in the pubs and clubs of the area. Which was another bit of luck, for as Alf had said in his dossier, Dennis Charleton was a man who 'liked to party'.

Forsaking the smarter clubs and restaurants, presumably through what Alf called 'lack of funds', Dennis had very quickly become an habitué of some of the more dubious clubs to be found around Praed Street. Clubs that Alf knew well. Well enough to have no trouble gaining access to old membership registers, where one or two of Dennis's changes of address were still faithfully recorded.

From then on, it had been easy, according to Alf's notes. Dennis had worked in a variety of different jobs over the years, each one more downmarket than the last. He had never spent more than a few months in each place and always, it was hinted, left under a cloud. He had moved house fairly frequently too, often doing what Alf quaintly described as a 'moonlight flit' to avoid settling his rent bills, thus leaving a trail of irate landlords in his wake.

The information Alf had been able to glean from aggrieved former landlords was of particular interest, and painted a grim picture of a man spiralling downwards into ever more sleazy accommodation. Sometimes Dennis was thrown out before he had a chance to leave of his own accord, and Alf's sources were vocal in their condemnation of a man described by one as 'a bleedin' menace, with his women and his drinking. I even caught him touching up my granddaughter once. Only six, she was. Dirty git. 'Course, I threw him out there and then. Gave me the creeps he did.'

Now that's very interesting, thinks Frank. I'd gathered Charleton used to knock Chris about, and according to these notes he still enjoys what Alf calls 'a bit of rough stuff' when he can get it. But I'd no idea the evil bastard liked little girls. That comes up again and again.

At last Frank is beginning to understand why Chris left her loving husband and why she had gone to such extraordinary lengths to keep Chaz away from him.

According to Alf's dossier, Dennis's working life seemed to have ended four years ago, when he was fired from a drinking club where he had worked as a part-time barman. At first, the manager of the club had maintained that Dennis had been fired for what he called 'dipping his hand in the till once too often'. But over several glasses, he had confided to Alf that Dennis Charleton had been nothing but an unreliable, drunken womaniser with a penchant for young girls. Oh, nothing proven, of course. No official complaint to the police or anyone else. Still, muses Frank, no smoke without fire, as they say.

At about that time, Dennis had suddenly left London, renting a shabby room in a an anonymous redbrick semi in Uxbridge, where he had remained ever since, keeping a low profile. Until now. What made him leave the area where he had spent so many years, wonders Frank. Upset too many people, maybe. The wrong people.

Frank closes the file with a sigh. Time to do something about Dennis Stanley Charleton, I reckon.

Sylvie Bates looks across the kitchen table at Dennis and wonders, not for the first time, why on earth she has put up with him for so long.

There he sits, chomping away at his meal, reading the *Sun* propped against the sauce bottles, completely ignoring her, as usual. Until he wants something, of course, she thinks bitterly. Like sex, for example. They're all the same, men.

She had been glad of his company at first, God help her. Liked to have a man around the house, did Sylvie. She shakes her head. Bloody fool I've been, ever since my Bob passed away.

Sylvie's husband, a builder, had fallen to his death while working on a new block of flats in Hillingdon, seven years previously. As his widow she had eventually received a sizeable sum by way of compensation, though not without an unseemly struggle with his erstwhile employers.

'Tried to tell me he wasn't wearing his hard hat, if you ever,' she was to tell old Mrs Fellowes, next door. 'Bare-faced lie, that was. Not that it would've made any odds either way. Not considering the poor bugger fell from the eleventh floor. Some cock-up with the scaffolding . . .'

She had burst into tears, and Mrs Fellowes had vaguely murmured something about life going on and how she wasn't to upset herself. Don't encourage her too much, Vera, Mrs Fellowes had thought. Or you'll have her and that brat of hers taking it out on your door knocker every five minutes. Didn't do to get too involved. Unless there was something in it for her, of course.

'My brief said that site was a bloody death trap,' Sylvie had sniffled. 'Reckoned I could take Bob's firm to the cleaners. But the case could drag on for ages, and what am I supposed to do for money in the meantime? What are me and my Mark supposed to live on? Fresh air?'

Mrs Fellowes had shrugged, growing bored with the conversation, until Sylvie added, 'So I've decided to settle out of court. That way I can pay off the mortgage and still have a few grand left over.'

'Quite right, dear. You wanna take the money and run, if you ask me.' And Mrs Fellowes ('Just call me Vera, dear') had smiled her gummy smile and invited Sylvie in for a cup of tea and half a packet of Jaffa Cakes.

A month or so after Bob's death, Sylvie found herself comparatively well off. By her standards. For the first time in her life she had money in the bank, her own cheque book with 'Mrs Sylvia M. Holdness' printed on it, having changed name by deed poll, and no mortgage to pay. And it was heady stuff, believe me.

'Why shouldn't you get out and about a bit, dear?' Vera had suggested. 'Young woman like you. I'll always babysit your Mark. Dear little chap.' And Sylvie had nodded appreciatively, her eyes filling with tears of gratitude.

'What shall we say then, dear?' Vera had continued briskly. 'Four pounds an hour and time-and-a-half after midnight? Better to keep it on a business footing I always say. Saves any awkwardness.'

So, to save any awkwardness, Sylvie had agreed, and Vera had wished she'd said five pounds an hour.

For a while Sylvie had been a regular customer at the Globe in the High Street, among other places. And it was here that she had met Gorgeous Graham, a six-feet-two casual labourer (very casual in his case) with black curls, matching eyelashes, a nice line in chat . . . and very little else.

Within weeks, and to Vera's dismay (''Spose that's put the tin lid on my baby-sitting money,' she had thought) Graham had moved in with Sylvie and Mark, and made himself thoroughly at home.

329

But Vera needn't have worried. Sylvie and Graham continued to enjoy an active social life, for a while, using her babysitting services more than ever. ('I've been thinking, Sylvie. Four pounds an hour's hardly worth my while, really. What say we put it up to five?')

With Graham more than willing to help Sylvie spend her money, it hadn't lasted long. Nor had Graham. And once he got wind of her pregnancy, he was off like a dose of salts.

Vera hadn't been exactly sympathetic either. 'Brought it on yourself, Sylvie, that's what you've done. Could've told you that Graham was a bad lot, but it wasn't my place to interfere . . . What d'you mean, he's had all your money? Well don't look at me, dear. I've only got my pension to live off, you know. And it's "Mrs Fellowes" if you don't mind.'

Pregnant and panic-stricken, Sylvie had advertised for a lodger for the back bedroom: 'Bed, breakfast and evening meal £50 pw plus some help in house and garden. Close to Uxbridge tube. Suit bachelor.'

The first lodger had lasted two years, and that was two years too long. Poor old Mr Cummings had certainly been in no fit state to help anyone around the house and garden. Sylvie should have been able to see that from the start. But she was desperate. Besides, she had taken pity on the old chap and had ended up nursing him until he was eventually taken into hospital, terminally ill. He had died very shortly afterwards.

Breathing a small, sad sigh of relief, Sylvie had re-advertised, and Dennis Stanley Charleton had entered her life.

How she regrets it now.

At first, he had been on his best behaviour. Nothing was too much trouble. He had been all over Sylvie and two-and-a-half-year-old Clare, Graham's child. He had played the perfect surrogate father to Mark, taking him to football matches, kicking a ball around the garden and generally ingratiating himself with the boy.

He was even willing to babysit Clare of a Wednesday evening, so that Mark could go to youth club, as usual, and Sylvie could have what Dennis called 'a well-deserved break'. He even insisted on bathing Clare himself before putting her to bed.

Not surprisingly, Sylvie was delighted with her new lodger. Predictably, and within a shockingly short space of time, she and Dennis had become lovers.

'Disgusting,' Mrs Fellowes had tutted to anyone who would listen, though most of the neighbours avoided her like the plague. 'Just a common tart, that Sylvie Bates. Well, she's bitten off more than she can chew with her new bloke, if you ask me. Don't like the look of him, I don't. Not one little bit.'

She was right, of course.

Four years on, Dennis has tired of young Mark, now a surly teenager, who thinks himself the man of the house and resents Dennis's very presence. 'Why should I do what you say? You're not my Dad!' Mark would shout, typically. 'Thank God for that,' Dennis would reply. 'Though if I were, I'd take my belt to your arse!' 'Just try it, that's all. Just try it!' And so on.

To make matters worse, having left school the moment he could, Mark has so far been unable to find himself a job and is thrown into Dennis's company for long periods of the day. For Dennis has long since tired of making any pretence of working for a living, preferring to sit around the house for hours on end, getting under Sylvie's feet, carping and complaining.

Sitting opposite Dennis at the kitchen, Mark looks up from his plate of food and catches the expression on his mother's face as she stands, leaning against the kitchen sink, staring at Dennis. Poor Mum. Obviously can't stand the bloke any more, so why, why doesn't she just chuck him out? They could get another lodger. Easy. Mark grins, in spite of himself. Yeah, that's what they oughter do. Young blonde tart with big tits, maybe.

Mark knows Mum and Dennis still sleep together occasionally. 'Specially when they've both had a skinful. He frowns. Not that it seems to give Mum much joy. Bloody row they make sometimes . . . Christ you'd think the bloke was half killing her at times. Certainly didn't sound like much fun. And Mark has seen bruises on her neck and arms more than once. Mentioned it to her even.

'It's nothing, son.' Sylvie had laughed unconvincingly. 'You're a bit young to understand yet, but, well, all couples get a bit carried away sometimes. It's nothing, nothing at all.'

'Oh yeah? And I suppose it's nothing the way he hangs round our Clare all the time, either, making her sit on his lap, pinching and tickling her all the time. Kissing her. It makes me feel sick to my stomach.'

Sylvie had given him a sharp cuff around the ear. 'Dirty-minded little sod!' she had exclaimed, cheeks flaming. 'He loves little Clare. Reminds him of a daughter he once had, way back.' She had gazed out of the window, sentimental tears springing to her eyes. 'Clare's the only reason he sticks around these days, I reckon. Told me his own daughter died when she was about Clare's age, and, well, he's taken a real shine to our little girl. Almost thinks of her as his own, and she adores him, that's obvious. After all, Dennis is the only father figure she's ever known.'

Placing a hand gently on Mark's arm, she had continued, 'Look, son. I know you don't like Dennis, but Clare would be heartbroken if I were to give him his marching orders, much as I'd like to now, I must admit. He's a funny bloke,' (Yeah, bloody hysterical, thinks Mark) 'but he loves Clare. He'd never harm a hair on that girl's head, I know he wouldn't.'

'He'd better not,' Mark had growled, clenching his fists impotently. 'I'd kill him if he did.'

Dennis pushes his plate away and stands up. Without a word or a look at either Sylvie or her son, he marches into the adjoining sitting room, where Clare is sitting watching television.

'Oh thank you, dearest,' says Sylvie under her breath. 'Lovely, that was. Best egg and chips I've had in years.' Mark sniggers. 'Give us a hand with the washing up, will you son?' she says.

'OK Mum.' Standing beside his mother, drying the dishes, Mark catches a movement out of the corner of his eye. 'Oi,' he calls, as Dennis and Clare appear in the hallway. 'Where are you two off then?'

'Just taking Clare over the park. You want to have a go on the swings, don't you, darling?'

Clare looks doubtful. 'It's a bit cold out,' she says tentatively, 'and it'll be dark soon.'

'Rubbish,' says Dennis breezily. 'Don't be such a little wimp. You'll be all right if we wrap you up well. It'll do you good. Bring a bit of colour into your cheeks.' He pats her face fondly.

'Can't you see the kid doesn't want to know?' says Mark irritably. 'She'd rather stay in and watch telly, wouldn't you Clare?'

The little girl looks dumbly at her brother, then back at Dennis.

'You don't have to go if you don't want to, Clare,' says Sylvie weakly.

But Dennis is admant. 'She does want to, don't you, Clare? Come on, we'll only be out five minutes.' Clare says nothing, standing still while Dennis zips her into her anorak. As he leads her down the front path, Clare turns her head to look at Mark, still framed in the doorway. But Dennis is holding her hand tightly. As if he's afraid she might run away, thinks Mark.

Dennis doesn't notice the car parked across the road. Doesn't notice when it pulls gently away from the kerb heading in the same direction as him and Clare.

But Mark does.

Returning to the kitchen to finish drying the dishes, he gazes out of the window. 'Here, Mum,' he says, 'That car was outside again. The black Vauxhall. It was out there last night, and the night before around this time.'

Sylvie shrugs her indifference. 'So what. 'Spect one of the neighbours has changed his car, that's all.'

'Could be, I s'pose. But why would he sit in his car for half an hour at a time reading the paper?'

'Wanted to get away from his old woman for five minutes maybe?' grins Sylvie. 'It has been known.'

'Yeah, but why park in the road? All those houses opposite have got bloody great driveways *and* garages.'

'Think it's all part of some sinister plot, do you, Sherlock?' laughs Sylvie, flicking some washing-up water at him playfully. 'Been watching too much of *The Bill* on telly, that's your trouble.'

But Mark will not leave it alone. 'Must admit it's a bit funny, though,' he persists. 'I'm gonna take down its number if it comes back again. I reckon the bloke in the car's watching out for . . . for someone.' Watching out for Dennis, he thinks, with a sudden flash of intuition. Getting to know his routine.

'Oh yes, and the rest. Definitely no more *Bill* for you, my lad.'

Two weeks later, Mark is feeling happier than he has in ages. Positively jubilant, in fact. He's actually managed to land his first job with the Parks Department of the local council. Nothing much, but it's a start, and it'll be a relief to be out of the house each day, in the fresh air. But above all, he'll be able to help Mum out with a bit of money. He can't wait for Monday, his first day at work.

His chest swells with pride. At last *he* will be the man of the family, and no one else. Poor old Mum. She's had a bloody awful time of it, but he will make it up to her. Her and little Clare. Oh yes, things were going to be much, much better from now on, especially since *he* had gone at last.

Mum had been a different person, after the initial shock. He had noticed a tremendous change in her after only a couple of days, as though a great weight had been lifted from her shoulders. Clare seems brighter too; chattier, somehow – more full of life.

The doorbell sounds and Mark gets up to answer it.

The man standing on the doorstep looks dimly familiar. Now where has Mark seen him before?

'Is Dennis Charleton at home?' asks the man politely. He has the slightest trace of an accent, but Mark is unable to place it.

'Not any more. Sorry.' Mark starts to close the door.

'Oh, I see. You don't have a forwarding address, I suppose?'

Hardly, thinks Mark. He gives a short laugh. ''Fraid not. Dennis is dead. Saw it with my own eyes.'

'Really? What happened?'

The man is all agog, hanging on to his every word. It makes Mark feel important, interesting. 'Well, he was crossing the road on his way to the pub as usual – practically *lived* round there – when he was knocked down by this hit and run driver. Right outside the house, here. Time the ambulance arrived he was dead as a doornail.'

'That must have been a terrible thing to witness.'

Mark shrugs. 'Not really.'

'You don't sound exactly grief-stricken.'

'Got it in one. Me and Mum both. Now, if that's all you wanted . . .' He begins to close the door again, but the man steps forward quickly.

'You were obviously able to describe the car to the police,

335

if you saw it happen.' His voice drops to a whisper. 'Maybe you even managed to get the number?'

Mark shivers suddenly. Now he remembers where he has seen the man before. It is the driver of the Vauxhall.

'Oh, er, n-no,' he stammers. 'Wouldn't know the car again, I'm afraid. It was all too quick and I was, er, too shocked to remember much.'

'I'm sure,' smiles the man. His brown eyes gaze into Mark's. 'That's all right then.'

And Mark gently shuts the door.

'Who was that?' says Sylvie, struggling down the stairs carrying the vacuum cleaner.

'Oh, er, no one. Only some bloke trying to sell us something.'

thirty-three

Frank adjusts his seat, smiling an apology at the passenger sitting behind him. She automatically smiles back, mouthing 'No problem' and wondering – not for the first time – at the average Brit's capacity to inconvenience a body with such charm.

With a quick glance at Chris, already nodding off next to him, Frank at last allows himself to relax.

Chaz had taken the news of her father's sudden death stoically. As Frank had expected. Well, she hardly knew the man, he thinks. Thank God. How old was she when they left Dennis? Four? Let's hope any memories she does have of her father are pleasant ones. Chris wants it that way. And what Chris wants, she gets.

Frank had organised their trip to Boston with a military precision that had taken Chris by surprise. ('Didn't know you could be so well-organised, Frank.' 'That's me, Chris. Hidden depths even you didn't know about.') Everything will go like clockwork or my name's not Francis Sean Kelly, thinks Frank contentedly. Gus and Trish Pannitti will meet us at Logan, and Chaz will marry her Ian in precisely two days' time. Gus's son by his first marriage will be best man and Faithful Frank will give the bride away.

Not Dennis.

Frank smiles. Definitely not Dennis. Perhaps now I can get some sleep. The sleep of the innocent. Now there's a phrase to conjure with.

And he breathes a sigh of deep contentment. All's right

with the world. God's in his heaven and Dennis Stanley Charleton is burning in all the fires of hell. Hopefully.

At Logan Airport, Chris and Trish recognise each other at once, even after a thirty-year gap. Struck dumb with emotion, they simply fall into each other's arms, tears streaking both their faces.

'Make the most of it, Frank,' grins Gus. ''Cos sure as God made little apples you an' me ain't gonna get a word in edgewise when those two gals get going. They gotta lotta catchin' up to do, I guess.'

And Gus guesses right.

Nothing short of World War Three breaking out is going to stop them now. Deaf to anything but the sounds of each other's voices they talk and talk, reminiscing, reminding each other of private jokes (much to Frank's and Gus's mystification), laughing uproariously one minute and crying the next.

Angel is quite jealous. *Don't mind me*, she says sulkily. *I was there too, y'know*. Ah, shut up, Angel.

So she does. For the time being, anyway.

Angel does attempt a brief rally when Gus's glossy black Lincoln finally pulls up at the Pannitti house, a handsome, colonial-style building complete with verandah supported on graceful, fluted pillars. *Jesus*, she says, *what a place. Gone with the Wind, or what. What ever happened to Scarlett O'Hara?* She is furious when there is no response from Chris. *OK, OK, I can take a hint. But you'll be sorry. And before you tell me to shut up, that's just what I was about to do anyway. So there.*

After Trish and Gus have given their visitors a grand tour of the house, after the luggage has been unpacked and the two women have modelled their wedding outfits for each other, only then does it dawn on Chris how tired she is.

'Well,' says Frank easily, 'we were travelling for, what,

338

fifteen hours? You must be exhausted.' He grins. 'And you've knocked back a fair bit of booze since we arrived. Why not call it a day?'

'And I'm pooped too,' yawns Trish. 'And I can hold my liquor better than you. Always could. C'mon girl. I'm for bed. How about you?'

Chris grins. 'God, you don't change, Trish. Always were too bossy by half. Right. Lead on Macduff.'

Having watched the two women make their giggly way upstairs Gus lifts a decanter invitingly. 'Nightcap, Frank?'

'Just the job. Thanks.' He wanders over to a side table and picks up a silver-framed photograph of Gus with his arm across the shoulders of a strikingly handsome young man. There is no mistaking the resemblance between the pair. 'The best man. Your son, Al, right?'

'Right. The one and only. Like I told you, you'll meet him tomorrow when he gets back from his vacation.' Gus pats the sofa cushion invitingly. 'Take a seat, Frank. Relax. You must be bushed.'

Frank sits down. But he doesn't relax. He takes a reflective sip at his drink. 'Where exactly did Al spend his vacation?'

Gus looks at him sharply. 'England,' he says shortly. 'Why?'

Frank shrugs. 'Just have the feeling I might have seen him before somewhere, that's all.'

It is a long time before Gus answers. 'It's just possible, I guess. England's not such a big place. But it'd be one crazy coincidence. Where do you reckon you saw Al?'

'Uxbridge area? Not far from Heathrow? Driving a black Vauxhall? I, er, had a bit of business to attend to in Uxbridge and—'

'Nah,' says Gus immediately. 'Al did hire a car at Heathrow. Took off to do England. You know, the Lakes, Windsor Castle, Shakespeare country . . . the whole bit.'

'In two weeks?' Frank raises his eyebrows. 'He must have been moving to cover that much ground.'

'That's my boy,' says Gus flatly.

He leans across Frank and tops up his glass. 'Wasn't it in, ah, whadyacallit, Uxbridge, that Chris's ex-old man was totalled in a traffic accident?'

Frank nods. 'Yeah. Hit and run.'

'And, uh, you heard about the, uh, accident from the police, maybe?'

'No.' Frank, drains his glass. 'I heard it straight from the horse's mouth, from an eyewitness. I found out where the bastard lived, and quite a lot about what he'd been up to over the past few years. He'd made quite a few enemies, one way and another.' He pauses, staring into space, shaking his head. 'I don't know, madness really, but I thought I'd pay friend Charleton a little visit. See if I couldn't talk him into getting out of Chris's life – and Chaz's – for good and all. Blackmail him, you might say. I'd got enough dirt on him, one way and another.'

Gus pours Frank another drink. 'But?'

'But I was too late. Young lad that answered the door told me Dennis had recently been killed in a hit and run right outside the house.'

'And couldn't identify the car?' says Gus, leaning forward slightly. 'Didn't get a good look at the driver?'

'You asking me or telling me, Gus?' says Frank softly. And Gus shrugs. 'Whatever,' continues Frank, 'apparently it was all done and dusted too quickly for the lad to see much.' He gazes thoughtfully into his glass. 'But here's the funny thing. He looked a bit shaken up, to me. Scared, even. Said I was the second person in minutes to call enquiring about Dennis, and it was a wonder I hadn't bumped into the fella at the front gate . . .'

'And?'

'And of course I did bump into a man at the front gate. I stood aside to let him pass. Stood on the pavement and

340

watched him climb into a black Vauxhall and drive off.'
Frank pauses, before adding, 'He was a dead ringer for
your son Al.'

'Well, whadya know,' breathes Gus, 'some coincidence,
huh? Old Al must have a whadyacallit, a doppelganger,
ain't that the word?' He smiles into Frank's eyes, raising
his glass aloft. 'Guess we'll never really know who got to
Charleton. Somebody from his past, maybe? Some drunk
that just didn't stop in time? Whatever, let's drink to a nice
neat result. Whadya say, huh?'

And Frank chinks glasses with Gus. 'Oh absolutely,' he
says. 'Couldn't be neater.'

epilogue

The wedding has gone like a dream. It has been a wonderful day. One Chris will never forget. She stretches luxuriously in her bed in the Pannitti house. I'm so happy, Angel. And fancy meeting such an interesting new man. At my age, too.

She frowns slightly. Angel?

In the darkness, inside her head, Chris is listening. Listening for Angel's voice. But there is no response. She begins to feel distinctly uneasy.

Oh come on, Angel. Don't tell me you're sulking. Don't spoil things for me, today of all days. You said yourself Gus's widowed brother, Ray, was an absolute dish. And I'm only having lunch with him tomorrow. That's all. We're not exactly nipping off to Vegas for a quick wedding ceremony and no questions asked.

Angel? Angel, don't leave me. Not now. And inexplicably, Chris begins to weep.

Oh, for heaven's sake . . . Angel's voice is very faint. She sounds weary, defeated. *I thought you were supposed to be happy.*

I am, Angel.

So why the drama queen routine?

I thought you'd deserted me.

Well, you don't need me any more. You've arrived, kid. Everything's coming up roses, for a change. Especially now you've met the gorgeous Ray. And don't try and tell me he's gonna go flying back to 'Frisco after your lunch date tomorrow, because I won't believe you. I've got a feeling about this one. A good feeling.

Got your voice back as well, eh? thinks Chris, grinning in the darkness.

For the time being, snaps Angel. *But don't hold your breath. I only stuck around all these years because you were incapable of running your life without me. Now . . . now I might as well piss off.*

Oh, I get it. This is where I'm supposed to give you my undying thanks for all your years of loyal service and pension you off, is it? Well nothing doing, Angel. I'm not letting you off the hook that easily.

And I love you, too, says Angel sarcastically.

Good. So you'll still be around when I take my final curtain call, will you?

What, like always?

Always, Angel.

Drop Dead Gorgeous
Anna Cheska

Imogen's marriage has hardly been an exciting affair but when her husband dies, she's alarmed to discover that Edward hadn't been nearly as predictable as she'd always thought ...

She's desperate to learn the truth but her best friend, Jude, thinks she should put the past behind her. Should she throw off her widow's weeds, don some war-paint and join the battle to find a single man who isn't bitter and twisted or still living with his mother? Imogen isn't sure she's ready for trial by dating agency and lonely hearts columns. But though everyone keeps telling her that all she needs is time, could it be that what she really needs is a date?

'Anna Cheska has a charming writing style and creates warm, believable characters'   Katie Fforde

Of *Moving To The Country*:
'a thinking woman's romance dished up with a good seasoning of wisdom'   *Irish News*

Redeeming Eve
Nicole Bokat

Can she resist temptation?

Eve Sterling is a 21st century girl with a hankering for the 19th. She wants her life to be as gracefully choreographed as a Jane Austen novel. However, when she finds herself pregnant after only a few months of dating the distinctly un-Darcylike Hart, she can't help but feel that she's living in an all together different genre.

Eve has the additional burden of being in the shadow of the imposing celebrity of her own mother, Maxie. Suddenly thrust into the limelight, Maxie has been transformed into a media darling just as her own daughter's career begins to falter. Can Eve ever learn to balance the demands of marriage and motherhood with her need to carve out a niche for herself?

'It is the modern woman's challenge to juggle career and family, and Bokat's likeable characters struggle gamely to survive the conundrum ...contemporary and amusing'

Publisher's Weekly